DARKNESS

ERIN EVELAND

AN INTERACTIVE NOVEL

Selladore Press
10246 Crouse Rd. Box 703
Hartland MI 48353

Darkness by Erin Eveland
Copyright © 2014 Erin Eveland
Published by Selladore Press
10246 Crouse Rd. Box 703, Hartland MI. 48353

All rights reserved. No part of this book may be reproduced or transmitted in any form whatsoever without the written permission of the publisher.

ISBN-13: 978-0-9903254-0-6
ISBN-10: 0990325407

eBook ISBN-13: 978-0-9903254-1-3
ebook ISBN-10: 0990325415

The characters and events in this book are fictitious. Any similarities to persons, living or dead, are coincidental and not intended by the author.

Eveland, Erin, 1978–
Darkness : a novel / by Erin Eveland. – 1st ed.
p. cm.

Library of Congress: 2014907150

darknesstheseries.com
erineveland.com

Edits and layout by Judy Berlinski
Cover art by Mike Mumah mumah.deviantart.com
Cover by Richard Piippo

Printed in the United States of America
Manufactured by Thomson-Shore, Dexter, MI (USA); RMA595MS676, June, 2014

The Darkness Code

darknesstheseries.com
Darkness incorporates the
Quick Response code to heighten
the reading experience with the
interactive addition of art and music.

—— Please Note ——

If advertisements or messages appear
during a link, they are the result of the
selected scanning app on the machine-readable
device and are not affiliated with
Selladore Press nor the author.

By Erin Eveland

— Novel —

Darkness

— Short Stories —

Snuffbox
The Way
The Thing Within
Trespasser
The Puppet

For Evelyn

PROLOGUE

PATIENCE

Searching the tomorrow of yesterdays, I have finally found you. Oh, my love, you have pulled me to you without even knowing. But as much as I long to take you, we have to wait, wait for the Darkness to enfold you, torment you, and suffocate all of your being. Only then can you be mine.

Flourish in the Darkness of this world. Feel its empty light. Reach its void, that vacuum of seduction, which would dare to drain the threads of your life away. But do not fear my love. I am your protector.

Know this.

The Darkness has eyes. It sees you Catherine. And you are so very lovely indeed.

Solitude will be your sister and agony your brother. Endure, for such has been my path. Knowledge must bleed, but the scars in the years to come will be the lessons of which you have mastered. Even raw in youth and ignorance, my Catherine, you are divine and I inhale you.

This is my final test.

When the years take away hope and numb your heart against the will of others, I am here. When you turn inside out, denying the world's trivial compassion and offerings, your dark teacher will be revealed. You will beseech my name, Artros, and I will take away your suffering with the rapture of Darkness. I am yours as the world is ours. Until then, the shadows embrace me. But I am always with you my love, my Angel of Darkness.

Ah, I can smell you, my black rose, standing on the street corner. You are a child now, but I will come for you in time. You see me now, but only this short spell, while I cover your eyes with dreamless sleep and blind the days before you. But it is I who will carry you, comfort your solitude, and replenish your soul when it is depleted. I am your keeper.

Frightened, you feel me near. I am the future before you. Grow in pain my love and blossom into the woman of power you will become. Until then, I covet your light. For as long as I live, you will only know Darkness and my love.

Will you be able to hold on? Are you strong enough to let despair set you free?

Patience, my love. Patience.

See me now as the shadow I adorn myself with. But remember, Artros is here, and it is in the Darkness that I will be waiting.

CHAPTER ONE

"The Devil is really an Angel," Margaret said to her granddaughter as they hurried along the cracked, uneven sidewalk, knowing her answer was insufficient. Late morning and the sky grew darker in front of them. Another gust loosened the silver hair from Margaret's bun. With one hand she held her hair out of her face, inhaled another shallow breath, and continued to allow her six-year-old granddaughter to pull her a few blocks farther away from the church they had just visited.

"Nana," Catherine asked, "how can the Devil be an Angel if he's so ugly?"

Coming on an intersection, their pace slowed, relieving Margaret's pounding chest. But the wall of clouds ahead rolled faster. Margaret groaned, knowing they would be forced to hurry again if they wanted to beat the storm.

Against Catherine's persistence, Margaret considered returning to the church for shelter, but decided to brave it and keep on. At the intersection, a blue sedan crept to a stop at the flashing red stoplight. Waiting to cross the street, Margaret watched her granddaughter's eyes jet between the church behind them and the sidewalk before them. "Tell me . . . how can he Nana?" Catherine asked again.

"Oh Catherine . . ." Margaret sighed, knowing these questions could not be answered on a street corner.

She had selected the church out of the Yellow Pages, hoping for spiritual guidance to their troubled times at home—*the shadows, the faceless man, and the nightmares.* She felt anxious leaving her grandchild with people she'd never met, but Catherine ran down the basement stairs for Sunday school before she could stop her, delighted to be with other children. Once dismissed, however, she raced back to Margaret and seized her hand. Waves of anxiety throbbed through the child's body. Margaret knew—she'd seen this before—her delving eyes and that pierced mouth. Catherine pulled Margaret out the church; her flight fueled by fear. Margaret didn't have a chance to ask Catherine what upset her. While Margaret knew the symptoms, she never understood the reasons behind her spasms of agitation. So often she would try to pluck the child's thoughts like a harp string with hopes of finding the right note, but she only succeeded in skipping beats. The wash, scraped knees, and piles of dishes in the sink—just caring for her granddaughter—kept Margaret busy. But she lamented when she couldn't comfort Catherine or protect her from the nameless terror that lived in their lives. Margaret knew that she would be the only one tucking Catherine into bed tonight, and she alone had to find a way to answer the child's difficult questions and the growing threat at home. She was an old woman in an unforgiving time and the earth grew larger the older she became.

Catherine was *different*—forever haunted by an unseen presence. Margaret knew it had to do with light—not the sun, or its warmth, just the light.

Catherine would dance in the sunbeams without rhythm. Her wandering eyes never focusing, just looking at emptiness itself. *The dance trance*, Margaret had named it standing afar, trying to make sense of the random movements. She worried the frequency of the dance was spiking.

A week ago, Catherine shrieked from inside the house and Margaret hurried from the mailbox to find the child in the living room just as she'd left her, playing in the sunbeams as usual. "See, Nana! See!" Catherine shouted.

"See what child?" Margaret asked short of breath.

"I stopped the light!" Catherine replied, extending her arms out to her sides, spreading her fingers wide. With her back to the sun, she faced the faded floral wallpaper and torn, green couch held together with a prayer like Margaret's finances. Against the wall, Catherine's shadow expanded in unnatural ripples. Margaret remained at the entry, questioning her eyesight, as Catherine looked at her shadow on the wall and said, "I thought I could and I did. I stopped the light!"

"Of course you can, child," Margaret whispered. She shuddered at the soundless disturbance in the air, like static waves on an unplugged television screen. The child's shadow stretched and throbbed fatter with every second. Margaret felt a tightening fear enter her flesh, but she continued to deny the child's grotesque shadow on the living room wall. She closed her eyes and said, "It's just a shadow. You know your own shadow, don't you?" She swallowed hard and opened her eyes again.

Cast by the light of the open doorway, Margaret's own shadow was on the floor of the hallway in front of her. An abstract to her natural form, it appeared as a short stick with a bobber in the middle. Outside green leaves swayed with the wind, but Margaret saw their shadows on the wall and floor of the hallway. They bent and bounced as if they knew a secret and were whispering it to each other, taunting her. Some of the shadow leaves broke off their gray branches. As they fell, Margaret reflexively moved her shadow-body to miss them. *This is ridiculous,* she thought, stepping back to avoid another gray leaf from touching her, but it was impossible to escape them or her own shadow.

Margaret looked at Catherine again, now giggling at her oversized, distorted shadow on the wall, her arms swaying to an imaginary beat. *The dance.* Margaret steadied a slight buckle in her knees. The limbs of Catherine's shadow flickered and spiked off the flat surface of the wall as if it would step onto the carpet at any moment and join the child in the dance. Margaret's throat constricted; she couldn't swallow. She tried to focus. *The shadows were the problem. No, not the shadows but Catherine. The child is doing this.* She uttered a false chuckle and spoke as if her voice could break this enchantment, "See my shadow? It looks like Miss Humpty Dumpty right now. No brownies for Nana for a while." She slapped the debt collection and junk mail against her solid belly. She looked at her shadow gut where nothing could be ingested, not even a conscience.

Margaret eased a little, seeing Catherine's shadow mirroring her granddaughter's movements again. As Catherine turned from the wall to Margaret, her shadow quickly diminished to its normal size. Margaret was able to exhale, but not for long.

"You can't see them . . . can you Nana?" Catherine sighed. "They're crawling on you, Nana. Just the little ones. There are always little ones on you, but more are coming, bigger ones." Catherine studied Nana's shadow on the carpet, the wall, and then all around the old woman.

Catherine's eyes locked with hers and Margaret gasped. *The trance without the dance.* The irises in the child's eyes were black, a dark void.

"The shadows are here," Catherine said. "They're coming for you, Nana."

"Shadows, Catherine?" Margaret asked, carefully closing the front door behind her to block the simple sunlight. Margaret's shadow disappeared as the hallway's parched paint glowed a maroon hue. Sunlight escaped into the living room from its parted curtains. Margaret side-stepped to close them, but before she crossed the threshold between the hallway and the living room Catherine moved into her pathway and stomped her foot.

"All kinds. They're everywhere," Catherine said slapping her hand against the wall. Margaret winced.

Catherine moved in a frenzy now, stomping the ground and hitting the walls. She batted and smacked the air as if to crush invisible insects threatening to devour them. Her thrashing increased as she moved closer to Margaret. "Sssssttttop that," Margaret stuttered. "Enough ggggirl." Margaret moved to grab one of the girl's flailing hands. Realizing she was still holding the mail she ended up waving it haphazardly in the air to shield herself from impending blows.

"Don't be scared Nana. They know when you're scared—there are more of them when you're scared, and you're scared a lot. When you're hurt they come, too, and you hurt a lot here," Catherine said, taking a fist to her chest. "When I'm scared," she continued between slaps, "they come for me, too, but I try not to be scared . . . and they go away. But you're scared and they know it, and they know you hurt inside, so they come some more too. And you must be scared more, and hurt more, because they come all the time now. They're all over you Nana." Her slapping hands turned on Margaret's chest, as though beating a disease out of her. Margaret yelled for Catherine to stop as she covered her chest with her arms, but Catherine's blows impacted deep within her.

"I'm going to make them to go away," Catherine said, suddenly calm, halting her attack. "I'm going to block them like I do the light." Margaret leaned against the wall to steady herself as the child stepped one foot forward and angled the other behind her. Raising her arms level from her sides, the air in the room rushed toward her. Margaret wheezed, feeling the wall behind her as if she would find escape. Catherine methodically brought her outstretched arms together in front of her as though she were compressing the air between her arms and hands. Midway she smacked them together and a blast of hot air flung Margaret to the floor.

Then there was nothing more. Margaret couldn't recall what happened in those fleeting seconds before the blast of air or how Catherine came to be kneeling at her side. Both were soaked in sweat and fright, but the moment was overcome. The color had returned to Catherine's eyes as she looked upon Margaret with a child's face of innocence and concern. Margaret felt her fear subside and the love of her granddaughter fill her. The shadows were gone and the air was still.

The night passed and Margaret could pretend everything was normal, denying what happened between them and the shadows. She was able to block the questions in her head as if they didn't exist. For a few blessed days the bond between Margaret and Catherine and the daily ritual was healed—until Catherine asked about the shadow man. She called him the "Darkest of Shadows."

"What does he look like?" Margaret asked, cracking an egg into the frying pan and missing.

"I can't tell, Nana. I told you, I can't see him. But I think he wears a hat, one like Papa wears in the old pictures you showed me," Catherine replied scribbling on a piece of black construction paper.

"What else does he wear?" Margaret asked, opening the fridge with a blank stare.

"I told you," Catherine said scribbling harder. "I can't see him."

"How do you know it's a man?"

"Because he talks to me."

"Talks to you?" Margaret's voice failed her.

"He talks funny. He doesn't talk like us—but I know what he says."

"Talks to you," Margaret repeated, closing the fridge door, empty-handed, staring at its cold, white metal.

"He says he's my guardian." Catherine paused briefly before she asked, "What's a guardian, Nana?" She continued without waiting for a response. "He tells me he's with me and one day he'll be my teacher and lover—or lover teacher—when I'm ready."

"Ready for what, Catherine?" Margaret asked, returning to stand in front of the fridge. The eggs started to burn on the stove.

"When . . . after . . . um . . . when I forget everything he says. He said I'm going to sleep for a while . . . so I can be . . . re . . . re . . . umm . . . reborn," Catherine said and held up her picture for Margaret's approval.

Margaret heard Catherine's crayon set down on the table. She heard the paper lift. She could sense it hanging in the child's hands behind her, but she couldn't bring herself to turn around. Catherine put her drawing on the fridge in front of Margaret with a magnet, and gave her a brief hug before quietly walking out the kitchen.

Black wax crayon upon black construction paper. Catherine placed it next to other pictures of spaghetti-lined rainbows, flowers, and sunshine. The scribbled figure on the black paper looked like a mound of black dirt with a brim and small hump on the top, nothing more. But the picture said enough. The picture was the breaking point.

That was when Margaret picked the first church she flipped to in the phone book. She had kept herself and the child emotionally corked from the world for too long. Now she was paying the price for their seclusion without another soul to turn towards.

They were alone and Margaret's heart was running toward death at a racehorse's beat, but she refused to let go of Catherine. She hadn't made plans for the great *what if*, not for Catherine or her, but mortality was creeping on her faster every day and she knew it.

If Margaret believed in reincarnation, she would have thought Catherine was an old soul. She would have accepted the blessing of Catherine's arrival as karma for "time well served." But she didn't believe in that stuff. She lost faith in God for a time—*maybe even still*, she conceded—but she needed guidance and direction for them both. Margaret had tired of trying to straighten the world, her past, and the heartaches left in its wake.

After Vietnam, when the bombs' craters collected dust, Margaret's experience of caring for the children on the west side of the county taught her all she needed to know about little ones, the affairs of people, and the havoc produced long after war. That was when all the men came home needing their women—wives, mothers, sisters, mistresses—to take time off and nurse them back—physically and mentally. The women were compelled to tune out their children for a while and tune their men back into reality, love, and the security of home.

Margaret didn't have her soldier anymore, just a baby girl left in his memory to care for, Kathy. Catherine's mother (the womb Catherine came from anyway). *Maybe*, Margaret always wondered, *she had been too concerned with the rearing of other children to be a fit mother for her daughter,*

Kathy. The widow-money ran out faster than she could bury her beloved soldier.

At first, watching other women's children with Kathy at her side seemed fit for the both of them, but the time came for school. Throughout the years, Margaret worked odd hours and time with Kathy became scarce. A great distance grew between them. The day came when Margaret realized she didn't know Kathy. She maintained she lost her only child to the casualties of war. That's how she chose to believe it. Now, Margaret knew (after years of trying to lay blame on the war or herself) that her daughter, Kathy, was born rotten. She was the stained seed of a young love's union. Margaret didn't know how it was possible—thinking back to her baby girl who entered the world plump and pink as a prized baby should—that her baby could putrefy and turn away from her mother's love and eventually into the arms of lust. Margaret hated the word lust, and shelved it in her mind along with a sailor's banquet of vocabulary used out to sea. The word was tasteless, yet full of bitter texture. That was the way she saw her only child. Kathy had a will for ruin.

Margaret never married after she had Kathy, and raised her alone. A few suitors came, while her skin was still taut, but hopes for a replacement father quickly washed away. Margaret knew why. It was Kathy. Her daughter was feral: always disobedient, scornful, and angry if restrained. She rarely spoke with civility; instead her words snarled from her mouth spewing hate, forcing Margaret to live in a constant state of guilt. What had she done?

Kathy eventually left without a trace until she called in need of money for an abortion. Margaret agreed to pay for all of Kathy's living expenses and the doctor bills, anything to see the pregnancy through. For a time, hope lingered that the pregnancy would change Kathy. Hope, yet fear, that she would come home to her.

The baby was premature, born from a sack of amniotic alcohol, the doctor explained to Margaret. Kathy discharged herself without a word and Margaret hadn't seen her since.

"Expect the possibility of developmental issues and retardation," the doctor warned Margaret before she signed the stack of forms in front of her, but that wasn't to be the case. Catherine thrived.

Margaret took hope home in a little swaddle. She named the baby after her birth mother, which seemed right at the time. A new beginning from the past and for a short time it was.

The baby grew, showing no signs of suffering from the toxic womb she emerged from. That was a blessing. They were together, that was a long awaited gift. Margaret had her Kathy in Catherine all over again.

Margaret thought about Kathy. Her daughter was a Devil, disguised in the soft pink flesh of a babe. But that Devil birthed an Angel. Catherine was Margaret's savior, and together they were fighting something nameless, dark, and deep.

The Devil is really an Angel, Margaret thought back to her answer. She wished she hadn't said that. It popped out of her mouth like a lost fairytale with an ending she couldn't remember. She didn't know the first thing about angels or devils. They were nothing more than black or white as far as she was concerned.

"How can something scary be beautiful?" Catherine asked at the intersection on the street corner, pressing her quivering hand into Margaret's. For a second it was as if the child read straight into Margaret's mind. A blaring car horn jolted Margaret out of her revelry, back to the here and now. They were waiting to cross the street. The blue sedan at the stoplight turned on its wipers. A mild mist fell on their Sunday dresses, dampening them as it fell in a gentle tease of what was to come. Margaret wanted to answer Catherine, tell her that she was afraid of raising a child so beautiful and loving. She wanted to tell her all things frightening could heal at the same time, and what she feared most of all: their time together was running short. Her heart not only raced from physical exhaustion now, but just by beating.

Once again, Margaret traced Catherine's gaze across the street, perplexed by her fixation. Margaret hoped it was the gray clouds tumbling their way that caught her absorption, but she knew different. Catherine was honed in on something else entirely. *Not now Catherine*, Margaret thought, *we can't do this now, little one.*

They were under attack from Catherine's unnamed, unknown phantom matter and a man without a face, but it was a threat that couldn't be voiced or breached. Right now, Margaret had to calm down. Thinking too much made her aware of her heart.

Catherine awakened Margaret's hand with another shake and pressed hard as she asked, "Are all angels . . . devils?"

"Forget what I said," Margaret replied. *Yes, let's just forget*, she thought, *forgetting is best.*

"Tell me, Nana. Tell me," Catherine said as she squeezed Margaret's hand.

The blue sedan rolled forward from its stop. "Sweetie, come on it's time to cross," Margaret said and took her turn carting them forward, but Catherine refused, pulling Margaret back with surprising strength. Margaret was stunned. Catherine continued to search the street where the eastern morning should have guided their way home. Thunder growled in the distance.

It's just the storm, Margaret reassured herself, *she's just afraid of the storm.* "Let's go back to the church and see if we can call for a ride," she said.

Eveland

"Angels *are* devils, aren't they Nana," Catherine stated. Her voice was flat, but her body trembled.

There was no sign of *the trance*, but that didn't mean it couldn't surface at any time. *We can't fight it now baby girl,* Margaret thought, *not now—let it go.*

Almost in a whisper, Catherine said, "I can't see."

Margaret crouched next to Catherine's face, but the child didn't acknowledge her. Catherine refused to move, studying the row of trees across the street they would soon pass. Margaret heard a rolling gust of wind heading toward them before the brute of the storm's squall line struck.

Windows flexed and trees bent. The wind pushed a path for the lashing rain behind it. Green leaves blew off branches while the howl of the wind gave way for its sister thunder. Black umbrellas popped up and people started running, holding bags and newspapers over their heads.

Rain shoveled water into their faces and beat upwards from the sidewalk. Margaret's free hand cupped her eyes in a feeble attempt to shield them, but Catherine didn't move. Her eyes were turning red, refusing to blink from nature's fury.

"This is too much!" Margaret cried, clenching her hands over the child's hands in desperation. "We have to get out of the rain. We need—we need to go back . . . find a ride."

Catherine was mumbling something. The edges of her mouth moved and the beating rain trickled in, only to fall out again. "The Devil is an Angel . . . an Angel is the Devil . . . the Devil and the Angel are . . ." but the storm muffled the words to Margaret.

"Catherine. Child! We have to get out of the storm," Margaret pleaded. Her heart. She must think of her heart. If only she could pick the child up and carry her out of danger. Damn her old bones. She tried to steer Catherine back to the church in the spattering wind and rain. "We have to get to the church until the storm lets up . . ." Breaking her hands free from Catherine's, Margaret grabbed the child's shoulders and shook her. "Catherine, listen to me. If you won't cross, we have to go back . . . we have to get out of the rain."

"I can't see," Catherine said aloud, her voice steadfast against the rain and trees she looked through.

"Can't see what Catherine?"

"In the shadow."

"There are no shadows," Margaret proclaimed, squinting her eyes to the dark world around them. The asphalt steamed from the cool rain, losing all the morning heat soaked into it.

"I know," Catherine lowered her voice, "*you* can't *see* the shadows."

Margaret's struggle turned into loss. She knew one lesson in life was not to tempt the tempest that brings about the temper. Old words, right words.

She played out her hopeless card.

"You can't see them because," Margaret sighed, "shadows are just that Catherine, nothing more. There are no shadows in the dark. There's no reason to . . . for this. We need . . . please sweetie . . . listen to me."

Catherine scrutinized the row of trees across the street. "I can't see *in* the shadow Nana. I can't see . . . if it's beautiful," Catherine said, straining with her eyes as she brought her hands up to Margaret's wrists where the old woman held onto her shoulders.

"You're hurting Grandma." Margaret's lips pressed together as Catherine's grip started to cut the circulation from her hands with unnatural strength. The two of them were in a stalemate and locked between unknown forces.

Margaret watched Catherine's determination to turn her head away from the other side of the street. Her face grimaced in desperation as she glared into Margaret's eyes. Margaret felt her grandchild pleading—*help me*—with unspoken words, but the only words she could utter were:

"Shadows cannot hurt us, Catherine. There is nothing in a shadow."

"Nana, have you ever seen the Devil?"

"No," Margaret answered.

"Then how do you know he can't hurt you? If you can't see it, can it hurt you?"

Margaret bent her head down to hide her face. Her next words would be a lie. "If you can't see it, then it can't hurt you, Catherine."

The dress coat of the storm passed and all that was left of its residue was the end of its coattails falling in lighter waves.

The child's silence grew into reluctance. Easing her hold, but not breaking it, she allowed Margaret, the only mother she ever knew, to guide her across the street to safety.

They made their way past the row of trees that held them captive for too long. Catherine looked to her shoes and felt the sloshing water within, knowing her grandmother failed to *see*. The shadow had moved on like the storm and left its stain upon her.

CHAPTER TWO

One week later, Catherine sat on a brown fiberglass chair flung outside of Nana's hospital room. The stench of iodine lingered like boiled metal. The soles of Catherine's shoes barely touched the floor as she brushed them back and forth along the scrubbed tile in marking wisps. These were the shoes Nana bought her for school. The first day she never went to. The new pair carried her from a sidewalk, into an ambulance, and finally Riverside Hospital after Nana collapsed on the street.

The Shadow Man followed. She didn't know where he was now, but the ambulance whisked by him on a street corner and once again in the hospital parking lot, tracking her. Multitudes of other shadows were here. Unlike the Shadow Man, they appeared as animals of all shapes and sizes. Void of smell and sound, she called them the creepers. Impossible to see, the creepers moved through the walls, floors and windows of the hospital. More were coming. Touching one was the same as brushing the air. They scurried, jumped and slithered—their movements as distorted as their shadow bodies. They were like a ringing bell without a sound or moving leaves without wind. Unreal and real all the same and Catherine knew she was the only one who could see them.

Catherine had asked Nana, *if you can't see it, can it hurt you?* The question was a test. If Nana were awake, she still wouldn't be able to see the creepers of the hospital and their shadow forms upon the people. But if she could, Catherine knew she would agree with her. The creepers funneled into wounds seen and unseen, drawing out a nebulous nourishment from the people they feasted on. These creepers grew fat and their form altered the longer they stayed on the body. If the creepers stayed too long, their host's illness and temperament worsened. The black masses infested Riverside Hospital, its residents and employees, like a plague.

When they arrived at the hospital, the staff kept her away from Nana. Catherine cried, begging to see her, be by her. But the staff told her to be patient while they questioned her for information about family and friends. "Do you know anyone we can call?" they had asked. "Someone close by . . . a neighbor perhaps?" Catherine looked at them dumbfounded. There was no one in their lives but them. Not one. The staff had nothing more than an address. Eventually, the inquisitors gave up and whispered something about social services.

Finally, they relented. "She's sleeping, Catherine, try not to disturb her."

As the nurses guided her into the room, Catherine saw the creepers moving about the room, and more entering. As she looked to the hospital bed, she saw them covering Nana and her heart. The sight of them made Catherine hot inside and without thinking she stepped in front of the nurses, raised a flat hand and waved it as if orchestrating the air in front of her. It was easy this time, when she was not frightened of them as she had been. The creepers spread apart and retreated from the room with her gesture. Since the day she used her full body and breath to banish them, she had grown stronger. Like the creepers in the room, the nurses stepped back and as they left, one of them mumbled something Catherine couldn't hear. Now, she was alone with her grandmother, the way it had always been and the way it should be. Catherine stood by her Nana's bedside for a long time, hurting and full of questions she couldn't ask. Nana's silver hair lay around her red-tinted face and Catherine remembered the time they watched the sunset together—before the evening glow of their picnic was overcast with clouds and they had to leave. Nana had said, "The sun eventually sets on everyone, Catherine." Catherine didn't understand her meaning then, but standing there beside the bedside she was afraid she was starting to.

Slowly Nana's eyes fluttered open and she gazed at her granddaughter; relief brought instant color to her cheeks. Her lips formed a gentle smile. Catherine patiently waited for Nana to speak. Placing her hands on Nana's chest, she moved them gently down her arm, willing her grandmother to find strength and comfort in the touch. Then in whispering puffs Nana spoke to her.

"You . . . you're a good girl . . . Catherine . . . remember that," Nana said and then gasped for another breath to continue. "You make . . . me . . . soooo proud . . . a good good girl . . ." And then she closed her eyes, relaxing all tension in her body.

Catherine's hands remained on Margaret, massaging her grandmother with harder strokes to awaken her. Bending her head to Nana's ear, she called her name over and over again in soft undertones. Tears streamed down Catherine's face as she confronted this impending loss—a loss she couldn't yet understand. Through her watery eyes she saw the shadow creepers moving back into the room and onto her grandmother. In rapid motion, the creepers quickly covered everything. Some on Nana were darting up

Catherine's arms and others up her legs from the floor. Overwhelmed by emotion, Catherine panicked. The creepers were like mice in walls, bats in window shutters, or hornets in the attic. Omnipresent. She flayed her hands brusquely to brush them off Nana and herself. Earlier, she banished them with her hands, but now, in her grief, she couldn't remember how. She couldn't focus. She hit them with her fist and stomped them with her feet, all to no avail. They rolled around her hand like an obstacle course, or popped in the air like a balloon filled with black smoke only to rematerialize into the same creepers. Catherine knew she could stop them. She had before, but attempting to stop them this time she realized her weakness—fear. No matter how she fought them, if she was afraid, they would not go away. At this moment, fear filled her.

Stop hitting them, Catherine thought, *you have to be easy, easy like you were when you came in the room*. It seemed impossible, even when she thought she was close, she could feel the tingle of her body and the pulse of her heart. Catherine closed her eyes and stepped back from her grandmother. She recalled banishing fictitious monsters looming under her bed or hiding in closets by just lying under the sheets with her eyes closed and willing them away. She now closed her eyes and imagined herself at home and in bed. It was enough for her to pull herself together and use the calm of her inner strength to thrust the creepers from Nana's room

Catherine swallowed. Her lungs pulled a bottomless breath as she lifted her arms to her sides. In the same instant she brought her hands together and expelled the air to pummel the atmosphere, discharging a power at the shadow creepers so great it seemed to come out of the very pores of her body.

A nurse walking by Margaret's room paused, stunned, watching Catherine flog herself, then the body of the old woman, and *then* everything within reach. As she entered the room to stop Catherine, the child's arms extended out. The nurse heard a loud slap before she was knocked down to the floor.

Catherine opened her eyes and sighed . . . the room was empty of the shadow creepers. Nana slept just as before. Startled, she saw a nurse pulling herself up off the floor, cursing threats Catherine couldn't understand and pointing a limp finger at her. The nurse staggered towards Catherine, her eyes inflamed. Her skin, open and raw and red with blood that wouldn't bleed, appeared to be pelted with sand. She grabbed at Catherine, and before Catherine knew to jump back, the two struggled, the nurse winning the effort to remove her from Nana's room.

She found herself in the hall surrounded by staff and onlookers as the injured nurse shrieked at her and pointed to her own blue and red face. Like cackling hyenas, others joined in. Catherine's wide-eyed silence made them all the more furious.

Creepers started to flood the hallway, landing on everything available, preferring the soft flesh of people. They scurried maniacally to become parasites upon the people. As they spit their muddled criticisms and disapproval of Catherine, the more the creepers rushed them, attaching themselves to their prickling, festering skin. Catherine bent her head. Her body sunk and she felt like she was being swallowed into herself as they chided her. Catherine couldn't stand the pressure. She needed to break from the crushing weight. Raising her head, she started swiping the crowd with her hands as she said in earnest, "They're on you and you and you and you and you." She rebelled, knowing they couldn't see the shadows like she did and she couldn't tell them why they were here, what they did, or why more were coming. She struck at the crowd harder, wanting and needing them to understand.

A doctor intervened. He came up behind Catherine and reached his arms around her, pulling her back while murmuring words for her ears only, but all she heard was ". . . going to be all right."

Nothing was all right while the world was covered in shadows.

The doctor pinned her at the shoulders, leaving her arms free to thrash about, to no effect. But the angry words stabbed at her from the growing crowd, fed her adrenaline and she stunned the doctor and the others by breaking free from his grasp. She turned to face the doctor with white-fire in her eyes and then swiveled around to the circle of people surrounding her. Catherine let out a despairing cry: "See!" Her words rang down the hall, through the rooms, and past the metal stairwell doors and elevator shaft. "See!" she screamed again and again until the gathering mob overcame her.

They thought to remove her from Margaret's floor, but decided to supervise her until social services could claim her, as she had no one else to claim custody. Heeding their threats, Catherine promised to remain calm and planted her small body in the chair outside Nana's room. "Stay put and wait here. Ya' hear?" *Wait for what?* Catherine only knew she had no choice; she had to protect Nana. She snuggled herself into a tight ball from the waist up and waited.

Catherine couldn't stop the big bullies and their threats. After a time, all she could do to keep her mind off the creepers sure to be covering Nana in the other room was scrape her soles back and forth. Back and forth, over and over again. A nurse behind the desk cocked a permanent eye at her. She had a scattering of shadow creepers on her, right above her waist. One of them had grown from a rat-form into a python that wrapped around her stomach. As the nurse grew frustrated trying to do her paperwork while keeping a watchful eye on the feral child in front of her, more creepers came. Catherine ached for someone to listen to her. But she was beginning to understand the world by the hearing aids they wore. She had no choice but to fight them. If the nurses tried to place her farther away from Nana again, she would bite and claw her way or even attempt to use the new skill—her secret key—inside her, which if turned right, could make the creepers disappear. And if it made *them* disappear, then why not the adults? She would try it on them if they made her move. For now she accepted this distance. Catherine waited.

Catherine's attention returned to the nurse at the front desk. Mesmerized, she watched one of the shadow creepers resting on her left breast. It grew fatter over time, much like the leeches she'd seen attached to the carp in the riverbed. But it wasn't blood they extracted; it was something similar to the flowing waters the carp swam in. The water of life.

In a disquieted state of waiting, Catherine started to think about the Shadow Man and his whereabouts. A touch of fear returned and she tried to purge it from her mind. He was getting closer. He had been at the street corner as the ambulance drove Nana. As they approached the hospital, she saw him standing in the middle of the road where cars didn't brake or swerve to miss him. She passed him heading into the hospital where people coming in and out of the doors walked around him as if he were a rock in the river they were trying to avoid. Keeping their distance, the creepers did the same, creating a clear radius around him, sometimes hopping off the people they latched onto as their host walked by the Shadow Man. Catherine didn't know where he was now and thinking of where he might be made her shiver.

The Shadow Man appeared as a dark lump with a hat, but she knew there was more to him. His shadow was so dark, she couldn't see through it, or into it. He watched her without eyes, never speaking to her in his shadow form.

Only after she discovered how to stop the light did she see him. It didn't take long for her to connect the Shadow Man with the night voice. They both manifested at the same time and something unspoken joined the two. Just as she drifted into sleep, the night voice came to her like a cradle, soothing and soft, swaddling her in a blanket of comforting confinement.

The heart attack brought conversations between Catherine and Nana to a halt. Questions remained unasked and unanswered. Catherine wanted to understand: was it an Angel or the Devil trying to steal her Nana away? She thought about the church Nana chose for them. It was an immaculate brick building with a steeple so tall Catherine imagined it as a secret elevator the church used to shoot people straight into Heaven. At the time she thought Nana brought them there so they could leave this earth together. Skyrocket that very day in their pretty Sunday dresses Nana bought for the occasion. The inside was as grand as the outside, with a beckoning smell of salvation.

Captivated by its welcoming charm, Catherine wasn't even bothered by the shadow creepers inside, or protest when the staff directed the two of them separate ways. Children advanced toward the basement for Sunday classes. Nana agreed with a nod. Catherine remembered how it felt to slide down the carpeted staircase in her flats. She beat the other children and took a front-row seat.

The teacher's vest was as tight as her lips. She said angels spoke to children within the bleak hours of night to comfort their hearts and minds. But children were vulnerable and the dark of night was like purgatory, balancing their fate on the weighted scales of heaven and hell which tipped according to their hearts and soul. This was when He would come to the children who dared listen to His voice, disguised as an Angel of guidance or desire. After all, He was an Angel, the greatest of them all before challenging the light of God in which He fell from grace in defeat. He was the deceiver of children and could drive them deeper into the sin they were born into.

Listening to the teacher, Catherine imagined *her* night voice bringing solace to her in the dark as it spoke of things she couldn't comprehend. The night voice soothed her nightmares and fear of the shadow creepers. It called her lovely. To insure she stayed that way, He insisted she sleep for long periods. Sleep felt good. But like many things the voice spoke of, she didn't understand what it meant about sleeping for a long time. She awoke every day like the morning before. But once the night voice manifested, she had fewer dreams until they trickled away completely. Now there was only darkness in her sleep. Even that darkness was devoid of the Shadow Man and his voice. Every day following, the creepers seemed weakened and they came less frequently.

"Repent," the teacher had said, slamming her brick bible on the table to ignite her young students, "lest that old wicked serpent wraps you up for the clutches of hell!" *Could the night voice be an Angel cloaked in black with a heavenly voice?* Catherine wondered. But for all the comfort the night voice brought, He could be anyone or anything as far as Catherine was concerned.

In Riverside Hospital, Catherine trusted no one. She braced for the whispers and lowered heads that directed their attention to her. Even when a nurse walked by dressed in pastel scrubs and a sympathetic smile, she secretly stomped her feet and scowled. Catherine's guard could not be let down to anyone.

Eventually Catherine remained quiet and still. When she was sure no one watched, she slipped into Nana's room. To her surprise, the room was empty of the creepers. Even Nana, who lay motionless on the bed, was free of them. It saddened Catherine to see her grandmother's motionless skin in its solemn state of slumber. She climbed on top of the bed, kneeled at her side and placed her fingers into the folds defining Nana's soft cheeks. Recollecting a game the two of them liked to play, Catherine started sliding Nana's loose skin around on top of her face. In this game Catherine would sculpt Nana's sagged cheeks and wrinkled brow into whatever face she chose: happy, sad, silly. Nana would then use *her* hands upon the girl's tight flesh and mimic Catherine's motions. Each mirror image of the other, gave way to raucous laughter.

Catherine's small hands moved to sculpt a smile, just enough to tell her everything would be all right . . . just a little perk in the clay, a bit of vitality, but Margaret's eyes remained closed. No matter how hard Catherine tried, no matter what form of grin she make-shifted with her hands, her grandmother's eyelids remained still. No sparkle, no laughter to capture what Catherine hoped for. She searched for the hope, the comfort that everything was going to be all right. They would go home soon and wake up tomorrow to repeat the first day of school under their own terms, a day that wouldn't involve respirators, needles, and strangers. Catherine looked for truth, the honesty in eyes that couldn't be pulled or teased. Replacing her grandmother's smile with her own grin, she lifted Margaret's china lids to reveal the truth.

Nana's eyes were gloss black. A piercing dark and deep, as if a tunnel ran straight through Nana's sockets and beyond. Terrified, Catherine made an effort to release her fingers from Nana's lids and turn away the soulless chasm threatening to pull her down. A voice sounded from within. It was the night voice and it resonated throughout the chambers in her head with no escape route to release it. It echoed and multiplied, filling her core. "The Devil is an Angel. An Angel is the Devil. The Angel and the Devil are one. One coming for you. The Devil is coming. The Angel is coming. You are the Devil and an Angel in one . . ." the night voice chimed on, teasing and taunting and blackening her sight. Her limbs rippled in waves which spread to the center of her body, immobilizing her. In that darkness, Catherine shut down, leaving her void—empty of thought, emotions, feelings—with nothing left of her senses. She became no more than a vessel for the night voice. The night voice had now taken over.

Nurse Beckwith walked into Margaret's room. She was making the last round on her shift when she found the child bent over the old woman's body, prying her eyes out of her teacup sockets.

"Stop that!" Nurse Beckwith demanded, carting an IV bag with her as she rushed at the girl. She hesitated when she saw the menacing grin spread across the child's face. "Stop that. You hear me?"

Her command was ignored. If possible, the child pried her fingers even deeper into the old woman's sockets. Her eyeballs looked ready to spring. "I said stop that!" Nurse Beckwith yelled again, letting go of the IV bags she carried, racing to the patient's bedside. With a swift backhand she swiped at the grotesque lock the girl had on her patient's lids, sending the child to the floor on the other side of the bed.

Peripherally she could see the immobile and silent child on the floor. Beckwith reassured herself she hadn't hit the girl that hard, but really she didn't know. It was the girl's fault anyway. *How outrageous,* she thought, *messing with the old woman like that. No wonder no one wanted to come near the child.* She examined her patient. It would take a miracle for her heart to recover. *Good grief, what kind of kid would butcher a dying woman's flesh?*

The last quiver of adrenalin left Beckwith as she changed the IV bags with expert speed. Her duty here was complete. She wanted to leave as quickly as she came in, but then she couldn't. She had to check on the child as well.

This was the last patient to see before ending her twelve-hour shift.

As Beckwith moved around the bed, she froze. The girl had levitated up, parallel to the floor. Her eyes were closed, as if in slumber, or death. Beckwith couldn't believe it. She wouldn't believe it. Beckwith had two teenagers and a pot roast waiting at home, she couldn't deal with this right now. She wanted to turn away, but the child levitated upright into a stance two feet off the ground, level to her height. Her head bowed as if hung by a noose and her arms dangled loosely at her side. In one swift instant, the child's head snapped up as if yanked by a rope. They were face to face.

It wasn't the sight of the floating child in front of her that caused Beckwith to freeze with fright. It was the loathsome, cold smile and piercing black eyes that burrowed through her like a snake finding its home. The monster child spoke with a man's deep, lustful voice,

"A brethren knows what a stranger holds
Whether he be the journey or the road
A brethren needs what a stranger grows
And into you, journey has withered the road."

As the voice spoke, Beckwith felt the breath of life sucked from her, shriveling her life form within. She could not move, nor gather collective thought, while her body responded to the rhythm of the voice. She felt invisible strings, like an unwinding web, tugging to snap back into place—strings that bound her body together.

The voice continued to pull. It suckled at Beckwith's defenseless fibers, craving to drain them whole. The child's smile grew wide within lips that receded back to show only teeth snapping up and down. The voice spoke once more, pulling the final string to devour Beckwith entirely.

"Travel no longer the world alone
She needs bread, and you are the soul."

Nurse Beckwith tumbled like a Jacob's Ladder onto the floor.

Catherine awoke on the recliner in Nana's room. Her body pulsated in warm rushing waves gently subsiding until it was followed by another throb of heat, giving her a lazed vibrancy. Brimming with a sense of renewal, she stretched her hands above her head where the pulse reached and wrapped over her fingertips to recycle anew.

This new sensation dazed her momentarily. But her newfound sense of peace floundered when she saw the foreign blanket on her lap. Collecting events that led to her sleeping on the recliner deemed to be more than memory could push. *Yes*, she thought, *yes, Nana was asleep*. She thought she recalled they were waiting to go home, but something else occurred, something . . . something she couldn't remember.

She spotted the nurse collapsed on the floor just feet from her chair and scrambled up, tossing the blanket to the floor. The nurse's chin protruded out from her head. Her shattered jaw supported a flat tongue, almost severed in half from the fall. Blood dripped into a little pool under the nurse's goose neck. Her eyes, open and immobile, stared out at nothing. Dread moved through Catherine as she stood over the nurse, staring at the still eyes—then they twitched.

Catherine startled at a deep-throated man's laughter echoing through the hospital room. In that laughter a word formed. A word she had never heard before, didn't understand, and didn't want to. The word was Artros. It seemed to speak out directly from the nurse's body on the floor, but then again everywhere. Aghast, she ran from the room for help.

Later they would say, with lowered voices of uncertainty, Nurse Beckwith suffered a brain aneurism. So tragic, they would remark, could have happened to anyone.

CHAPTER THREE

Everyone that came into the room was a stranger, doctor or nurse. One eventually replaced another, their conversations low and filled with mystery. After Nurse Beckwith's misfortune, the nurses approached the room with suspicion and left with relief. Catherine didn't know what happened to the nurse on the floor, but she felt an invisible finger pointing at her each time someone entered the room. Catherine heard the nurses murmuring in the hall, "They said it was an aneurism, Sheila . . . Look Linda, I've been working here a helluva lot longer than you, and I've never seen the brain short-circuit anyone like that . . . Well, there's no way the girl had anything to do with it . . . I'm just saying we should watch out for each other, understand?" If a doctor or housekeeping wasn't in the room then the nurses came in two at a time. "Well there has to be someone who can take her . . . No, that's just it . . . I guess they've been having a hard time tracking anyone down. It's as if the grandma was a recluse or something, I mean, she had the girl but . . ." They spoke in whispers *about* her, but never spoke *to* her. For the most part, she was ignored.

One of the housekeeping staff took pity on Catherine, even though the girl didn't recognize the gesture. She brought her a package of licorice sticks and an oversized, pink, prickly sweater left in the lost and found, reminding Catherine of how much she missed her shabby blanket from home. Soiled with food stains, spotted with holes and frayed edges, her blanket had been her life raft. Catherine yearned for her grandmother tucking her into bed and snuggling her "bankie" under her chin. A lullaby always followed. But now, the only voices Catherine heard before she fell off to sleep were the nurses' murmurs. "Someone's got to get that kid outta here. Why hasn't social services taken . . . They were coming . . . they located someone . . . the woman was supposed be here an hour ago. When she shows up I have to call them, they wanna talk to the woman . . . they think she'll take her . . . When? . . . hellifiknow, soon I guess . . . "

That night Catherine curled into a ball and sang herself into a dreamless sleep. As her eyes drifted to sleep, she vowed no one was going to take her away from her Nana.

The morning staff worked their routine in the room. They brought Catherine food which she only poked at. They insisted she shower, despite her protests. As the day dwindled, she remained quiet and the staff changed shift. Catherine settled on the recliner and doodled on a small pad of paper provided by the kind housekeeping woman, along with a box of crayons. She left the box of crayons alone and instead drew with a black felt tip from the nurses' station. She drew ovals and circles at first, thinking to make birds of some sort, but once she colored in their round bellies with the permanent black ink, her gentle birds transformed into creatures of all sizes, irregular at the edges, all filled in black. A faceless stick figure of her stood in the middle. In the picture, the creatures surrounded her, as if watching her without sight, and waiting. In the corner of the drawing, she drew a tall black figure she could not name. Pressing harder on the paper, her misplaced memories were trying to connect something to the creatures she created. She scribbled inside and outside of the lines now. Her scribbling intensified. *Struggling to remember the importance of... something... what... what was it?* She pressed harder. It was important... *Shadows yes? Shadows no?* She worked the pen and paper to the point she was tearing through and onto the next layer and the next after that, unaware of her actions. She stopped when the ink ran out and the notebook was ruined, hollowed out in the middle where her figure had been, and shredded into paper guts.

The creepers Catherine witnessed had vanished from her memory and the Shadow Man along with it.

By late afternoon, another stranger stood in the doorway. Shoulder against the entranceway, she slouched and spiked her upper lip at Catherine. The scent of soiled ash and burn spilled about the room, scorching Catherine's nose. Catherine greeted her with a grimace. The stranger's denim jacket scarcely covered the tummy roll jutting out at her midriff. Her ruby red lipstick and blue eyeliner appeared smudged and haphazardly applied. One high heel tapped like a metronome. The rapping made Catherine cringe. Previously in the day, Catherine heard a couple of old men complaining about the staff. She heard one of them say, "That nurse is meaner than cat shit," causing Catherine to giggle at the time because she never heard talk like that. She didn't quite understand the meaning then, but looking at this stranger in the doorway she realized what the old man meant. *This woman looks meaner than cat shit all right.* This time it wasn't funny. Catherine's sensors were on high alert after the death of Nurse Beckwith.

A clipboard lady in soft flats and narrow suit called the high-heeled thumper into the hallway. Catherine was grateful to be rid of her.

"Now Kathy," the clipboard lady said, "I understand you're going through some financial hardships right now and that you don't have . . ."

"I'm gittin' it all," the stranger interrupted without a jitter-skipping beat with her heel. The clipboard lady swooned from the pungent air between them. "I'm the only child—the only one—so," she said, smacking the gum in her mouth, "get ta' it."

"You're not the only surviving heir," the clipboard lady stated. Once her words soaked in, the stranger's clacking and smacking abruptly stopped. Then she continued, "The inheritance has been left to your daughter, intended to be distributed by her guardian, with the understanding it is to be used for her well being. This is what Margaret wants . . . it's just a matter of time now . . ."

The stranger spun on her heel and gave Nana a venomous glare. The clipboard lady placed a slow hand on the woman, trying to attract her attention before she continued.

"Kathy, there won't be a whole lot left after your mother's medical bills are paid and . . . please Kathy . . . we need to know what your intentions are so we can move forward . . . forward with this process . . . are you listening to me?" The clipboard lady continued, "We believe children should stay with their parents. There is help available for struggling mothers . . . such as . . . yourself."

"That bitch!" The stranger's temper exploded as she headed down the hall in disgust.

Their words were a puzzle without a picture. Significance was lost on Catherine. She had nothing to do with this scene.

A piercing, insistent pitch sounded, signaling a rush of nurses and doctors to Nana's bedside. An unending hum overtook the waves of the heart monitor previously climbing and falling in a mountain terrain. Its broadcast was a chilling flat pulse.

Catherine was shuffled against the clipboard lady and out into the hallway where the stranger backtracked.

"Clear," someone said as three zaps hit the air in rapid succession, cutting into the infinite hum. Whoopasha . . . Whoopasha . . . Whoopasha . . . the process was repeated each time followed by the hum. Without forewarning, the urgency quieted and stillness replaced chaos. Only a lone, bold drone occupied the space in the room. Padded feet paused briefly as they passed her. Once again, whispered voices returned, but she didn't listen. For the moment, Catherine thought all had been restored to the way it was before.

"We'll let you two have a moment," the clipboard lady said, guiding Catherine back into the room. She closed the privacy curtain, cornering Catherine with the high-heeled stranger.

Nana rested on the bed, showing no pain. But something quiet and suffocating lingered in the air.

The stranger offered no words. Instead, she charged to Nana's bedside. Looking on, Catherine watched the back of her bent body wrestle with something on Nana, grunting as she moved. Her elbows jerked back at her waist while her hands fidgeted with Nana's fingers. Catherine tiptoed to the other side of the bed. She knew this woman wasn't here to treat Nana, so what was she doing to her?

The stranger's actions, cut short when she realized she had a witness staring on, offered an explanation. Holding out her hand, the stranger spoke with false delicacy, "See here . . . she wanted me to have it." Resting in the palm of her hand was Nana's wedding ring. A thin, plain, gold band. It was a perfect circle. A bond created out of love and the only thing remaining of that love had become a grave robber.

Catherine looked to where the ring rested. Since she could remember, Nana's hands were soft like lilies, thin and fragile. Her stomach cramped when she saw the once delicate finger torn apart by the nameless thief.

Catherine let her guard down. She let a stranger get too close to Nana and now she was hurt. Catherine stared defiantly, narrowing her eyes at the woman now straining to cram the ring onto her own finger.

"You don't look like an Angel to me."

The righteous façade shattered the stranger's face. Her head tossed around in frustration as she glanced between Catherine and the ring stuck on her knuckle. With a final push, the woman succeeded. Her head snapped up and her hands flew to her hips.

"Now what in the fuck is that supposed to mean?"

The last hour fell into Catherine's mind like a Rubik's Cube and by shifting its minutes, Catherine realized, with gutting horror, Nana was dead.

CHAPTER FOUR

10 years later

In the wake of a dark dawn, before the native birds broke the iced air with their morning song, Catherine walked the sidewalks of town that lay to rest the predators of the streets, the junkies of the night, and children released from comfort's arms. It was the time of morning that is still—only broken by a small lamp in a window, a whining dog let out to roam, or an elderly woman rising for possibly the same reason she did, breakfast.

Moving a little faster, hoping the chill might run off in her steps, Catherine headed for the local donut shop. Only baker hours applied this time of morning, but she was not headed there to purchase. She was on the lookout for yesterday's stale baked goods of long johns and cream puff pastries left outside the back door in brown paper bags for Farmer Richard's pigs. If she heard Richard's tailpipe bubbling a disgruntled noise out of its holed belly, then she was too late. She'd turn around and go back home after watching her breakfast drive away in the back of his pickup. She usually made it before the farmer, but even if she didn't, there might yet be time. Howie, the owner, allowed Farmer

Richard in before business hours. They'd sit for a while and gossip about the townies and squabble in a friendly match over politics. Howie would serve Richard coffee and doughnuts, fresh off the baker's rack. Catherine could smell the sweet dough alongside the brick walls of the building. It made the flat taste of the crusted doughnuts easier to digest. Catherine only came to the shop in the winter. Summer pastries brought bugs and worms she could not identify.

Farmer Richard's pickup was parked out back. Catherine wasn't too late. She peeked through the window before dodging to the back door to collect her loot. Farmer Richard stood at the counter with his hands in his oil-stained Carhartt jacket and bibs talking to Howie. This morning, the men were taking turns complaining about the new developments in town: The useless new streetlight. The suspicious coffee shop where all the hoodlums were gathering and old man Chide's practice which had just turned over to a young doctor who moved here with his wife and children. They detested change. They were born here and would die here, proud their names would be an addition to the local cemetery. No matter how long you lived in this town, you weren't considered a local unless your last name was engraved on a tombstone or street sign. Listening in, Catherine wondered what type of men they would be today if they would have left the town decades ago. What would become of her if she didn't get out of this homespun shell of ignorance and submission? The town was a cult, stricken with disease, Catherine felt, one which brainwashed and seduced outsiders with its country charm along with those born into it. And the more she stayed apart from it then she couldn't become another victim to its trap of deception. The dreams she desired were simple enough, but none of them she envisioned here. For the last few years she spent most of her time wondering how she would escape the town, Kathy, and the tin tomb she called home.

Howie smiled as he sealed the lid on Farmer Richard's second cup of bean-water brew. The men fell into another conversation about a new town ordinance. Dawn was coming soon. There was little time. She ducked down from the shop's side window and rushed to the doughnuts in the brown paper bags. Her expert hands picked through the top of the frozen and stale goods to the middle for a softer morsel. No one ever missed a bit of food left out for the pigs.

Coming back from the donut shop, the dawn's sunlight emptied its fire into the air. The blaze cast an orange radiance against the white crystallized rooftops and ice-covered trees as if to blanket them in warmth and awaken residents in a sleepy town fifty miles from nowhere. She tried to inhale slowly so the air wouldn't burn her throat.

Holding her doughnuts, Catherine passed the last steel fortress that marked her way home, a battered shoe factory in an almost abandoned industrial park. Soon, the first and last mother of them all would raise smoke from her rusted pipes. The stench would follow Catherine to the trailer park where she lived. The burnt soles of leather and plastic lingered between the mobile homes, almost disguised by fresh air on a Sunday, only to resume and grow thicker with the following workweek.

Sometimes rejects were left in a small bin outside the shoe factory. Catherine would rummage through them in the mornings before the first-shift employees could inspect and separate them into categories of which ones would be stripped down or repaired. Remnants were shipped off and recycled. Occasionally she would find a matching pair her size. It was better luck to find shoes that coincided with the season she needed them for. This fall the factory had an issue with their military line and Catherine found the bin chucked full of black leather boots. Once she figured out her size in men's, she retrieved two pairs. It was early March, but winter held strong and the soles of her second pair was wearing thin. The first pair wore out the same as these. The thick black treads on the bottom of the first shoes cracked and finally split all the way up to the inner lining where her foot bent in motion. While she walked, snow and pebbles compacted into the split and packed in harder with every step. Now the second pair did the same. The cold numbed her feet but she was grateful for the snow. She would take the snow instead of icy water that would eventually come with spring's thaw. When the thaw came, the water would seep its way up the cracks of her soles and soak her socks. Once that happened, the misery would last all day.

The trailer park came into sight as she turned the corner. Divided like the classes of society, manufactured homes had different levels themselves: upper class, middle class and lower class. In an unspoken awareness of mobile home society, it was translated: Upper class, some cash and trailer trash.

The trailer park grew from the inside out to form a domino spiral figure. Inside the coil were the rickety seeds which started the park. Through time, it extended out with newer makes and models of homes, but like a nasty secret a family holds, the core of the park was filled with those society dismissed, the outcast and the wayward. Catherine lived within the center. Everyone was snuggled in tight with the sniffer outers, curtain watchers and park police. When the jobs started leaving town fifteen years ago, the invasion of trailers slowed until it came to a halt altogether and left a large field adjacent to the park undeveloped.

Catherine stepped onto a thin path in the trailer park's glazed field. Petrified Goldenrod twined with Queen Anne's lace between the tall blades of brown grass. They were bent in a permanent bow from the western winds. An ancient oak tree stood defiant in the field surrounded by thorn bushes with frosted stars glistening on their stalks. They brushed

Catherine's legs as she walked through this simple patch of spared land.

In the beginning, the trailer park was erected along with the shoe factory. Both expanded with growing industry. Decent jobs, good homes and new beginnings resided here forty years ago until hope packed a suitcase and forgot to leave a note. On the brink of abandonment, the trailer park and shoe factory were dire reflections of each other. Catherine thought if one stood long enough, one could hear them falling apart in their sediment. As long as the factory held on, the trailer park would too.

Quietly, with her head to the white earth, Catherine crossed the field. Instead of using the park's roadway, she would cut through multiple rows of trailers. It was a walk she could have made blindfolded if it weren't for the debris abandoned for the ice to claim, a tricycle, spare tires or fallen folding chairs. She jagged the path thoughtlessly as she had traveled it many times before.

When she came to live with Kathy as a young girl, she was the one who started this path and since beat it down with each passing year. After Nana's death, Catherine learned to survive by building walls around the emptiness inside of her. In these distracted steps of food, clothing and shelter, Catherine clung to courage and hope, while ignoring her black hole of solitude and neglect. An outsider from the world too long, the void inside her was transforming into a substance of nameless retribution. Like the thin air she gasped for in longing, Nana wasn't coming back from the dead. Catherine spent her time gazing at the walls of her room like she was window-shopping for the future. She was starting to see her reflection in that imaginary windowpane of yearning. Still, Catherine trudged forward, wanting to purchase her desires without a dime to hold. Upon Nana's death, Catherine understood how love couldn't be explained, nor the loss of it. She felt herself choke up at times, as if trying to swallow or throw up a nameless feeling. Lost love and a time past, and it could not be replaced.

In the aftermath of Nana's death, they sent her to live with Kathy, under the strict supervision of the clipboard lady and other government social workers, which thinned out through the years. Oblivious at the time, Catherine had the youthful spirit of new adventures aside from her grief. Once she stepped into Kathy's life, she learned of a deep strength within her, a cut off mechanism that would harden her thoughts and body to her new warden, and the outside world. Years of battering developed this trigger to flip on its own accord. Catherine never thought about it. It was a part of her when she needed it.

At the time, innocence was Catherine's fault, and her assumptions upon the world that everyone was loved in some measure. Assuming Kathy allowed Catherine to live with her would mean Kathy wanted her, simple for a girl of six years then. But growing up meant that the world had turned and there were those in life who only loved the self, and those who didn't know how to love themselves and took from the world whatever they could steal. That was Kathy, a grave-robber and a vixen, single-mother martyr. Catherine was an object to Kathy, one to obtain gains from welfare. The death money slipped through the woman's fingers faster than spilt whiskey in the purse.

When Catherine first came to Kathy's trailer, there were speeches drilled into her and rough skits to act out when the clipboard lady arrived.

"Makes sure you're calling me *Mommy*, understand?" Kathy had said. "If they don't hear you callin' me Mommy and this place ain't clean of all the shit layin' round, they're gonna take you to kids' jail, see? You know what kids jail is— don' cha?"

"No," Catherine responded wide-eyed.

"Kids' jail is for kids that ain't got no mommies,"

"Or grandmas?" Catherine asked.

"Or grandmas," Kathy spat. "And those kids are gonna kick ya' round," Kathy said striking Catherine in the shin with her foot. Catherine bent over speechless, placing her hands on the blow. "And other kids are gonna drag ya round," Kathy said gathering Catherine's hair into one clump, pulling her off the couch and onto the floor. Catherine's tears spilled in anguish.

"Shut your spoilt trap, cuz you are spoilt. You know that? You'd got it so good I took you in. You'd best be thankin' me you smelly little brat cuz this is nothin compared to what you'll get at kids' jail. And you just forget about coming to me for help—understand?" As Kathy drooled her venomous demands at Catherine, the child struggled to recall the way she had cast out fear before. The dark fear which came in the night. The fear which covered Nana's sickness, and how she washed it away. But she couldn't remember. Eventually she learned how to fight fear with fist and blood and the glory of guts.

"Yyyyesss, ah . . . ah . . . yessss Mommy," Catherine said, gripping herself.

Kathy stomped a quick-heeled strike on her head, temporarily damaging Catherine's eardrum. "Do you see any case worker bitch here?" Kathy screamed. The only words Catherine heard through her ruptured eardrum were a muffled "Don't call me Mommy!"

Hopeless, Catherine stared across the shagged carpet in pain and terror, too scared to know if answering something or nothing was best. Later, she would understand neither mattered.

Kathy's domain held many rules, but Catherine was a quick learner. They played the coexisting game. The rules were simple. All Catherine had to do is pretend she didn't exist and Kathy wouldn't have to remind Catherine of how to play.

Catherine became good at pretending. She was even better at lying to herself than to the social workers. For a long time, she closed herself off to the world, but years later with a simple act of kindness the door of her sheltered mind widened. Nathan cracked it open. He had been the one to show her a bit of mercy and kindness three years back when she was on her way home from the library. Catherine was thirteen. It was daylight when she had been heading down a dirt alley through town. Three classmates were smoking cigarettes by a couple of trashcans. One was a girl she knew as Freda, with a mouthful of tongue that lapped every boy she hung on. The other two were boys, one of which was grinning as he zipped up his fly. When Catherine walked by, the second boy lifted a trash lid and pulled out a flimsy grocery bag, dripping of leavings. It sailed right at Catherine and he yelled out: "Hey, put that between your cooter—ya skint!" Catherine turned her head as he yelled, causing not only her clothes and books to be soiled but her face as well. They burst out laughing as Catherine wiped coffee grounds, a banana peel, and the swollen particles of a urine soaked diaper from her face. While they laughed, Catherine bent down to her books where another diaper had busted open, oozing green shit laced with undigested corn.

If there was one thing Kathy taught Catherine after all these years of living with her, it was how to fight back. Catherine walked over to the pack and waited for the first one to look at her. It was Freda. Without hesitating, Catherine smacked the buck-faced girl with the diaper's green shit, pressing and smearing it into the girl's face so hard Freda fell back from the pressure. Catherine savored this small victory, watching the girl heave. It felt good. But this small triumph would be challenged. At once the two boys were upon her, and even a fighter has to know when to flee. Catherine would have escaped if she hadn't stopped to pick up her books. That was all the time it took for one of the boys to grab her hair and throw her to the ground. *Always the hair*, Catherine fumed inside, trying to spring up. The boy's grip remained strong, even though it pulled clumps of hair out of her head. The other boy kicked Catherine relentlessly. Catherine didn't cry out. Living in the trailer park taught her that even though people heard a plea for help, no one would come.

From nowhere, Nathan appeared. Older, and with a few swift right hooks on his side, the boys and shit-streaked Freda dragged their injured pride down the alleyway and out of sight. Grateful, but reluctant, Catherine allowed Nathan to help her up, gather her things and walk her home. During that short walk she discovered Nathan also lived in her trailer park. His father had taken a job at the shoe factory and they needed a place close by to save for the future. Three years later, like everyone else who lived there, they were no better off than the day they landed.

Nathan and Catherine's time together didn't end there. Nathan offered to walk her to and from school for a while after her encounter with the classmates and she gladly accepted. Not out of dread that the trio would attempt another go, but for the fire inside her that longed for connection. Nathan accepted her friendship, and they grew closer, sharing tedious thoughts about the night before, the morning of, and the day to come. To Catherine, it was fulfillment. She felt the rush of life and hope when she saw him, but the void resurfaced when they parted, and the emptiness which refused to leave her gut, which was coated by his presence, returned.

They walked together for two years until the third when he graduated and took a job as a dishwasher and line cook at Donnie's Bar, the same tavern where Kathy worked. Sixteen now and Catherine had this year to finish and the next. Ahead of her classmates, she had nothing to do, but study and work through the process of graduating, but she worried that if she didn't finish school soon she would lose Nathan. What started out as a young friendship evolved into another desire, one which contained Nathan in her future, but Catherine felt Nathan still looked at her as that same girl he had found in the alley—a scrapper just trying to make her way home.

And maybe, Catherine lamented carrying her doughnuts across the field and past the third row of trailers, he would be right.

Catherine fought the frost in her bones. Sometimes she would purposely pass by Nathan's to see if he was awake. He was living the second shift life now along with his father. Not a single light would illuminate for her at this early hour.

A few yards away from home, Catherine was about to pass Mrs. Zinger's trailer. It was the last marker along her trek before entering her own cubical yard, where faded pink flamingos grazed upon frozen debris alongside the brown aluminum skirting which sometimes sheltered a critter inside.

Suddenly, the doughnuts in her hands spilled to the earth when the path betrayed her feet, almost sending her to the snow with it. A curse erupted inside her throat and she bent to gather her donuts from the ground. It had been cold for so long, the snow refused to fall any more, stitching the mud, gravel and piss into the once delicate flakes of its fiber.

Inspecting the landing place of her morning harvest, a shimmer of red and blue flickered over her reaching hands and startled her into a stance. The colors were now accompanied by glints of yellow, green and brown. Taken in by the winter rainbow rays that moved closer to landing on her feet, Catherine hesitated with a step back and looked for the light's creator.

Mrs. Zinger's bottle tree cast the light of its colored glass onto Catherine. She stood mesmerized by the crude lawn ornament, which the neighbors had said was Mrs. Zinger's final undoing. It was an iron stick spliced with twisted limbs where glass bottles adorned the ends for leaves. Mrs. Zinger called it her daemon catcher. The evil spirits, she said, were attracted to the colored light of the glass and drawn inside for a closer look, where they would become trapped. When the wind whistled past the opening, the daemon's agony could be heard moaning in the breeze. "That," she had stated, "was a sure sign one was trapped." The bottle tree would change from time to time when Mrs. Zinger corked a daemon inside and cast it into the river. "The only proper way to dispose of them," she would tell onlookers who needed to be educated on such things. They never questioned the woman in rollers and housecoat throwing bottles into the water. Best to leave that one to itself.

Now, with dawn's light illuminating the cast iron's fruit, Catherine was captivated by the beauty that escaped her before. Frost covered the bottles and when the light hit them, Catherine thought she could hear china crack against the delicate heat of the sun. No moaning to be heard this morning, just the soft broken tinkle of frost warming with the sun.

Lost in the gaze of the tree, she had forgotten her mission for a moment. Then a rancid smell broke the air.

Catherine was speechless discovering Mrs. Zinger standing right next to her. Weeks passed since she'd seen the old woman. Patches of Mrs. Zinger's snarled hair had fallen out and flapped in the breeze. The woman was almost bald with scabbed patches and blisters covering her head and skin. Catherine was ready to make her apologies for trespassing on Zinger's lawn, but she couldn't find her voice looking at Mrs. Zinger who parted her mouth with a charcoal grin.

Even though Catherine thought her nose was frozen shut from the cold, she could smell decay coming from the woman's toothless mouth. It seeped into Catherine's nose. A glance at Mrs. Zinger's bare feet under her yellow floral nightgown, confirmed the nickname the park children chanted when they rode their bikes past her. *Mad Hag*, Catherine recalled. They called her the Mad Hag. Her feet had been in the same place for so long they melted the bitter earth around them and now they were freezing in place.

"Caught one this morning, I did," Mrs. Zinger said in a deep-throated cackle. "This one lived east of the sun and west of the moon, she did. Took me a long time to find her . . . it . . . did."

Catherine hurried to depart from the Mad Hag.

"I'm sorry Mad Ha, ah . . . Mrs. Zinger. I just dropped a . . . a few things."

Mad Hag's eyes glanced at Catherine's doughnuts and then at her. "What do you think a daemon eats, Catherine?" Mad Hag toyed, rolling the "r" in her name to an articulated dream Catherine couldn't place. "Are you filled with legends? Does your belief surface only upon the desire of flesh like a daemon in your book would relish? Those which suckle intestines and leach their victims dry in gluttonous delight until they putrefy the soul? Do you think a daemon is only full of bloodlust without a purpose? What does a daemon eat Catherine? What is its purpose?"

Catherine didn't want a lesson on the bottle tree, or anything else it might contain. "I'm sure I wouldn't know. I–I'm not . . . a daemon catcher."

"Light my love," Mrs. Zinger said clapping her talon hands together in one smack, pressing and twisting them together. "Ah, so simple. They feed off of light, and in the glass they are chasing it back and forth trying to catch it before it escapes. Bottles cannot hold them inside. They moan out of misery. The misery they face when they realize they can taste the light, but never have the power to hold it. So they wait, as I have waited. Patient. Watching. Longing and dreaming as I have dreamt of you. But you don't dream do you Catherine? That will all change soon. Soon you will dream of only me."

Catherine's heart quickened, but the thumping beat couldn't budge her stiffened limbs, the pulse was not strong enough to allow her to run from this voice which trapped her. She couldn't believe this vile woman was somehow holding her. The longer Mrs. Zinger spoke, the more her cackle turned into a profound rumbling of a man's voice, one that almost sounded familiar, and impossible, but Catherine couldn't deny somewhere she had heard that voice before.

The Mad Hag leaned closer to Catherine's pained face and said, "But the wait is almost over, my love. I have been patient long enough, and soon I will have the light, the light of my hunger. I have waited for you far too long, and soon I will come for you."

Catherine's blood rushed through her. She swung her arms in motion to run, but they were quickly drawn back behind her, bound by one stone hand that wrapped around her wrist while the other cupped her screaming mouth. *No,* Catherine thought squirming for freedom, *this isn't the Mad Hag. This is someone or something else.*

Catherine's body was pressed against the Mad Hag, who rocked her like the beat of a pendulum. *Oh God*, Catherine thought, *it's smelling my hair, smelling me.* The scent of decomposition wrapped around Catherine's head and neck. Through the rotted breath, the Mad Hag spoke again in a haunting verse.

"East, she called and came I did
Sun, she cried and light I bid
West, she swallowed and dreams were rid
Moon, she rose and darkness was hid."

Nails dug into Catherine like spikes, but she refused to submit. The voice grumbled as she fought against it.

"We will be united," Mad Hag said. "And we will discover how to hold the light. Until then," the voice grew hard in her head, "stay away from that which you do not know."

Mad Hag's fingers separated enough to break the frost inside Catherine's throat. She unleashed a scream frozen within.

"Let me go!" Catherine yelled.

The cackle in the Mad Hag returned with laughter and said, "I will for now my love, but not for long. Artros will never let you go." With her captor's release, Catherine fell to the ground.

Her wrist throbbed from the hold and her throat felt shattered from her screech. But she was free and sliding her feet up under her legs, getting ready for a second chance to run. Nothing stopped her now while she moved her body into motion, directing it towards her door adjacent to Mrs. Zinger's.

She was a heartbeat into her own yard, aware of every inch of her boxed world, but in haste tripped over one of Kathy's pink flamingos belly up and frozen in the snow. *Damn it*, she thought, *damn . . . damn.*

Catherine stole a glance at Mrs. Zinger's trailer whose occupant moved around the rectangle box with an eerie grace which almost made her pause before jetting a second time for her door.

"Don't be talking to outsiders now dear, cause if you do I'll know, I'll be right here watching and," Catherine caught the tail end of the words as she slammed her aluminum-safe house on them, "I will know."

She caught her breath on the inside of her metal shield and prayed the hands of the Mad Hag wouldn't come to her door. She couldn't trust the lock. It was known for giving way or not latching at all. Catherine had no choice but to hold it shut or make a break for her bedroom door and latch the dead bolt from the inside of her room. She wasn't sure what she'd do if the Mad Hag got into the house and lingered to . . . to . . . *No,* she thought, *better just hold onto the door for a while.*

Nothing moved up the porch, she was sure the creaking steps would have warned her, but still she wanted to see if the Mad Hag was in her yard. She let go of the knob with one of her hands and tried to look out the living room window close to her, but she couldn't reach far enough to see anything out of it. An icicle crashed to the ground, or was it Mrs. Zinger's footsteps on the porch? She grabbed the doorknob with both hands again and held on tight.

She didn't know if Kathy was home or not. Kathy worked closing shift at Donnie's Bar downtown where all the townies went after work. Donnie's was only closed from 2 to 6 a.m. The bar opened early to catch the third-shift employees from the shoe factory who wanted a drink at the crack of dawn, to them it was all relative. Catherine never liked the bar to begin with, but now Nathan worked there as well. Now she had two reasons to spurn it.

Kathy was asleep or never made it home. Half the time Catherine didn't know. Even so, calling for help was wasted breath. It was best to hang on to the knob of the ice box a little bit longer and listen for whatever sounds to come.

In the kitchen, magazine clippings overlapped each other, covering one of the walls entirely. Kathy's once prized collage, she now neglected for years. The faces in the clippings stared back at Catherine holding the doorknob. Once they beamed bright eyes of life, the fulfillment of a better place everyone was welcome to. A magazine reality where everyone should truly live. Now, the corners of their glossy pages were chewed by moths and yellowed with age. Cigarette soot coated the once white smiles of the celebrities that hung on the wall. In the last years their admirer failed to add anyone new to the wall of fame. Catherine felt like the clippings were watching her, taunting her, years after she had tried to put a picture of herself on the wall of perfection—the only picture to be ripped off.

Catherine could still hear the comments Kathy made as she stapled the clippings to the wall. "Would ya look at thay't ayzss," she would say, smacking the glossed paper to the splintered plywood, rubbing it back and forth as if she could feel a firm lump under her touch. Their smiles promoted Ten Tips for Top Sex. Firm Abs. Luscious Lips. The Hottie of the Month, Divorce of the Year, and Cellulite of the Celebrities. Movie stars and fashion divas all adorned Kathy's wall.

Tightening her grip on the doorknob, Catherine digested the walls of her confinement. Usually she traveled the path from the front door to her bedroom, everything else she tried to avoid, but pieces of it soaked in every time she moved between the front two rooms of Kathy's domain.

Bathroom towels hung for curtains. Layers of soiled blankets covered exposed springs and rips in the furniture. The orange carpet looked as if the shag had melted into the dirt, holding the slippery patches in place forever. Clothing draped at random around the living room and spilt nail polish stuck to a *T.V. Guide* on the warped coffee table across from the foiled rabbit-ear television. The ceiling bubbled, surrounded with a molding stain from water damage the previous year. Now that obtuse ring looked as though it would cave in with spring's frost.

Memories went from bad to worse in these small confines.

With the phone shut off, pipes threatening to burst, and an electric bill on the fringe, Catherine didn't know how she would survive through the next year of high school. She wasn't sure if the place would hold together that long. If they were forced out of the trailer, chances were she would never see Nathan again. She never dreamed while she slept, the Mad Hag was right, but daydreaming of Nathan, her only friend, saved her sanity in the times she would have come undone living in this crater she called home.

If she had a phone, Catherine would have put her mind to rest and called Nathan, even taking the chance he'd deem her crazy for holding the doorknob against an old woman she feared wandering the park in her nightgown. He would have come over, she was sure. She used to think of Nathan as a big brother. He was a measure of safe, even in small doses, but her emotions matured from friendship to the longing of love in this past year just when he slowly started to drip from her life.

Nathan's hours doubled once he graduated, slapping twilight gruel in Donnie's Bar for Kathy's late-night patrons. Like Kathy, the only time Catherine saw Nathan was in the passing moments of work and sleep. If it was a school day, chances were she wouldn't see him at all. She didn't want to think of him pulling double shifts at Donnie's Bar in this cursed town she longed to be free from, but she couldn't push college on him, not yet. She didn't want Nathan to leave town without her. Even if the future felt light years away, Catherine supported herself with her daydreams of a roadmap, packed bags, and a full tank of gas. Without Nathan, she would have nothing to hold onto.

Catherine was making the same motions she had for years, but Nathan's life changed and she was afraid her dream of their future together was fading. Upon finishing school, Nathan felt a duty to help his old man pay the bills and the debt collectors. She didn't blame him for what he chose to do. Most of all she was jealous his duties demanded him elsewhere, because every waking thought she had surrounded him. As long as he was around, and she was here, then there was still hope that one day they might wake up next to each other, forever.

Catherine thought about the reality of the events with the Mad Hag. It was ludicrous to think the neighbor looked and smelled as though she was rotting from the inside out. It would have been complicated to explain the deep, familiar voice inside the old woman, which trapped her as much as the hands that held her back. She could hardly convince herself of it, even though she could still smell the decay and hear the dark voice spoken through its black-gummed mouth. Catherine would never have been be able to tell Nathan why she was out so early in the first place. She couldn't hide the way Kathy and her lived, but she still had pride. She could never confess her humiliation of picking breakfast out of the pig feed bags. No. She wouldn't have called him. She placed the imaginary phone down.

The trailer park was one big metal house and the yards were the hallways that divided space like rooms, but somewhere in between she felt that as long as she was here she could reach out and find Nathan if she needed him. Days would pass without a sighting of him, but he was close enough that she could hang onto his presence, even if seeing him might have to wait one long day and into the next.

Trapped like a door jamb in place of a faulty lock, Catherine's thoughts filtered away telephone wires and the simple complexity of communicating. A part of her was angry. She didn't even have a damn telephone to call him with. Another part of her swelled with shame. She hated herself for being a coward and she blamed the greatest part of her hesitation on the confines of her life and the filth Kathy soiled it with. Why would Nathan want her anyway? She was trash, just one big heap of it and it was no wonder he didn't stop by anymore. He just wanted to get rid of her. Toss her out like the garbage he once rescued from the alley.

Catherine's anger expanded. She ignored the reason she was holding onto the doorknob and let it go. Her resentment was building and she had a sudden urge to rip the magazine clippings off the wall. Kathy probably wouldn't notice, her days were spent in oblivion. The snide faces had been staring at her for too long now and she would make a clean spot in the trailer, starting with that wall.

Catherine just released her grasp on the doorknob when it started to turn. Her fear returned and she gripped it tightly, afraid to breathe. The handle twisted both directions. The door was the only barrier between her and the Mad Hag.

As the doorknob turned, Catherine could feel someone pushing against the other side. She wanted to scream, but didn't dare. Then the twisting and pushing stopped for a second. A hand hammered on the door causing Catherine to jump, followed by a hollering on the other side. Catherine never thought, not once in her life, she would be relieved to hear Kathy's voice, but she was.

"Open the door!" Kathy yelled, banging on the door. For a second Catherine didn't move. She stood holding on the door, thankful it was Kathy and not the Mad Hag. "I said open the fucking door!"

Catherine flung the steel casing wide. Kathy stumbled through, holding her purse and a paper bag, casting accusations at Catherine who stepped back into the kitchen. Her mini skirt teased to split as it moved back and forth with her rear. The pleather jacket refused to close over the sagging nipples that threatened to pour out over her low cut top. Brunette roots pushed up through fried bleach hair sticking to the caked layers of makeup around her coon eyes. Her ear lobes swung heavy from burden. Growing older hadn't influenced Kathy's wardrobe, but now she looked like a worn Barbie doll that had been played with for far too long.

"What the hell? Were you holding the door shut? You little . . ." Kathy accused.

"No I wasn't, I was just . . . the lock was stuck, I was trying . . ."

"Yeah, I bet it was," Kathy said slamming the door. It bounced back open.

Catherine rushed to close it, glancing quickly at the frozen landscape to see if Mad Hag was still outside. She was nowhere in sight. As Catherine looked, a word entered her mind. A word she could almost recall through some faded memory. Artros. The word held no meaning and yet somehow it was stamped into her mind. She shut the door thinking about the word and then it was gone like a whisper. Catherine tested the lock again hoping this time it would stay in place. She pulled at the doorknob to chock, but even though it stayed shut she could never be sure if it was truly locked. Kathy took no notice as she dropped her purse on the table.

"You think that shit's funny huh?"

"No that's . . . I was just out and I saw . . ."

"What do you mean you was out? Where the hell you got to go other than school? And you betta still be goin to school or else those sonsabitches are gonna come here. That's the last fucking thing I need."

Catherine brushed back the clothes on the kitchen chair making a space to sit down. Her feet were still numb from the cold as she peeled off her boots and said, "I don't have school today. It's Saturday. I just went to the baker's shop."

Kathy struck a match along the splintered paneling on the wall to light the cigarette dangling between her lips. It was a trick, years in the making. She tossed the match on the kitchen table where it singed the tan Formica top before extinguishing.

"Oh yeah, with what money? You got some cash you betta cough it up quick cuz you can't be holdin' out on me." She plopped down in the only other chair across the table from Catherine.

"I don't have any," Catherine said.

"Where'd ya git it?" Kathy asked.

"Get what?"

"The money,"

"I told you, I don't have any money."

"Bullshit. How you gonna eat if you ain't got no money. Ah huh, I know. I bet your gittin' it from Thomson's boy."

"Nathan?"

"Yeah, Nate," Kathy said. "He given you money for something . . . for a *favor?*" She exhaled smoke and rapped her nails along the table top, collecting a smile in her thoughts. Catherine knew that smile. She knew what favors meant to Kathy.

"I'm not . . . sleeping with Nathan."

"You're a little lyin bitch. I got your number. You got some money don't cha? You ain't got a job like I got and that means you're making it somewhere else. You sit on your lazy ass all day not givin' a damn about nothing . . . spreading your trap . . . while I'm out workin' . . . "

"Donnie's closed at two. I'm sure you weren't mopping the floors this long."

Kathy raised her cigarette hand to cut Catherine off with a slap, but it was a false warning. They both knew it. Cheap swings through the years taught Catherine how to strike back.

Their eyes hardened against each other until Kathy curved her hand to flick away her ash.

"You'd best shut that hole of yours. You don't pay for shit around here. I gotta pay the bills," Kathy said pointing her burning tip at Catherine. "Not you."

Catherine held her tongue to this useless fight. Glancing at the electric bill on the table, the bold red print warned shut-off at the end of the month. As usual, Kathy would take it down to the welfare office with a rehearsed tale about the hardships of a struggling mother raising a child alone, squirting out a tear if need be. Any story she could spin to avoid paying from her own pocket. Electric and Lot Rent were the only bills Kathy had left, paying one with her "special favors" to Sam, the park's owner. Lately Sam picked up the bad habit of showing up unannounced, especially if Kathy wasn't home. Catherine put a dead bolt on the inside of her bedroom door now that the lock on the front would give way.

"There's no harm in doing favors for people," Kathy said relaxing back in her chair. "If you're not in school, then the checks'll stop coming. And if that happens, then you'd best be earnin' your way round here. You're getting old enough now. You should start makin' somthin' of your sorry ass."

"I told you, I'm going to school."

"Ya can't be keepin' that shit from me. I know ya got some trick cash ya ain't coughin' up."

That was it. Catherine thought she was going to explode, she didn't care what the hell Kathy thought of her, apparently the warden already knew. "I was getting some of the doughnuts they leave out for the pigs behind the shop . . . before they get picked up, all right? I'm going to school Kathy, so you don't have to worry about the checks not showing up!"

Kathy put out her cigarette, smashing it with her two fingers into the overflowing ashtray. She smiled again as if she had a rat in her trap and lit another cigarette. "Where are they?" she asked inhaling.

"Where's what?" Catherine asked.

Kathy leaned across the kitchen table toward Catherine. "The fucking doughnuts," Kathy said, exhaling smoky words through her teeth.

Catherine's hunger turned sour after her encounter in Mrs. Zinger's yard. She forgot the doughnuts entirely.

Kathy drew back in her chair, pleased she snared her little rat. "Lemme give you some advice baybee," Kathy said.

Catherine hated the way she said baybee, she called everyone *baybee*. "I don't need any advice, *Kathyee*."

"They don't want nothing from you 'cept what's between your legs and that's that."

"Nathan is not like that."

"Where'd ya think you come from?"

Catherine knew nothing about her sperm donor other than he had come and went as fast as the rest of the men did in Kathy's life. Catherine never wanted to know, especially if it was someone like Sam, the landlord. Her gut warped with the thought.

"Let me tell you something," Kathy continued, "I get to spend time with Nate, a lot a time. And he spends a lot a time with that new waitress Donnie's got. He's givin' her rides to work and waitin' for her to close and . . ."

"That doesn't mean anything."

"Oh yeah, doesn't mean nothin' now does it?"

"I don't care. He can do whatever he wants to."

Kathy relaxed, the mark had been hit.

"Hey baybee . . . I'm just lookin' out for ya. I'd personally like ta suction cup that boys ass between my hands too, yah know. He'd make pretty babies. Though can't say the same for you. But if he aint gittin it from you, then he's gonna be gittin it from her. And if you want a piece of it then you better hurry up cuz he'll get tired of you quick. If she's knocked up, well, then you can just lowball the money. She'll suck all she can outta him in daddy support . . . course there's the welfare . . . but if he's workin' both of ya at the same time then there's gonna be less to go round."

"Is that all you think it's about, get knocked up and . . . and . . ." Catherine said waving her hands as if it would manifest her frustration.

"Yeah, I know what it's all about. Now that we're talkin' the same track, I'm gonna give you a few pointers. First thing, you will be cuttin' half with me . . . and I'll know if you're not. Then buy some makeup and get your hair done, boyz like that. You can turn tricks as long as ya givin' me money, but if you're thinking about somthin', a more *steady*, you'd best hop to it cuz he might just shake you with that Melissa. She's got the look for him ya know."

All that talking made Kathy thirsty. She pulled a whisky bottle out of the brown bag she carried inside. It didn't matter what time it was, every hour was Ten High Kentucky Bourbon Whisky. Years ago she might have mixed it with coke or something else to water it down, but now Kathy was beyond polite society's views of how one should work their liquor. Three quarters empty, just enough for a night cap.

Catherine usually ignored Kathy, trying to displace herself from the world she lived in, but the thought of Nathan with another girl brought about new nerves. They were surfacing along with thoughts and images of him with someone else. She tried to push it from her mind. She had to say something to cool the heat that was boiling inside her.

"I saw Mrs. Zinger outside this morning," Catherine said, hoping to dispel her anger.

"And . . .?" Kathy showed no interest to this new subject.

"Well, she had to have been outside for a long time. She was . . . well she looked like . . ."

"Who the fuck cares about that old bag."

"She didn't have on any shoes . . . her teeth . . . she doesn't have any."

"Rat poison," Kathy remarked.

"Rat poison?" Catherine questioned.

"Yeah, rat poison. She tryin to sell ya some?"

Catherine hesitated, thinking of the encounter. "She didn't try to sell me anything. She grabbed me and . . ."

"She knows ya got money too," Kathy said nodding her head to sleep. It sprang back up to let her finish. "She's sellin' the drugs she makes on her stove. That rat poison makes ya grind yer teeth down. Why'd else ya think she'd be outside?"

"I'm not . . ."

"She wasn't trying to steal anything, was she?"

"No."

"Good. She better keep her hands off my stuff. She was either lookin' to sell or steal to sell. The kids run out on her a long time ago." With that finish line, Kathy's liquor grew tired and she headed for her room.

The woman moved as if on a ship, her high heels swayed and bent trying to steady the waves underneath of her walking down the narrow hallway. One cheap spike heel broke off her sole. She didn't pause to curse. Kathy just swung her rubber leg in front of her, hurling the broken shoe at her door, somehow managing to catch her balance as she did. The boat steadied enough to take her to shore, to her bed where she would eventually pass out with the other shoe still on her foot, clothed and saturated in whisky.

Watching Kathy close the door, Catherine felt she had let the Mad Hag in after all.

CHAPTER FIVE

That morning, Catherine watched for Nathan through the front window above the kitchen sink. The water-soot, stained curtains were parted as she washed and rubbed the silverware to a clean polish. Hazed in thought, Catherine tossed the silverware into a matted utensil drawer which lost another piece of particle board when she closed it. She walked from the kitchen and found herself standing at the living room window. Creating a slit into the red, sun-bleached curtain-towel covering the window, she waited to catch Nathan walking past. Her eyelids shuttered like a camera, but the only photos her mind captured were those of a diluting day. Her finger etched the crack in the edge of the windowpane. It collected cobwebs and dust along her finger's bloody track.

Since Nathan entered her life in the alley, she'd felt like a girl in waiting. He never spoke of other girls, and now she felt a fool to think he would have. Another girl had entered his life, possibly others, but this one was named Melissa. She was something Catherine was not, a woman. Dating or not, they worked together at Donnie's Bar. Catherine tried to ignore Kathy's remarks about Nathan and Melissa. She knew how Kathy perceived the world, twisted it and worked it in her mind, but the roots were planted in a landfill and sprouting. Catherine searched harder for him today than she remembered for a long time. Nathan was the one thing, the only thing, wholesome in her life. She couldn't bear the thought of him disappearing. Nor could she stand the thought of being alone, even if alone was all she ever was.

Catherine gripped the towel-curtain and it swung down in one heavy lump. Dust flew up. The living room was a cave from the walled-out sun. A thin vertical shaving of light shone into the living room. The illuminating ray only amplified her dim dwelling. The glimmer of light was a false hope of the outside world and everything she waited for.

Times like these, Catherine stood still in contemplation and froze in place without knowing. Her eyes were wide open even though she looked at nothing but inner thoughts. Minutes passed, but each one was a second to Catherine. Now, looking at that shaft of light, the Mad Hag entered her mind. Even though she'd been searching for Nathan, the desire to see him took over her fear of the old woman—the old woman who didn't appear to be a woman at all but something else, something profane. And yet as Catherine studied that shimmer of light coming into the trailer, she thought about the sunbeam and the Mad Hag's lesson about daemons chasing the light inside the bottles that hung from the cast iron tree. The living room was like a bottle and that ray of light was false hope. It emanated from the outside world, full of promises and dreams which Catherine wanted to grasp. Within that light she envisioned Nathan walking by. She could almost touch his mirage. Reach and free herself from the bottle. Step into the light. She could see it, yearn with all her heart for it, and yet she could never hold it. Catherine didn't know how.

Catherine could hear the deep-throated cackle of the man's voice inside the decaying body of the old woman, "*Light my love . . . so simple,*" the voice said before explaining the bottle-tree daemons, "*The misery they face when they realize they can taste the light, but never have the power to hold it.*" Arrested by her thoughts, Catherine related herself to one of the daemons trapped in a bottle, one she couldn't escape. She sought to hold the light coming in from the outside world, the light of thirst and desire in one. A light that looked obtainable, and yet here she was, running her fingers in motion across its rays as if she could strum it. She pushed her hand into the light along with her arm and bent elbow. Nothing. Pulling back, she insisted to believe something about the light could be grasped as she looked at her empty hand.

Like the daemons trying to grasp the light, Catherine cast a net into a pond of gold only to harvest emptiness, and she would do it again. If she didn't try she would become as empty as the bottle which shafted the light. She knew she couldn't stop chasing after it.

For now, Catherine let Kathy's comments pass about Nathan and Melissa.

She turned away from the light.

Catherine had to wait until the afternoon to stop over at Steve and Nathan's place when they'd be eating their cereal or toaster waffles. Both would be groggy from the night shift before, but rolling for the night to come. Sometimes, Nathan would be helping his dad make a sandwich-dinner for the factory. Their life was simple, but Catherine envied their connection, plain father and son love. Mystified, Catherine watched them care for each other, gravitate around each other through the years until it was hard to tell which one was the father. Being around them made Catherine taste something she longed to experience. Steve never missed a day of work, or touched the bottle for that matter, but he was fragmented inside. Catherine thought it had to do with Nathan's mother who left them years before, but she never asked. Nathan nurtured this part of his father. But for all the fostering, Steve needed reconciliation from a past Nathan could never provide. Steve never demanded anything from Nathan. He embraced the love Nathan willingly gave him, even if that love couldn't mend the cracks in his heart. And Nathan loved his father, every broken piece of him.

Morning dragged to a painful noon when Catherine ceased waiting. She threw on her coat and boots, but before stepping outside she double-checked to make sure the Mad Hag wasn't afoot. Confident, she ran outside and down the road to Nathan's place.

Her heart dropped. Nathan and Steve shared a battered Celica. Pieces of rust and oil trailed from the driveway and into the road. It was hard to tell if it was from this morning or yesterday. Most of the time, Steve walked to the factory. Catherine assumed Nathan was gone, but she wouldn't leave without checking first. She knocked for a little while, pausing in polite breaks to see if anyone was coming to the door, before she started rapping freely and her knuckles turned red. Nothing.

Catherine walked back to her trailer.

She hadn't given up on seeing Nathan today, but for now she was deflected. Closing her bedroom door, she sighed sliding its bolt in place. Catherine flopped down onto her mattress on the floor and eased a little looking at the aged paneling of the wall. For many years this wall gave her comfort. She had made friends within its grooves before she found her one and only in the flesh. The paneling channeled and swirled in its fake rendition of wood. Long ago she pulled faces from its warped knots. Marks of her little fingers indented grooved lines traced in the paneling, defining the faces which once surrounded her rubbings. Her friends lived in the wall. As a child, they popped out of its labyrinth. Catherine would name one and then all of them as they surfaced as if in waiting. She envisioned them, recalling most of their name's from long ago: Sadie, Ursula, Kitty, and many more—the voices of her imagination's enduring isolation. Dancing and singing for them, they were her playmates for every fable she created. Although childish, she believed she heard them speak. They told stories of places yet to discover, the blossoming rose she was, and the rare petals of a child she contained. Wearing the neighbor's used goods, the voices described the elegant dresses she would be adorned with, just like Guinevere in the picture books. *All she had to do was wait they told her. Endure, they said between the play. Suffer like the lady in the story. Wait just a little while longer and all of the fairytales would come true. Patience would reveal itself, they had said. Be patient like they had been patient waiting to find her. Her prince would rescue her and they would be together, forever.*

Artros, Catherine thought. One of the faces in the wall was named Artros. *Wasn't it*, she asked herself? Her brow arched as she thought of the Mad Hag and her rat poison concoctions. Within the swirls and lines that talked to her as a young girl there was an Artros. His wooden face resided in the middle. Center stage, he retold a story to her every night before she went to sleep. A fable about a gentleman who would come in black and rescue his lady in white, and Catherine had all but forgotten.

Rationalizing the Mad Hag again, Catherine honestly wondered if her fear didn't create some sort of connected delusions to her childhood mind. It was possible that the Mad Hag said Artros. Impossible, she concluded staring at the faceless wall. She had heard the name out of the forgotten memories of her playmates in the paneling.

Artros' knotted face disappeared with the rest of them. She couldn't recall what he looked like, only the place in the wall where his face had been. Still two knots, close together, held the everlasting imprint of where his eyes were, eyes that moved with her as she danced, praising her. Catherine didn't know how it happened, but one day they stopped talking. *Child fantasy*, she thought, but looking at the wall, she wondered when the lines were drawn between the child she was and the woman she was becoming. Was she the girl drowning shoulder-deep in living a life of fantasy to survive, or one who would be salvaged from her bedroom and enlightened by the world?

Alone, Catherine longed to see her imaginary friends again, to feel their comfort. "I miss you," she whispered, "Speak to me . . ." The breath of her words swirled stardust galaxies through the air, glistening in floatation from the sun that sparkled upon the speckles in mid-drift before falling and rising to become again exactly what they were. Dust. Catherine folded her body into a fetal position and fell asleep into a river of oblivion.

CHAPTER SIX

Saturday passed. For most of the day, Catherine's attention remained on the tobacco-streaked, front window willing Nathan to come home. But neither he, nor the Celica, appeared in the driveway. By late afternoon, she quit. Closed off in her room, she finished her homework and tediously organized some books and roadside trinkets. She placed a miniature gargoyle between assorted rocks and dusted discarded metal pieces she had made into trees, flowers, houses and people—some missing parts until she perchance passed by another piece in her travels. She placed these back on and within a dresser barren of drawers long ago. Three garbage bags were lined in a row. She picked up one rattling with cans to return for laundromat change and reached for the other containing her dirty clothing, but set it down without the heart to venture out again today. These rituals consumed time, but didn't take away the nagging sadness plaguing her. Nathan and Melissa. Were they truly a couple? Catherine plopped onto her mattress on the floor, biting her nails. Grabbing a pen, she started scribbling random doodles on the wide ruled, blue lined notebook paper. The pen moved easily over the paper, indiscriminate of where it landed. She didn't care; it was a simple exercise to relax her mind. She rubbed her chin with the side of her palm and felt the wet ink streak her face. She stopped to look at the singular mess on the notepad page before getting up to wash. A large, muddy black mound in the middle of the disorder seemed to be growing and pushing something to the top. A hat. *Stupid*, Catherine thought. Around the mud mound were other smaller, unidentifiable black shapes and smudges, almost in purposeful placement. She touched them, feeling a thick indentation from the pen tracks, still wet and slick from her vigor.

An abrupt, vivid flash blasted inside her mind. She recognized it as a hallucination or a past memory of something she knew as a child. Either way, its intensity chilled her.

Nana's kitchen. She remembered Nana cooking something. She could almost smell it—Nana's perfect fried eggs. Nana was jittery as she moved about the kitchen. Catherine saw little, black shadowy blobs moving randomly over the room. Some crawled up her grandmother's chest, but Nana was ignorant to them. They roamed freely. Nana's frustration grew evident when she accidentally split open an egg on the countertop, knocked over a jelly glass filled with orange juice, and then walked into an open cupboard door. With each misstep, the number of shadow things spiked. Catherine strained to remember them clearly. She saw herself as a child sitting on a chair at the kitchen table and scribbling something on a piece of paper. Her child-self lifted her head, acknowledged the little shadow critters moving about, and then lowered her head back down to her drawing. Her child-self was not troubled by the things in the kitchen or on her grandmother.

In an instant flash, her child-self faced her. Catherine was looking into a mirror of her former self. But the little girl now confronting her had soul shattering black eyes. Pleading to Catherine, she said, "You can see them. You need to see. Wake. Wake us." The child's eyes dripped black tears. "He's here."

"Who?" Catherine asked. The child moved aside. On the table sat the little girl's drawing of a black hump with a dark hat. Catherine moved from the vision staring back at her to staring at her own pad of paper on the bed.

Catherine ripped the paper out of the book and crumpled it into a ball, throwing it into the pink plastic bucket beside her bed. She went to the bathroom and washed her hands. She looked into the mirror while she splashed soap and water on her face, relieved to see her own reflection. Suddenly, her child-reflection was behind her in the mirror, dry black eyes staring forward. "Wake up," she said, her voice now harsh and demanding. Reeling, Catherine spun around, but the bathroom was empty.

"I'm awake. I'm awake . . ." She rushed to the bucket, grabbed the discarded paper, and returned to the bathroom. Frantic, she flushed and flushed watching the shredded, ink-soiled paper spin down the toilet's mouth into sewerland. She wanted the picture gone and the vision destroyed.

At the onset of evening, she gave up on Nathan completely. Comforted by the scent of her newly cleaned blanket she pulled out of a third garbage bag, she nestled deep into her bed and listened to the settling sounds of the trailer foundation as it expanded and shifted against the winter night. There was no stopping the cold outside, or the daydreams freezing within. A purse knocking against the hallway meant Kathy decided to leave for work, always a miracle. The woman was getting worse. Catherine didn't know exactly what time Kathy needed to be at Donnie's Bar, but she knew the wait staff shouldn't show up after dark for the night shift.

Once Kathy closed the front door, Catherine relaxed and fell asleep imagining the whirling snow lifted by the heavy, winter wind outside, whistling at the windows. She wondered how she would survive Sunday.

She awoke to a dark Sunday. A clouded sunrise threw a gray aura into the room. The blankets, cocooned around Catherine like a nest, no longer protected her from a biting chill. That was a bad sign, either Kathy hadn't paid the electric bill or the furnace broke down. Neither sounded good.

Catherine slid the bolt back on her bedroom door and sighed. She stepped out of her room to meet a blustery, winter wind crossing the threshold of the open front door. She rushed to close it, grateful nothing was broken or shut off. The only thing cut was the temperature. Within a few hours it would be back to its normal toe-chill.

On nights when Kathy worked, Catherine rarely saw her before noon. So, it surprised her to find her crash-landed and passed out on the Lazy-Boy (that failed to recline after years of wear). Catherine turned in disgust, not questioning the vomit covering Kathy. She usually had the decency to make it to the bathroom, not necessarily the toilet though. Some of the vomit would hit the bowl while the spew left behind found a home imbedded in the carpet. Puke lingered in the air long after a good scrub, but it was always the piss that got the best of her. The piss would settle into the floor like mold on bread and there wasn't any ventilation good enough to filter it. The bathroom contained a small fan Catherine left running long after pushing watered-soaked, t-shirt rags across the floor. A small window above the bathtub became a source of fresh air after the fan finally gave out, but the window even gave way to stick and it couldn't be trusted, especially in winter.

Catherine looked at Kathy sprawled on the chair. The smell was as revolting as the object it came from. The acidic blood and liquor cocktail mixed into her hair, creating a plaster around her face and neck. The winter wind was freezing it into slush on her faintly rising chest.

Jet-black mascara and blood red lipstick melded together at her sagging chin and oozed down into her neck. The split flesh at her knees was bloody and wet under the torn denim jeans. Catherine bent over to find gravel imbedded in the wounds. Her bare feet told the same story. *Where are her coat and shoes?* Obviously someone had dropped her off and left her to fend for herself. *Figures*, she thought. She debated cleaning Kathy up in the chair or dragging her to a frosty shower to shock her out of her drunken stupor.

She kicked Kathy's shins and yelled her name. "Kathy . . . Kathy . . . KATHY!" she said in unison with each swing. But nothing fazed her. Catherine continued to shout her name, stopping only when she heard a gurgle followed by another gurgle rising from Kathy's throat. Kathy was choking—choking on the misery she brought them.

Catherine's stomach churned. *She always knew this moment would come. Why hadn't she prepared for it?*

She actually debated with herself: bend Kathy over to relieve the percolating blockage? Or, let her swallow it whole and wait for one big gasp of air. This was the balance of fate. She had one last option: she could retreat to her bedroom and let nature take its course. What would happen if there was no more Kathy in the world?

For the first time she could remember, Catherine was allowed a choice. Time was not on her side, however. And then another alternative presented itself—a choice that took inevitability out of her hands. She would call an ambulance.

She threw a sweater over her thin nightgown and slid on her unlaced boots. She would go to Nathan's. He would help her. He cared about her, after all. *He did*, she told herself.

She pounded on the door, crying out for him, "Nathan. Nathan. It's Catherine!"

Instead, Steve opened the door in a camouflage sweat suit. He shaded his squinting eyes from the dim, morning sun.

"Catherine, you all right?"

It shouldn't matter who answered her plea, but she wanted Nathan to be the one. She ached for a sign of hope he would be close to her when she needed him. In this moment, his absence wounded her.

"Is Nathan here?"

"No. Ain't seen him. He didn't come home last night. Girl," Steve asked, "what's the matter?"

"Kathy's passed out and she's not breathing right," Catherine said.

"You want me to take a look at her?"

"No . . . I . . ." Catherine said hesitating, "I need to call an ambulance."

Steve led her to the kitchen and grabbed the receiver of the wall phone, extending it to Catherine. The heat in the kitchen warmed her fingers as she punched 911, still hoping Nathan would arrive any second.

The dispatcher needed little more than an address and cause for urgency. The keyboard clicked away on the other end of the line as a woman asked, "Is she still breathing?"

"I can't see her right now. I had to . . . to borrow a phone."

"You should wait with her for the ambulance. If she stops breathing . . ." the voice carried on with instructions for mouth-to-mouth resuscitation. She dropped the line to her cheek as the dispatcher rattled on, praying for Nathan. Where was he?

"Head home. Help is on the way," the dispatcher said.

"Okay." Catherine said handing the phone back to Steve.

"Where's Nathan?" she asked again, but Steve didn't hear her. She knew she showed more concern for Nathan's whereabouts than she did for Kathy's safety. She didn't care. The only reason to stay in the trailer park was to be near him. If the situation were reversed, she knew the only remorse the woman would feel was grievance for a cancelled welfare check.

"Do you want me to come home with you 'til they show up?" Steve asked.

She thought about going back to Kathy, alone.

"If you don't mind," Catherine said.

The snow crackled under foot as they moved in rushed silence. Once inside the trailer, the smell hit Steve's nose straight on, but the sight of Kathy soaked the picture in.

"Oh, Catherine . . . oh shit . . . ohhhh . . ." Steve's timid feet didn't want to move beyond the doorway.

"Do you think they'll take long?" Catherine asked, brushing Steve aside as she stepped into the living room. She reeled at the sight of Kathy again.

"God, hope not."

A light, rhythmic jerk lifted Kathy's body up and down, but no sound other than a fizz spilled from her mouth like a cork trying to burst open. Steve moved closer to Kathy's caked chest. His pinched fingers moved around her body as though trying to grab a hopping flea. He couldn't bring himself to touch the lug on the chair, and Catherine wouldn't budge to assist him.

"Let's bend her over some and see if that helps." Steve reached for Kathy's arm and moved it up and down like a marionette. "Come on girl, she's dead weight. Help me bend her over."

"No," she mouthed, without a sound.

"Come on. Move it. Grab her other arm and help me pull her up." Reaching for her other arm, he pulled, not expecting her weight to shift forward so fast. With the move, her head flung down to her chest and her mouth released the last bit of spew it held. Her body followed and fell headfirst to plant the floor. Steve's knees hit the ground, grunting as he struggled to flip the unresponsive slug onto her back. He put his hand to the side of her face to see if she was still breathing, a useless attempt. He looked to Catherine.

"Catherine, help me."

"No," she said in a whisper.

A faint cry of sirens looped their way onto the winding streets.

Relief came over Catherine when the time for decisions and consequences weren't hers any more, fate could take over from here. She rushed outside to greet the ambulance.

The paramedics came well-equipped. They didn't flinch, they simply moved to work. In parted pieces, Catherine saw Kathy tipped on her side. The acidic food and liquor that had blocked her passageway lay splattered on the floor. Standing in the open doorway, Catherine looked away to the muddy dawn and back again. Kathy was on her back as a paramedic covered her mouth with a breathing apparatus. Her chest rose and fell. Kathy spewed more vomit. Everything happened so fast. The drowning victim was pulled from the bottom of the bottle, and with a thwack, given life again.

Catherine examined the choices she made—her decision to do nothing. She felt defeated and didn't know why. In the end Kathy always won. Kathy would live to see another morning and another day after, and that meant Catherine would see it with her. It would be the same as all the yesterdays before and the tomorrows after.

CHAPTER SEVEN

The standup shower in Riverside Hospital had a small seat tiled into the wall. Catherine sat on it with her head bent down. The water poured over her, turning her skin red from the heat that promised not to fail. Again and again it came. Slowly turning the dial farther to the left and into the red, she challenged the scalding water against her limit of toleration. The dial was at the end of its thick red line. Still, she wouldn't surrender to its merciless burn. Her skin was on fire. She inhaled the choking steam of thick air. Catherine snapped the dial to the blue side and off before she passed out. But she didn't remove her hand. A part of her didn't want to. She wanted to flip the dial back to the left like a switchblade and see if it were possible to cook like an egg. Just boil away in the water until her body hardened and her eyes popped under the pressure of well-done. If living was alone, what was living worth?

It wasn't the first time she had the notion of putting herself to the test. Every time she crossed the smaller of the two bridges in town, she considered jumping into the river below, but it wasn't high enough and the water was shallow.

Tommy Higgins was a testament to that. He jumped off the bridge, for pleasure or otherwise, she didn't know. Once was all it took. He was never in a position to jump again. His legs were shattered from the impact on the rocks.

The thought of being in a wheelchair like Tommy was too real. *To give it a whole-hearted go*, she thought, *it has to be good. Real good. Get the job done right. End it right at the finish line and none other.* She couldn't risk the chance of failing and being left handicapped. *No, not with Kathy. No, never that.*

Catherine stepped out of the shower, dizzy from the heat. She pressed her face into the towel, inhaling its crisp bleached linen. She felt the antiseptic air cleanse her pores even after the steam settled damp on the wall and her body. Catherine relished the feel of the purified linen and cleansed air. Being at the hospital was like a vacation of sorts, and she didn't care if the package contained wheelchairs, IVs, and the occasional visit by a social worker.

She brushed her hair slowly, looking into the streaked mirror. The thick steam coated it once again, but it didn't matter. She had time to kill, and for a change she would soak in this little peace.

What next Catherine, she thought, *what next?*

This one room had more amenities than her entire trailer: a reclining chair that actually worked (which she didn't use); a television with access to more channels than she dreamed possible (that she wouldn't turn on); warm, healthy meals served with flawless flatware (which she did enjoy). For the most part she avoided these comforts. They were just other reminders of things she would never have.

The doctors said Kathy *should*, no, they reassured her, Kathy *would* awaken from this unconscious state. All the same, Catherine tiptoed around the room in case she might be the one to stir her. Catherine wasn't ready. Silence was best. But Kathy would recover; they all but guaranteed that.

Catherine tried to enjoy the silence, but questions came at her again and again. Why had she called the ambulance? She knew why. She was calling for Nathan. And now she felt the sting of betrayal in his absence. She was selfish, but she couldn't help it. He had yet to make a call to the hospital room. Alone again, as before.

She didn't trust Them. Not even after They came to the trailer park to give her a ride to the hospital. They used to step in and out of her life, issuing warnings to Kathy, threatening her that if They found a bruise on the child . . . if she didn't make sure the girl went to school . . . if-if-if. *What would happen if . . . ?*

Kathy caught on quickly to the boundaries necessary to get a check every month and the paper food stamps she used to trade for booze. The one thing an alcoholic will do is find the means to a supply. She practiced the art of "perfect aim," leaving no visible marks on Catherine. In the beginning, Catherine was old enough to dress herself and walk to school. Neighbors handed clothing donations to the single mother—that is until Kathy's uncensored mouth turned them away. Free hot lunches applied for anyone on welfare, so Catherine was assured she wouldn't have to fend off hunger five days a week. It didn't take her long to figure out how to survive on weekends. She stashed her pockets full of food to a cubbyhole in her bedroom when no one was looking. Instinctively, she scoped Kathy's hospital room for simple articles she would take with her when the woeful departure date arrived.

This time they said Catherine would receive help. Upon Kathy's recovery and release, she would have to attend meetings for her disease, the newfangled word for drunk.

In the aftermath of paramedics and police cars, Kathy was stabilized. Others showed up to collect Catherine. While she gathered a small bundle of clothing, the house was inspected for the first time in years.

There were two this time. One, Catherine thought to be in training; she saw the revulsion in her eyes. The older one hid it well.

Only the elder spoke, "You know, Catherine, you don't have to go to the hospital. We can take you to the Teen Connection House, where you could . . ."

"No. I'm going . . ."

"There are people you could talk to."

"I'm fine. Forget it."

"Well . . . you could even get a little rest, freshen up. Talk to one of the counselors and then . . . go to the hospital."

"I need to be . . ." she stopped herself from gagging while she spat out the tastless words. "I need to be with *my mother.*"

Kathy lay on the hospital bed, breathing heavily in sleep. For the first time, she saw this woman without makeup. She was aging fast. Without the caked face paint, her crinkled lines drooped one towards the next. Her face wasn't contorted in its usual charm. Kathy was exposed and Catherine took the opportunity to study her. Sporadic gray roots crowned her head, mixing in with the brown, before the bleach took over. A piece of Kathy, no matter how hard to uncover, resembled a face Catherine fought not to remember. Sheltered memories, in a time that seemed so long ago it never existed. The only other time she'd been at the hospital, when . . .

Catherine wanted to turn away. This woman, her lawful guardian, looked so much like the woman who once cared for and nurtured her.

Hate filled her. She wished the haunting memory dead. Her warden looked too much like her beloved Nana and the hurt was beyond scars. She wished Kathy would die, and with it suffer all the years of torment the woman brought her. Her anger stirred deeper still, with the hard fact she alone made the choice to let the woman live. Catherine clenched her fists, using all her strength to restrain them from lashing out toward Kathy on the bed, along with the memory of Nana—her one and only true love in the world. The one who left her in the hands of Kathy.

"Why did you leave me?" Catherine asked aloud, trying not to break. Tears ran down her face, released after years of dormancy. "Why did you leave me with *her*?"

Catherine heard Nana's tender voice, and inhaled her scent of lavender filling the room. At first Nana's voice came softly, eventually growing louder in her thoughts, until she heard the words clearly. Her voice carried across the room, and not out of memory. "Oh sweetie, had I but known . . ."

The illusion continued, without prompt or invitation from her. It traveled outside her head, past Kathy on the bed, and to the other side of the room. Through a haze the voice formed an image, a perfect picture of Nana standing, hands clasped together, against the white wall. She wore the starched, simple blue calico dress with ruffles at the sleeve. Nana spoke again loud and rich, "But my child, I have little time."

Catherine stood motionless, allowing this breakdown to completely consume her, sure her shell lay cracked on the floor.

"I have come to warn you," Nana said with a troubled voice.

"Nana," Catherine sighed, reaching to embrace her.

"No child, I cannot . . ." Nana said. "You have to listen now, Catherine. Listen, and listen right. Do you remember the day we left church, and you were so frightened?"

Catherine tried to recall, vaguely thought she remembered, but then there was nothing.

"You asked me if the Devil was an Angel."

Catherine recalled a little . . . walking, the rain . . . was she afraid of the storm . . . no, not the storm, there was something ahead of them.

Nana looked steadfast into Catherine's bewildered eyes and said, "You must see them again, Catherine. You have to see the shadows I denied you. See inside the shadow. It's in the shadow that the Darkness lays. They are one. You must remember that. The two are one. Ohhhh," her grandmother sighed. "See, baby girl, sssseeeeee," her words hung in the air as her image faded, leaving only the small trail of her voice. "They are coming for you. Run, Catherine, run." Nana and her scent had vanished.

What was happening to her? She thought her isolation must have brought the vision to life. Still, she could reach for it, couldn't she? If Nana was created from mere delusion, it didn't hurt to reach out and try to touch her. Maybe if she just thought hard enough, reached far enough, she could bring Nana back.

"Catherine?" Nathan stood at the door to the hospital room. He had been watching a dazed Catherine as she waved her hands up through the air as if to catch something. Stepping in, he jingled keys to gently warn her of his presence. Her face was stained with tears that dripped off her chin and soaked into her shirt. He never saw her cry before. Not once in all the swells of fights with Kathy, or taunting from schoolmates. *Isn't that what girls do?* he thought. *They cry, at least sometimes.* He lifted his hand to touch her, just her shoulder, or maybe her hand.

Nathan knew her for three years, but couldn't remember deliberately touching her. She wasn't the kind of person, let alone a girl, who made it easy. Fighting the touch was hard. He couldn't stand the thought of her rejection. In the last year, his thoughts were incessantly drawn to her. Finished with school, a new life was drawing him away. In the rare times Catherine allowed him into her home, he saw its shambled state, but he never knew Kathy, not then. He hardly saw the two of them together. Catherine didn't talk about Kathy or their home life. Now, Nathan understood why Catherine couldn't speak of it. Catherine lived in a seeded-hell and Kathy was the gardener. He had his fill of Kathy working with her at Donnie's Bar. He'd witnessed the woman, in full form, working the joint along with the men who had an eye for an easy snatch.

Nathan tried to construct a plan to bring him closer to Catherine. He missed the simple times he took for granted, like walking her to school or ordering extra carryout to have an excuse to share with her. Any little thing he could think of to see Catherine's rare smile, the way she carried herself amongst others. She pulled everything in the room towards her as if gravity were hers to control. At times even the imprint of her body seemed to linger after she moved away, as though it burned the air surrounding her. He was mystified she couldn't see it. Catherine was oblivious as to how she affected other people. She stood as an impenetrable fortress nature itself wanted to break. This distinction set Catherine apart. But like anything people cannot understand, it made them uneasy, and sometimes overcome with an unwarranted threat they saw around her ragged beauty and silent strength. That also made physical contact hard. She intimidated him sometimes. Watching her childhood beauty transform into the curves and definition of a woman drove him senseless.

Simple attempts at contact went unnoticed or avoided, and frustration wasn't helping. With other girls it was so easy, Nathan didn't have to try, but with Catherine . . . he didn't know how to get close.

Work wasn't the only thing keeping him from Catherine. There was the man in black, and he demanded almost all of Nathan's spare time.

The townies ostracized the man in black who came in almost every night tipping his fedora hat towards the hem of his long black trench coat. His desire for seclusion in a room filled with people was unnatural in this town, along with everything else about the man. He was striking in demeanor along with the dark austerity he was cloaked with. His silent authority, and heavy wallet, repelled the men at Donnie's Bar. He didn't belong and it compelled people in different ways, especially the women who appeared weakened with infatuation. He could have the woman of his liking, but he politely refused their offers, always a gentleman, and that brought them back for more. Rumors circled as to why the man carried a knot-twisted cane he'd swing, but never lean on. Donnie, the owner, held spit in his mouth for the man as well as anyone else, but the man in black paid a generous price for his presence and solitude.

When the man in black first came into Donnie's Bar, his charm shined against the brigade of checker-flannelled townies lined up on bar stools. The man sat at a table and ordered a Straight Sour Mash Bourbon Whiskey—a long name for a short drink. Serving him, Kathy asked, "What's the fix?" He obliged her by saying it reminded him of someone.

At first, the locals left him alone. Then he came back, and back again, until his presence became a regular itself. He sat in the same mended chair and table, placing his heavy boots on the seat nearby, always relaxed in black and wearing a sly grin.

Kathy wiped down his table at least three times during those nights without a nibble from him, hanging her chest lower and lower with each swipe. Some of the old oil-riggers were envious of the attention she draped on the outsider. By the third night, there was talk at the bar, not the sport updates or the shoot-shitting factory talk, however. It was of the weeding kind.

A couple of weeks after the man in black stamped a routine presence in the bar, a few of the regulars wanted to create a no-vacancy understanding when it came to the newcomer.

That night, Dick, another lifer at the shoe factory who came in after his day shift ended, got up and walked over to the man in black's chair. Movement in the bar stopped as Dick came up behind him. Everyone watched Dick draw his hand back behind the man's head and swing, attempting to knock his fedora off. The man in black was smoking a long pipe which curved down to his chest. He kept puffing, bowl billowing on, as he drew up his free hand, catching Dick's swing in midflight behind him. Some in Donnie's that night said they could hear the bones in Dick's hand shatter. Dick fell to his knees holding his crumpled dart-shooting hand.

Tom and Howie, coworkers of Dick and relics of the old high school football days, kicked their bar stools back. Pushing people and chairs aside, knocking drinks over tables and on patrons, they headed for the man, snorting for a fight. The man in black never turned towards them, or at Dick moaning on the floor. He sat smoking his pipe, grin wide like the brim of the hat which shaded his eyes. Howie reached for the man's shoulders to hold him while Tom drew his arm back, threatening to land a blow to the side of the man in black's head. Before they could touch him, the cane jabbed through the air, striking Tom in the left eye. Tom screamed in pain, cupping his eye. His second mate changed course and attempted a chokehold around his neck. The cane then sailed back and around as if cracking a whip, slicing across Howie's neck and hurling him onto the pockmarked table, forcing his head and back down. His veins popped out of his neck. Choking on his saliva, while spit streamed from his mouth, he rolled his eyes to the man in black and pleaded, "Done, man . . . done." As quick as it started, the man in black released him and puffed another drag of swirling smoke.

The bar grumbled with whispers for the rest of the night. The man in black remained placid, swiveling his ice. Content, he stared forward without looking at anyone or anything, sometimes smoking, sometimes not, yet aware of everything around him. Cordial when spoken to, tipped more than his share, but the man in black didn't belong in the Chapel of Heathens. That night the man in black left a hundred dollar bill on his table and said, "I shall return." True to his word and money, he came back many nights after.

Then, one night, the man in black introduced himself to Nathan.

Kathy had grown accustomed to working with a white Styrofoam container near at hand. Donnie, the owner, didn't question its contents, as she sipped a bit from it now and then—as long as she got the work done. Donnie called her "Old Faithful" or his "Seasoned Girl." But when she started coming in late and refilling her container more than usual, Donnie knew something had to be done. Her bathroom breaks had become more frequent and longer. Kathy wasn't draining the radiator in there. She was speaking Dutch in it. Like a dirty dishrag, Donnie knew he'd hung onto her long enough.

At first, when the regulars commented on Kathy's behavior, Donnie would shrug and say, "She's got a kid."

A kid? Nathan thought, *not anymore.* Catherine was a woman now and he was trying to find a way keep them from the gutter, but at what cost to him? He watched Kathy's deterioration, forcing him to keep a vigilant eye on Catherine. But this couldn't be the rest of his life, a never-ending drudgery of work and sleep. There had to be a way out of it, a way for them both.

The night Nathan spoke to the man in black for the first time, he was thinking through different alternatives regarding Catherine. He thought about inviting her to stay with him and Pa, but that was awkward, they only had two rooms and Kathy would be nearby. He thought about getting his own place, but Pa's rheumatism was getting worse, causing him to leave the factory line earlier each week. This meant scrimping paychecks. Lucky enough for the old man, Nathan finished school and could work full time to help with the room and board. Fortunate for the old man, but not for Nathan. College was riding on the tailgate, out of sight and about to fall off the bumper. Thrown in the work cycle right after school, Nathan didn't have time to plan the future. The only time he could think was while he was at work, in-between the mop and slop. And when he was free from it, he'd fret about when he'd have to go back and muck around in it again. Exhausted from a night of washing the same dishes he'd slapped food on, he'd go home, unwind and find himself waking up on the one-way road again. No exits or U-turns allowed. Nathan started to worry he would lose Catherine for good, if not himself first.

And then everything started to look up.

Nathan was driving the mop bucket, moving bar stools and chairs, and pushing dirty water across the floor. Then he'd rinse again and swash some more. One night the man in black lingered later than usual. Nathan was cleaning the floor near his table when, without a glance, the man spoke to him.

"What's on your mind, boy?" he asked.

Boy? Nathan knew he was speaking to him, but this man was far from an old-timer to be calling him boy. It was hard to tell his age. Nathan thought he might be in his late twenties, but his youth was offset by an antiquity in the air that surrounded him. Nathan was surprised the man in black spoke to him at all. Other than to order his spirits, Nathan couldn't recall him ever speaking voluntarily to anyone else.

"Nothing," Nathan replied with a shrug.

"I have seen far into nothing my boy, and I can tell you have something more than nothing eating your mind," he said with his back to Nathan.

"Well, it's nothing," Nathan said rinsing the mop.

"Sit down and tell me about this nothing you're thinking of."

"I can't . . . gotta work," Nathan said looking to see if Donnie was watching them.

"Never mind about that," the man said, without turning around, removing his feet from the chair and kicking it towards Nathan as an invitation. "That's nothing . . . only the ignorant concern themselves with nothing."

"Just for a sec I guess," Nathan said, his interest perked by the man's comment. People only talked about the obvious, as if words were a way to hide from reality. Even he was guilty. But no one called it out like that before. *Yes*, Nathan thought, *all people did was talk about nothing.* He felt an odd privilege, being the first one asked to sit at his table. The man must think he is someone who has something to say. Nathan sat down, still clutching the mop.

"Does this nothing have a name?" the man in black asked, refilling his pipe.

Nathan's face flushed. "I guess so," he said.

"Only a rose would make a man turn the shade of his desire," the man said, looking into Nathan's eyes.

Nathan looked down, wondering why he was sitting so close to this man and why he suddenly thought about being a little kid again with a box of candy-cigarettes, wishing they were real. Another feeling overcame him; he didn't know if it was because he was thinking about Catherine, or if this man somehow reminded him of her—her "off" part. The part that made strangers stand at a distance from Catherine, the part Nathan admired. This man intrigued him in that way.

"Your face is red with the desire you think upon now." Had this man looked right into his feelings? Thinking of Catherine, he could feel his cheeks grow hot. "Ah, and she makes you burn inside. Tell me, how does she make you feel so *red* right now?"

"Red, um . . ." Nathan said bemused. "Gosh, I don't know."

"How does the color red make you feel?"

"The color?"

"Yes, the color," he stressed, "because, my boy, she casts a reflection on you that makes you feel, and see red. Whereas my rose is as black as the darkness she was created from."

Nathan tossed the handle of the mop back and forth between his knees. "How can you think of a woman as a black rose?" he asked.

"Because, she absorbs all of my love," he said, and then was silent.

Nathan looked past the man in black, to Donnie and the few stragglers left in the bar watching them. "Well, I gotta get back to work if I'm ever gonna get outta here."

"We shall talk more. And you will tell me all about your red rose, and I shall teach you more about the colors of the world."

Nathan thought he didn't hear the man's words correctly, but he wouldn't dare ask the man to repeat himself, and be considered one of the ignorant. He couldn't sit any longer though either. "Donnie's already giving me the eye," he said standing up. "Maybe I'll catch you tomorrow."

"You don't want to be *that boy* forever, now do you?"

"Whaddaya mean? Everyone's got to work."

"Ah, but as long as you answer to another, you are just the fetcher to the call, chasing another man's coattails, aren't you. A cock outside the henhouse. A servant. A slave. A boy, until you learn to become your *own* master."

"That's kinda harsh, don't you think? I mean everyone's gotta answer to somebody."

"I answer to no one."

"Well, I tend to think that's cause you got money. I don't mean bad by it. I mean who needs to worry about anything, if they got money, right?"

"Money is nothing. What I have is more powerful than all the money that drives the world."

"So, what is it?"

"Ah yes, we will get to that. But first, I will teach you colors."

The man in black was talking about colors, Nathan thought, how odd. "You're a strange one. I mean no offense by it. I mean anyone can tell you . . . well . . . you, you . . ." Nathan stammered, wishing he never opened his mouth.

"Let me show you a little bit of what one color can do. Just think of this . . . as a parlor trick for now."

"Ok," Nathan said intrigued, but doubting anything the man would do could top the idea of cash and its poker-faced charm.

"See that girl?"

"Yes," Nathan said looking at Melissa refilling ketchup bottles behind the bar. A year older than Nathan, and what the locals called a looker, she was also the hook and sinker type, waiting to bait and date the first man who came around. She tried working Nathan over when she started, but the flattery deflated. It didn't take long for Nathan to realize she was just another tracker on the prowl, a younger version of Kathy minus the spitfire. Soon Melissa's loose behavior would sway that way too. No matter. He wanted Catherine. He didn't dare tell the guys, at nineteen, he was still stiff in the plank over her. Sometimes he felt like a ham trying to match the guys and all of their pussy talk. He'd nod and make remarks along with the cook's comments about some of the girls who came in the bar, but that was gristle talk. He felt above it and yet he was a part of it. Melissa had already made the rounds with a few of them.

"I just called for her," he said.

"No you . . ." Nathan's voice trailed off as he watched Melissa look in their direction and set down the ketchup bottle she was emptying. For a second she looked away and wiped her hands with a dishtowel. Then she walked straight over to the table, staring into the man in black's eyes.

"Can I get you something?" Melissa said with a faint sigh. All the women leaned into him, even if they weren't aware of it.

"No, my dear," he said.

"Oh, I'm sorry. I thought you wanted me . . . are my ears burning?" Melissa chuckled, "You guys weren't talking about me now, were you?"

"We were just discussing the length of your legs," he said. Melissa gave a schoolgirl giggle. "Tell me," he continued, "do you dance with those legs, or just torment men's hearts with your every step."

"No," she cooed, tucking in the wayward springs of loose curls from her ponytail.

His voice dimmed as he said, "No to what—dance or torment?"

"To . . . to neither I guess," Melissa said with a fading smile, unsure of the question's meaning.

"On your toes," he snapped.

Melissa attempted to say "what" before she abruptly stood on the tip of her toes, her arms curved out, creating a bowl formation. Posed, she looked like the gears of a wound clock, tight and waiting to spring. Her astonished eyes locked with the man in blacks. His rotating finger pointed to her legs. "Dance for me a fouette adagio so Nathan can see my favorite color work its silent arpeggio." She extended one leg midway in front of her and then brought it back, as if the air propelled her. She spun full circle before repeating the process twice more. Her contorted face contrasted the elegance of her newfound ability. All her movements were slow, controlled, and profoundly unnatural. Melissa was spinning in time with the man's rotating finger like a ballerina on a jewelry box, finally running out of coil once his finger dipped down and touched the table. Melissa nodded a slight bow, and then landed on her flat feet with a thud.

"Oh wow. I didn't know I could do that!" Melissa said physically exhausted.

"How did you do that?" Nathan asked the man in black while he looked at Melissa who reeled on like a jukebox.

"I don't know, I guess I just always . . ." Melissa started.

"Shush," the man hissed at her and brushed her away with one wave of his hand.

"Oh. Oh, Okay," Melissa said in a daze. "If you need anything, just let me know and I'll . . . I'm . . . here." She pranced away on her sneakers, looking back to the man, waving and willing for his every whim.

"I have to know how you did that," Nathan said aloud to himself and the man.

"That is nothing, my boy, for all the wonders I have to offer you in time. Nothing is time. But for now we will start with colors."

That night turned into countless stars. During their midnight walks and never-ending discussions, Nathan felt the man was offering something he could almost grasp. This was going to unlock everything for him and all he had to do was get the key. Nathan felt the man was showing him the door, the wood it was made of, which way the grain ran, its different inlays and how it would feel upon his hand if he could only touch it. But the man didn't show him the key. Not yet. He didn't know exactly what it was, but he didn't have to. He felt it and it overwhelmed him. This opportunity would only cross his path once and it was too great to be denied. A way to quit the bar, break out of town, skip college and save Catherine. Save them both. He wanted to be the man in black, and he was willing to do anything to learn how to become him, even if he didn't yet understand who the man in black was.

No one in the bar knew his name, no one except for Nathan, and he was warned never to reveal it. Artros made that point very clear. He was his teacher. "And the teachings," Artros had said, "all begin with trust. Punishment comes to those who betray trust." Nathan understood, without knowing. To betray this man could not be even a whisper of a thought in his mind. Whatever the repercussions, they would be long and lasting. This he did know.

For the next month, Artros discussed colors with him, expanding and extending ideas of a simple color wheel to the surroundings of the entire world, down to the back of a simple laboring ant. At first, Nathan thought the notion of deliberating color charts to be absurd. He was the one who forfeited art class in place of auto. Nonetheless, Nathan was fascinated. Artros spoke of every color having its own energy, depending on the color itself, the hue it cast, and the wavelengths in which it traveled. He said there were two colors that ruled above all others. The mother of all colors and the father. When Nathan tried to open them up for discussion, Artros said that too would come in time, but not yet. Patience would reveal itself.

Artros' intense discussions aroused Nathan's curiosity and the awareness he built studying his surroundings. They walked together after Nathan's shift and the talks with Artros made him feel stronger and self-confident. Even though Artros only talked about theories and ideas, Nathan saw his mind opening to the new concepts Artros presented.

One night, Nathan was cut from his shift early. This was becoming routine now that Donnie, along with everyone else, knew he was hanging around the man in black. Once his shift ended, the two men would take off. Donnie figured this the easiest way to get the man in black out and boost business—cut Nathan's hours. Since the man appeared, some of the regulars were seen patronizing Saddle Tavern, a competitor down the street. Donnie was teetering on his bank account as to how much money he lost from those regulars and how much the man in black left to counter it. Donnie knew more customers would follow the exit door if he didn't get a hold on this problem. Even during the day, no one sat at the man's table, as if he never left. Nathan took grief from the crew as well in slighted comments and work mishaps directly aimed at him. Even his best friend, Ricky, an old schoolmate who worked alongside him, joined in the banter. It wouldn't be long before Ricky would treat him like an outsider as well. Didn't matter to Nathan. He was starting to understand, along with the teachings of Artros, that those taunts were nothing. They were nothing and it was best to treat them as such. Expelling unnecessary anger on them, as Artros would say, only unleashed a color best suited for a purpose, other than wasting its strength on nothing.

One night, during their long walk, Artros said, "I can see you have grown." His cane tapped alongside his step. Nathan never asked him about the cane, although it was obvious it wasn't used for any infirmary. For Nathan, it was just another part of the mystery surrounding the man. They were the only ones on the street that bitter night, following the lampposts that illuminated their path, no matter the temperature.

"Grown?" Nathan asked.

"Knowledge is power. I can see the knowledge of my teachings growing inside of you."

They walked further down the street and through a city park, concealed from the rest of the town by an embankment on one side and the river on the other. Red taillights from an idling car flashed in a distant parking lot, past a ball diamond and tennis courts. Other than that, they were alone.

"How can talking about colors have anything to do with the knowledge of the world?" Nathan asked.

Artros stopped and turned to Nathan. His wide eyes blackened. He said, "It has to do with everything I've been teaching you!"

Artros' voice exuded anger. One by one, the lamppost lights exploded like glass balloons on a string, all the way down the row until the only lights in the darkness were the distant taillights of the car parked far away. Nathan covered his head and closed his eyes from the shattering bulbs. He was afraid, but in fear he understood this was the sign he'd been waiting for. He knew this man was more than just one dressed in black who talked endlessly of colors.

"Ah, that's better," Artros said, now composed.

Nathan opened his eyes, brushing off glass shards, aware none landed on Artros, humbled with envy by this man's ability. He witnessed Artros use this same inner skill at the bar, with the regulars who jumped him, and the way he manipulated Melissa like a doll. But he never showed a reaction to those others. But Nathan angered Artros, caused him to expose emotion. He had an inkling of control over this man in black—a tiny notion that Artros fed off his existence. This man had something, and he was going to share it with him.

"How did you do that?" Nathan squinted into the night sky above. Beneath the overcast cumulous clouds an illuminating circle of light glowed through—the hazy light of a hidden celestial moon.

"The father of all colors," Artros said turning from him. "Let us continue our walk and discuss colors some more."

Artros walked a steady stride while Nathan tried to keep up, dodging the chunks of glass crunching under his slippery, grease-stained tennis shoes. Some of the shards stuck into his soles as he walked, forcing him to look down so he might kick the broken bulbs away.

"You haven't told me what the father of all colors is."

"Some believe the night is without color. But I tell you, there are many colors in darkness."

"How can that be?"

"Let us consider a rainbow, for the moment," Artros said, maintaining his stride in silence, waiting for Nathan to respond.

Nathan recalled other conversations, but none spoke of colors as a unit. They'd always been singled out and dissected. "A rainbow has seven colors," Nathan said, hoping he was close, knowing Artros would fill in the empty holes of his mind.

"Seven you can see, five to another, but I can see more than any eyes envision."

"How?"

"Imagine a truth, in which a rainbow continually surrounds you and yet is hidden. When she is exposed, it is not the full measure of her colors you witness, only the fragmentations of the gown she has chosen to captivate you with, while she finds a means to escape your sight. Deception is her weapon, lest you part her lapels and expose her breast, where the splendors of pure white light exist – the power she refuses to let anyone wield. The greatest power of all. The rainbow foils your eyes to the true waves of infinite energy that emanate out of sight and reach, akin to the colors of the night. For all of these colors, there is one that cannot exist in the rainbow. It is the one I use to harness light. It is the color of the father. Now tell me what that color is."

"Black," Nathan answered, thinking he should have known all along.

"From now on, we will refer to the color as Darkness. Because it is in the dark of blind eyes and hidden light that Darkness obtains its power. Darkness is the father of all light."

"If Darkness is the father, then what is the mother?" Nathan asked.

Artros stopped and turned to face Nathan. "Around others you may call me Artros," he said with a bottomless voice. "When we are alone, you will call me Master."

"Master," Nathan said, thinking the notion absurd and wondered what *others* Artros was referring to. He was warned never to reveal Artros' name. "You said I would stay a boy until I became my own Master."

"And who better to teach you the discipline it takes to become the Master over your domain than me," Artros said sneering in the dark. The wind kicked with a sudden gust of rushing air. Nature swayed to a bend, and the clouds blanketing the sky began to roll. The wind grew in force, causing the trash in the containers from the park's litter to rise into the air. Shingles flew off the pavilions, while some of the chain-link fencing of the ballpark came unhinged, one connected piece of metal after another. Broken twigs, leaves, plastic, and cardboard flew past Nathan. He ducked as the dead limb of a tree broke off and sailed his way, but Artros encompassed them with a barrier Nathan couldn't see. The limb hit the barrier and shattered to splinters. The moon broke through the rushing clouds. Its ominous glow shined upon them. Dixie cups, pizza crust, paper plates and broken branches flew past, but not just beside them, over and around, where even the wind could not penetrate the dome Artros created. Nathan heard everything whooshing by as it popped and whirled. It sounded like thundering air forced through a tunnel where objects collided and bounced, only to shoot further down the shaft with a ricocheting echo. Nathan heard the squealing of tires burning rubber. He looked and saw the distant car struggling against the wind like a metronome, even as it slid into the grass and closer to the river.

Nathan saw the headlights of the car submerge into the river. Its belly was soon to follow, but it appeared to be hung on the rising river's rocky embankment.

While Nathan soaked in the remarkable dynamism at work around him, Artros directed his attention towards him.

"Turn away. They are nothing," Artros said. Nathan turned back to Artros who disregarded their chaotic surroundings and the car. "This is nothing," Artros said, "other than the pleasure of the Darkness cast out for you to see at play."

"This is—is awesome!" Nathan said beside himself. He stopped worrying about the car. They would make it, he reassured himself. They always did in the movies.

"This is the father at work. The father of all colors. Tell me, Nathan, what is the name of that father?"

"Artros."

"And who is Artros to you?"

"Master."

Nathan was determined to keep Artros and his mysterious powers secret. He felt singled out from the crowd for the first time in his life. When Nathan punched out of work, he could take a butter knife to his grease covered arms and scrape it off like a salve, but once he started walking with Artros during the long winter nights, he could feel the mop-bucket blood drain out of his pores. It was replenished by something he'd never felt throb in his veins, pure confidence. While Artros called it knowledge, Nathan felt a transformation stirring inside of him, an awakening, and he hadn't even touched the power yet. He accepted Artros, and his teachings, blindfolded. The man said one day he would reveal to him all the wonders of the world. The power of colors, the Darkness. And Nathan wanted it.

Since he devoted himself to Artros, it was even harder for Nathan to see Catherine. In the spare time he managed, he wanted to spill everything about Artros, the events he'd witnessed, and why he had to keep this secret locked from her. That was the paradox. He wanted it for them both, but he couldn't tell her anything about it. Days passed since he was able to see her, and even though he constantly thought about her, work and Artros consumed him. He found time to sleep during brief spells, but even that was thinning. He was starting to walk the plank, leading a double life, and ready to drop off the deep end from exhaustion.

In the hospital, watching Catherine cry and reach out to an empty wall, he willed himself to touch her. He knew the distance between them could be broken, if only he could bring up his hand and make a connection.

Nathan placed his hand on her shoulder. Instantly, she recoiled in surprise and moved away. His confidence was lost. Only Catherine made him feel like the boy Artros claimed him to be.

"Oh, Nathan, oh . . ." Catherine said wiping her eyes with the back of her hands, trying to hide her flushed face with them. She inhaled and recoiled. To Nathan she was adding to the impassable wall she built around herself. Catherine wouldn't tell him what upset her, she never did and that made the mortar stronger between them. It didn't help Nathan would have to lie. He had to protect his association with Artros and invent a tale about why he wasn't there when she needed him.

Seeing her grandmother, and now Nathan, knotted conflicting emotions within Catherine. She didn't want sympathy from him. She didn't want the pity she'd grown accustomed to seeing in stranger's eyes. She felt ashamed, mistaking his compassionate look as one which saw weakness. And even though she missed him, she felt resentment. She came for him the one time she truly needed help and he wasn't there. *Of course*, she thought, *Nathan couldn't be around every time Kathy got hammered. That would be every night.* He couldn't wait on standby and jump when she needed help. He was her neighbor and nothing more. It wasn't any of her business why Nathan hadn't come home this morning after the late night shift . . . *just like Kathy would . . . just like Kathy does all the time . . .* "Stop it," she said to herself, "just stop it! He's here now and that's all that matters." Maybe that was the true problem, she thought, maybe she was scared he was off doing the same things her mother did after work. She felt guilty thinking these thoughts. She knew Nathan. She put it out of her mind as much as she could. She cared for him. He was the only person alive she cared for. She wished she could tell him that, she wished . . .

"I didn't expect you to be here," she said with a sigh.

"Of course I'd be here . . . Well, I'm sorry I couldn't come sooner. My dad told me you came to our house when your, um, Kathy passed out."

Passed out, Catherine thought, *that's a way to put it.* "I had to use someone's phone," she said. "It was nice of your dad to let me use yours."

Nathan combed his fingers through his hair and turned away from her. Stuffing his hands into his coat pockets, ready to mix lies and truth together, he fanned them out as he turned back to her, saying, "I stayed out late and crashed at Ricky's house. I saw you leaving the park, but my ol' man caught up with me and . . . man he was . . ." Nathan paused and then cleared his throat before he continued, "Anyhow, Donnie, he can be . . . all right sometimes. He said I could come and see you before the dinner rush, so I can stay a while if you . . ." Nathan fidgeted his hands in his pockets. "You know I would have liked to have—you know, I would have been there had I'd known . . ." Nathan tilted his head up to the ceiling, then back to her before he tapped his foot and said, "Damn Ricky, he loves the pool halls, they're open till 4 a.m., can you believe it, and he's always looking for a partner. I lost twenty bucks last night . . . when I should have been . . ."

"I don't care . . . that's fine . . . I mean, I'm glad you're here. Your dad's a good guy. He offered to drive me to the hospital so I wouldn't have to ride with . . . anyone else . . . but I didn't. But it was nice of him to offer, really nice, working second shift at the factory and . . ."

"Yeah, he's trying to get me a job there," Nathan interrupted, wondering why he said it. That part was true. A couple of months ago he might have considered it, but not now. Still it was something he could ramble on about—just spill more words into his burgeoning pothole of lies to cover his tracks and absence. Suddenly his twiddling stopped. He stood a few feet away from her. Instead of pacing and flapping his hands with his words, his body slackened as his head tilted down to the floor, ashamed deception came easily.

Hearing Nathan speak of the factory made her cringe. The shoe factory was a death sentence full of willing victims and shattered aspirations. The young were bait to feed a never-ending production line of missed opportunities and lost dreams. Many who started the factory, never left.

"You're not going to do it are you?" Catherine asked.

"What, the factory?"

"Yeah, I mean, what about college? You used to talk about it."

A silence sat between them. She knew Nathan's father to be an honest blue-collar type, but the few times Nathan talked about school anymore, the look was in his eye for consideration. She assumed it was the factory. She shuddered to think he could become another soul feeding the black rubber line. Money was always the issue, not only for her, but for him. They hadn't seen much of each other since he graduated. Looking at him now, Catherine felt college slipping away with the slipknot of the factory tightening its grip.

"It's not like it would be a bad thing," Nathan said scuffling his feet a little. "It's more than minimum wage, and it sure beats cooking and mopping up after . . ."

"You need to leave, Nathan," Catherine interjected. It pained her to say these words. "Don't settle. Not for the factory, not for this town, not for . . ." she wanted to say Melissa, but instead continued, "Even if you don't know where you're going, you know, you . . . you just have to get the hell out of hell."

"It's just . . . it's not that simple," Nathan said looking into her worried face, a reflection of his own. He wanted to tell her about Artros and how he thought that would link their futures together, but he couldn't. If he did, he might never see the man in black again, and what he could gain couldn't be turned down. Nathan needed to think of something to stall time, why he wasn't moving forward with school, or with anything else in his life, even her. He continued, "My dad needs me. His joints are acting up on him and . . . I don't even know where I would go. I never really picked a school, and I was never sure what the hell I would go for anyway. You know it all breaks down to money. I thought maybe I'd be able to save a little, and help him out if I worked for a while."

That's what they all said, Catherine thought, *and then they found themselves twenty years later shelving shoeboxes blindfolded.*

"Nathan, you just can't be hanging around here. You know what happens to people when they don't—well—you know, get outta here," Catherine said, with her stomach churning in nauseating thoughts about Nathan sinking deeper into the town. Catherine couldn't help but ask, "Are you staying here because of Melissa?"

"Melissa? What?" Nathan questioned in puzzling thoughts until he realized Catherine must have thought he was seeing Melissa on the side. "Oh, no. She seems to . . . to get around, if you know what I mean," Nathan responded with a little smile.

"Know what you mean," Catherine said a bit lighter-hearted and filled with relief. "Come on, Nathan. I live with a Class-A-Kathy-Wailer-Banger, if you know what I mean," Catherine added trying to ease the mood, pleased he showed no interest in the mention of Melissa's name.

"God, after working with her, an' seeing her tits flash at every guy who walks in . . ." Nathan stopped himself short. "Sorry Catherine, you didn't need to hear that."

"Did you forget I live with her? I've been watching her flash guys for years. As much as they're sagging now it's no wonder they don't fall to the floor when she lifts up her shirt." Catherine's comment made them both chuckle in nervous laughter.

"Seriously though," Nathan asked pointing over to Kathy lying on the bed, "is she going to be okay?"

"She better be," Catherine said tossing Kathy a glance, "because there is no way I'm taking care of a vegetable."

"Ouch," Nathan responded with the thump of his hand to his chest.

"Don't worry," Catherine said unable to face him. "I'd take care of you." She smiled a little and looked at him. "I mean as long as you promise to pack your bags and go to school."

"Hey, what are you trying to do? Get rid of me?" Nathan poked at her.

"If I wanted to get rid of you, I'd kick your ass right out of here," she shot back.

"Right down the street?"

"Right out of town," Catherine said, swinging her foot in the air. They laughed a little and felt the rift between them weakening.

"I haven't had breakfast yet," Nathan said, as his stomach growled.

"You know, I haven't either," she said, even though food was tasteless at the moment. She was happy Nathan was here and the tension passing, but Catherine felt something wasn't right. The feeling wouldn't settle. She looked at Nathan's bright smile and let the feeling pass, for now.

"So," he said tapping his chin, "we can't order takeout yet, and there's no butler in sight . . . is there a vending machine or something in this joint?"

"God, you are hungry."

"Where there's a stomach there's a way," Nathan said patting himself.

"On the table is an order form for breakfast, but it might be too late now. I'm not sure when they cut eggs off around here. Maybe we could wait for the lunch menu," she suggested, but the look she got in return told her he couldn't wait now that they were on the subject of food. "Or," Catherine snickered and continued, "you can just take it down to the second floor kitchen and see what kind of leftovers they have."

Nathan was more than willing to hand deliver the breakfast ticket. "What do you want?" he asked picking it up.

Catherine was never picky about food hot from the oven. "I'll just eat your scraps," she said with a grin.

He took the order form and pen with him, reading it on his way to the door. Catherine turned away from him, already anxious for his return. She heard the door open as she started to pace the room. She didn't care about food, but if it gave him a reason to stick around longer she would use dinner as persuasion. Whatever excuse she could use to keep him. But for all her elation something was amiss with Nathan, and she couldn't place what it was.

Once Nathan came, she pushed aside the vision of her grandmother in the hospital room. But glancing at Kathy reminded her of the hallucination, asking herself why it came, and what did it mean? How could her mind make up such preposterous things like the darkness laying in the shadows? Yesterday, her child-self told her to see the shadows. As much as Catherine tried to push the voices down, they grew until they sang out in unison, *see the shadows, and run.*

CHAPTER EIGHT

Jorgen watched the people walk in and out the hospital, taking innocent steps into the world of pain, sickness, death and birth. Man's intervention of the inevitable. Humanity would fight to keep its breath alive.

The end of each society boiled down to loss and mourning. In this place of contemplation, the elderly felt the sting of mortality, hoping the breath of life would be gentle to the born, strengthen the resurrected, and spare the dying within pain's cradle. No matter the tribulations in life, the end would be the same. Death greeted them all at the same door.

Rejuvenating life through generations long forgotten, this place held no use for Jorgen. He walked a different path than his brethren now. The path of Darkness. His journey led him to this hospital, shrouded with the power.

After shutting himself away for decades, the quest called for him once more. Even when Jorgen wanted to abort, he was pulled like a sailor to the sirens. The blind voyage led him here, to an old brick hospital in a remote country town. But it wasn't the building; it was the mystery within. He was drawn by its strength and the power of attraction, only one like him understood.

A dark shroud covered the building, one that could only been seen by those who knew the Darkness and its veiled truth. It was not death, nor the river's fog broken from a cool night. It was stationed power. A shield used to protect the core of a Master's keep. Jorgen studied it with caution. Ordinary eyes could not see this stirring force, the deadly defenses of the shield, or its venomous guardians. Shadow Men and Shadow Creatures defended the hold and would fight to the extinction of their profane bodies, even if it meant dissipating into the shadows they were created from.

Jorgen tried to connect to the core of the shield, to the source of what was coveted. Could be a human, maybe not. With the shroud in place, it was impossible to tell, but it was powerful. Strong enough to radiate across state lines and airwaves and into the root of his pores. Whatever lay inside the hospital was well-protected against someone like him, a Master of Darkness. If he were to enter the building, the shroud would defend and attack against the power of Darkness he harbored. It was made by another like him, and against those of his kind.

His inner power tensed and willed itself to move forward, causing him to relax the dark energy within. He'd not used the power in such a long time. Darkness had a nature of its own. It was a wild power and to control it took decades to master. Like poles of magnets, opposites attract, and the Darkness stirring within him repelled the shield. Even the swell of it, expanding inside of him, might warn others of his kind he was near. His actions must be quick, before the power inside him took over, lest his mounting energy led to discovery.

Solitude hadn't brought the answers Jorgen searched for. Nor surfacing into a world of technology, where science surpassed its creators who attempted to grasp the mysteries they solved, only to succeed with another one to unravel.

Long ago, Jorgen felt himself an artisan, but the dexterity of the Darkness fooled him. Nothing was eternal. Energy needed to be rejuvenated, shaped or controlled in its unstable environment. The concept of pure form, be it the Light or the Darkness, eluded him.

The weary search became a dull charade and, when he forced the quest, a muddle of madness. He wandered in and out of humanity's discord trying to discover the connection which would join the whole. Theories displaced themselves into fallacy. The union of Light and Darkness was a riddle that taunted him, boldfaced, between the two of everything, the two that held substance and isolation, together. Everything forgotten and found, blade to grass, fingertip against touch, silence and sound. Attempting to balance the weight of the two would cause one to thrust or pull. Neither side of the equation equalized to join the elements. When he thought he was close, one outweighed the other. He no longer searched for the power of Light, but it was the same quest for pure energy that afflicted his past and haunted him still. All Jorgen hoped for now was to understand the balance. Before he died, he needed to know what tied Light to the Darkness, and the Darkness to the Light. Even if he couldn't understand how to harness the elusive Light, at least he would be at peace knowing how two opposing forces could be connected at the same time.

The decision to enter the building wouldn't waver.

The threads he gathered to sustain solitude were thinning. The aging process crept into the grooves of his flesh. Time colored his hair, marking him with an elder's appearance, a deception of truth. Jorgen was filled with power, but against mortality, he should have been nothing more than dust.

Driven from isolation, he traveled aimlessly. Fear of death weakened through the miles, as he committed himself to an end, even if the result led to the last mystery everyone in life is forced to solve. He let the wheel of his mind go and allowed the road to gravitate him to this hospital covered in a Darkness he had no choice but to stir.

If he were to penetrate the shield, he would have to release his power elsewhere, in hopes to enter the hospital and survive. He would attempt to sneak past the guard as normal human's did.

Before entering the building, he would have to unleash the very essence holding death at bay, but most of all, his darkest of defenses. He would need to become akin to his distant brethren walking in and out of the gray glowing shield, ignorant and exposed, making himself almost one amongst them.

Draining the dark essence thriving inside his intricate webs of power could be disastrous and even fatal to those who encountered it. He would have to disperse the power with a purpose, a direction, and unfold its energies harmless upon the innocents and attempt to leave nature herself untouched. He could neither afford calamity or the undesired attention that might alert the kraken protecting the mysterious pearl within.

Darkness could dissipate as well as transfigure. It was a power that might fizzle into the cracks of the earth or breed and feast off the environment. Darkness was ruthless innocence like nature. The dark power could not be punished, scolded nor rewarded, and yet it was volatile in temperament, a true dynamism of its own. He had to decide how best to release the dark power before entering the hospital, which in turn may reveal his presence as well.

A steady river ran nearby. Thick layers of ice and snow topped the waters beneath. Jorgen felt the Darkness could be cast into its slumbering waters until it would finally dissipate and filter through the freshwater life, boulders and sand along the shoreline and upon the roots that drank from the river's flow. The dark energy could ride upon the hidden waves underneath the ice and snow without harming boaters, fisherman or children playing along its banks this time of year. He'd never attempted anything like this kind of release, but he prayed the dark power could be purified into harmless currents within the water's flow.

The electrifying waters charged him as he drew near the river, a natural way his body identified flowing energy. Jorgen's arms extended to alleviate the pressure of his restless dormant power urging to advance. The swelling began in the center of his body, with tremors that quaked through his blood, beating the temples of his forehead. Then the surge expanded, threatening to shoot out from his limbs in all directions if he didn't compose the power quickly. This control was something only a Master could achieve, yet looking at the white river, quivering and holding back the power inside, Jorgen doubted himself and his purpose. He hadn't expelled the Darkness in such a long time.

Jorgen stood on a wooden bridge created for foot travel and directed his attention to the waters beneath the snow. His body shook as he extended his arms to the side and then in front of him. Creating a triangle with his thumbs and fingers, Jorgen directed the energy through the triangular hole. The power rattled his mind as he tried to control the instinct of the dark power from taking over. He attempted to move the power in one slow steady stream beneath the ice and snow and into the calm waters beneath. Jorgen could feel the power channeling faster. He tried to hold its reins. The Darkness commanded a flow of its own. The more he resisted, the faster it traveled until it pulsated against him and he couldn't deny it any longer. He met its beating wavelength, like a kite unraveling against the wind. He was left no choice, but to hold on and ride the surge.

DARKNESS

The ice started to crack as its sisters' growing waters beneath were filled with power. It too charged and expanded. All at once, the ice exploded like dynamite and released the top coat of winter's sheath down a raging river. The mounded power recoiled upstream as well. Boulders of ice and earth exploded from both directions, riding on the river's great tidal wave. Compassion and understanding were beyond the tempest flowing out of control. Darkness knew no mercy.

The loud thundering roar continued with the crashing of ice and aberrant waterfalls. Jorgen witnessed his grave error. The power inside hid deeper than he fathomed. He chastised himself for this reckless undoing, but he could not delay to sway its outcome, or attempt to ease the damage. Movement without a purpose was the most dangerous form of all, a hard lesson learned. Jorgen would numb himself to the consequence of the Darkness he released, at least for now. He hoped it might be merciful to whatever suffering lay in its path.

He had to move quickly now that the Darkness was drained. He couldn't afford discovery at this vulnerable time. It would be his undoing.

Defenses were not out of reach. Jorgen could harness the Darkness once inside the hospital if the shield detected his presence. To him, it was a vulgar way of gathering protection, but a way all the same.

He stood in front of the hospital's shield thus far undetected. Without the power inside, the Darkness which sustained his mortality and gave him endless internal anguish, he felt his flesh, its withered skin and hardship lines. His internal strife and what he truly was inside, an old man walking into a hospital, to meet death through this final door and never walk out again.

An ambulance turned its siren off, the engine idled, while its red light throbbed against the side of the emergency entrance. Jorgen walked in like any other human, invisible to the shield's Shadow Men and Shadow Creatures within. Jorgen glided past the reception counter and waiting rooms. His pace left little to question from the few who noticed him. Receptionists answered one call after another, until the circuit boards filled with flashing lights. A woman's voice came over the intercom, calling all available staff to the main foyer immediately. Rumors of a crisis spread through the hospital like a spinning vane broken from a windmill and cycling out of control. No one knew the details of the calamity that struck the river and its town. Nonetheless, the aftermath of it was coming towards them. Nurses shouted at one another and told people to clear the hallways. Aides rushed to pull out gurneys and first aid equipment for triage, lining them up one by one for patients that had yet to arrive. The ambulance headed out, sirens blaring.

Jorgen ignored them. The concern of others would be still to him until the mystery of the shield was solved. Instinctively, the urgency surrounding him tempted him to gather the Darkness for defense, but he warded off the desire. Not yet, he wavered, not yet.

He took the stairs to the middle of the building where the protected jewel lay.

Opening the stairwell door, he gave pause. He almost backtracked. It was close. It was human. The walls pulsated with a vibrancy of *one of his kind*. He was vulnerable and the urgent need to gather the Darkness returned, but he could not. He would trigger the shield's alarm. No, not yet he fought. He had to see first. He had to know what had the strength to pull him out of isolation and to this abandoned town. Patience. He had to exercise control, no matter how exposed. He would see first, and then decide.

This human was a separate entity to the maker of the shield. The walls inside the hallway gave off a wave different from the exterior of the building, a distinct rhythm and speed. His index finger rose to the hidden vibe. It was soft, warm, and full of all the sensations a blossom waits for anticipating spring. For a moment, all faded from Jorgen: the chaos, the fear of discovery, and the future. A feeling overcame him, a connection which hit his enduring solitude and ruptured it. He wasn't ready. He felt connected to the creator of this vibe. He understood the inner pain and suffering, and the raw purity behind it. Just like he once was, before the Darkness overtook him. Connected to its maker, letting the touch alone guide him, Jorgen weaved in and out of wheelchairs and carts, past the people who hustled from the news down below and to the direction of its source. Hospital staff barked orders to aides, visitors, and custodians, while they moved trays and gurneys in the hallway. Never taking his finger off the pulse, it guided him to a door that blended in like all the rest. Jorgen knew, as a phantom knife wrenched its way into him, it would change his life forever.

215. His fingers touched the numbers. 215. He etched the numbers again and then slid his hand to the doorknob, daring to turn it and enter. A young man opened it for him. Jorgen stepped aside. This was not the one he pursued. Although this boy was ignorant, his mind was being manipulated toward the power of Darkness. Jorgen could see it inside of his inner threads which were developing awareness, a knowledge, which would soon lead to the dark hollow cave of questions without answers. They glanced briefly in passing before the young man became distracted by the commotion in the corridor. He walked down the hall and questioned a janitor about the events taking place before stepping into the elevator with him.

Jorgen stood in the doorway of 215. Mesmerized, he watched a girl pace the room, unaware of herself or anything else around. However, her inner-self spindled, weaved and projected forth as much as it could stretch given the binds placed upon her and the pulsing power she held within. Jorgen saw Catherine for the first time.

Fighting the presence in her head, Catherine paced the room. Why hadn't she gone with Nathan? She finally plopped in the recliner and gave way to the visions whispering to her; they wouldn't let her be. *Nathan was here. Nathan was real,* she reminded herself. She shot out of the chair to pace again.

A picture hung on the wall of some sort of nun. The woman's face tilted up. Her eyes squinted within her wrinkled skin. She wore a white headdress with a blue line striking its band along the top of her head, not the attire Catherine associated with nuns. She studied the picture, focusing on the hands clasped in prayer, holding a rosary. It calmed her. The woman's serene face beamed in solace and hope against some hidden sun which beat upon her weathered skin. This face knew hardship. Her tribulation grooved its trials within the lines upon her face, putting Catherine to shame for no reason she could gather. This woman had been through some war, and still looked towards the light.

"Do you know who that is?" a man's voice asked from the doorway.

Catherine was startled. It didn't sound like an inquiry, it sounded like a command waiting for an answer. "It says . . . The Saint of Calcutta," Catherine said reading the title at the bottom of the photograph.

"So she is, and a woman to be respected. She is also known as The Saint of Darkness," the man responded.

Intrigued, Catherine turned to the man. His hair was silver like the stubble of his beard, left undecided to grow or shave. It shimmered throughout its shagged lining. He was clothed completely in black, a bit disarrayed in dress, but it was fitting attire for a priest. His thick coat collar was folded at the back of his neck and twisted. Beneath furrowed brows, his eyes studied her, causing her to feel exposed and defenseless.

"Who are you?" Catherine asked.

"My name is Jorgen," he answered. Catherine thought he bent slightly, as if to bow, before he continued, "And what is yours?"

He couldn't be a priest Catherine surmised. He was missing the white band around the collar. But something else rested there, a ring of silver, a necklace perhaps. Yes, it was a necklace. In the center of the solid ring around his neck, a silver square rested with an engraving on it. Catherine caught herself drawn to its centerpiece. Half of the design looked like an R, one side straight like the letter and then folded, opposite of itself. A double R, one forward and one reverse. His chin dipped down, catching her attention, and she looked at his face. The only one who asked her name would be a social worker or the hospital staff. All interest in the photo, the man, and the necklace faded.

"Catherine," she said, assuming he was one of Them. "What do you want?"

He seemed to sway. His hands rested at his sides. His presence filled the entrance, but he did not enter. He made her uncomfortable like They all did. She was on guard to protect her future. Catherine felt They might place her in a shelter, a place They liked to call a home. But she could care for herself. His stare unnerved her. She wouldn't make it easy on him. She wouldn't give anything away to displace her from Nathan.

"Ex-ca-ussse meee . . ." Nathan said from behind the man.

Catherine didn't think he was going to let Nathan pass, but the man abruptly spun aside. He moved with a grace and speed unnatural for anyone, let alone a man of his age. He then vanished out of sight and down the hall.

"Who the hell was that?" Nathan asked.

No point in lying since he would find out anyway.

"Just another case worker," Catherine said. "I think he wanted some answers from me, until you so rudely interrupted us . . ." she tried to tease, but Nathan's face made her uneasy.

"Haven't they poked and prodded you enough?" Nathan asked.

"You know *Them*," Catherine started to say, remembering Nathan never had to deal with the system. "They have to have all their Ts crossed and . . ." Catherine trailed off noticing Nathan's distracted behavior. She heard rushed voices and a climbing commotion outside of the room. "What happened to breakfast?" she asked confused, realizing his hands were empty.

He walked to the window and upturned the shades. "You didn't hear?" he asked, surprised no one had told her.

"What?"

"The river . . ." Nathan began and waved Catherine over to the window, "Something happened on the river and the dam broke. Rumors are spreading like crazy. People are saying something like a . . . like an iceberg plowed through it or something. Isn't that nuts? They're saying it just exploded. It's been taking out bridges and houses on its way. I heard houses and cars are being washed right into the river."

"No," Catherine gasped, putting a hand over her mouth walking to the window.

"See," Nathan said, still holding onto the blind's string, stepping aside for Catherine to see for herself. She saw cars piling into the parking lot, parking randomly on the sidewalk, curbs, and earth to get close to the hospital doors. Staff and a few security guards were trying to keep the road open to the emergency entrance filling rapidly with vehicles of all makes and models. They hollered to the drivers, but they went ignored. Some were wounded, some not. One driver almost fell out of his truck, but used his swinging door as support, and Catherine saw why. Half of his left leg was almost torn off. The only thing that seemed to hold it together was his bloodied, ripped pant leg. Another man grabbed him and helped him into the hospital before the blood loss made him pass out. Some were carried by others. Some looked as feeble as the dead. A driver helped a carload of wounded passengers. One was a young woman Catherine's age in pink pajamas stained at the shoulders from the blood spilling from her head. The driver directed her to the entrance while the three others emerged. They were a family—a father, son, and daughter. Dressed as if they had gone to church, but covered in blood and rubble. Catherine watched the boy about the age of ten, attempt to carry his older sister into the hospital, followed by his father who staggered as if he were blind, or blinded from shock. Another driver hopped out of his vehicle, only to collapse onto the pavement. With his hands to his face he sent out a heart-rending wail. Catherine didn't need to see to know why. It was the cry of mourning and no closed window could hold it out. The suffering mass of people was rising. Catherine looked away in disbelief.

In a low voice, Nathan said, "We're the only hospital around for miles."

"How did it happen?" Catherine asked.

"For all anyone knows, they don't know yet," he said. "They don't know. Not yet. But they're preparing for the worst, setting up the cafeteria as a second triage center."

"We need to help them. We need to . . ."

"Wait," Nathan cried as he pointed down to the people below. Catherine heard the sound of gunshots, and saw a man, dressed in plain farming clothes, brandishing a revolver high in the air. He held a wounded, unconscious woman in the other. Her housecoat dragged along the ground as he moved toward the entrance, swiveling his gun at anything that moved. People tried to calm him. Their hands motioned for him to put the gun down. He shouted something, pointed the gun to the woman in his arms, and then back to the crowd. He yelled something at the nurse closest to him and moved his revolver, nodding its six-shot barrel to point at her. She tiptoed in slow motion toward him and the woman in his arms and carefully lifted her away, calling for assistance from another close by. They took the woman into the hospital. Once inside, the man dropped his revolver and allowed himself to be overtaken.

Sirens started to ring, like the people's cries, through the masses rushing for the doors of the hospital.

To use the dark power meant destruction; in the end it would destroy everything it touched.

Jorgen knew before entering the hospital he caused a catastrophe. He refused to acknowledge his actions until he found the source of power the shield protected. He never fathomed the treasure of its keep would be a human, let alone a girl completely unaware of the power she held within. It swirled at her feet like a cyclone, expanding and collapsing, matching her thoughts and feelings. Darkness wrapped around her fingertips, head, and feet like black ribbons pushing and stretching against knots created by a Master to keep her from using the power. Not only was she protected, she was bound and blinded from seeing the Darkness that stirred within and around her. Jorgen saw the binding knots would soon break. When that happened, the consequences of her ignorance would be destructive. The girl would have no way to protect herself from it, or anyone else.

In all Jorgen's travels, he'd never seen anyone who was *made* like her. The dark power was always taught to another. It was an art that took years to master, but a Master knew the power could never be tamed. No one was born with it inside, until now. That mystified and alarmed him. She was dangerous. If the binding knots suddenly broke and she became aware of everything at once, the tragedy of the river would look like a playground for all the power she held inside. Even though she was born with the dark power, she had no idea how to control it. Fear alone could unleash it. She was so powerful. It took great strength to bind her and protect her at the same time. Whoever placed the shield around her was a deadly Master. Time for questions would have to wait if he was to make it out of the hospital alive. Jorgen knew he didn't deserve to live. Today would be another mark on his death path of memories.

The Master of the shield would know another was near. The unnatural floodwaters carried the power of Darkness upon its crash. His carelessness alerted his presence and fashioned mayhem. The Master would not be far. Jorgen had to gather the Darkness and risk the wrath of the shield and its guard. The delicate part would be collecting energy. The more he harnessed, the greater the force of the shield would become. Even in its lifeless awareness, the shield was alerted to an intruder and stirring. He needed to defend himself. The shield was searching. Jorgen needed to pull all the threads of energy he could before battling the shield and possibly its Master.

Walking from Catherine's room, he snapped his arms down with his palms facing out from his sides and called the Darkness to him. It was eager to fill his depleted vessel. He was ruthless in its gathering, paying no mind to the sick or wounded he might harm or the working staff in the halls passing word of the patients to come and the rumors of what happened to bring them. He gathered the Darkness wherever he could. He must. He consumed all threads of energy through the people crossing his path. He pulled at the white fire shooting from the core of their bodies which gyrated in sparkling offshoots. This was their life essence, burning with different intensities until death extinguished it. Threads were the extension of that life force, each unique depending on age, health, and strength of mind. Threads illuminated a brilliant white light, but once he snatched them, the threads resembled glistening black bands he would absorb and transform into what his kind called Darkness.

Occupied with the calamity Jorgen brought upon the town, he had no trouble collecting threads. With tragedy afoot and the hospital in urgency, he pulled their life essence to him with ease. Distraction and emotional turmoil was a tool a Master used to collect threads. The thickness of an individual's barrier came with their character and determined their strength. But everyone had a weakness, and natural defenses became feeble as greater external disturbances and wayward emotions rose. It left them unprotected, and all the more beneficial to Jorgen. As he collected their energy, the people would feel it. They would disregard the random threads he soaked from them, oblivious to the knowledge that the greater part of their exhaustion came from a thief passing by.

He spared no one. The elderly, the nurses, and young were all victims to his indiscretion. A pregnant woman held her belly in the hall and Jorgen glimpsed her own life force and the child within as he drew from them both. He didn't have time. He could feel the shield's force advancing the stronger he grew.

The shield came at him. Slowly it sent in the bottom ranks of Shadow Creatures littering the hospital which resembled lampreys, to leech away at the tail end of the threads he collected. They suckled and nipped at the threads he gathered, attempting to extract what they could. In return, some grew, swelling in the process and ballooning to the size of small rodents. When the transformation took place, it was as if they'd grown legs and instead of slinking in their shadow form some came directly at him, scurrying in jagged movements along the floor and walls. Jorgen reversed the tail end of the threads and whipped it back at the Shadow Lampreys and their mutated comrades. They made no sound as they retreated. Some disappeared into the walls and ceiling, while others withdrew to the bodies of the people from which they fed.

Next, the Shadow Creatures like boars came. Their silhouettes filled out as they rushed him. Jorgen reached the stairwell door in time to close it with a temporary block. Fortified by his rejuvenated dark power, Jorgen created a seal around the door, wall, and floor so the boars couldn't seep through and devour him piece by piece.

Halfway down the stairwell, Jorgen halted just in time to duck a blow from a black orb hurling forward. It flew over him as he crouched on the steps, contemplating the orb's next maneuver. The orb launched a boomerang attack. He sprang himself above it, touching the high ceiling, before landing on steady feet. The orb was back where it started, hovering in front of his escape route, denying him passage, and ready to launch again. Jorgen didn't want to use the dark power, but he had no choice. He was trapped.

It rushed him, threatening to drill a hole in his chest, but he thwarted the strike. Jorgen extended his right arm, palm out, and unleashed the dark power upon it. The orb spiraled down the stairwell and exhausted all of its energy colliding with the exit door. The impact exploded the solid steel door off its hinges, taking chunks of drywall and tile floor with it.

Jorgen stepped through the gaping hole where the exit sign once hung. A thick haze filled the emergency room foyer. People cried out for help, calling through the ashen smoke and debris to one another. Some moaned in pain. Others lay still. They didn't see the man who stepped across the fragments, the one they would later blame without identifying. He could see the people and threatening Shadows manifesting through the dusty air. Their silhouette bodies cast a shadow of the human form revealed in a cape of Darkness. But they were featureless, without limbs or the need of clothing to cover them. These were the Shadow Men, even though men they were not. Varying in size and strength, they gathered together without eyes and focused their energy on Jorgen. They were the strongest of the shield's defense, triggered assassins. They advanced. Annihilation their only purpose.

Jorgen would not challenge them and bring more death and suffering to the innocents. He'd seen what the shield protected and that was enough. The only thing to do was flee. He pushed his way through the emergency door crowded with paramedics and police officers. Bumping into onlookers and victims of the river's wrath, he moved ahead, still gathering the threaded life essence of those around him while he passed.

Jorgen didn't turn back until he was out of range of the perimeter. The Shadow Men halted against the border of the shield they served, swaying back and forth, watching him. Hungry and restless, they had been in the servitude of their Master too long and craved to unleash their fury.

A rush strummed Jorgen's veins. He'd been reckless gathering the Darkness so fast. It boiled inside. He needed to calm it before it brewed and spilled over him. Walking with a slow stride he soothed the current, tying it to his step and thoughts. He cooled the power and tamed it only like a Master could.

He could still hear shouting and sirens from the hospital ringing into the barren woods he stepped into. A sigh escaped his lips. Jorgen had buried himself away from the world due to the dark art. It always found a way to unleash its callous nature onto the innocent, but Jorgen knew he was to blame. *Too late now*, he moaned in his head. The damage was done. He saw the girl and knew more would come.

Jorgen made his way through the small snow-covered woodland of dead grass and leaves. He almost cleared the distance to safety when he heard a voice behind him. A voice he once trusted, traveled through the desolate forest. The man spoke words of an ancient tongue. The voice of Artros spat a spiteful verse at him.

> "Little thief, little thief, on the path
> Drawing big waves as he passed
> Not wanting to break the slumber
> Of Artros' oceans thunder
> Jorgen tiptoed through the grass"

Jorgen halted, reeling inside. The first time he heard that voice, in an old age, the man spindled the same rhetoric he spoke now. The man came to his village, a mystic in disguise, and reaped the only thing Jorgen loved. He fell for the enchantment the voice carried, trusting and following every command that came from it. Until the day came when Jorgen could open his eyes and see the Darkness, in all its possibilities, for what it truly was, a blind-sighted path in eternal night. By then it was too late.

Jorgen knew the stinging truth. He knew who created the shield, and yet he chose to ignore his instinct. Once again, he tempted fate. He tossed his prison of solitude away and all the years of contemplating Artros' demise, in one careless heartbeat. He stirred an old ghost, a bitter past, and his execution with it. The voice that pinned him in the woods knew how to spin words into power, and even actions, that would seem meaningless to another, into a movement capable of directing or pulling energy. Jorgen had to tread wisely if he were to walk away, or crawl if need be.

Jorgen wanted no interactions with the man, but the call for decisions was over. He was involved now. It was too late. The world was too limited to hide from anyone, or himself, any longer.

"Artros," Jorgen said.

"Apprentice," Artros said behind him.

Jorgen choked on the name. *He is close, too close*, Jorgen thought. If they were to fight this time, it would be the end of him.

"I was just passing through," Jorgen said, closing his eyes. He swallowed hard before turning around and opening them again upon his old Master. Artros strolled closer swinging his staff in hand, a layman's prop aside his walk. Artros' black fedora tipped down to hide his thermal eyes, while a polite white smile covered his snarl. Yards away from Jorgen, Artros old blood nourished a face of youth and strength more powerful than Jorgen could fathom.

"Trespassing through," Artros snapped. "Risen from the grave have you Jorgen? Out of my world, my reach so long now . . . I am curious how you managed to stay beneath my watch, hiding without a trace. Coward. Been licking your wounds, have you? Are you healed now, Jorgen? Healed from your self-righteous pit of squalor? Ready to kneel and beg forgiveness? If not, then woe to you for troubling me with this tedious affair. You should know better than to walk on the grounds I claim." Artros leaned into staff, both his hands cupping the top. The staff tilted forward. Artros appeared relaxed and forgiving. Jorgen knew better. He was positioning himself for battle. "I am, however, pleasantly surprised to find you here. I thought I'd drained your every essence, but obviously you were stronger than I thought.

Remarkably stronger. I am a man of great measure, forgiveness if you will, so I hope you have come begging for mercy, because I miss having a dog by my side."

"Yes, Artros," Jorgen said, feeding Artros' victory to survive this encounter. "The last time you taught me well. A lesson I will never forget."

"You must tell me what you think," Artros said, soaking in Jorgen's humbled defeat.

"About?" Jorgen asked, trying to deceive the master of deceivers.

"You know Jorgen, I thought you were dead. It seems even I can be humored by a mistake once in a lifetime. But dead or alive, I know you . . . beating your head against the cobblestone, believing that's where answers will come from. But you were never a liar. That was one thing I enjoyed while you served me. There's nothing like having a disciple of truth under the rod, now is there," Artros said as his voice rose, "But you challenged me. Me! I took you in, gave you an unfathomable gift and you . . ."

"We both know why you taught me," Jorgen interjected. "I served as an instrument, a pawn you controlled to feed your never-ending lust for the Light."

"Ah, young love," Artros said. Jorgen recognized his false smile as a prelude to danger; he retreated. They both knew Jorgen's accusations crossed an old, but open wound and the woman he'd lost to Artros in the search for the Light that didn't exist. Maintaining his grin, Artros continued, "But you were ignorant to her desires, weren't you, Jorgen? You were the farm help, the stable boy, anything and everything underneath her feet. You could never fill the yearning of her heart. You were just a boy then, and now an old man before me. You have allowed all the gifts I gave you, enlightened you with, to become nothing more than a brittle soul. One squandering the gutters for answers, allowing my teachings of truth to drain by. The truth, the light for which you seek and even deny as you hunt for it. On my ground, nonetheless."

"You are correct Artros," Jorgen said, trying to calm his rival with words of submission, biting his tongue in order to survive. The last time he'd challenged Artros, it almost cost his life. "I have no purpose here. With your permission, I will be on my way."

"Oh, no Jorgen. No," Artros said. His voice dipped into reprimand. "You up heaved my pleasant residence, stirred the town with your reckless behavior and risked your life without even giving me a compliment as to what you witnessed under my shield. Ingenious, I must say, deposing the great power with behavior unbecoming of you. I was surprised to find it was you who penetrated the shroud and you who dropped your defenses to get past my guard . . . and the destruction . . . unlike you, valiant old man. Clever. I wonder what it was like for you to feel exposed. Vulnerable. But that is . . . unimportant. After all this time, you may have discovered how to lie with words, but your emotions deceive you. You will not deny the fact you saw her!"

Jorgen had no choice but to answer Artros. "I cannot deny that I have seen what you hold dear, but I no longer have interest in your affairs," he said trying to contort his feelings into indifference.

This appeased Artros, if only for a moment. "But you have yet to tell me what you think of such a mystery. She is fascinating, is she not? A creation of nature herself. The one we have been searching for!"

His words hurled needles into Jorgen's pores. Artros used the word *we,* an invitation for Jorgen to join him. No, serve him. Through countless years, Artros still tried to weave virtue into the path of Darkness with his justification for all the souls he consumed along the way.

"She holds power," Jorgen said, "she is power, in the rawest of elements but how she . . . how she's been able . . . how she was born . . ." Jorgen tried to understand.

Artros interrupted Jorgen's thoughts, "She is lovely. I have been nurturing her, protecting her, and teaching her the hardest lessons of Darkness. *Patience.* Particularly patience."

"But how can you be teaching her when she doesn't even know?"

"She knows exactly all she needs to know right now, and that is nothing!"

Jorgen thought about the restraints, the dark knots, Artros bound around Catherine. He had so many questions to ask, but he must speak carefully, lest Artros know of his building intentions. "It's not like you . . . I wouldn't have thought it was you who shielded her. It doesn't fit your nature. You were always one to take anything you desired."

"Jorgen, you have never understood my nature. You have always been fighting me to learn anything from it. Have you forgotten what happens to the young when they are taught before their time?"

Yes, he remembered and would never forget. Death abound, wielded by the hands of innocents unable to control the Darkness. The young led themselves to oblivion.

"But I don't understand," Jorgen said shaking his head. "She is powerful, too powerful. She'll come undone. She will unravel—"

"She is," Artros said, his courtesy running thin, "under control. She has proven herself above all expectations I had from the beginning. The dark power is natural to her being. She has been able to hold more than you could ever conceive."

"She is swelling, Artros. I can't imagine what will happen if the Darkness takes hold of her."

"I have sustained her in a life you know nothing about!" Artros said in anger, "I have given her strength when death would have seen otherwise. The age is ripe for this child to become the woman bequest with the knowledge. She will do the bidding of the one who has been her greatest comfort, her only love."

"Yes, Artros, I understand," Jorgen said, attempting to distract Artros' fuelling anger in another direction and treading with anchors as he did so. "Who is the boy?" Jorgen asked, thinking about the young man who entered room 215 as he was leaving. The boy contained the awareness of Darkness, but he will not be a threat until he learns how to harness it. This is how the path to dark art started. Artros would enlighten the boy soon. Another pawn.

"Curiosity drives you to be rude," Artros said. "It's tempting to relinquish you of that insolent tongue which cuts questions that are not yours to ask."

"Pardon my disrespect. It is just that . . . you have changed your ways since the last time we met." Artros studied him. Jorgen knew he was surveying him for inside thoughts. "It's not like you either," Jorgen continued, "to allow another so close to that which you covet."

Artros' anger stirred the icy wind around them causing a slight inward bend of the trees in the block of woods where they stood. Artros lifted his hands from his staff. It spun in free motion between his palm and the ground. The whites of his eyes blackened from the strength that lay in his fingertips. Jorgen could not fight him. He was not even a whisper to the power that stood before him. His old foe could snap him like the twigs around them if he chose, but not without first withstanding a fight that would clear the small forest, attracting attention neither of them wanted. That alone might be saving grace. Jorgen was a trespasser, but not a threat. Not yet. That might bide him a little time.

"Forgive my intrusion, Artros, and my ignorant speech. You are correct on all you say. I have been out of touch too long and have no authority to question you or your affairs,"

Jorgen said.

The spinning abruptly stopped when the staff halted in Artros hand. He said, "I see you have traveled far, and so I offer this last answer as a parting gift. The boy is leverage. One can never have too much, as you well know. Now you will have a gentleman's warning. Come near her again and I will eat you alive, spit out your entrails, and feed the last threads of your life force to her."

That was his true nature, Jorgen thought. Time never changed anything, nor anyone. Jorgen nodded in understanding.

In the old language, time long ago, but never out of memory, Jorgen heard the speech of parting not spoken in centuries.

"We are all brothers in our quest. But before we part, tell me brother are we friend or foe?" Artros asked.

Jorgen could not lie to Artros.

"I will part a friend of my foe."

They bowed briefly to each other. Each knowing they would meet again.

CHAPTER NINE

During the passing hours, the hospital's parking lot, and hallways filled with victims and their loved ones. To get the flowing crisis under control, the staff was merciless in not allowing more than one support visitor per patient. Some brought in had yet to be identified, and others, their family informed. Nathan wasn't asked, he was told to leave.

Kathy's small, one-bed room would be recycled soon. Catherine felt the walls shrinking. Occasionally a drifting visitor would poke a head in the room, looking for a loved one or longing for an ear to hear about their hardships.

Kathy's eyes opened briefly and stared vacantly out, then closed. Catherine took a permanent stand in the corner and watched the woman slowly regain consciousness. An hour passed before she opened her eyes again, tossing them around as if in a fish bowl. Kathy awoke once more, this time into a world of thirst and Daemons. Her limbs thrashed and her tongue slurred, and she hollered as if tormented by unseeable forces. "Ratzzs! Deeemoonn ratzzs! Git. Git, git off . . . off me!" She assaulted the air around her, as if possessed. Catherine studied her delusions, she understood they were created from withdrawal, but never witnessed them. After the deviants in her mind subsided, she hollered again. This time for a drink. The mother of all grains. Kathy's body twitched on the bed, begging for it, foaming through parched lips pleading sustenance, until a seizure weighted her back into unconsciousness.

A young doctor eventually made his way to their room and diagnosed Kathy with Rum Fits. Catherine thought Whiskey Fits was more appropriate.

"What are Rum Fits?" Catherine asked the doctor, standing at Kathy's bedside. This was the first time he'd been in the room. The doctor didn't give his name. He simply walked in, just as ready to walk out.

The doctor had the duty to inform, but facts could be sweetened if necessary, bent into laced taffy if need be. He had urgent business on his hands and he knew he'd be here through the night, possibly into the next. The hospital needed to be relieved of as many patients as possible.

"Rum Fits," he answered like a textbook, "are the reaction from withdrawal of prolonged inebriation, causing seizures and spasms as you have witnessed in your mother. I know they can look a bit . . . unnerving, but I assure you it will pass. Chances are she probably won't remember her hallucinations, so you don't need to worry yourself."

"So that," Catherine asked pointing to Kathy on the bed, "won't happen again?"

"I can't say what Kathy's body will or won't do, but she will recover," the doctor said, milking the stethoscope around his neck as if it didn't fit right. He continued, "Now . . . I don't want to alarm you but patients with Rum Fits have a slight tendency to develop Delirium Tremens. However, it's a small window and you'll know within the next 24 hours if she is going to continue . . ." the doctor paused and cleared his throat, "I just want you to be prepared in case that happens." He was sprinkling sugar over the facts and felt confident about wrapping and sending it along like a razorblade in Halloween candy. "But in your mother's case, she's recovering, aside from her slight step back, and I don't believe this is anything you're going to have to worry about," the doctor concluded, denying his patient crossed the border into the land of the Tremens.

"What is Delim Tremons?"

"Delirium Tremens," the doctor corrected.

"Yeah," Catherine said.

The doctor cleared his throat again and said, "It's the greatest shock upon a body that is detoxifying from the pollutants of its system. The body can become distressed to the point where the mind suffers profound confusion and sometimes vivid illusions from withdrawal. When your mother was admitted, she should have been one of the walking dead, or at least slipped into coma for the level of alcohol in her system, but she didn't. She's improving. But aside from her improvement, she could still suffer delusions and tremor agitation. The next few days will determine whether or not Kathy has crossed the bridge onto the road of full recovery."

"But you guys just sedated her. I mean, why can't you just keep her that way until . . . that passes?"

"Sedation is not the cure to controlling addiction. She needs to face it. She'll be an alcoholic the rest of her life. Her body is going to go through detox. Withdrawal can create reactions that appear frightening. However, this is what she has to overcome in order to cleanse herself of the poison she's abused her body with. I don't think I need to stress the importance of throwing out all alcohol in the house. One sip is all it takes to start the cycle again. If she drinks herself to her previous level of consumption, well . . . it could kill her."

Catherine looked at the doctor as if she were viewing a soap opera for the first time, acknowledging the fact she didn't know anything about his big words and explanations, but questioned how much the actor in front of her knew as well. She stared at the doctor and wondered if his script had been edited. Catherine hadn't thought about going home, going back to life with Kathy. But the doctor looked back at her like he was spreading the earth to plant a seed, throw some wakeup water on it, and call it a day.

"Please understand," he said, "these are extreme circumstances . . . we have done all we can for your mother—"

"Kathy," Catherine interrupted.

"Yes, but we are under severe strain right now from the disaster. We need to relieve the staff . . . the pressure . . . we need to get as many beds free as possible."

"Just what are you telling me?" Catherine asked.

"Kathy has made progress. Her bodily functions have stabilized. Soon, she will have the ability to feed herself. Once the sedation wears off, you're going to see major improvements. She is," the doctor stressed, "recovering."

"Look at her!" Catherine said, feeling a wasted fight brewing. She wanted the doctor to see how sick his patient really was. How she might lose her sanity having to support the one thing she despised in this world.

"I am," the doctor said without turning to Kathy. "And I tell you there is nothing more we can do for her except for monitor her at home."

"You expect me to take care of her?" Catherine asked in disbelief.

"We have to first serve those that need our care the most. Rest, and the commitment to stay dry, are the only things required of your mother to see her through this . . . this difficult time."

"I can't believe you're saying this. You're just going to kick us out? Kathy can't even walk."

"The sedation will wear off . . ."

"I have school . . ."

"School has been cancelled until further notice. There has to be someone who can help you. Isn't there someone, somebody you can call?"

"I don't even have a phone."

"You have a support system," the doctor paused as he looked at his chart and backed up again to finish with, "Catherine. You're not alone in this. She will be mandated to enter rehab. Social Services is scheduled to make sure Kathy is compliant with the substance abuse program, and they'll be checking in on you. We'll give you all of the supplies you need to cope with her at home, her medication and . . ."

"Her meds . . ." Catherine shot back, feeling abandoned and betrayed by a system in place to look after her, yet always failed. Her frustration was growing into anger as her hands flailed in aggravation. "What are you talking about? What the hell am I supposed to do with her? What if she if she flips out on me with one of her delirium frigging delusions, huh? What then?"

"We are taking the necessary precautions you will need to make sure she is of no harm to herself or you."

"This is bullshit," Catherine said landing in the reclining chair. Hopeless and deserted, she folded her hands into her face, questioning her solitude and the burdens it bared. Why did she always have to be alone? Alone again. Alone.

"One of the nurses," the doctor said, "said they would try to stop by tonight on their way home, if you really need them to. It's very decent of them to volunteer. The staff is extending themselves beyond the call of duty. They're going through a lot," the doctor said and then added, "as I'm sure you have. The next 24 hours are going to be the hardest. She needs your support right now. She needs to know you care. One of the best medicines is being at home around the ones you love."

Catherine didn't budge. A part of her was afraid to move. She didn't know if crying or laughing would make her feel better, or tip her over the railing.

Her words pushed through her fingers, where the moisture growing inside hid her watering eyes. "Leave," Catherine managed to say.

"Catherine, please think of others at this time," he said, relieved to wash his hands of this sticky mess, and left Catherine alone with her thoughts.

The bulging backpack couldn't fit all the items she intended on bringing back with her. Catherine decided a double layer of small trash bags would have to suffice as she crammed the last of her treasures into the bursting sack of stolen loot. One of the last items to go in the bag was a sandwich container. It pressed against saltine crackers, other nonperishable snacks, and a small pillow next to bathroom toiletries. She packed everything she could squeeze into the last plastic bag, down to a washcloth and towel. She struggled to knot the top of the thin bag and used her fist to push the hard plastic sandwich container further down. The top cracked under pressure causing Catherine to slice her knuckles. Thin blood soaked the lines of her skin, stinging her, as the sandwich container sailed through the room in defeat. It hit the wall, cracking the seal, and spilled its ham and cheese to the ground.

Catherine closed her eyes to slow her breath building since the doctor left. She clenched, trying to swallow the abrupt news that they were going to throw them out of the hospital like barn cats in the house.

The staff informed her that a hospitality van and two recruited paramedics would take them to the trailer park. The paramedics would help Kathy into bed where she would ride out her purification. Catherine thought about bolting, leaving the damn town for good and putting Kathy behind her forever. How long, she wondered, would saltines and a few packages of condiments last? How long before her boots gave out? When would she see Nathan again, the only one she felt tied her into the real world?

A light knock came from the door. Catherine acknowledged a nurse's aide with olive skin and black hair that shimmered blue as she moved her head. The aide held on to the door as she said, "S'cuse me miss, I just wanted to let you know I'm on my way down to the wash to get your ma's clothes. When I come back I'll get her dressed. They'll bring the wheel chair round when the van is ready . . . so it shouldn't take long."

Catherine gave her a small nod of understanding and then bent down to place the sandwich pieces back into the container. The aide walked over with a small offer to help.

"Here, I'll get that for you," the aide said.

"I got it," Catherine said as she pitched the container toward the small trashcan. She missed and it spilled all over the floor again. "Augh," Catherine said, grabbing the pieces, and slamming them one by one into the trashcan, flicking her hands of the meat sticking to her fingertips.

The aide quietly turned away from Catherine to leave, but collided into a man entering the room. It was Sam, the park landlord. Catherine felt nauseated by the sight of his port flesh and fish-scale scent. He pushed the aide off his brown soiled jacket with one hand and brushed it, as if the foreign woman left invisible particles behind. He held a gas station rose in the other.

"Goddamn it. Watch out!" Sam spat at the aide, squeezing the protective plastic around the rose in an attempt to mold it back into proportion.

The aide stepped back, head down, and muttered an apology as she left.

"Is this place crawling with skunks or what?" Sam said looking at the passing aide. "They got more halfricans working here than I knew lived in town. I don't let'um in my park, that's all I gotta say. Skunks no better than the niggahs breeding um. All on my dime too. Ain't no better than the redbones. I don't let those wood chippers in my place and I don't know what the hell they let them work here for. Probly all illegal immigrants if you ask me," Sam said thrusting the wilted rose out to Catherine, "Damn skunk 'bout broke it!"

Catherine recoiled. Sam's intentions were as good as a treed coon, and reasoning was a one-way bullet.

"We're leaving soon," Catherine said, closing the plastic bag for distraction. She tried to touch and grab anything to keep her eyes from grazing his. She would fuss with the air if need be.

"You guys coming in tonight?" he questioned, as if they were on a plane, a journey home, and the landing strip his trailer park.

Catherine picked up wet towels off the bathroom floor. She started folding them and said, "Yeah . . . they said they need the room . . . because of the . . . what happened."

Sam tossed the rose on her bag and tucked his hands into his pockets. He stood on the balls of his heels and repeatedly smacked them down with the thump of his boots. Each smack made Catherine cringe.

"That was some messed up shit," Sam said all the while thumping. "It's a terrorist attack all right, but they aren't saying yet cuz they ain't got nothing to prove it. No bomb, no trigger—nothing. Can't find nothing. I heard in the lobby someone down there saw a guy after he set the bomb off in the hospital, but they don't got it on the security cameras, so they aren't saying a goddamn thing right now. What they need be doing is callin' out the militia is what they need be doing. I heard they're planning their own attack against those dune niggers. They're gonna send a rocket straight up their ass so high the explosion will be seen across the ocean. Payback's a bitch. That'll show 'em we ain't fucking around." Sam paused before his face bent into a grin. He bobbed his head from side to side. "Well, at least some of us ain't fuckin' right now." His rant was subdued by the one word he had in mind, while his hands fingered about, connecting his thought aside the thin-lined pockets of his brewing excitement.

Sam laughed to himself and stepped closer to Catherine who padded and fluffed the recliner cushion.

"Course you know what's better than explosions?" Sam continued, welcoming Catherine's agitation. "You know what I like? I like implosions," he said and thrust his hips.

"You're disgusting!" Catherine said not able to stop herself.

"Your rent's due," Sam said.

Catherine moved to pick up her backpack, but Sam stepped in front of it. Now she had to confront him. "When we get back I'll get you the money," she said.

"You can say whatever you want, but when you get back there ain't nothing you're gonna find. I saw Kathy last night and if she didn't have the money for the lot's rent then, she ain't gonna have it now. Now is she?"

"Ah! You dropped her off like that . . . wasted? On me? You're a real asshole, you know that?"

"You better watch that mouth of yours, girl. I've been taking good care of you—makin' sure you got a roof over your head when your ma ain't got the cash to settle her debt," Sam said nudging a deadpan elbow at Kathy on the bed. "Looks like she'll be outta commission for a while. Means you're gonna have to find a way to lick the slate clean. Know what I mean?"

"She has a stash somewhere. I'll get it from her or find the money," Catherine said. Lies were better when they had hope.

"How 'bout I give you a ride back and we can look for the money together."

Catherine knew he wasn't just jingling keys in his pocket. She said, "The van is going to be here any minute so don't bother."

"Hey, come on now. Why ya gotta be like that? I'm a nice guy. Kathy wasn't holding her liquor so good, so I took her home. Where's the fault in that, huh?"

Catherine didn't think she'd be anticipating the van, but she turned and looked out the window hoping liberty would be parked at the main entrance. She couldn't see anything but her reflection in the glass and Sam behind her.

He stepped closer, as if he wanted a turn at the salt block, and said, "Look at me when I'm talking to you."

His command was answered with a jab of her elbow to his rib cage. "Get the hell away from me," Catherine said.

Sam freed his hands from the pockets keeping him at bay. He had an invitation now to use them and rush Catherine. She dove under his arms and picked up the first thing she could grab, her backpack. She swung it at him as he advanced, but he caught the straps and used it against her like a battering ram, slamming her against the wall. He pushed harder the more she squirmed for freedom. The backpack was the only thing separating him from her and she could smell his stale breath inching across the top of the backpack and down to her, threatening to muffle any scream.

"I *said* I'm a *nice* guy," Sam said pushing the pack harder on the words he wanted to emphasize while grinding his teeth on the others. "So I'm *gonna* tell it to *you straight*. Get me the *four-fifty* by the end of the week or *else* you're gonna find out just how *nice* I can *be*."

Catherine didn't utter a sound under his weight. Sam waited for an opportunity like this, to get her alone and educate her on the way things were going to work between them. With the backpack between them, she could see the hunger burning in his eyes. Their eyes locked into a bitter stream of hate and lust.

Sam savored this arrest. His emotions escalated in his growing desire. Attempting to control the excitement brewing in his head, he was losing at suppressing his hunger all the more. She knew, without thinking, the thoughts he envisioned, detailing her body into his dogging grin. The hatred Catherine felt at this moment turned inside her. It whirled into her core, writhing and waiting to erupt. Suddenly her repulsion shot itself back out from her eyes and into her oppressor. Her hate burned into him. She saw him blinking his eyes before they turned a beet red, as if suddenly filled with splinters. Sam was forced to look away, but he didn't drop his arms, not yet. Catherine's disgust scorched into his body. In a rapid wave, an itch came over him. Minor at first, like poison ivy, but it grew deeper, dragging as cats' claws would. The sensation stung his flesh, grating into his pores and beyond. His shoulders twitched, his legs quivered and he let go of the bag's handle with one hand, attempting to scratch at the phantom pain grinding deeper into him. Sam felt as though he was beading drops of blood, draining from invisible wounds upon his flesh and from the sweat he had aroused himself with, until he did indeed bleed by his nails alone which scraped his exposed flesh.

"Fucgerrahhh . . ." Sam cried, crushing a last shove at Catherine before he let go completely, rolling his head to the side while the pain twisted into him.

Catherine had no thoughts or words in her mind, as she shot her hate into Sam buckling on the floor. Other than pure antipathy, Catherine's mind was empty, blank and running on emotion alone. She didn't notice the nurse's aide walking back into the room holding Kathy's clothing, cleaned of vomit and blood.

"Mister, you alright?" the aide asked rushing to him.

As Catherine looked away from Sam and to the aide, Sam was released of the drudging burn plaguing his body. Catherine gazed at the aide as if she had just nodded asleep during a movie, and after the blackout, tried to rationalize what just happened between Sam and her. He stood up, disarrayed and dazed by the enigmatic pain that ceased as quickly as begun. He rushed past the aide and bolted out the door without looking back. Catherine was grateful whatever came over Sam had saved her, but he would be back, just like he said he would. She would have to be ready with more than just a backpack to keep him at bay.

Throughout the day, the town rolled with sirens. Local traffic clogged the streets between emergency vehicles blaring horns through the congestion. Some locals volunteered by observing the aftermath of the powdered bridges and papier-mâché homes along the river. Those who stayed home peered through their windows or stood on sidewalks, holding their choice of beverage in hand, and commenting at the passing wheeled mob.

Jorgen was the only one who drove out of town that day, never intending to leave. Not after seeing Catherine. She was brighter in the essence of life force than he'd ever imagined, but born with the crux of Darkness within.

Artros had said, *"The one we've been searching for."* Jorgen knew his words to be true, even after denying it was her energy alone that drove him here and not the overbearing Darkness that enveloped the town harboring Artros and his army of Shadow Creatures. Coming to the heart of this desolate countryside, Jorgen discovered a girl. A naive child who knew nothing of herself or the way she was a part of something immeasurable. She was a victim, but her innocence could not be used as an excuse once the dark power was revealed. Why providence chose her to carry this burden was impossible to unearth. Only the mystery remained as to what she would do with the knowledge once she became aware, or the consequences to pass if she couldn't be controlled.

Jorgen first followed the path of Darkness upon the footsteps of illusion, believing Light would be his ultimate end as a man entering paradise without death. Artros wanted to intersect the power of Light with Darkness and create a crossroad union of supremacy. Jorgen's path was one of knowledge and answers, but the discovery of Catherine was an enigma. How could she be the answer when she was a question herself? He couldn't let Artros use her like a tool, a weapon, as he'd done to all in his distorted quest for the Light.

Jorgen drove past the milling people. Some were concerned, others morbidly entertained, and both thankful ruin didn't come to their front porch. There was a charm in devastation and its darkness showed throughout humanity. Numbed by decadence, Jorgen was tasteless for society's lure when it came to misfortune. Impoverished to prosperous, people evolved with its impact and the cleansing of its aftermath. But no matter how people swayed with it, it was an attraction all the same.

Jorgen was not under any delusions driving past the witnesses and victims of his error and carelessness. He was aware his negligence drove a mother now to scream on her knees at the loss of her son, and the absent eyes of a man waiting for word from his brother. He caused this misfortune. He unleashed it. Jorgen built a fortress around him, lest the inevitable break him down with the knowledge more would come to the people in this discarded town. Darkness was here, and its presence would be known.

A part of the shadows now, he embraced them to hide from Artros' guards and the Master's arrogance. Jorgen relied on Artros' pride, a crutch to Jorgen's benefit, to help keep him safe.

Jagging along the perimeters of town, Jorgen drove on autopilot. He strung out thoughts in his mind, trying to surface the answer within, as if he would understand what discovering Catherine meant. Impossible. While his thoughts webbed, he mapped the roads out of town for escape routes, seaming alternative directions together. He was thinking ahead without a plan. Every crossroad, two-track, house and barn was stapled into his mind for a decision he hadn't made. He was unconsciously planning to abduct Catherine. There wasn't time for reasoning or understanding, only action. If he were to stop Artros from obtaining the greatest energy Jorgen had ever seen, he needed to steal that power and not look back. This was the cold part of him. The part that kept his emotions and heart distant from others, and himself. The path he traveled. The pitiless road of Darkness.

Jorgen wasn't without reservation. Doubt tainted his mind, confusing him in its unfamiliar presence. He was a man of direction, but discovering Catherine was challenging his perception. Compassion seeped in. Time diluted this feeling, but touching Catherine's hidden pulse caused bricks in his emotions to break down. He didn't know how to build them back up. The sentiment was strong. He fought it with the logic of Darkness, his evolution from society, but the girl was getting inside. He wanted to banish it, but feeling wasn't an object that could be tossed, it was a poison. He didn't want to submit to this revelation. After all this time of solitude, hopelessness, and the scream that would never be unleashed . . . he was nothing more than human. He couldn't cope with the thought he might be thinking of rescuing this girl, as opposed to seizing raw power.

Catherine, Jorgen thought, *who, what are you, Catherine?* He risked his life to get close to her. The one he felt would lead to his demise. Yet, he couldn't leave. He felt her as he drove, as if the power she emanated reached for him with its thoughtless light, touching him in its thoughtless embrace to the effect it had over him. Rescue her. Jorgen tossed this foreign instinct aside. Ludicrous. In a great battle with Artros he tried to be a hero and failed. When the bandage of love was torn from his eyes, the world was foreign and he walked amongst it in a shell. The man within himself, the one he thought drained by love's betrayal, was showing its shadow again, cast out by the light of a girl, Catherine.

Tempting Artros' wrath was reckless suicide. Jorgen had to make sure his decision wasn't fueled by vengeance. Retribution was a part of the Darkness and he wanted nothing more than to overcome it. Thus far, no one had ever conquered the dark power they wielded. Not even Artros.

The country roads were long and endless. Jorgen could drive out of town, destination unknown and never return. Hide. That time was past. He turned onto a main road leading out of town, spun the wheel and peeled pavement and dirt aside. He simply couldn't leave. He was involved now.

Jorgen turned down a seasonal road and parked his cratered black '69 Chevy Nova off the small rutted trail. Contemplating, the car idled awhile before he turned the ignition switch off. The engine rattled to sleep. Jorgen laid his head back to think more.

Why was he here risking his life? Deep down he knew why he didn't leave town. Jorgen had nowhere to go. This was the great loop of truth, and its farce was revealed. Time led him to this dead zone of another mystery and consequence to start the loop anew. Time never changed.

Jorgen gathered the Darkness before he left town, but even its overwhelming rejuvenation was no match against Artros. His old Master harbored more power than Jorgen thought could be contained without losing control. Artros' strength was to be feared, but Jorgen's confidence grew in that. As long as Artros thought himself to be invincible, then the probability of Artros searching for him was diminished. That alone might allow Jorgen to pass undetected once again.

There would be risk, but Jorgen was committed now. While he planned his next move, the emotionless man he was accustomed to returned. The shadow of the man, who once knew how to love, vanished where it belonged. He wasn't going to rescue Catherine. He would steal her like the thief Darkness had taught him to become.

Jorgen was ready to travel again. This time, he would move without his body. First he had to remove the object that kept his celestial body in place. Jorgen gripped the necklace around his throat. Hesitating, he fingered its silver. Centuries ago, he made the necklace. It was empowered with binding properties. Only under extreme consideration would he remove it. The necklace stopped him from traveling outside of his body on the astral plane, but more importantly, it stopped others from entering his body to take control of it, or his mind.

Even though his power had charged the necklace, he wasn't able to pass through its barrier. He must remove it in order to see Catherine with spirit vision. It was the only way to get close to her and inside of the town, leaving his body empty and vulnerable. He dared not physically enter the town, not yet.

Jorgen unfastened the necklace like a locksmith with a combination twist only he held the key for. He set the necklace on the seat next to him and placed his hands to his sides. He tried to ignore his conscience which challenged his absurd intentions. Inhaling repeated deep breaths, he slowly lost the sensation of his physical body. With one great exhale, the essence of his mind heightened to be his only awareness. This part of him ascended through the roof of the car. Now Jorgen was on the ethereal plane. A place he didn't like. One he wouldn't spend time discovering, as it was unknown and rarely documented. People of his kind disappeared here. Shadow Men were rumored to be born here. This plane was a different dimension to the one he lived, and yet it attempted to appear the same in its watercolored shadows moving like seaweed in a haze. This replicated world was an alternate reality which made Shadow Creatures stronger. Even the lesser ones could drain the spirit dry in a matter of seconds. Jorgen soared past its trees, rising as he followed the rutted trail he parked his car on, down to a main road with pot-holed asphalt. Its craters lined the road straight into town.

Normal sensations eluded his form without a body. In this state, Jorgen had to maintain strict control, lest the astral plane unpin him from the earth, cutting the astrophysical umbilical cord from his body and spirit. It had been decades since he attempted travel by astral projection. He tried not to think about his exposed body left behind in the car. He concentrated on moving through the astral plane world, its breathless air and alien beasts.

Focus was the main technique to this slighted world. He maneuvered through it, documenting more parts of the town the astral world revealed to him and he banked numerous insights based upon its layout. Delusions and dreams were a doorstep away if he couldn't hold his sanity. Colors were diluted in this realm, but Darkness remained true and void of emotion.

Jorgen thought to himself, *Catherine, where are you . . . I need to see you Catherine.* He placed fence posts as mile markers in his head and proceeded into town. Eventually, the hospital came into sight. Even here the sun rose and fell and right now the realm was darkening.

The shield over Riverside Hospital was still in place and reinforced by more Shadow Creatures. Artros was taking extra precautions now that Jorgen snuck past his guard. He had no idea how he would penetrate it again. Artros' Shadow Men were doubled. Jorgen never saw a Master control so many. They wavered like black flags upon the terrain. The perimeter was extended and Jorgen wondered if Artros was stretching the limits of his power, or stronger than Jorgen fathomed.

The streets and parking lots were full. People stood around the hospital grounds, and cars, in assorted groups, parting as another car or person came past. Jorgen could not hear the vehicles, voices, or the unassuming breeze that appeared to be gaining speed. Sounds of static airwaves pinned individual motion or groups in different frequencies. But here, unlike the earthen plane, Shadow Creatures made a distinct sound. In accordance with people in and around the hospital, they came rushing as feral trackers hungry for the feast of suffering, shrilling like a piper's rusted flute.

Jorgen couldn't linger in this state. The Shadow Men's acute sense of this plane would detect him any moment. He didn't want to think of his celestial body being ripped apart if the Shadow Men overtook him, or his flesh rotting away as he left it. Briefly, he wondered if he would feel death here at all. This was a part of their world. The one they walked between the living and the other. They couldn't leave the confines of the hospital they were placed to serve, but Jorgen didn't think this plane held borders, or any Artros could maintain. No matter, the Shadow Men would alert Artros of an intruder. Artros couldn't be far. Like sight with the eyes of the flesh, Jorgen tried to see Catherine and failed. The shield's energy coming from the hospital blurred this plane in a thick unsettled fog. Jorgen knew she had to be here if the Darkness was. Observing the density of the shield, Jorgen assumed she would be there for some time.

Jorgen was about to return to his body when he saw Catherine walking behind a nurse out of the dark shield covering the building. The nurse pushed a wheelchair with a patient rocking her head from side to side before being lifted her into the back of a van. Catherine was oblivious to the nature of the Shadow Creatures and Shadow Men that watched her every move, surrounding her even as she entered the van's back doors. Jorgen watched the van pull away with Catherine inside. The guards remained in place, anxious and unable to follow.

Jorgen witnessed Catherine's departure, while the Darkness around the hospital stood still. Artros didn't know she left.

One thing Jorgen could count on from the astral plane was that even though traveling took time, returning did not. Jorgen snapped back into his body. His flesh was numb with shock from the abrupt return. He could open his eyes, but nothing else in his body moved for a short spell. This inability to move tortured Jorgen. Awake, staring involuntarily at his chipped windshield, he waited for the numbness to pass while his physical form and the astral essence of him interlocked into one again. He felt his fingers and toes tingle with an awakening sting. He willed them to move. He had to take action. This may be the only window he would have to get close to Catherine again.

Finally, Jorgen was able to turn the ignition. The car grumbled. Jorgen whipped the necklace back around his throat. Revving the engine into reverse, he backed up and then sped down the two-track road and into town hoping time didn't close on him.

CHAPTER TEN

Eyes peered through parted curtains in the trailer park at the van passing. Its diesel engine idled as Catherine walked into the trailer. Catherine turned in disgust to the chair where she discovered Kathy with its crusted vomit stuck to the armrest and floor. The paramedics came inside and Catherine pointed down the hall to Kathy's door. Kathy was incoherent as they guided her to her bedroom. Catherine cleaned the vomit as the two men settled Kathy in. She couldn't remember the last time she was in Kathy's room. Embarrassed enough having the paramedics in her house, she was more disturbed as to what they would find as she walked down the hall where a single dusty light bulb glowed in the pit of Kathy's domain.

The men laid Kathy's head down on a crushed pillow atop a barren mattress and used a matted blanket from the floor to cover her. Catherine watched them turn away, side-stepping magazines and clothing on the floor. One of the men chuckled at the nude images he slipped on, but the other tried hard not to look at the glossy pages or anything else. It was inevitable, like his embarrassment realizing

Catherine was watching them. Their faces flushed brushing past her in the tight confinement of Kathy's sty. Catherine took her turn in the room and cleared Kathy's nightstand of plates breeding mold between cigarette butts and torn magazines. She swiped the rest of the nightstand clean with the back of her hand, dropping the remaining litter on the piled floor.

The paramedics left with hushed words. Closing curtains fenced in the trailer park gossip that would spread long after Catherine shut the door against them.

Catherine locked the front door. She reinforced its lock with a chair from the kitchen table, jamming it between the ripped linoleum floor and the knob.

She dropped the plastic bags from the hospital on the kitchen table along with a white paper bag containing Kathy's meds. She poured a glass of water and grabbed the paper bag intending to head back to Kathy's room when she realized she never took off her backpack. Catherine set the water and bag of pills down on the coffee table. She reached for the straps around her arms and hesitated. She couldn't bring herself to drop the backpack. If she did, then she would be fully committed. No turning back, or away from Kathy. No more ideas of running off into the unknown world of yearning dreams. This was it. She walked to the front door and stood there for a long time. She tightened her grip on the chair securing the lock. She thought of Nathan. He promised her, no matter how late his shift, he would come and see her tonight. That could be well after midnight if he couldn't get out of work earlier. This assurance was the only thing overriding her internal struggle. She relied on him to see her to the dawn. She tossed the backpack down.

She returned to Kathy's room. She had to. A quarter-filled whisky bottle knocked her foot as she crossed the corner of the bed. She tucked it under her arm. *"I don't think I need to stress the importance of throwing out alcohol in the house . . ."* the doctor had said. *"One sip is all it takes to start the cycle again . . . If she drinks . . . it could kill her."* Catherine squeezed its thick glass between her arm and side. She set a glass of water on the nightstand and placed the pill bottles down. At the hospital, they rambled instructions to her about times and doses to administer them, starting tomorrow morning. Instructions she didn't listen to. She had looked at Kathy on the gurney as the nurse tried to dress her limp body. Even then, Catherine couldn't think about anything. They were sending her home to nothing.

Kathy slept in her bed with her mouth gaped open, heaving in the slumber the nurse promised would last through the night. Catherine unhinged the bottle from her arm. She was holding the choice once more in her hands. She could let Kathy die. She could help Kathy live. It was all in the bottle.

She set the bottle next to the pills and looked at it.

She picked it up. She set it down.

Kathy heaved on.

Catherine picked up the bottle again and chucked it under the bed where she found it. The glass struck tin. Catherine didn't want to investigate the pile of filth under the bed, but she thought that if she were to last another month here, she needed to start searching for some sort of cash to give Sam. She looked at Kathy again with an awkward sense of trespassing, as if the woman would spring up like the dead and reprimand her for snooping. Catherine slowly knelt down and started pulling clothing, trash and unspeakables out of the way. A tin box came closer with each dig of her hands.

Crouching at the end of the bed, she held the small box. It was silver and rusted around the seams. Catherine couldn't imagine what it contained. From the looks of it, Kathy forgot a long time ago. Catherine looked at Kathy again, attempting to pry the box open and failing. She scraped off some of the rust with her nails, but the lid wouldn't budge. She decided to take it out of the room, praying it might contain some loose bills for the lot rent.

A wad of ones, a scratched lottery ticket, and rattling coins lay in the bottom of the box. She unfolded the money. Twelve bucks. That left four hundred thirty-eight dollars to go. She lifted the scratched ticket. It was an outdated game of bingo, a worthless two dollars. She dumped the change into her hand. A few coins dropped on the floor while the rest spilled into her hand.

With despairing hope, she counted the change. She fingered through the dimes and quarters, between the lint and dirt that fell from the box. Sliding her finger through the change, she saw a simple gold ring. At first, Catherine wondered why Kathy hadn't pawned it. It looked like real gold, compared to the costume jewelry the woman usually wore. It was thin and small. Not much worth pawning. Catherine lifted the ring and looked through its small perfect circle.

Then she remembered. Through the hole of the wedding band, Catherine saw a memory. One she sheltered to protect her mind. The first time she saw Kathy, at the hospital, where her grandmother lay dying.

Once Kathy removed it from Nana's hand, the ring disappeared into Catherine's withholding closet of recollection. The circle indented her flesh as she clutched it, feeling her Nana's passing once again and the monster she was forced to shelter with years since.

She reached for her backpack on the floor, holding the ring tight. She stood with the ring in one hand, backpack in the other, staring down the tunneled hallway to Kathy's closed bedroom door.

Push. That's the only feeling Catherine felt. With every forward, a shove back. Push to stay. Push to leave. Anything she did, or didn't do, pushed against her. Decisions weren't choices. They were another road of obstacles and consequences ahead. The door was inviting. Catherine pressed her head against its cold-rutted steel. The other side of the door was a mystery to her fate. Running was enticing. All she had to do was simply open the door to the world, instead of allowing its suffocating push to smother what was left of her depleting will. Catherine squeezed the ring tighter, admitting she made the choice to come back. That angered her the most. She was pushing against herself. Catherine's head turned numb against the door, but still, she left it there.

A thief of the night. That was Jorgen, walking across the trailer park's field to Catherine's insatiable vibe. He answered to no one, yet moral laws haunted the walk he justified. Her energy pulled him. His past trailed behind. He refused to be a part the revolving world and its civilization, living a recluse life trapped in time. His search for answers left him wary of the world around him and its volatile people. Upon defeat, and the loss of the woman he loved, he had nothing else to live for except the quest. The search for the Light was the only thing that kept his sanity from breaking. The Darkness swallowed everything he cared for. His life and love. The only way to overcome the Darkness was to find the Light. The Light he could feel just out of his grasp for all the knowledge he obtained. Yet, he moved forward, as if he would discover it, hold it and learn from it. Only then, would Jorgen feel his pain wash away in that single moment of revelation.

For now, here he was. A thief coming for a girl. He tried to defend his shame for the greater purpose. The Light. He despised this man he'd once been, creeping upon him in the dark. The one who was once an honorable man, turned bitter with resentment and loss.

Coming closer to Catherine's place, Jorgen knew he had to be quick. Neither Artros nor the Shadow Army was in sight. If Jorgen was discovered, Artros would snuff him out. It astounded Jorgen that Artros let Catherine slip out of his reach, if even momentarily. His old Master must have other workings in the town as well. What they were, Jorgen couldn't be sure, but it was deeper than the boy he saw at the hospital. This was his last opportunity to get close to the girl and stay alive to celebrate the sunshine in the morning. Jorgen was grateful to see another weakness shining in Artros, his confidence. He came here for one reason only and he mustn't lose attention to his surroundings. Luck had a way of spinning. Artros' army could be on the horizon at any moment. Jorgen proceeded with caution. Thus far, nothing was coming for Catherine, nothing but him. Catherine's energy pulsated like a wave so strong he felt it radiated only for him. He picked up something else inside her flowing energy. Between the waves, a disturbing thump interrupted her pulse. He was alarmed by its beat. Without laying eyes on her, he could sense something unsettled her. This disturbance could stretch her to the point of snapping the knots Artros bound her with. If that happened, there was no telling what would transpire. Anything could come from the Darkness.

Given her emotional state, Jorgen realized stealing Catherine away from Artros might not be as easy as he once thought. He had little time and the roulette wheel was starting to turn.

Jorgen stood on Catherine's porch, feeling her on the other side. She was close. Her pain closer. It had been a long time, such a long time since he felt these feelings. He tried not to let them touch him and manipulate his intentions, but the feelings seeped in and he felt shards of her pain intruding his emotionless shelter. Her suffering made him want to turn around, leave the town, and never look back. The pain was unbearable. Somehow, he choked it in and rapped gently on the door where she stood on the other side.

Catherine felt a tapping pound into her cold forehead. She lifted her head and cautiously placed her backpack on the floor. She slid her grandmother's ring inside her pocket and held onto the chair in case she would have to reinforce it. She didn't respond. She was afraid to breathe as though it would be heard from the other side. The knocking came again, harder this time.

"You said I had until the end of the week, Sam." Catherine yelled. "Give me a break already. I'll get you the money!"

"I'm sorry for bothering you this late," a man's voice answered. "I would just like to . . ." the voice trailed off and then said, "talk with you for a moment, if I may."

Catherine flipped the porch light switch, but the bulb burned out as soon as it was lit. She went to the side window, but the night coated the stranger on the porch step.

"Who is it?" she called.

"I saw you at the hospital. I just have a few questions to ask you," he replied.

"What do you want?"

What did I want? Jorgen questioned himself. He dropped his head and answered, "Just a moment of your time." Maybe for tonight that's all he would take. Silence came from the other side. Forcing the door open would be as easy as the flick of his finger, but Jorgen didn't want to approach Catherine like that, but he would if forced.

Reluctantly, Catherine slid the chair back and opened the door a hairline crack. The man outside was dressed in black, identical to the older man at the hospital. She eyed him through the slice of light cast from the kitchen. A bright flicker struck her eye from the necklace around his throat. She recognized this necklace as the one the social worker wore, but this man looked like the son of the man from the hospital. She pried the door open a little further.

"So you guys work any time of night now or are you just some overachiever?" she asked.

Jorgen sensed the gap widening, but tension stood between them. He formed a polite smile to hide a lie as he said, "I can come back tomorrow if I trouble you."

She opened the door a foot wide, perplexed. Everything about this man was familiar except for his age.

"I don't remember talking to you," Catherine said in suspicion.

"It was brief," Jorgen replied, afraid to disclose too much. He could see Catherine working out the decision to let him in or not. Then the door started closing.

"The Saint of Darkness . . ." he said in hope.

The door halted as she said, "You're not the same man."

"No, pardon me. You spoke with my senior," Jorgen said cupping a swipe to his chin in understanding to her confusion. Between the time of their brief exchange, he regressed to the youth of someone in their thirties, or so he suspected. But he didn't want to think about it. There was no face for the man he was. The gray vanished from his head when the luster of his hair returned around tight rejuvenated flesh. The fine lines which indented his skin, like windswept mortar, were gone. He could not identify with these hands. It was a deception of the truth, for which he was, and his age. He refused to look in the mirror after recharging the power again, not yet ready to look at the face of a man he had once been. The transformation was not created by his desire, but by the effect of gathering the dark energy. He attempted a false smile, one that could intrigue as well as deceive. It was inviting and a skill he learned how to employ well over time.

Doubt rode Catherine's suspicion, but she opened the door all the same. *Let's get this over with,* she thought, as she moved her backpack out of the way and tossed it on the couch. She wondered if Social Services were breeding a new kind of cult. She waited for him to close the door and interrogate her as They all did.

"You know," she said, "you guys could have come by tomorrow."

Whoever Catherine believed him to be, he had to choose his words carefully. Somehow, he managed to make it through the door without conflict, but her charging emotions were at a sensitive state. His steps must be light.

"Were you going somewhere?" he asked.

Catherine looked at him and then turned away and said, "There's nowhere to go."

Jorgen sensed the broken pulse he felt walking up to her door intensifying. Examining her, he noticed some of the knots Artros placed around the girl had snapped and others were stretching. Only two people were capable of breaking them, Artros or Catherine. Something had happened to Catherine. Whatever it was caused a distress great enough to break a few of the knots, but still Catherine was as ignorant of her power now as she was at the hospital.

"You know," Jorgen said, "you have the decision to stay, or leave. The choice is yours."

Catherine's head snapped around and Jorgen realized his words triggered her frustration into anger. Her fury grew, not just with her voice, but along with the power swelling inside of her.

"That's a joke, right?" she growled. "You got a speech to back that up as well? You going to feed me the round-off drill you practiced in your visor's mirror before you got here. Stay in school. Say no to drugs. The future is mine to hold, bullshit. There's no choice here. Every time you guys show up, you're just showing me a dead end."

"What's the bag for?" Jorgen said, not trying to upset Catherine further, but only to understand her intentions.

"That's none of your business," Catherine said, her dark power swiveling with her motions. "Unless you want to check it for drugs or something. But that's something you guys never did before, so why not," she said storming past Jorgen and picking up her backpack. She turned back around and headed for the kitchen. She threw her backpack on the table next to the other plastic bags from the hospital. "Here, here, you wanna see?" Catherine asked, unzipping the backpack. She started to throw clothing out of it before suddenly stopping. She moved to one of the plastic bags on the table and ripped the middle open to expose its guts. All the while she said, "It's all the same with you people. In and out. You don't give a fuck, you just wanna make a buck. You don't care. None of you. Just want to write me off for another few years—until another incident—and leave. Never coming round unless you have to. You want the speech I've given you people for the last ten years, so you can shed a rehearsed tear for my sake, check it off in a box, and say you're going to make it all better. You going to wave a magic wand—send a check, because that makes it all better. Puts it out of your way, gives you a reason . . . an obligation to care when you don't give a damn about me!"

"I asked you what the bag was for," Jorgen said in a tranquil voice. "Not what's in the bag." He tried to remain calm. Catherine was a tidal wave about to crash. It was too easy to let the Darkness take control. Anger fuelled the Darkness, and it didn't help that her young spirit was already broken. He turned away from her. *Relax*, he told himself, he must maintain control for the both of them.

"No. No here. Let me show you what's in the bag," she said grabbing random items and lifting them up, identifying each one before slamming it down. "Toothbrush. Pen. One bar of used soap. Smashed crackers. Wet washcloth," she said, continuing to name other toiletry items until the bag was almost free of its contents. Her temper flared. Her pulsations expanded, vibrating the ground and walls of the trailer. Engrossed in her frenzy, Catherine didn't realize she was causing the trailer to tremor. The defenses inside Jorgen were reacting to the threat of power inside of Catherine. If she unleashed it on him, no matter how innocent, the Darkness inside of him would retaliate. He might not be able to call it back before it caused serious damage. He wanted to say something to her, but even speaking might distract the composure he was trying to sustain.

"There!" she continued. "You satisfied? Any other questions? I got nothing to hide cuz guess what *baybee*—that's all there is!" A horrified look came over Catherine's face and she covered her mouth in shock. Her body shuddered and with it the power she was emanating receded slowly back into her. Another one of Artros' knots was broken.

Jorgen's power cooled its black waters. As the Darkness inside of him withdrew, another sting of feelings and revelations caved in on him. Jorgen understood clearly now. He understood why Artros kept her in this pit of solitude and fear, alone, frightened and angry. This is exactly the way he wanted her. These were the emotions of Darkness, and the ones that made the power come stronger. He wanted her this way, near the breaking point. In the fog of fear and rage, he would sweep her away. Come as a savior to her aching heart, only to let her fire burn for his every whim. That was Artros' nature. That was why he hadn't taken this girl, not yet.

Jorgen stood silent, feeling her pain soak back to the place where it would lay dormant until the inevitable happened. Who knew what her callous years of sorrow were capable of unleashing? She pulled back the throbbing agony he had known, and still knew, after all these years pretending to shut the world out. Somehow, this girl penetrated him. From now on, if he couldn't find the Light, at least he would try to give Catherine the light of life before Artros took it away from her, as his old Master did from him. And maybe that alone might give a small amount of purpose to this long and endless journey. Maybe that was the only Light left in the world.

Catherine sat on the kitchen chair, bent over, and slowly slid her hands over her face until her mouth and eyes were covered. Knees pressed together, she trembled. Jorgen didn't need to see her to know there were tears in her eyes. He walked over and silently knelt down in front of her.

"Catherine," Jorgen said softly, not believing his own words. "I have come here to protect you. Nothing more."

Catherine moved her hands low enough to uncover her bloodshot eyes and stared, bewildered by the man kneeling before her. His proximity was too close for comfort, but she sensed something coming from him. An invisible serenity which soothed and calmed her grief. She was too baffled to move or speak.

"Everyone walks a different path in life, Catherine," Jorgen said. "Walk with me for a while and maybe you will discover the direction of yours."

"Who are you?" she managed to say.

"I will be your guide, if you let me."

"But, who . . . who . . ." Catherine was cut short as a moan came from the back of the trailer. Jorgen's eyes closed. The moaning escalated, breaking their moment apart.

Kathy was awake and yelling in agony, "Ah . . . get off . . . get off of me . . ."

Catherine's eyes filled with dread looking down the hall to the back room. She moved to stand, but was halted by Jorgen's hand.

"There is nothing for you there. Only the past behind you, if you so choose."

"I, I have to . . ." Catherine sighed, almost ready to collapse into a sob.

"I will go," Jorgen said, angery his hold was broken by the tension Catherine felt from that voice. He stood and abruptly turned from her and headed down the hall.

Catherine sat in the chair confounded. Who was this man she let into her house? Watching him enter Kathy's room and shut her bedroom door, Catherine stood up. For a second she didn't know what to do. When she allowed him inside, she thought he was something he wasn't. Now that he walked into Kathy's room, she didn't know his name, let alone what he was doing here. She was never so careless. No matter what she believed, this man was nothing but a stranger in her house.

She walked through the living room and entered the hallway strewn with ashen light from the kitchen. Her thoughts directed on the strange man in Kathy's room. Something on the floor caught her eye. It moved out from underneath Kathy's door. A mouse perhaps, they were known to come in from time to time. Another something moved along the wall. She stopped, distracted by the scurrying streak. Her head twitched, trying to see what it was, when a flood of them came from Kathy's room and down the hall. They didn't just come from underneath the door. They seeped and sped from the ceiling, walls, and floors past her.

Stiffened by the faceless creatures around, she screamed out of primal fright. To her horror, the sound made the creatures change course. Instead of passing, the multitude came directly for her. One touched her boot. Another leaped for her hand she braced herself with against the wall. She tried brushing them off, but more came after her until the faceless terrors rapidly covered her body. The more she flung and swiped at them the faster they moved, like frenzied piranhas. For all her efforts, her hand swiped at nothing but black shadow air, passing through them untouched and only encouraged. Catherine tried to fend them off. She felt nothing other than her own hand hitting, swinging, and whipping across her body. Still, she couldn't feel the creatures. She only saw them and their movements upon her and the others coming for her. She was certain she was being attacked. She didn't know how, but these creatures were taking something from her, devouring something to fill their hunger. She twisted and turned, trying to fight them off. She felt something grab her shoulders. Automatically, she swung out and thrust her hands forward to expel the hold that griped her. It wouldn't let go.

"Fear feeds, Catherine." It was the man's voice speaking to her now, strong and anchoring, and holding onto her. Instinctively, she continued to struggle against the creatures covering her. "You have to release your fear, if they are to go away."

What was he saying, she thought, watching them crawl and squirm all around her. He took her face in his hands, forcing her to look directly at him and said, "If you don't fear them, they will go away."

She looked into his eyes, brimming with understanding of the terror she felt. He was clean of the shadow vermin. He was not afraid. Only concern lay in his eyes. In that truth, she tried to comprehend what he was saying. *Don't fear*, she said to herself, *no fear*. It was impossible.

"Close your eyes," he said.

Catherine did as he willed her. Looking into the dark, she could hear nothing, feel nothing, except for his hands upon her face, lifting the terror she felt inside. After what felt like endless time, she parted her eyes just a little to see most of the shadow terrors dispersed. A few remained. One crossed her right eye, causing her fright to rise again.

"Keep your eyes closed until I tell you to open them," he commanded.

She didn't know how long they stood in the hallway. Eventually her shoulders relaxed and her breathing eased. His hands slid gently away from her face. Even though he had not told her to open them, she could feel him staring at her. She opened her eyes without waiting for instruction. The things were gone and only the natural shadows remained in the hall, but the man's face was covered with a profound ache unlike Catherine had ever seen. It was directed at her.

For all the questions she had spinning in her head, she asked only one. "Who are you?"

"I have introduced myself before," he said with a sigh. His face eased. His composure returned as he continued, "My name . . . is Jorgen."

Jorgen, Catherine thought. The man at the hospital was named Jorgen, but they couldn't be the same man, yet she just witnessed the impossible. She needed to know more. Her questions spat out in random. "What were those . . . those things?" she asked.

He paused for a moment in thought and then he said, "To some they look like pests, parasites or leeches, but they are bottom feeders all the same, the weakest of Shadow Creatures."

"But how—where do they come from?"

"They are everywhere, if you know how to see them. Here, they were feeding off of the woman."

"Kathy," Catherine said aghast.

"Yes. As I cast them away, you saw them. Your fear turned on you, allowing them to feed off the fragments of your threads."

Catherine gripped her shoulders, thinking of the things swarming her body. She shook her head and looked down the hallway and said, "They're not real. They can't be."

"They are very real, but the least of your concerns right now," Jorgen said gravely. "The world around you spins in an ignorant deceit for things of this nature and others . . . that are much stronger and very powerful. And you, Catherine, are in the middle of it."

"What . . . I . . . this is . . ." she stammered hopelessly, trying to grasp everything she witnessed and his answers.

Jorgen's face grew alarmed. Before she could comprehend his words, he grabbed her hand and pulled her down the hallway into the living room, heading for the door.

Catherine yanked back, releasing her hand and cried, "What's going on?"

"We don't have time," Jorgen said in earnest.

"This is crazy. Tell me what you're talking about."

"I will tell you everything," Jorgen said. "But you must come with me now!"

"Come with you? Just where do you think we're going?"

"Anywhere. Anywhere you want. I'll give you all the answers to the things you have seen and anything else you ask of me, but right now we have to leave."

"No," Catherine said.

Jorgen's voice rose. "There is nothing for you here Catherine. Nothing. Don't let your decision waver for any trace of pity for that woman," Jorgen said pointing down the hall, "Or any feeling of hope you may have on another!"

"You are telling me to leave with you, when I don't even know you," she protested.

"You don't have to know me, or the thing coming for you. But you need know this, it is very real, very dangerous, and it's headed this way."

Catherine recalled her vision at the hospital, her grandmother's warning she believed to be nothing more than a manifestation of her delusional mind. She struggled with the memory, and touched her pocket where the ring lay. "Run, Catherine . . . run," she remembered Nana saying. Now she believed that maybe, just maybe, the vision had been real after all.

"But, Nathan . . ." she found herself speaking aloud, rubbing her hand against the ring in her pocket. She couldn't abandon Nathan.

"Leave him behind you," Jorgen said pleading for her to come with him.

"I - I can't . . ." Catherine said in turmoil.

"Then, for now," Jorgen said in defeat, "all I can offer you is this." He moved with inhuman speed. With a wisp like a breeze, her hair lifted and fell. He stood in front of her again. She looked at him, aghast, and struggling to understand everything taking place. "I will be close, even when you can't see me. I will protect you Catherine, even if it means . . . the end."

"The end of what?" Catherine asked, mystified by this stranger walking to the door, not wanting him to leave, and yet scared all the more of the questions that came along with him.

Jorgen turned the doorknob and paused. "The end of me," he said and pulled, leaving the door wide open as he left.

Catherine felt something around her throat as he vanished. Touching it upon her neck, she realized it was the necklace he'd worn around his throat.

She heard footsteps on the porch. She ran to catch the enigmatic man in black and instead discovered Nathan at her door.

CHAPTER ELEVEN

Nathan stood at the bottom of the porch steps a short while before Catherine's door whipped open. A strange man's voice came through the thin aluminum walls. The few words he picked up were "nothing for you here" and "leave him." But he couldn't pick up her response.

After receiving Catherine's phone call, he spent hours trying to get out of Donnie's to be with her. He was only successful in buying a stretched hour before he'd have to go back and finish his shift. Finding her with another man was the last thing he thought he'd discover tonight. The intensity from the voices sounded like a lover's quarrel. No one was close to her. No one but him, or so he thought. The jealousy stung within.

The boy he was a year ago would have walked away, but not now. Not ever since he met the man in black.

A month passed since Nathan committed himself to Artros' teachings. Nights were still filled with concepts of color, color that blended into all light forms and the metaphors as to how Darkness absorbed them. Artros continued to meet him at Donnie's bar with an unspoken agreement that the man would reveal the secret of this power, this Darkness. Artros said knowledge was stronger than any weapon a man could wield. His attention made Nathan's esteem rise while the teaching's continued to open his mind to the intricate concepts, and the stagnation of the world around him. He felt the nights when Artros came into the bar he was there for him alone, and had been the entire time.

Tonight, Donnie's bar was blockaded with people and the grill tickets never ceased. The crowd was one moving mass of a gossip exchange. Some spoke of those lost in the river's wreckage and others retold stories of heroism and kindness. No one knew how, but the townies consensus was the explosion at the hospital and river were related. The town's disaster spiked an adrenalin rush without a way to come down. While the townies reiterated what they witnessed there were two in the tavern who dismissed the venting crowd. Nathan looked through the moving fence line of people and saw Artros sitting at his table as usual. Tonight, however, a woman joined him. Even from afar, this woman's beauty shone. Her locks rolled about her, down her back, and against the beaten chair she sat upon holding her black coat. While Artros eased into his chair, her posture remained square and taught, like the flawless features of her skin. Dressed in black like Artros, Nathan wondered if this was the *black rose* he spoke of. People froze mingling by, captivated as if in a trance. Conversations paused, catching a glimpse of her, along with Artros' rare grin. Artros' courtesy, Nathan grew to understand, was an artificial display for all the knowledge and power the man held. But tonight it looked genuine. Tonight, Artros looked satisfied.

Nathan, along with everyone else in the tavern, stole glances at them every chance they could. Longing to know who she was, his excitement grew. *One day*, he thought, *he would be the third member of their party. One day, he would be a man of power and hold the attention of those who would desire to befriend him, or hate him for it.*

Then the phone call from Catherine came. Nathan took the call in the back of the bar in Donnie's office. "Nathan," Catherine said, "They're sending us back."

"No. They can't do that . . . they said you'd be there a couple of days," Nathan replied in disbelief. "What about Kathy?"

"She . . . she's not good. They said they . . . they need the room," Catherine replied in a stark voice.

"Listen, I'll see if I can get Ricky to cover my shift, or else I'll be there right after work, okay? I promise. Just hang on. Okay?"

"They got Kathy in the wheelchair. I have to go," Catherine said.

It was an hour later when Nathan was finally able to contact Ricky. They settled on twenty bucks for an hour of work. That was the best Nathan could get out of him. *Some friend,* Nathan thought as Ricky came in red-eyed and half-baked.

"One hour man," Ricky said punching his time card into the clock on the wall. "Any longer and you owe me another twenty, plus a bag. But, you'd better be back."

Nathan gave Ricky's back a good hard slap, as if in thanks, but his old friend stumbled forward from the blow. Nathan said, "I will. Thanks for covering for me. I just gotta check on Catherine," and punched out. He thought about telling Artros, but he knew he'd have to come back at some point, and moving through the mob would waste time. Nathan assumed this night of colors would be dismissed given the woman at Artros' table, but he would be back in time to find out, and possibly meet the mysterious woman with him.

Nathan grabbed his coat, shot a look at the woman and Artros still absorbed with each other at the table, and slipped out the back door. To his disbelief, he nearly ran into Artros before the man's cane landed on his chest, stopping him.

"Where are you going?" he asked.

Nathan looked in awe at Artros and back to the bar, wondering how Artros moved so fast. He tried to compose his gawking shock. He knew Artros was aware of his surroundings at all times and would have known he left. "I was coming back," he said. "I just got a call from a friend who needs . . . some help, and then I was going to come right back. I was going to tell you, but you were with the woman . . ." Nathan trailed off, speechless and unsettled, looking into Artros' probing stare.

Artros lifted the cane from Nathan's chest and held it high above him. His eyes grew dark, almost black, and Nathan feared Artros was going to strike him with it. Instead Artros pointed it north and held it there. He continued to look at Nathan, but Nathan realized Artros didn't see him. It appeared as if the man was looking past him, searching for something, scanning the unseen. Suddenly, Nathan ducked as Artros whipped his cane in the air around to the east. His dark stare eased and he set the cane down.

"Always a pleasure to know chivalry is not dead," Artros said, returning to his normal poise. "You may leave."

"Thank you, Master," Nathan said, although perplexed as to what Artros had just done. He hoped he would get the chance to ask him.

"I will speak with you later," Artros said walking past him and back into the bar without another word.

When the door of Catherine's trailer swung open and the man came out, Nathan was taken off beat by the his black attire and thought it was Artros at first. Something about the man was vaguely familiar, something he thought he remembered, but couldn't place. This man carried himself with assured grace, like Artros. Master, Nathan liked the idea of that word. If it wasn't for Artros he would have turned around on the porch steps, but not now. Nathan was curious if this man had anything to do with Artros, but immediately dismissed the thought with his questioning anger and jealousy brewing within. He wanted to know who was involved in Catherine's life.

As the man flew past him their eyes locked. Nathan pursed his lips and gave a discerning stare, but the man looked back at him with contorted misery. *Whatever happened between the man and Catherine?* Nathan thought, *was good*. The man was leaving in sorrow, as Nathan watched him walk down the street and out of sight.

The door was wide open. Catherine hadn't moved to close it and that in itself was strange. She had a thing about doors, especially locks. Placing his hands on the doorframe he moved to peer inside, but Catherine ran to the door, almost running into him as if she were chasing after the man. Looking at Catherine, his jealousy turned into the bitter anger of a scorned lover.

Her shirt was twisted about her waist. The top button undone. Her hair was tossed in a frazzled mess and her chest rose and fell in a quick, shallow rhythm. At one point she had been crying. Crying for the man who left, Nathan gathered. Didn't look like he was going to be gone from the bar that long after all.

"Looks like you called somebody else too," Nathan said, as she stepped back in surprise. He came inside and saw her backpack on the table, her clothing thrown about along with a ripped plastic sack of items from the hospital. He was just about ready to turn back around and walk out, when suddenly Catherine wrapped her arms around him, burying her face in his chest. For a moment, he held his arms down his sides. He thought the last thing he would find at her place was another man, but now she was holding him, breaking the touch. He melted into it.

Returning her embrace, he held her. Moving his hands along her back and sides he felt her trembling. He held her tighter and laid his face across the top of her head, inhaling the sweet essence of her, wanting more. She hadn't moved, but he lifted his head and brushed his hand along her hair, cupping it behind her ears. She looked up at him as he drew back the strands left on her face. He wanted to touch her for so long, too long. He savored the feel of her cheeks and brow beneath his touch, the curve of her mouth. If there was ever a moment for him to finally show her he was in love with her, it would be now. She broke the distance between them. He continued to stroke his fingers along her face. She looked at him, inviting him. He slid his hand underneath her chin and lifted it so he could kiss the flesh of her petal lips. Lips he waited years to embrace.

Then he saw a necklace around her throat. It made him pause even though she continued to grip his waist, harder, pulling him closer. His hold wavered. Catherine never wore jewelry and he knew this had something to do with the man. Jealousy returned. Even though she may have broken it off with the man, the thought of her touching him, him touching her, lingered around her throat. For now, he couldn't bring himself to kiss her inviting lips. He had wanted to be the first.

Struggling with the feeling of betrayal, he blamed the greater half of his jealousy on himself and spending his free time with Artros. While his love for her hadn't dissipated, he couldn't bring himself to kiss her. Not right now. He felt like it wouldn't be genuine if she wanted his affection as a replacement for the man who walked out on her.

"You've had . . . a day . . . " Nathan said, moving his hands down to the sides of her arms enveloped around him.

He unwrapped her arms around him and held them. She looked hurt and confused. He felt the need to apologize, for what, he didn't know exactly. Somehow he felt that if she sought out another's affection instead of his it was because he deserved it. Even if there wasn't a day he didn't think about her, he'd been so engrossed in his own life, in Artros, that he hadn't taken the time for her. He blamed himself, but the necklace around her throat stung inside the love he felt for her. Catherine hadn't said anything yet. It was as if she were lost for words. He wanted to shut-up, take her back into his embrace, but he couldn't. He had to know if it was over with the man, completely over and finished. If he was to continue to trust, there had to be something to believe in—the love he thought she once shared with him.

"Since when did you start wearing necklaces?" he hated to ask, but he had to know. Nathan released his grip as Catherine brought her hands up to her throat and grasped the hard ring around it. She fingered the silver pendant hanging in the center. She rushed to a broken soot-covered mirror and viewed the necklace. The chain was a solid ring of silver. The pendant hanging down was also silver, but it had an odd sort of etching upon it. It looked like two letter R's, sharp in the circle where the top of the letter's would have curved around, one normal and one reversed. But otherwise they were equal. Catherine started spinning the necklace around and around her throat, struggling to find a clasp to undo the ring around her neck. Finally, she gave up and walked back to Nathan, who seemed pleased she wanted to be rid of it.

"Would you help me take it off?" Catherine asked, turning around and lifting her hair.

Nathan was more than willing to help, thinking he might take it with him when he left and dispose of it for good along the way. He studied the soft white flesh of Catherine's neck, where the V line of her hair stopped at the base of her head, yearning to touch it and kiss that point over and again. *Soon*, he thought. He found himself turning it round and round her neck, just like she had in the mirror. The necklace appeared to be without any sort of latching device. Nathan started to pull the ring in various places, thinking it was a trick of an eye, but the chain remained bound around her neck.

"I can't get it," Nathan said.

"What? It can't be stuck," Catherine said.

"No, well it's not stuck. But I—I can't find the . . . the doohickey thing to get it off. How did you get it on?" Nathan asked.

"Jorgen put it on me," Catherine said turning to him with her head down, still pawing at the necklace around her throat.

So that was his name, Nathan sighed inside. *Woe to you Jorgen*, Nathan heard the Master's voice trailing into his thoughts and feelings. Nathan didn't want to be the boy, a coward, and let someone take what was his. If he saw Jorgen again, he would make it very clear the man was not welcome. Nathan thought about cutting the necklace off, but considering the close proximity of her throat he decided against using a pair of tin snips, at least for now anyway.

"Are you going to see him again?" Nathan asked with bitter curiosity.

"I hope not," Catherine said dropping her hands to her sides in defeat.

That was good, Nathan thought satisfied. He smiled to her and said, "Don't worry, we'll find some way to take it off."

"I'm just so . . . so happy you're here," she said.

"Me too," Nathan replied. "Me too."

Nathan helped Catherine pick up her scattered belongings while she talked about what happened at the hospital and the ride home. She failed to mention what transpired between Jorgen and her. A part of Nathan was relieved, because he didn't know how he had let her fall so close to another man, and yet another part of him painfully wondered how it all began. When he graduated, he continued the monotonous beat of life, and thought she would also until she finished school. Once she did, that waiting period would be over and they could step into life together. Then Artros became a significant sideline of his free time, consuming the hours he slept and those he would have otherwise spent with Catherine. In the muddled wash of trying to maintain work and Artros, Catherine slipped by. Life tricked him with its deceiving repetition. Nothing remained the same. Maybe he was the fool, thinking Catherine would always need him, and her life would never change without him. He never wanted to feel the way he felt tonight walking up her porch steps. He never wanted to think again about the possibility of losing her. He couldn't bear the pain of thinking of her with another man. With Jorgen.

Nathan caught her looking in the mirror again at the necklace around her throat.

"Do you want to talk about it?" Nathan couldn't help but ask.

"No," Catherine replied, trying to stuff the necklace inside her shirt. No matter what she did, it stuck out.

Nathan turned from her and noticed the clock on the wall. *Damn*, he thought, *damn*. Time couldn't have passed by so quickly. He hated the thought of telling Catherine he had to leave. It was just the thing he always said to her—gotta go—gotta run—see ya later—another reason for her to find someone else to keep her company.

"Listen Catherine, I gotta . . ." Nathan stopped himself short before he continued. "Ricky covered my shift for a while so I could come and see how you were doing. I . . . I have to close the bar down, but then I'm coming right back here, okay?"

Catherine's face was troubled. "You promise?" she asked.

Nathan chided himself for leaving. How could he bring himself to it? It would just be for a little while, he thought, just a few more hours and he would be back. Back for her. "It'll be late, but I . . . " Nathan said looking at her broken face. He walked over and slipped his arms around her wilting frame. "I promise. Just hang on a little longer and I'll be right back."

It was another moment, another touch. If he held on he knew he wouldn't be able to stop. He had to leave. Not only for work, but to Artros and the Darkness. Stealing a soft kiss at the top of her head she wouldn't feel, he let go. She stood in the living room, feeling the affection of his desire coming from her as he closed the door, fully intending to keep his promise and return.

Jorgen scanned the horizon for the Darkness making its way to Catherine. It was coming to cover her in its shielding shroud. Bouldering at the head were the Shadow Men, followed by other desolate creatures of Darkness Artros retained. They resembled the wildest beasts in nature. Jorgen watched the stallions, bores, coyotes, ravens and many more settle a perimeter around the land, trees and air. They moved upon the earth as shadows. In the air they swooped and spun off each other like a flock without destination, restless to be set free from the Master who called them and held them captive. The magnitude of their looming presence would eventually dampen the innocent souls within the shield. Inevitably, lovers would quarrel, hate would be expressed through the fist, and those weak in the physical body would become ill, and those ill, would perish. All of this would transpire. The black mass of Shadow Creatures would feed off the residents, draining them of their strength, heart and mind. They obtained energy through the same life force as the Masters of Darkness, the threads of life. Now they were contained and Artros would allow them to drain all the life out of the people, as long as he could maintain control over Catherine. Now it would be hard, if not impossible, for Jorgen to reach her again.

Thus far, Jorgen was content believing Artros did not suspect him so close to Catherine. His army would have been sent to find him in the night, and beyond, if he knew Jorgen was nearby.

The paved road turned into dirt as Jorgen walked to his vehicle. Only he could see it through the cloak of Darkness he created to blanket it, and himself, while he made his escape. Undetected for the moment, but never out of Artros' grasp, his pace slowed. Jorgen tried not to think about anything other than distancing himself from the Shadow Creatures, but the decision to leave Catherine frustrated him.

As Jorgen walked, his breath shot out in front of him like fog, slapping him in the face as he pressed on. He couldn't hear his heavy breathing, or his boots stomping louder with each step. The world was silent, except for the provocative voice in his head and the haunting path of his life that brought him to this moment.

The night was a dusty memory dragging chills up and down Jorgen's spine. The past lingered in his mind, vexing him in waves of torment, restless to remind him he gambled before and lost. Walking with bitter memories, he wrestled the commitment he made to Catherine, a promise of unwarranted protection, and one he couldn't justify. Plaguing thoughts chastised the vow he made to her. Its bladed voice slid up and down him, sharpening his conscience against the strop, ready to release its ferocity. Every step struggling between the man he claimed to be and the man he was. His conscious butchered him, allowing no room for mercy and he fought against it.

"I will listen to the decisions she makes," Jorgen said to his conscious. "I will not force her. I will only attempt to guide her through the journey she will inevitably have to make. The vultures of Darkness hover around her, and she is but a child to the power that seeks his claim upon her."

You're weak! Time has debilitated you to become nothing more than the pathetic man you were when Artros found you. A woman started this and now you will let a woman finish it. She doesn't want anything to do with you. You saw her. You never learn! Trying to be a hero to the fallen, Jorgen?

"This has nothing to do with the past of my beginnings. This is part of the quest."

Liar! You live in lies. Lies are safe. Look at what happened to you. Look at what you've become. See your reflection, Jorgen? Look at the lie of what she has done to you.

"No. I have done this to myself. Everything . . ."

Oh, pity the self-righteous that blindfold themselves. Cover your ears so she can't tell you she doesn't have any answers for you. Only questions that lead to insufferable pain are felt here, and the only release you will find, will be in death. You deserve the worms. All step aside, Lord of the Worms is passing by.

"She could be the Light. She could unlock the mystery of the quest."

Did you see her Jorgen? Did you really look inside of her? Or were you too busy looking straight at her! Ha. Ha. You're falling for her Jorgen. You'd best pretend harder not to feel because your savior is bringing out the lie in you.

"No. There is purpose in this. She is innocent."

She is a beast. She is raw. She is not innocent; she is ignorant. Remember what ignorance does Jorgen. Remember? You were ignorant once. You pulled the Darkness faster than you could tame it. See what you've become.

"I am no longer that man. I will never be that man again."

Really Jorgen, really? You may have the face of a young man but you are a stupid old fool. Stepping back in your old ways. Falling for the same trap. You gave her your necklace Jorgen. You gave her a piece of you and now you are already more vulnerable than you were when you came here. Maybe you should crawl back to Artros, because before all is said and done, even the worms won't be able to feed off of you.

"No!"

Yes, all because of a woman. She's not even a woman, she's a child left in a pen of despair, just like Artros wants her. Just like you want her. Want her to be ignorant for you? Want to seduce her like you were seduced and manipulated? Want to take her Jorgen? It's been such a long time and you're starting to feel again. Starting to become a man instead of the Master you claim to be on the path of knowledge, the quest, the . . .

"Silence!"

You are nothing more than a man filled with the weaknesses of the world.

"No. I won't touch her. I won't. This is the *Darkness* talking. I—am—not—that—man!"

Then you are a coward. You want her, but you wouldn't even take her. Take her for yourself, away from Artros, because you're a coward. Go, crawl back in your cave, coward. Won't fight Artros. . . couldn't take her. You ran when you saw Artros coming to claim what was his. You won't have another opportunity. You know that. But you can blame it on honor—now can't you—say it's all a part of the quest, your hopeless lie. Artros has grown stronger than you could have ever imagined. He is the true Master of Darkness—a man who knows no weakness—unlike you. Pathetic! Tail between your legs Jorgen . . .

Jorgen's hand slammed on the hood of his car. Engrossed in dueling thoughts, he didn't know how he reached it. Isolation spawned the voice, and no matter where he went, or didn't go, the voice was his offspring. It chewed, and with each bite, Jorgen felt its sinking teeth.

You've fallen for her Jorgen and now you can do yourself a favor—kill yourself before she does. Let's return to the days we planned it out, the days when selfishness ruled and you were the martyr of Darkness. That is the only destiny you have left. The one thing, the only thing, that you have left to decide—the entertainment of how it will end!

The voice grated his body, slicing him apart. He wanted to silence it. He grabbed his hair and pulled at it, yanking his head down. Twisting his head to the sides he yelled, "Get out of my head!"

His voice burst into the night as a thunder of nothing but emotion, enraged by his plague of truth and justice, against the Darkness and its lust. His explosive voice tunneled into the dirt road, riding underneath the packed earth, shattering the road to crumbs as his voice carried away from him.

Ashamed of the uncontrolled release of power, Jorgen drove away, to hide once more, distancing himself just enough to be in reach, where he could watch Catherine and not feel the taxation of emotions overcoming him. He left Catherine alone with her mysterious power and the shadows of Darkness surrounding her.

Walking up to Donnie's Bar, Nathan groaned. The street was still lined with cars. People mingled on the sidewalk and others flowed in and out of the bar. Nathan overheard an unexpected dump of snow would befall the town. There was always something about an impending storm that made people anxious. When the weatherman called for a foot of snow, townies drove the streets until the last moment, eventually to make it home or ditch in trying. People rebelled and the packed bar showed it with those overcome with cabin fever before a single snowflake had fallen. Townies were ready to get their last call in, whether it was water or spirits, before the town came down with a cold. This one professed to be heavy enough to weigh down power lines and barricade roads with fallen limbs. The last blizzard. Mostly the emergency crews and county road commission felt the toll of the approaching storm. With the morning's unexplained disaster, their help and exhaustion trickled thin.

Nathan punched in. Ricky punched out.

"You owe me," Ricky said with a smirk, reaching for a pack of smokes out of his coat pocket, ready to infuse himself with the bar crowd.

"I'll get 'cha back," Nathan said, thinking *asshole*, as Ricky mingled into the people across from the bar and grill. Ricky wasn't doing anything aside from what he would have done during his shift other than talk, flirt, and take a drag with every opportunity. Nathan tied a white grease-stained apron around his waist and walked to the grill in the heavy choke of the smoke-filled air. Waiters hollered and food tickets hung above the grill like a white sheet clothesline where flames sizzled afire for the swelling orders. Across the bar, regulars attempted to talk to him, but tonight he drowned out their words. Tonight he didn't care. He thought of Catherine. Tonight was an awakening. He thought he lost her, but the touch was broken. Somehow, her embrace empowered him like Artros' teachings and opened his mind. Everything here meant nothing. Just like Artros said, *these people were nothing*. No feelings or aspirations other than wanting and fill, thirst and drink, and never satisfied. Nothing. Love and the knowledge of Darkness were the only things that mattered. The crowd talked, laughed, and spoke of the chaotic events at the hospital, the river, and the storm, but to Nathan they talked about nothing. Only two things mattered, Catherine and Artros. The barrier was broken. He was filled with Catherine and he rode on it. That was sustenance. Something he could hang on to until he was able to punch out of the noose like the slave for the man Artros said he was. *It wouldn't be long*, Artros had said. He had to exert patience. Patience took great control. Patience was power.

The bar was a hive of voices. They shouted, while others demanded Nathan pick up the pace at the grill. The mass stood shoulder against shoulder. Artros' table was hidden by the multitude. Nathan dove into work, thinking about the day he would end this never-ending stubbed ticket line of wanting, and cater to his own desires. Soon. He could feel it.

Donnie joined Nathan on the grill, quick at hand, slapping ground meat into burgers. He stayed late, as they were understaffed and flooded by the locals and weekend regulars that only came out on a night like tonight. Tonight was madness. Even Donnie, a man of his tavern-time, couldn't predict when these moments would hit.

"So, ah," Donnie began to ask, handing Nathan a plate of food to place under the heat lamp, "your man going to pay for his drinks or you going to cover him till he gets back?"

"What are you talking about?" Nathan responded, watching Donnie flip burgers faster than money could burn.

Donnie passed him another plate for the lamp and said, "Your buddy walked out without paying his tab. You just remind him 'bout that and I won't hold hard feelings against him, or you, alright?"

Nathan realized Artros wasn't in the bar. He never left without a word to him, and never without paying. Artros might skip town as fast as he appeared. Nathan thought that was a possibility. Artros was a secret. That was the first time

Nathan was worried he could lose Artros like he almost had Catherine. Nathan said, "He's paid for his drinks triple over Donnie. If you got a problem with him then tell him yourself."

"His money don't make up for the regulars I've lost, and I've lost a good amount of money since he's been coming in here if you haven't noticed. The bar is cranking right now, but the people won't sit at his table. Ever notice that, how people won't sit at his table? He's not here and I'm still losing money. People are talking. They don't like him. I don't like him. Wish he'd get done whatever he's doing in town and get the hell outta here. He doesn't belong here."

Nathan didn't want to discuss Artros around Donnie, and it wasn't just the warning Artros gave Nathan never to mention him. It was none of Donnie's business.

"I'll tell him when I see him," Nathan lied and then yelled, "Order up," the same two words he would repeat the rest of the night, long after regular closing time.

Artros didn't come back to the bar. When Donnie locked the doors and the last couple stumbled out, Nathan checked the little square window inlay to see if Artros' hat might pass by, wondering and worrying what he would feel like if Artros never stepped back through the door.

The bar looked like it had been ransacked. Liquor glasses and mugs covered everything, along with dishes and napkins. Glasses were stacked in the bathroom stalls, where even the walls needed a good swashing. Nathan swept the floor, lifting up chairs and sliding back displaced tables. Normally the bar would have closed at 2 a.m., but given the storm, and the chance of losing money for the next couple of days if the town was quarantined, Donnie squeezed another hour past the legal cutoff hour for booze.

Melissa begged for a ride home, complaining her tired feet couldn't possibly walk home in the snowstorm now covering everything with four inches and counting. Nathan said no twice, but she followed him out to his car like a lost cat, whining behind. It was a quarter to four and Catherine was sure to be waiting.

His Celica was a beast of burden. The brake sunk just enough at times, when in park, causing the taillights to turn on and drain the battery. Usually he'd leave a can of wax beans under the pedal to stop it from dropping, but when he came back to the bar for the second time that night, he realized he'd forgotten. The battery was dead. Fortunately, it was a stick shift and he could pop the clutch once he got it rolling and start the 4-cylinder. As ill fate would have it, tonight he needed Melissa's help to get the car rolling. In return, she bartered for a ride home. She was an obstinate mule, but with some coaxing from Nathan, they succeeded and were fishtailing down the road.

Melissa's apartment was only a few blocks out of his way. Driving, he thought about Artros, wondering if he would come back to see him again at the bar, and Catherine. Melissa chattered on about the tips she raked in and something about the snow. Nathan was distracted in thought until Melissa broke them by sliding her hands underneath his leg working the gas and brake.

"What are you doing?" Nathan asked, shifting into second while lifting his side so she would remove her hands.

"Come on, Nate, I'm freezing." Melissa moaned.

"Put 'um between your own legs."

"They're cold too. It's your fault. I helped you push, didn't I?"

Nathan grumbled. They weren't too far from her place, but fighting the snow-covered roads was a challenge and he was losing time. All he had to do was get her out of the car.

For a while neither one of them spoke, but Nathan could feel her hands each time he moved his foot off the throttle and back down.

"You know your guy?" Melissa said. Nathan rolled his head to the side. "He told me you and I . . . well he thought, we should get together."

"That's pretty funny, Melissa. Did you tell him you get together with a lot of guys?"

"That's not true," Melissa said pouting. "I've just been waiting for you. Waiting for you to get your mind off of that one chick. Anyway, isn't she still in school? That's so lame. Really, Nate, you should go out with a real woman," she said moving her hands from underneath his thigh to the top and proceeded to move her fingers, like a spider up and down it.

"We're here." Nathan stated, pulling into the driveway and moving the stick to neutral. Melissa gripped his thigh.

"So whaddaya say?" she asked.

"About what?" Nathan snapped.

"Say about us looking good together? Your guy thought we'd look good together. He said you and I should make purple."

"What?" Nathan asked, shaking his head while he spoke, not believing Melissa would understand anything Artros had to say. "What the hell is that supposed to mean?"

Melissa cocked a coy smile and said, "You know . . . when you're a kid they say girls are red and boys are blue so don't be making purple."

"Get out," Nathan said pushing her hand off of him. Melissa opened the door. Nathan pressed harder on the brake and clutch waiting for Melissa to leave.

The passenger door hung open as Melissa stretched and stepped out, turning back to him and continued, "Look, it'll be fine. I mean if it's your first time. Come on up. I'll do all the work. I'll show you how boys and girls make purple."

Nathan let the clutch out and eased on the brake, allowing the car to slowly roll back on the inclined slope. The passenger door pushed on Melissa.

"Gawd, Nate. You're such a drag," Melissa said. "The cooks are right about you. Your Jonny's so wadded in the sack you couldn't even let it fall outta the bag if a girl untied the string for you," and slammed the car door.

Finally, Nathan was heading to Catherine. The roads were coating fast. He wasn't driving on them, he was skiing.

By the time his car was parked in his driveway, half of the predicted snow had fallen. He wanted to change and wash the bar-sludge off, but it was past four in the morning. He headed straight for Catherine.

The snow was silent in its heavy fall, thick in the air and everything it covered. Everyone was asleep except for a small light in the distance, Catherine's place. Nathan was uplifted, thinking she was awake after all.

Passing the trailers, he looked down at his soaked tennis shoes when something caught his eye to the right of him. He turned, but nothing was there except for a row of cars covered in white. A dark flash swooped aside him and into the air. He turned around and back again, glancing from side to side. All was still. He proceeded to walk in the quiet snowfall with the ominous presence of being watched. The feeling unnerved him even though his tracks in the snow were the only ones to be seen.

Ahead, he saw a black figure standing in front of Catherine's kitchen window. Nathan paused a moment in suspicion before making out the image of a man, one he knew well.

The wide rectangle windows in front of Catherine's trailer cast a foggy light through its double window frame. Walking up, Nathan could make out Artros' hat and coat, almost covered with an inch of snow. Artros was standing directly in the middle of the windows where the seam of the parting curtains cast a shadow down the middle of his face. The dividing line streaked his forehead, nose, and basking smile. There were no footprints around Artros to determine when he got there or from which direction he came. His trench coat pulsated towards the windows, and the light she left on for Nathan.

"Artros?" Nathan said, questioning his teacher in front of Catherine's place.

"What did you call me?" Artros asked without waver.

"I . . . I apologize, Master," Nathan said. The word was still foreign. Nathan was relieved to see his Master again, but unsettled finding him at Catherine's. "I didn't expect you here."

"I knew I would find you here," Artros simply said. "This is the only light on. The only light in the world right now. Tell me, Nathan, do you know what lays the heart to rest when the night is dim and the soul is broken?"

"No."

"Of course not, but you will." Artros said turning to him. "Darkness lulls the heart to sleep, and in Darkness the heart will be awakened." He started to walk down the carpet road of white, away from Catherine's. Nathan sighed looking up to Catherine's window and back to Artros. For now, he told himself, he would have to follow Artros.

Artros swung his cane round and round his side, grazing the snow without a mark. They came to the field where the snow couldn't be trusted for its depth. Nathan caught obscure shadows moving at random and questioned his tired eyes.

In the middle of the field Artros stopped. He turned to Nathan and said, "Tell me, how is your rose?"

"Catherine? How did you . . ." Nathan began, but then dismissed questioning Artros. He shouldn't have been surprised the man would know everything about him or where he went. "Her ma, Kathy, isn't doing so good. She was at the hospital with her. She's an alkie, an alcoholic. They were supposed to be there awhile, but because they—well I don't really know, but they sent them home early cause of the shit that went down today and I guess . . . I guess they needed the room . . . at the hospital," Nathan finished, regurgitating some of Catherine's words and his disturbance. Something didn't sniff quite right with Artros tonight. He hated sounding juvenile around Artros, but something was hidden, like a dirty bag, and Nathan's leeriness was coming through in his cold, chattering voice. He wondered if it was the reality that Artros was so close to his home and Catherine, or that the life he lived and the fantasy he indulged with Artros were merging. But Artros was real, like his cryptic power, and Nathan was walking the tightrope. If he kept moving forward with Artros, the future was indefinite. If he turned around, an application for the shoe factory sat on the table at home. Either way, he could fall. He almost lost Catherine. Trying to balance that wire could lead to a cutthroat end.

"I am a gentleman, and dispose of all others when my lady calls," Artros said with smiling curiosity. "Tell me, apprentice, how was the young rose when you came to her aid?"

"Well," Nathan began, relieved that Artros looked appeased and might understand why he would ask to return to Catherine, once he could find the strength. "She called me at work and said they, her and Kathy, were coming home."

"And you came like any nobleman would," Artros said.

"Yeah, of course," Nathan said stuffing his hands in his jacket. "But when I got there, there was this other guy there and he was . . . dressed, like you, in black," Nathan continued, feeling as though the dip of earth he was standing on was starting to vibrate. "But he left, and Catherine doesn't want him back, at least as far as I can tell. No, she doesn't. I'm sure of it." Nathan looked down at his shoes, caked in snow, where he could feel quivers moving up his frozen feet.

"Does this adversary have a name?" Artros said in a low rumbling voice.

"She said his name was Jorgen, but she doesn't want to see him again." Nathan said looking at Artros' marble face. Alarmed, Nathan continued, "But he gave her a necklace, and she can't seem to get it off . . ."

A sudden shockwave exploded from Artros, blowing Nathan back and onto the ground. As Nathan fell, the snow on the earth and air blasted away. Nathan's eardrums pounded. He couldn't hear Artros' bellowing voice streaming in fury, but there was no mistaking the anger residing in the air. Lying there, Nathan feared Artros, but not as much as what he witnessed coming out of the dark, straight for them. What he saw, terrified him beyond any fear he had ever known.

When Artros' power detonated, the rushing Darkness expanded. Nathan saw the Shadow Creatures for the first time. The air whooshed and hissed as they advanced like razors. The power Artros released didn't hinder these creatures from moving against it, or through it. The night was dark and the winter white, but the Shadow Creatures were as pitch as a black hole. They were defined as beasts of the land and air. He couldn't hear them, but he could see their emotions in the movements they projected in disregard of their Master and his pupil. They moved, all shapes and sizes, like a hoard wanting nothing but flesh for vengeance and a soul for penitence. Nathan wrapped his arms around his face, as if he might protect himself through this physical measure. He rolled on the cold barren earth and peered through the white wash in his eyes. Artros' coat tossed around him from the air-streaming force of the Shadow Creatures moving in attack. Artros threw his cane in front of him. It landed in the air, suspended and spinning. Nathan's blown eardrums relentlessly beat along with the foreign words Artros shouted, commanding the Shadow Creatures back, along with the pressure of power revolving from the cane. The Shadow Creatures were held at bay. They writhed and snapped their empty mouths. Some flapped their wings in jigsaw like patterns while others pawed around the defending circumference Artros created. Slowly, they calmed to submission and vanished into the dark where the faint sigh of the morning was about to break. Nathan wiped the snow from his eyes and stood up. His heart raced and his legs wavered, but he held his ground. He felt as though he might heave, but choked it in. Not knowing what to do, he stood, aghast. He understood those were Artros' creatures. His Master imprisoned harpies, longing escape.

Artros recalled the spinning cane to his hand and held it again to his side. His anger was far from expelled.

"A lesson, Nathan," Artros said with a cynical stare, "an adversary of yours will be one of mine. Another," Artros spat in disgust, "fear feeds, and you *boy* are reeking of it!"

CHAPTER TWELVE

After Nathan left, Catherine continued cleaning. She took care of her clothes and hospital souvenirs, stashing them around the trailer. She was exhausted, but driven by the fumes of elation. After all this time, Nathan returned her affection. Years of embalming solitude were touched. The tomb breached. When she saw Nathan at the door, she gathered the courage to embrace him. Feeling his warmth, the longing within was quenched, however brief.

The memory of a loving touch was lost after Nana's death. Catherine had dreamt of someone to hold, dare love her in return, and it brought everything she thought love would bring, but more. It burned. Smoldering into his arms, Nathan nurtured her soul and melted the hard layers of her being. At that moment, she was nothing more than a girl trying to hold onto a boy. When he released her, love's lining tore as fast as it was bound. She rebuked love for this torture. After submitting herself to it, she was stranded once more in the desert where her desire would wander. How, she wondered, was love fulfilling and desolate at the same time?

The sting of love's reprisal was new and confusing. It pained her awakening heart. Catherine thought enduring years of isolation could be masked by love. Instead, her solitude was magnified, and she felt like she would suffocate. The encompassing loneliness was reinforced by the dread of wondering what would become of her if Nathan were to vanish. The pit would be infinite. Without its homecoming, she was suspended in the clock of her mind, waiting to be rescued.

Catherine worked through these conflicting emotions as she cleaned the trailer. The chore of mindless movement helped ease her mind. Nathan would return. She tried to ride on his word, against an itch in the back of her mind. It wasn't disbelief in Nathan, but doubt afflicted her. *Why he would ever have anything to do with her in the first place? What would he want with someone who had nothing to offer?* She ridiculed herself, searching for the justification of Nathan's love, into a hopeless dead end of reasoning.

Catherine stood in front of the stapled magazine clippings Kathy once revered on the kitchen wall and held a butter knife in her hand. Without anger or jealousy, she used its dull tip to pry the staples out of the wall and took the pictures down. This was her home too, she thought. Removing them one by one, she regarded the two-tone bare spots they created in the veneer paneling. Catherine regarded the square markings in the wall where the clippings once hung. They were like an empty photo album, one where she would create new memories supported by hope. This was her place, and she was going to stay here as long as someone wanted her, as long as Nathan needed her.

To create a future, a home, she had to purge the trailer of as many wounds as possible. The walls and floors would hold the scare, but she could heal, couldn't she? At this moment she had to believe it, or the roof of her mind would cave. Thoughts charged her, picking up and shuffling through the clutter. A heavy ache pounded in her head with weighing thoughts she dismissed walking around as though she were cleaning a maze. The only truth she knew beat against her like warning signs in the road, and she was driving straight ahead in denial.

Amid rifling and tossing, she felt the necklace around her throat. The encounter with Jorgen threatened to eradicate reason from her. Catherine scrubbed harder, trying to push Jorgen from her mind. It was impossible with the memory choking her neck. She strained to block his voice, but his words persisted and they grew louder with her resistance. *Walk with me. Nothing for you here. I will be your guide . . . the thing coming, very dangerous, headed this way . . . leave him behind you. Close. Protect you.* Who was he? What did his warning mean? Recalling the shadows along the floors, walls and ceiling, her skin shivered. She touched the pendant of the necklace, afraid, and heard his parting words, *the end of me.* Not possible, she thought, closing her eyes. She gripped the pendant and pulled. The back of her neck grew red and raw in her struggle to break its invisible clasp. *Stop it*, she said to herself, *this is my turn—my time—my chance!* Catherine let go of the necklace. Heavy in breath she turned to the walls with a bucket of water and started raising them with a hard swash, rubbing the paneling down long after her rag fell to pieces. She balled it together and continued to dip its tattered ends, netted with splinters and paint chips, and resumed the cleansing. Dirty water splashed as she plunged the rag in and out of the bowl, rinsing and wringing it over and again, trying to rinse out the particles embedded in the weave of the worn fabric.

White rusted flakes from the refrigerator door filled the water bowl. She opened the fridge to wash the drawers and shelves inside, ignoring the slivers and fine cuts on her hands. Expired condiments filled the inner door while a few of Kathy's takeout containers from Donnie's Bar, cold in molded grease, lay on the shelves. She threw them into a trash bag aside her. Finishing, she emptied the bowl of water into the sink. Leaning against the counter, she listened to the dirty water trickle down the drain. When it clogged from chips of metal and wood, she pulled them away, feeling she was straining particles of the past within her pruned fingers and crimson hands.

Turning around she looked at her night's accomplishments and regarded them. *What once is opened*, Catherine thought, *is never closed when you know what's behind the door.* The trailer never looked so empty. Her optimism waned, remembering Kathy's closed door at the back of the trailer.

It all depended on Kathy. She walked back to the fridge to the one place in the kitchen she failed to clean. The freezer. Ice cube trays and liquor bottles lined its single shelf. Without hesitation, Catherine threw them in the trash. One by one they clanked, filling the bag to the brink, until the freezer was empty. Catherine looked into the icebox and felt its cold cleansing. The gutting invigorated her.

Slipping her feet into unlaced boots, she threw on a sweater and headed to the door to dispose of the trash at the park's main dump. She reached for the handle, and then withdrew in apprehension, recalling the bottle she tossed underneath Kathy's bed. She wondered how many more bottles of tomorrow's future littered the woman's bedroom. *Not now*, Catherine thought. She wouldn't be detoured.

Kicking the trash bags aside, Catherine walked across the living room and down the hall. In the dim hallway, she stopped in front of Kathy's door and reached for the courage to open it, but there was none. Awakening the woman's thirst, or Shadows Creatures, held her back. She would become undone if she were to fight them now. All the same, she moved to face them.

The light she knew threatened to defeat her. The door was a smokescreen and the future hazed. She worried her efforts were that of a child playing pretend and in the end the only cheat she could blame would be herself. Even if Kathy remained sober, the past was a vat of toxic waste that would reek long after the watered down rags of her labors were clear. Aside from penniless wishes, that was the only truth she knew. She was terrified to open the door and see the room for what it was.

Recalling the Shadow Creatures, she panicked. Light from the kitchen cast abstract shadows in the hallway. Catherine felt any one of them might suddenly move, even as she strained to deny their existence. Jorgen's voice echoed in her mind, *fear feeds*. Without his guidance, she felt they would reappear. Catherine back-stepped quietly out of the hall with closed eyes and soft footsteps, as if they only existed in the confines of that narrow rectangle.

Catherine made her way past the living room and exhaled. Leaving Nathan a note in case he returned, she headed outside, stunned by the snowfall.

Dragging the trash bags, Catherine trudged to the dumpster along the road which didn't look like one anymore. Potholes blended in with the grass and dirt of its borders, all in white. Her hair and clothing became saturated. She came to the dump. The lid was weighted with snow, and collecting more. This was a quiet storm, one that just emptied its fill silently, without howling threats or warning winds. It just poured on and on.

Her tracks on the way to the dump were already coated with a thin layer of snow. Walking back home, she tried to retrace her steps so the snow couldn't dig deeper into the cracks of her soles and soak her boots for tomorrow. It would take a day at least to dry them out.

Hopping in her foot-marked trail, a long black streak, like a wave's ridge, crossed over her feet. The agitated, flowing streak headed for the field, lengthening as it slithered to the end of the asphalt and spiraled up a basketball hoop relic. The snowfall was thick as a moving lace curtain. A large dark mass, like a weightless dog, passed before her and then three more of the same size followed it. Suddenly, the trailer park was streaked with shadow blazes, all of different proportions, accented against the glaze of the white they belted through and between. They whip-tailed around her in a blur, but she recognized them as Jorgen's shadows all the same. A few smaller ones ran across her path and she inhaled. Holding her breath from a scream she was sure would attract them, she didn't stop. Catherine thought of Jorgen's words again, *fear feeds*, and in those words she tried to make it back to her porch step, gulping her breath lest she expel her fear. She dispatched his words in a numbing march, her only guidance to bring her back home.

Catherine closed the trailer door with her shuddering hand and exhaled. *They're not real*, she said, repeating doubt over and over in her mind. Not real.

She wanted to confide in Nathan as to what had happened with Jorgen and the terrifying Shadow Creatures, but she didn't know how to begin. Doubt kept her from unburdening herself to Nathan about the man in black, the one she tried all night to push from her mind. *What if he was the one who created the shadows*, Catherine pondered. *What if he were outside right now summoning these things around her?*

No, she thought. Jorgen's parting words haunted her . . . "I will protect you Catherine," he had said, "even if it means . . . the end of me." Catherine silenced his voice in her mind and thought, there is no such thing as Shadow Creatures, *there is nothing in a shadow . . . just my mind and the shadows I create inside of it.* For the time, she was able to shut the creatures out, and Jorgen, but her subconscious knew they were there.

Easing her wet boots off, she placed them by a small grate humming thin warmth. Catherine felt the dread of isolation overcome her. Losing heart, she sat down on the couch. The clock on the wall showed it was almost two in the morning. Nathan should have been back by now. Maybe he was delayed due to the snowstorm, she thought, or maybe something happened to his car. He would return she reassured herself. While she stared at the clock in front of her face and created more excuses for Nathan's delay, her optimism dwindled. She was thankful she hadn't seen any shadows moving inside her house. Even thinking about them, she was afraid one would appear. She knew her mind would crack if she did, and probably worse than the last time. Focusing on the clock eased her into a trance-like state while she waited for Nathan. With each painful tick and tock, she believed time would bring him closer to her.

Sleep threatened to overtake her. The last thing Catherine saw before succumbing to it was the clock on the wall. Catherine thought about Nathan, the stranger Jorgen she inadvertently let into her house, and the brief time in which Kathy would awake. It all ticked down to the sunrise when new beginnings might leave the man in black and his shadows behind. Thoughts shuffled like cards in her mind and for each one played, she was challenging a house that always won. Two fifty-nine clicked to three. Soon after, her eyes closed for good, sitting upright on the couch with her hands folded in her lap.

Asleep on the couch, Catherine's body relieved itself of the tension from the day's events, and the nightfall of emotions. Her body relaxed and rejuvenated in a long awaited rest. Underneath the lids of her skin, her eyes moved back and forth in rapid motion, experiencing something foreign to her. A dream.

In the dream state, Catherine hung suspended in the starless night, thinking, seeing and feeling nothing other than the sensation of drifting. Pain and loss didn't exist. Soundless, black waters of rocking waves swayed her back and forth like a cradle. Her body received warm vibrations, creating a secure state of slumber. The pulse dipped into her and gave her solace. The dream was a familiar sensation of sanctuary. As a young child, these types of dreams came, and somehow its gift of unseen dynamism would offer her solace for the days ahead. Long ago, when strength threatened to falter, this sensation replenished her as it did now. Catherine felt swaddled in the dark dream of night, and she surrendered to it. She accepted its silent lullaby which embraced her in the hypnotizing waters of its dark abyss.

Here, in the embrace, time didn't exist, even the dread the dream would end and release her into the world she longed to escape. Awareness was nothing. This place didn't contain Kathy, Nathan, or the future. She existed without a conscious string of thoughts. It was dark peace.

The rhythmic pulse of the darkness started to dissipate and shift her to another state. The sensation of drifting in a black ocean of rocking waves ceased as she became weighted and gradually aware of her surroundings. Catherine felt as though she was now being carried. She felt her body sink into unseen arms, but she was not alarmed. They continued to soothe her as her body materialized in the arms of another.

Catherine felt her hands on top of her body, folded into each other as they were when she fell asleep on the couch. Her left arm pressed against the form of the one who carried her, one she could not see. She felt an arm under her neck as her hair hung down and swayed with the walk. Another was underneath her legs which brushed each other from the gentle stride through the night.

The darkness closed in. Catherine submitted deeper into the one who held her. She was accustomed to this grasp, its devoted hold, and without knowing it, she had been waiting for its return.

They came to a stop and Catherine protested. She found her voice in the darkness. Shallow and weak as it was, she heard her words, "Don't stop. Carry me. Carry me further. Don't stop now."

The arms brought her intimately closer and whispered, "Oh, my love." The voice, a soothing haunt from the distant past, drew her deeper into him. "I have carried you always, and forever will. But I cannot tell you how long I have waited to hold you. Hold you like this."

"Don't stop. Don't let me go. Just hold me...hold me forever like you hold me now."

"Long, so long my love, have I waited. This is but a tease to the embrace I will consume you with once you are fully mine. I can see you accept my love in the darkness, and in the darkness your love for me will grow. Remember that, when I come for you," he said. "And do not be frightened of me."

Catherine listened to the familiar voice that spoke to her in dreams when she was a child. The voice poured into the subconscious of her memories and resurfaced now in the dark. Her senses rose and she was afraid of losing the sensations of the dream, the sense of protection, and the feelings of desire. It was seduction. In his phantom arms, the pain of solitude and loneliness washed away. Catherine couldn't bear the thought of it ending.

"I am frightened only by the thought of you letting me go," Catherine said.

"My dear," the man said with an ache, "even though we suffer our inevitable parting, I will never let you go."

"No," Catherine moaned. "Stay . . . please . . . I don't want to be alone . . . always alone . . ."

"Soon, my love, we will be united under a dark sky for eternity. But you will have to wait a little while longer, as I have waited for you . . . My love, I must scold you a little, but just a touch my dear, because tonight I was coming to take you in my arms forever. Alas, you have broken my heart."

"Broken?" Catherine said twisting her body, confused and unsettled. The man's tender words grew darker in reproach.

"Shush your mind and settle yourself into me," he said, but Catherine continued to squirm with an alarming feeling that writhed its way into the solace waters of the dream. The man continued, "Although you have tested my love against another, I will give you a chance to prove yourself to me."

"I don't know what . . . I don't understand," Catherine said.

"The necklace, Catherine," the dark voice responded. "You must remove the necklace."

"I can't," Catherine protested, uneasy in the tightening arms around her which felt more like a lock than embrace. He lifted her face to his, but still she couldn't see him. His voice was close enough that if breath existed in the dream, she would have felt his heated words blow upon her face. "I can't take it off. I tried. I . . . I . . . I don't know how."

"You must *will* it off."

"I don't know what you're saying. I tried. Nathan tried . . ."

"Don't make me punish you, my love, because if that's what it takes to push your will, you will force me to teach you a lesson in strength. Defy the one that would dare intervene. I don't want our fore-longed unity to be scarred by this affair, but if it must be, so be it. If you cannot will the necklace off by your hand, I am left no choice but to correct you. I shine when it comes to discipline. But I only want the light of your gifts, the one that is inside of you, to shine upon me."

"It's not my fault. I didn't . . ."

"Ease yourself, my angel. Had you heeded my words, when I gave warning, I could have taken you by now. You refused me. The world is full of deceiving dogs and one has led you astray. I offer you the way back home. Understand me and do not challenge me, lest your perfection be stained."

"I didn't . . . you didn't warn me. Please, you're frightening me."

"Listen, so I will not have to come to you this way again."

"Don't hurt me."

"Hurt you? That is another blow against my heart. I have no desire to harm you, only to help you unbind yourself. If you cannot find a way, then others will be forced to assist you."

Catherine couldn't deny this man's warning, or the enigmatic circumstances which now surrounded her life. The dream swelled with a foreboding heed. If the man in her dream threatened her through another, then she could only assume that other was Nathan.

"Don't hurt Nathan," Catherine said and then wished she retracted her words in case she singled him out.

"Consider this, my love. If you do not find a way to release yourself from that necklace, then whatever befalls him is of your doing."

"Show me how. Help me. Please. I don't want it. I want it off. Tell me how to take it off and I'll do it. I'll do it for you. Anything . . . please . . ."

"If tears existed in the place I hold you in now, then I would see yours fall only for me. My love, you weaken me. It has been such a long time since anyone has moved me the way your suffering compels me. I am a man of many things, but for you I will show you a side of mercy I do not bestow on anyone else. Think of it as a gift of my love to you, even if the taste of it leaves me distilled with displeasure."

"Anything, I will do whatever . . . you wish."

"Ah, your words are silk around my neck. What I would destroy, and become, to have you say them to me over and again."

"Just tell me what you want me to do."

"This isn't for me, Catherine, this is for us. So we can be together unabridged by those that would seek to come between us, even your pet Nathan. Listen to my instruction."

"Yes . . . yes," Catherine said. His arms released her. Although he no longer held her, her body retained its position as though he was. Her body floated in a dream-state mold. She saw his hands in a darkened glow, lined with the flesh of veins and strength, swirl in movements over and under her suspended body. Then his hands paused above her face.

"Say it again," he commanded.

"Anything . . . " she said and a moan escaped him. His hands touched her forehead and slid down to her cheek and brows, moving as a blind man would to dictate every crevice into memory. He outlined her lips with the tip of his fingers and then moved them down to caress her neck before gripping her suspended arms. His hands lingered there, only for a moment, with intensifying strength. Catherine's dream-eyes searched for his face in the dark, but she could not see him. She felt the longing in his hands grip her harder. Whatever afflicted him was now released as his hands moved over her entire body with a caressing force. Catherine felt like a doll, immobile and without choice, but at the same time yielding to this embrace. As virgin as her isolation was, his touch was that of an artisan. She succumbed to it, along with her shame for bending to his touch. Between yearning and fear, her emotions stirred. No one touched her like this before, and its enticement relapsed her back and forth from the cradle dream-state and into the threatening revelations that came with it. Almost lost by his touch, her senses gripped her when he brought his arms underneath her again, as if he carried her.

"When you awaken," he said, "you will leave your home where my guard is stationed, although I will never be far behind. I will never let you out of my reach, again."

"The guard," Catherine questioned with returning fear and wondering. "Where do you want me to go?"

"Anywhere and nowhere, so that together we might deceive the deceiver. The one who will come to you and attempt to sway you to leave with him. But you mustn't be tempted, lest you anger my wrath. And that, my love, is something I do not want you to see."

"Who am I looking for? What am I supposed to do?"

"You will walk endless streets, until you see the one," the man's voice rose in angering lashes, "who ensnared you with that necklace around your throat!"

"Jorgen," Catherine whispered. Her anxiety arose like the awareness of her dream.

"You let him in, Catherine. Now you will have to find a way to persuade him to unbind you, unless you find the will to do it yourself. I offer you a chance against reprisal. Do not fail."

"I didn't know . . . I didn't know he was going to put . . ."

"I warned you," he interjected. Catherine's body shook in violent tremors from his hold. "I warned you against outsiders, and this is the repercussion you have brought upon yourself. I do not forgive thee unfaithful lightly. Do not betray me again."

Catherine recalled the words of the Mad Hag: the walking corpse who spoke with a deep, thatched voice, similar to the one threatening her now. She flinched at the memory of the rotting stench of the woman, her putrid gums and talon hands. Catherine realized his voice and the Mad Hag's were the same. *Don't be talking to outsiders now, dear, cause if you do I'll know. I'll be right here watching and I will know.* Foolishly, she denied the realism of the Mad Hag, the dream, the warped fate of a life she now tread and the mystic forces surrounding her. Terrified, she was stunned by the thought of who held her in the unsteady dark.

"Unchain yourself," he commanded.

"I will," Catherine managed to answer, praying to awaken from this nightmare.

"Oh, I know you will. And you, my angel, shall return a gift to me for the mercy and understanding I give you," he said drawing his voice back. "Show me your love. Breathe into me. Give me a taste of your essence. The one I have sought for centuries to kiss. Surrender to me the kiss of power."

Catherine's eyes darted in the darkness, searching for an escape route. Her arms struggled for freedom as she sensed his face coming down towards hers. Lips, of pressure and weight, parted hers. Even as she fought against them, they overpowered her. Concentrating with every aspect of her being, she stopped struggling and fixated on the inert parts inside of her. Catherine thought of nothing other than the instinct to freeze. She iced her mind. The lips in the darkness were positioned for theft. The part that brought dreams, nightmares, and hope to life. This was the essence, she felt, he was after and she was countering his advance.

Catherine crystallized. She didn't understand how she achieved this, but she sensed her efforts could shut down the one who sought to steal a part of her away. In a draw of breathless air, he pulled with unyielding strength. Catherine was a glacier against him. Entwined in a silent battle, their bodies quaked, rumbling like a volcano before eruption. She couldn't hold much longer. His draw threatened to shatter her, like lightening against ice. She held against him as long as she could. Suddenly, without surrender, the glacier blocking her core exploded. The force didn't allow him to enter her. Instead, it detonated against him and released her from his arms.

Catherine cascaded into a torrent of black waterfalls. Released from his grasp, she could hear his defeated howl ringing in echoes as she fell. She descended down an endless tunnel of darkness until his thundering voice was nothing more than a faint scratch against the abyss. Just when she thought this black hole was eternal, she awoke on the couch where she'd fallen asleep waiting for Nathan.

Her arms lifted as her body snapped awake. She felt the jolt as she hit the couch in her fall and rolled to the floor landing on her back where she watched the water-stained ceiling spin. Her stomach turned in seasick bounds, but she was grateful to have landed. A drip of saliva slipped from her quivering mouth. She wiped it away thinking the dream impossible, but her body contested the thought. The necklace throbbed with a cold beat against her throat, as if it understood the forces at work in her dream and the menace behind them.

Gripping the cushions of the couch to turn herself upright, she tried to ease the ferocity of the dream. For now she overcame the man in her dream, but not the dream itself. She feared its haunt and dreaded retaliation. But it wasn't a dream. It was . . . was . . . she tried to make sense of it. The buzz of Jorgen's voice rang like the push of wind against a window pane, *and you Catherine are in the middle of it.* She must free herself of the necklace for Nathan and herself.

Catherine's head rested on a hard spring of the couch's cushion. Its spike dug into her thoughts. She laid between the couch and floor wondering how she would find Jorgen to remove the necklace. She feared for Nathan's safety. She was nothing, no one. In the dream's cradle of black soothing waters she was nothing. Nothing was comfort, and she had tasted it. The cradle made her whole. Catherine thought with a sigh, if she could find a way to enter the embrace of darkness within the realm of life, any obstacle she faced was possible. The calming numbness would override. In the arms of the man, even before she feared his presence, she knew he was connected to the dream, the rejuvenation, and all of the comfort that came without caring, without needing, and the reality—that in nothing, there was nothing to fear, even the man who threatened her. And in the state of nothing, she was lulled by its bittersweet hold on her.

Catherine's thoughts lingered on the mystery of the darkness, how it made her feel whole for all its emptiness. She stared out the window, the dawn brightening the white faded aluminum on the trailer across from hers. In the night of the dream, she was at peace. Nothing could harm her. Even when the man manifested in the dream, she felt ashamed to admit it now, but she would have stayed with him in that place forever to escape the pain of life. But then his admonition stirred her into reality.

A dream, Catherine thought. No, it wasn't a dream. It was another state of reality. Its contrasting soothing waters and threats were real. The Mad Hag was real. Nana's apparition was real. Jorgen was real. The Shadows, and the man of the darkness, was real.

The morning rose as one gray blanket under the clouded sky. The snow had stopped falling. Lost in thought, Catherine hadn't moved. Her glossed eyes remained open and unfocused, until something moved at the edge of the hallway adjacent to where she lay. Startled, Catherine looked to it.

It was Kathy.

Dressed in a stained negligee, Kathy braced herself between the walls. Her head bobbed as she attempted a step forward, but stopped. She eyed Catherine with a contorted grimace, until she was capable of speaking.

"Git me a drink," Kathy said with a quivering voice.

Still deep in thought about Nathan, Jorgen and the man of her dreams, she hadn't mentally prepared herself for Kathy. The purging of the trailer was supposed to lead to new beginnings, and it did. This was it.

"There's some medicine you're supposed to take next to your bed. Did you see it? You're supposed to take the . . ."

"Ya hear me? I said," Kathy paused with a dry swallow of air, "git me a drink."

Catherine recoiled from the beast that continued to dwell in Kathy's gut. After years of inebriation, this was their first chance. Catherine thought she wouldn't care. She wished she didn't, but if she were to live with the woman and her health, she at least had to make a stand for the decision if they were to survive. There was never a time that Catherine felt more alone than in the presence of Kathy, but that wouldn't deter her. She wouldn't stand down.

"Did ya hear me?" Kathy said raising her voice like the words of slurring anger she spat when she was hot and heavy in the drink, "You little . . ."

"I heard you," Catherine shouted, "but you can forget about me finding you anything to drink other than the goddamn water next to your bed. Did you forget where you were yesterday, cuz I sure as hell haven't. Or have you fried your mind of that memory as well, just like the rest of the fucking years you've spent in a bottle."

The monster Catherine saw before her now was a different breed than the one she knew. It was thirsty and ready to use whatever means to suckle the glass teat. Catherine was thankful Kathy's strength was crippled. That would bide some valuable time.

Finding her footing, Kathy staggered towards Catherine who stood steadfast, watching the woman walk closer. Attempting to balance herself with each step, Kathy said, "What I do ain't nothin' by you. I make the livin' . . . round . . . here for your yappin' trap who doesn't give a fuck 'bout . . . but . . . herself." Kathy made a feeble lunge at Catherine who slid aside, causing her to miss her target and land face first on the couch. She flopped herself over and slurred, "Git me a drink, you little peeze a schlitt."

"There's nothing in this place to drink other than water. I made sure of that," Catherine said. She tried reasoning with lies, "And I'm going to tell you something else, Kathy. If you start drinking again, then they're . . . they're going to stop sending the checks. Because they said they're going to stop by today and . . . for a long time after that. And if you're not dry, then they're going to pull me outta here. What will you do then? What are you going to do if the money stops coming, huh? What are you going to do if they do that?"

"You're a lyin' little shit. Thatz what you are. Pull you outta here . . . that's rich. Ain't nobody want you. Not them, not me, less you get your ass out right now and git me a drink. Else you can forget about coming back," Kathy said, flapping a hand in the direction of the door.

All the times Catherine thought about leaving, she'd never been more tempted. She paced in a slight weave around the living room. *Just leave*, Catherine thought, looking to and from Kathy on the couch. Kathy closed her eyes in what Catherine assumed to be the hangover of a lifetime. Catherine glanced outside and saw the aftermath of the storm and sighed. Nathan was somewhere, but it wasn't here.

If only she could evaporate into the arms of nothing again, where complexities didn't exist. She wondered if the man would discover her there, like a bloodhound of nightmares.

He threatened her with Nathan. She believed in the dream. Upon awakening, she still felt controlled by the man inside of it, and that feeling weighed on her each time she looked at the door. Running would endanger Nathan. She didn't know what the consequences would be, but they existed, and he was innocent. His fate depended on her and even though he failed to return, if she never saw him again, she would always love him for bringing her hope. Hope that one day a foreign tomorrow could change everything. If she were to again reject the mysterious events surrounding her, then the necklace was there to remind her of it.

Figuring Kathy couldn't kick her out with force, at least not in her present state, Catherine walked to the kitchen and filled a mason jar full of water. The tap sputtered just a little before relinquishing its cold water into the glass. She turned around, meaning to head back to Kathy on the couch when the door of the trailer burst open.

At first, Catherine was alarmed, she never left the door unlocked, but did through the night anticipating Nathan's return. Anxious, she hoped this sudden gust of cold air coming in the trailer might be him.

But it wasn't Nathan. It was Sam.

Catherine's grip tightened around the threaded markings of the chilled glass in her hand. The snow was over a foot deep and it tumbled in with Sam's arrival. Carelessly, Sam stomped the snow off his boots and shut the door with his heel. He made a white path of tread marks across the floor to Kathy on the couch.

"Hey, how'sa my girl doin'?" he asked walking over. Double fisted, he carried a large brown paper bag in one hand and a dry snow shovel in the other.

Kathy greeted the bag with a smile and said, "Bout time you got here, baybee. I was begin in' ta wonder where you'd been all my life."

Sam plopped on the couch next to Kathy. Leaning his shovel against the couch, he tilted forward and dangled the paper bag just out of reach from Kathy's hands. She pawed at the air in an infantile struggle to grab it.

"Come on-n-n," Kathy drawled, knowing she was only a swallow away from being fulfilled. "Give it ta me."

"Tell me, whose yer friend? Whose got yer back? Tell me how much ya missed me."

"Oh baybee," Kathy said slapping her knees together, "I have misssssed you." Sam swung the bag back and forth, lowering it just enough for her to grab it out of his hands. He hoisted it again. Kathy's puckered lips started to smack as she played Sam's game, becoming more frustrated.

"How dare you!" Catherine said advancing into the living room. "You're a slimy piece of shit, you know that? Just what the fuck do you think you're doing?"

Sam disregarded Catherine with a sharp grin. He lowered the bag down and squeezed it between Kathy's legs. Wrenching it as far down as it could go, he said, "You can hold it. You can hold it can't ya baybee." Kathy didn't open the bag. She tore at it. Humored by her fever, Sam took the bag out of her objecting hands and said, "Here, lemme get that for you." He pulled a half-gallon of whisky out of the bag by the hook of its glass handle and cracked its seal. He took a swig before handing the bottle back to Kathy's shaking hands. With a wink, he turned to Catherine, licked his lips, and said, "Kisses are always better when wet."

Catherine tossed the glass of water she was holding on Sam's face and said, "You're one sick bastard."

He wiped his face, like he was removing a large teardrop, and flicked the water from his hand towards Catherine. Kathy imbibed, oblivious to anything but the jug. The bottle tipped, but never rested, as Kathy struggled to hold the weight of it in her unsteady hands. While moving to stop Kathy, Catherine chucked the Mason jar towards Sam and missed. It split in two. Half of it fell on the backrest of the couch while the other half fell behind it. The jug drizzled with whisky and Catherine struggled to latch onto it with Kathy pulling back. Sam, who moved to intervene, struck down Catherine's arms with one blow.

"It's about time someone showed this girl a thing in manners," Sam said looking at Catherine.

Catherine grabbed half of the broken Mason jar off the couch and held it to her right side and said, "You're going to get out—right now—or else I'm going to . . . to . . ."

"To . . . to . . . to . . . what?" Sam taunted. "That's right. You're not going to do anything, because this is your Ma's place and your Ma, she wants me here. There's nothing you can do about it."

"You tell her, Sammy," Kathy said, waving a spare hand at him. He turned to face Kathy, his face frothing, like it would burst from the pot, as he tried to control his temper. Kathy slurred, "Help me up. I wanna go to my room and cellebrade."

Sam gripped Kathy's hand and pulled so fast she almost fell forward. Sam yanked her back and steadied her. Kathy palmed her face in the sudden tip, anchoring herself with the bottle, and realized she wasn't wearing her paint, the veneer she used to cover her age. She patted her face repeatedly as Sam watched her compose herself under the influence of vanity's grain.

"Hey beautiful," Sam said with cooling ease, "How 'bout you go and get that party all warmed up for me."

Looking down, Kathy's hand dropped from her face and back to her glass pacifier. "You're comin' aren't ya?" Kathy asked.

Forgetting the broken jar in her hand, Catherine made another swipe for the whisky jug. Sam countered her movement by reaching his arm out to stop her. The jar in Catherine's hand sliced the side of his arm. Without a word, Catherine stepped back, wondering what retaliation may come. Sam spun to look at her through slitted lids before turning to Kathy and shuffling her into the hallway with coaxing words. "First I have to have a word with the little snapper here. Then, I'm gonna tortilla you inside a fiesta you'll never forget."

"Okay baybee. I'll be shakin' my maracas," Kathy said, attempting to move her chest back and forth, which countered her walk. Sam let her go and she wobbled in the remaining stretch to her bedroom door. "I'll be waitin' for ya," Kathy said and closed the door.

Satisfied, Sam turned around and moved slowly toward Catherine in the living room. He rapped his fingers against the side of his thigh where a thin trickle of blood was making its way.

"You know," Catherine said, "you should have brought a different shovel because you just sent Kathy to her grave."

"Hey, Cath. You need to relax. I told you before . . . I'm a nice guy."

"My ass."

"Oh, come on now. What would you have done with Kathy if I wasn't here to help you out? She ain't gonna change her ways. As long as I've known her, she's been a lambasted, sauced up, stumble fuck, slick on the dick she's riding on," Sam said, inching closer to Catherine, who countered each move with a back step, slowly raising the broken jar in her hand. Sam pointed toward the hallway and continued, "And she . . . she ain't going ta change her ways. Not for you, for me, for anyone. She's got what she needs right now. She doesn't need nothing, doesn't want anything but what's in that room. And I'm going to tell you, you don't need anything but a nice warm place to stay when your waxed mama goes in the . . ."

"I'm telling you," Catherine said holding the broken jar at him, "stay back."

"Little girl got some balls. I like it. I like it a lot," Sam said nodding his head. "You gonna show me what you got? Huh? What you got?" He walked to the door, grabbed her boots and walked back, tossing them at her feet. "You got shoes. Put' um on."

The broken jar in her hand was heating. Catherine thought it was the warmth of her grip, but its temperature was increasing and it started to tremble, causing her hand to shake with its growing force. "Fuck you," Catherine spat, holding fast to the hot glass, "I'm not going anywhere with you."

"Oh yes," Sam replied, glancing at the glass she held, "you are." He took another step forward, leaving only a few feet between them. Catherine felt like the glass was melting around her fingers from an invisible furnace, but it didn't melt or burn. "What you gonna do? You . . ." Sam was cut short by a pounding at the door and stepped towards it. In the same instant, the glass in Catherine's hand ejected on its own, just missing Sam, and shot across the living room, shattering on the wall behind him. Shocked, Catherine looked at the glass stuck in the wall and the pieces of it falling to the floor. Sam halted, turned to the wall, and back to Catherine. She was stunned by the glass rocket. Sam charged her and she ran for the kitchen. In haste, he stumbled over her boots, buying Catherine a second to escape his grasp.

Bracing herself against the kitchen sink, Catherine heard the pounding again at the door and hollered, "Here. Here. I'm here," like a panic button. Her shout forced Sam to skid on the threadbare kitchen floor in an attempt to revert his step to the door and block it. He was too late.

Nathan burst through, throwing his duffle bag down, and looked for Catherine. His flesh bagged with gray tones and his jeans were soaked to his thighs from his white-ice encrusted shoes. "Catherine," Nathan said, spotting her in the kitchen. Sam extended his arms out like a barricade, blocking Nathan from his captive.

"Nathan," Catherine slipped under Sam's arms and made it to Nathan's side. Sam moved, as if to stop her, but halted.

"I'm so sorry I couldn't . . ." Nathan started to apologize, but Catherine cut him off with an embrace. Their reunion was short.

"Turn around and shuffleboard your ass back the way it came," Sam said taking a step forward.

"This isn't you're place," Nathan said locking eyes with Sam. Nathan eased Catherine's arms from him and guided her behind him. The light winter wind stirred her hair as she stood by the open door, but no one moved to close it. "If anyone is going to tell me to leave, it'll be her."

"Well. Well. Aren't you just a pimple popping chewer if I ever met one? Cath and I were just going through this, weren't we," he said tossing her a glance and then looked back to Nathan. "This isn't her place—it's Kathy's. And I own it, just like your old man's place, who's behind in the rent. You're gonna get your puckered ass outta here right now, or I'm gonna take you home myself and evict you and that flea shoe picker."

"No you're not. He . . ." He knew his pa was trying to squeeze down some credit damage. He should have known that included backed up rent as well. Each week Nathan handed over half his check to Steve once he started working full time at Donnie's Bar, but that didn't matter to Nathan right now. He had to leave that behind, maybe forever. He was here for Catherine only.

"Pussy got your tongue in a ball, boy, or you going to leave before I have to unravel you myself?"

Nathan had to think quickly if he was going to get Sam out without a fight. "You can try Sam, try." Nathan said. "Either way, I know about the dealings you been making with the bigwigs at the factory. Word is they're producing more than just shoes behind the sidelines of that barn you got across Miller's Pond."

"Millers . . . you tell anyone, anyone . . . and I'll . . . I'll . . ."

"Don't worry, Sam. I don't have anything on me but a four-letter word, but then you know lotsa' um don't ya? Especially ones that begin with the letter m."

"Motherfucker, you think you can . . ."

"Nope, too many letters. Let me spell it for you. M-E-T-H."

"You think you can play a man's game? Keep it up and Steve won't have a job and you won't have a roof to pop your ass pimples under. How you like that boy? How's them words for ya? That'll keep your mouth . . ."

"Leave my pa outta of this and I'll forget every word I know. But, if you don't leave right now, then you might have some visitors in blue stopping by your place today, understood?"

"You think you got me," Sam said seething. "You think . . ."

"I think you were just leaving," Nathan said, guiding himself and Catherine from the door. Catherine and Nathan stood still as if they were waiting for a train to pass. Nothing happened. Catherine moved to the living room and grabbed Sam's shovel from the couch and threw it at Sam. He snatched it in flight and swung it like a broken wing.

Sam walked towards the door and drew his elbow back and popped a white knuckled fist forward, stopping short as a warning toward Nathan. Nathan didn't flinch, nor move. His inflamed eyes followed Sam who tilted the shovel at Catherine with his other hand. "I'll be seeing you." He turned his back to them and walking out the door said, "The both of you." He marched down the porch stairs as Nathan closed the door.

Nathan stood tense as if he waited for Sam to come back. With a heavy sigh of release, his composure faltered.

Catherine realized how exhausted Nathan was and that he reserved his last bit of his energy getting Sam out.

"I waited and waited," Catherine said in relief. "You came back. What about your dad? Do you think Sam will–?"

"Don't worry about Sam . . . or my dad," Nathan said, but his face was full of concern. Catherine looked at him, confused, but grateful for his return. Nathan wanted to embrace her the way they did in the forever ago, in the eternity that distanced itself from then and now. But everything changed since he last left her house. He was here for a reason. No, not a reason, a purpose—a word he recently learned could mean many things. A word he now understood would be in every footstep he took for the rest of his life. That is, if he were to live long enough to survive the risk he was taking.

"Catherine," Nathan said, simply staring at her, finding the words he had to say unbelievable, and the great question he had to ask of her. "I'm leaving town."

"Leaving?" Catherine melted as she looked at his duffel bag on the floor.

"But, I need you to come with me," he said, directing her attention away from it. "Please say you'll come with me."

CHAPTER THIRTEEN

Nathan hadn't been to sleep. He wasn't anywhere he planned, walking with Artros through the dark morning to its gray rise. He trudged through the snow matching Artros' stride, through the cocooned town. They walked along abandoned railroad tracks, before crossing the bridge over the river, and down past Main Street to the other side of town where the affluent lived. The Victorian and Colonial architecture was a testament to the town's unspoken divide of Us and Them. Nathan lived on the Us side, east town, where the trailer park belonged. The elders still called it Parishville, from a long forgotten memory of the logging days, when a small sawmill joined the prosperous lumber drive which built its first humble log homes. Traces of Parshville's past could be seen on a summer day through the river's crystal waters. Its majestic timbers lay imbedded on the floor of its river grave. Living on the Us side of town, Nathan thought if he were born in that time, he would still be the hired hand of the Boss Hogs who drove the gold down the river.

He would never own one of their relic homes on the west side of town, the Them side, in which he now walked with Artros. Through the years, envy had grown a quiet resentment for those people. Now, he didn't want to join Them, he wanted to overcome them. He didn't want to admit it, but that was the singular reason he was attracted to Artros in the beginning. In Artros' world, there was no Us or Them. It was only Artros, and Nathan had wanted it.

The river was the only thing not completely covered in snow. The black ruffling waves stood out against the white banks of its borders. The wreckage of the previous morning hid underneath the layers of the heavy snowfall which fell through the night, blocking the roads in town. Limbs had fallen and some were bent to the ground, but the town had electricity. Soon the County Road Commission would be firing up the trucks and whatever fresh meat was available from yesterday's disaster to drive the plows and clear a one-way path through the main streets.

Walking, Nathan didn't protest his tennis shoes and jeans were soaked, or suggest he wanted nothing more to do with the man in black and his mysticism. Nathan understood Artros was not the trickster he perceived him to be at the bar, and darker than the howling winds in the park. Nathan scolded himself for being careless and desperate to fall for this man's invocations. Artros was the black wizard from one of his fantasy novels as a kid and Nathan the ignorant boy longing to try on the wizard's hat, unaware of the consequences. Nathan wished this was a story where the outcome and enemies were clear, but he was tripping on the line that defined hero from villain. He just didn't know how to get out of the wizard's castle.

Nathan caught traces of the Shadow Creatures in dark streaks and flashes. Artros disregarded them. What does he see? Nathan wondered without wanting to know, but he had to consider the world he'd fumbled into. Why would a man of power want anything to do with him? Another blur of large dark mass crossed their path. Its tail streaked the air and imprinted it like a black smoking flame. Bracing himself, Nathan walked through it. It broke apart as smoke, without any sense other than sight to know it was there. But the Shadow Creatures were more than apparitions. They were defined with abstract details for the creatures they represented. They rushed the Master like wild pit bulls, ready to devour the one who chained them and anyone else in their path, including him. Nathan wanted out, and it wasn't going to be as easy as saying goodbye and finding another street to turn down.

Artros glided through the heavy snow, his woolen trench coat seemed to cast the snow from him; he appeared to float above white water. In his black attire, richer than night, he radiated in the Darkness he sheathed for the time. Nathan tromped alongside, trying to keep pace. His legs felt heavier with each step. His gut twisted knowing he was the apprentice of this man who expected him to become like him. Nathan didn't understand what Artros was, but it was like bile on the tongue through the taste of frosting.

Again, Nathan sighted two Shadows Creatures. One was above him, no bigger than a small bird. He traced its path and saw a large, slow-moving shadow behind him. Both were impossible to identify, but the one behind him reminded him of a tall man. It seemed to be following them. Before he could focus on either, they became nothing but a trace of something he thought he saw, but knew was there.

"You are sensing them," Artros said. Since they started their walk from the field, he had been unusually distant. He continued, "Do not follow them with your eyes for they can look back into you with their own sight of perception, and you would not want them to stare into the threads of your soul."

"I . . . I don't know what I'm seeing. The second I see it, it disappears."

"They are everywhere," Artros replied with the same distance in his voice. "More than would normally anchor a town such as this, but they gather in strength because I am here. Even the ones I have not yet called upon are attracted to my power. However, you cannot construct them as anything more than obscurities in your fragile mind. You sense their presence because you have been enlightened to them, not because you hold power. The knowledge of my teachings has opened the subconscious within you, and now you are starting to see the shift of the world that is hidden. Until I teach you how to control them, it would be dangerous for you to acknowledge them. They spawn from the same energy that empowers the Darkness, and they like to hide within the shadows that created them. Without holding the power to control them, they can feed off you, as they do others, and steal the essence of your energy. Ignorance of the unbelievers is one of our greatest assets when it comes to harvesting power. In time, you will understand this well."

Nathan shuddered and said, "They were all around us in the field. I thought they were going to . . . to attack us."

"Next lesson, boy. Anger feeds. It will become one with you and the dark power, but you must always keep control, lest the ones you command have an opportunity to bite back. Anger is the strength of a Master. However, without control, anger is loose in its emotionless strike. It is a tool, akin to Darkness. Without a Master, it commands itself without direction. Power without purpose is wild. Dangerous. It can leave us exposed if we do not maintain control over the power we unleash."

"Were they—those things—trying to get you, because they looked like it? Because you . . . you . . ." Nathan wanted to say *lost control*, but didn't dare.

"My power extends farther than you can imagine. They were attracted to the . . . displeasure I felt against your adversary. As the father of Darkness, I am in complete command. Nothing can touch me."

Nathan was sure the Shadow Creatures in the field tried to attack his Master and inevitably him. For all Artros' confidence, Nathan doubted him.

"I don't know if I can . . . I didn't know . . ." Nathan hesitated. He searched for the right words to tell Artros he wanted out, knowing it would take more than words to release him.

Artros stopped walking. He turned to Nathan with a hard stare that softened into a sympathetic sincerity, unexpected for the man in black. "We do not choose the Darkness," Artros said, "it chooses us. Once you have accepted it, it will never leave you. The only choice you have is to follow."

"I . . . I . . . I'm not that . . . that," Nathan struggled, reaching for words to rebuke the Darkness and his Master. He turned away from Artros and said, "I promised Catherine I would see her after I got off work. If I could just stop back at her place for a minute . . . you know . . . so she won't be . . ." he almost said *angry*, but that word didn't fit after Artros' explanation of anger. Instead he said, "Upset with me. She . . ."

"She is asleep, Nathan," Artros said with distinct pleasure that gave Nathan a prickling sensation along every hair of his body. "And sleep is an ocean of eternity when one dreams."

"Asleep? How do you know?"

Artros sighed and said, "She is dreaming of her lover, and we mustn't disrupt a dream that carries the desires of the one we long to hold."

Artros beamed the same elation Nathan saw him basking in through the light of Catherine's window. Had he dragged Catherine into this stringed mess of affairs with the man in black? How could Artros possibly invade Catherine's dreams? He hoped Artros was taunting him. Shocked by his words, Nathan couldn't say anything to Artros, whose face was soaked in gloating conquest.

Artros inhaled and closed his eyes. Nathan tried to construct another way to escape the man in black who had not only found a way to seduce him, but possibly Catherine. He didn't want her to become a victim of his careless actions.

Artros' eyes opened and looked ahead down the empty sidewalk. He said, "She is coming."

"Who?" Nathan asked, searching between the rows of houses and back and forth across the empty streets. In terror, he thought Artros was referring to Catherine.

"She is the Mistress of Darkness," he said with a smug smile that rose to one corner of his mouth. "But, you may call her Esa. She is a tribute to her name, which means 'to stir war.'"

A woman, cloaked in black, walked around the bend of the street ahead. The dark power was with her like the elegance she carried herself with. She reminded Nathan of the snowstorm with its purity and destruction in one. Her unfaltering grace glided towards them. Her hands warmed inside a fur muff and her hair flowed down in long waves against the black cloak of her breast. Her flawless flesh shimmered against the fallen snow. Even though her brows were tipped down to the grimace of her lips, she was the perfection of eternal beauty.

Fearless, she stood before Artros. She ignored Nathan's presence, but Nathan recognized her as the woman who sat with Artros in the bar. Mistress, she may be, but she was also a Master of this cryptic power of Darkness.

"Finished here, Artros?" Esa asked in disgust.

"My dear, your temper becomes you, but you must smolder it with patience. A small trial from now and we will have what we've sought to achieve here," Artros replied.

"A decade since you last called for me and still you have not acquired . . ."

"A decade, my dear?" Artros interrupted. "You sound as if that were a measure of time, when it is only a heartbeat closer to the Light we have been searching for."

"It is too long to not be at your side. You have kept me in the shadows," Esa protested, espousing shadows as if the word were a toy between them. "Take her and let us be done with this."

"You know it is not that simple, my Esa. Patience is one quality of power you . . . you . . . fail . . . to . . . to," Artros said in a tremor of words. He struggled to maintain focus as his face knotted. "Rec-og-nizze . . ." Artros managed to say as his body broke in vibrations. For the first time, Nathan saw him lean on the cane at his side.

Astounded, Nathan watched Artros buckle to a kneeling position, supported only by his cane. He was brought down to his knees from an unseen affliction—a force even Esa could not comprehend. She clutched his shoulders to support him from falling headfirst into the snow. Her alarm magnified when she couldn't determine what was causing Artros to falter. As bewildered as Nathan, she watched him quake in violent spasms. She looked to Artros, to Nathan, and even in the air for an answer.

"The—kiss of—power!" Artros roared. His pupils expanded, coating the sclera to the end of his eyes where black veins shot into his flesh and pulsated through his face. As dried earth, the black veins expanded, cracking and wilting his graying skin. "Give—it," Artros demanded. His clenched fist raised his cane into the air. "Give—it—to me!" With one swift move, he slammed the cane into the earth, generating lightning bolt-like craters in the snow. The ground quaked, causing the snow to fall off the trees and houses along the sidewalk. His body thrashed and Esa could hold him no longer. The fallen Artros let out a wail, one that echoed with a force that could have caused an avalanche to befall the entire town.

With Artros' howl, Esa shot her arms into the air. Palms out and fingers splayed, she moved her hands above her, creating an effect far beyond her reach—an invisible shield encapsulated them. Nathan watched her, mystified by the events unfolding, but it didn't take long for him to understand. As Artros writhed in pain, Nathan saw the Shadow Creatures with clarity. They advanced with determination to taste a piece of the Master who called upon them to do his bidding.

At first he saw only a rushing few, some moving like crows or black dogs, but then hazy stallions galloped in streaking strides, racing alongside jackals and snakes. Esa's hands wove about the air in the direction of each attack. Nathan ducked or cringed with each advancing Shadow Creature. To the left, above and behind, Esa spun her hands around in figure eights, ovals and long brush marks until she created an unseen web of defense around them like a vault. The mass became indistinguishable as they gathered together and swarmed as bees to a hive. Esa managed to block them all. Nathan's eyes caught three larger shadows in the distance, advancing little by little, their gait ponderous and menacing. Their slow progress and stalking posture told Nathan they were men on a mission. These man-creatures approached methodically, as if they thought and planned their steps with each movement. In the chaos, Nathan caught a clear outline of one of them. Its body was like an empty cavern, waiting for its void to be filled with something that could never satisfy. Nathan saw its burning red eyes without a face, so unlike the other Shadow Creatures or Shadow Men around them. Caught in inertia, Nathan stared into the depths of its hollow belly and felt the emptiness within it. More Shadow Creatures came, releasing his gaze from the Shadow Man's vacuum.

A whirlwind of shadows hovered around Esa's barricade. Upright, Esa held her arms above her and then brought them down to her sides like stretching wings. The air flowed towards her as she raised her arms back again in an arch gathering. She repeated the process, stepping clockwise, until she made a full revolution. Her hands came together and she braced them tightly before she simply let them fall to her sides. Her breath, however, heaved in shallow spurts as she looked at the Shadow Creatures pacing in looming knits and strides around them. She spoke in a language Nathan didn't recognize. The rhythmic words were a soft pulse, like an enchantment to his ears. One by one, the Shadows Creatures dispersed into the thin air from whence they came. Nathan could not see them, nor was he sure they were gone.

Artros knelt in silence, his head bowed. Esa regarded him without pity. Her attention turned to Nathan. "What do you know of this?" she demanded.

"This? I—I don't know . . ."

"I can see you are nothing but ignorant," Esa spat looking him up and down. "Still, Artros doesn't indulge himself on your kind unless you are of some worth. So tell me, boy . . ."

"My name is Nathan,"

"We'll see if you have a name when this is over," Esa said, cocking her head. "Tell me, boy, what is it you hold that would make Artros submit himself to your . . . company?"

Nathan didn't know what brought him to this dark madness of creatures. He couldn't answer why Astros chose him. He gave a simple answer: "Artros has been teaching me . . . Darkness."

"Teaching you?" Esa mocked, "More like teasing you. You have no secrets. Your blood is thin and tainted to the breed you cling to. Everything about you is hollow. Nonetheless, any simpleton can be washed with knowledge. In time, the Darkness will fill you, but this knowledge never comes without surrender. You must surrender yourself or another close to you." Esa searched Nathan for discovery. "There is a consequence." She stepped closer, "The consequence is always the exchange you pay for the truth. The power. You cannot have it without sacrifice. Darkness comes with a purpose. Tell me, what is yours? What have you paid for the truth? What is your purpose to him?" Esa asked, not hiding her aversion to him.

Nathan heard that word again. Purpose—the word was trapped in a brick that needed to be chiseled.

"I don't know," Nathan answered.

"Yes, you do," her taunting voice accused. "Discover what your purpose is to him. Discover that purpose, and you will have your answer."

"What do you want from me?"

"Ask yourself what *he* wants from you? What do you have that he wants?"

Nathan dragged back every memory he could think of starting with Artros and the Darkness. Although Artros announced Esa to be the Mistress of Darkness, he realized this was not the woman who Artros said consumed his love. No, he didn't think it was Esa at all. Wherever she came from, Artros fixated on something else. Something he wanted to obtain. A desire. Nathan dug deeper trying to discern what Artros wanted in this remote town.

Without a dime to his name, he had nothing but four walls and a pa he loved. And one other. Every day he awoke, she was with him. Days would pass without seeing her, but his thoughts held her close to his heart. Others passed by her like a wildflower grown by the roadside. No. He fought with himself. He remembered Artros' words, "The only light in the world right now." No. Nathan said her name over and over in his thoughts, recalling Artros' intimate knowledge of Catherine's dream state. "No!" he shouted, raising his palms to his temples. "Catherine," he moaned, bending over from the pressure of the truth.

"That's her name," Esa said with satisfaction, watching Nathan's anguish from the sudden discovery. "Darkness never comes without a purpose, and purpose never comes without payment."

He let Catherine down. He was tied to the dark forces coming for her. He should have known, but then what did he know. Nothing.

Artros had power and knowledge, Nathan thought, *but what else could he possibly want? What does he need? More,* Nathan thought. *More.* The Light. The Light, like Darkness, was in and out of everything Artros spoke of. The Light was an infinite color that Darkness absorbed, but the Light could banish the Darkness. "The Light," Nathan repeated. The Mother of Colors. Catherine's innocence was tied into this. She'd been swept into this fray, but why? Somehow, he would figure it out, but for now, he had to escape.

Helpless, Nathan studied Esa and Artros. They were coming for Catherine. Why they wanted her didn't matter. He couldn't let her be deceived the way he had been tricked into Artros' palm. Then there was another—he recalled the stranger in black and the necklace he attached to Catherine's neck. He didn't distinguish the man in black for what he was then—a man of power. One thing he did know: Jorgen was the enemy of Artros.

"Jorgen," Nathan said aloud to himself, attempting to place Jorgen in the picture of events.

"What did you say?" Esa peered at him from under her furrowed brow.

"Jorgen," Nathan said louder, surprised by her reaction. Without knowing what Jorgen needed from Catherine, he suspected the worst. Just the utterance of his name inflamed her. This name might be the only weapon he had in his arsenal right now. Trying to gain a foothold on the answers he sought, he honed in and played Jorgen's name to the best of his eight ball cracking abilities. "Yeah, Jorgen," he said, not knowing if he should direct the ball to the right corner pocket or if he'd scratch the table doing so.

"Jorgen is dead," she said with a heating fury. "Dead. Impossible!"

"Guess you've been out of town a while," Nathan said.

"You are filled with lies," Esa said with a gluttonous pride, "Jorgen died for me."

"Well, he was kicking the last time I saw him. You mean, you didn't know? I mean everyone has a purpose here, right?" Nathan asked testing.

"Lying tongues flap on the floor," Esa said, taking a step toward him.

"Interesting you didn't know Catherine's name when Jorgen knows it," Nathan said, halting Esa's step. She looked at Artros, regaining his strength, and back to Nathan. For a woman of confidence, she was struggling for control.

"Where is Jorgen?"

Nathan hesitated, not wanting to involve Catherine any more than he must, but he knew he couldn't afford to lie at this point either. "He was at Catherine's tonight, but he left," Nathan said.

"What is he doing there?"

Hell if he knew. He was just a pawn, outlined in the block on their board, trying to cut corners and maneuver himself out of their game. He was standing against the black queen, scrambling to rescue the white, and his skin was that of a sallow gray. "He gave her a necklace.".

"Gave her . . ." Esa hissed, breaking her porcelain veneer. Nathan saw a furious Master before him, unlike the cool and patient Artros. "He would never . . . ever . . ." Esa said with fury. "He wouldn't! You lie!"

"Artros knows Jorgen is here," Nathan continued. He watched the man recover slowly. Artros had a weakness, Nathan thought, even though he didn't know what that was. He wondered what would have happened to Artros and him if Esa had not been there to stop the Shadows from coming down upon them.

"You have enlightened me with more information than I would have guessed to come from one who looks as you do. But that is of little matter, considering what I am to do with it."

Steadily watching Artros regain his strength, Nathan knew his chance to escape grew thin. "I just want out," Nathan said. "I . . . I want to go home."

"Of course you do, now that you understand. Such is the price for purpose. I will speak with Artros. I have no time for you, nor the lessons Artros has dusted upon you," Esa said turning to Artros, "in his ancient ways." As Nathan turned to leave, Esa admonished him: "Remember this, boy, you cannot hide from that which conceals. When Artros calls upon you, be ready."

Released, Nathan ran across town, over the bridge and railroad tracks, and down the street of the Industrial Park. His legs felt like rubber bands, expanding and contracting and pulling him forward. Protesting, his body threatened to stop, but he knew he couldn't or else he would collapse. Exhausted, he tried to think of a plan. Only one came to mind, grab Catherine and leave town as quick as possible. He didn't know how they would get by, but he would panhandle if need be to get them another mile away and another town further from this one and Artros' grasp. The only obstacle might be trying to get Catherine to come with him, but he had to convince her. The Father of Darkness wouldn't be crippled for long.

Nathan passed Catherine's place as he headed for his own. He desperately wanted to stop, but needed to grab a simple bag for the road and what little cash he had stashed at his house. His pa slumbered from the late night second shift. Nathan tossed the idea back and forth to wake him. He didn't want to say goodbye, not forever, but he didn't know what tomorrow or next year would bring. Looking at the old man, deep in sleep, he thought about his father, weathered by life more than years. What would his pa look like, one, ten, or twenty years down the line? How much hardship would his pa face if he wasn't there to help support him? *I don't have a choice,* Nathan thought, watching him sleep. Nathan hoped one day he could come back and tell his pa he was sorry, sorry for all of it.

CHAPTER FOURTEEN

Jorgen stood on the edge of a steep embankment which sheared to the river below. Throughout the night, he stood like a talisman on the highest elevation in town, scanning the sky above Catherine's home from the cliff. His tire tracks and footprints in the snow vanished underneath the barren bleached land. Jorgen looked like a lost man in a white desert, thirsty for answers. Heated by the Darkness throbbing inside of him, the snow melted, trickled and dripped from him into an icy pool at his feet. Unwavering, he studied the air. Struggling thoughts swelled his mind and he fought with himself over and again as to why he made the decision to protect her. In haste, he'd given her the necklace along with a vow of protection. One she didn't deserve and one he couldn't justify.

Catherine was just another face in the portrait of humanity's suffering. One he'd witnessed all his life. Aside from her power, she was nothing. No different than any other person who walked the earth in misery. Yet a fighting spirit lingered in her hopelessness and this set her apart. Jorgen didn't know if the Darkness inside of her magnetized him, or if it was something else. His logical mind told him to treat her like the object of power she was, but he was surrendering to a young woman of the flesh, allowing her pain and solitude to sting him. The brief contact they shared opened a vulnerable slice in his insulated soul.

Seasons blurred into nothing more than hot and cold. Time wasn't a word when it felt like an eternity of iniquity. Attempting to control the quest caused him to lose his purpose. Surrendering, it led him to this town. Here, he was confronting the ghost of his past, the first sign of the Light he could touch in years, and death. For the first time, Jorgen thought that maybe the Light wasn't his to hold, and his only purpose was to protect it. No matter now. The road of endless wander was past. And if death be the end, then so be it.

Standing this close to Artros was suicide. Esa stabbed his heart once, when she allowed their love to be forsaken. Jorgen thought that even though Artros had failed to kill him, the heartache would. But, it didn't. He was a testament to pain.

Esa. Was it Artros' presence that made her feel so close? After all this time, he couldn't be sure. Recalling her, the pain would come and cause him to lose focus and rekindle questions from the past in which he didn't want answered. He swore he didn't care. Yet, if she discovered he was still alive, would it matter to her? Was she capable of remorse? These questions were a vice which resurfaced through time, and Jorgen feared that even questioning them at all meant he still cared.

They were young then, even younger than this deception of age. In the aftermath of the battle with Artros and defeat, Jorgen still believed a part of Esa had loved him. Time had a way of tapping into that vein of false belief and he had to cut it out, lest it bleed him dry. Alone, on the road of the Light, he extinguished love, lust, and feelings for humankind. Chastity and solitude became brothers to him, and part of the quest. Jorgen thought of love like a rattlesnake which mated, yet carried the spirit of venom. Even blind eyes heard the rattling poison of its nature. Jorgen denied love, because if he were to feel it again, it would be the defeat of his life. His life was all he had left.

But, he gave Catherine the necklace. In haste, he had given her a part of his essence, something he'd never allowed Esa to have. Now, that silver link was a flag of war on the battleground. It was his symbol and he staked it on the girl as something worth fighting for, without knowing why. That was the quest at work, he resolved, and he would allow his thoughts and actions to become wild in nature when he was possessed to do so. In an age long ago, when he couldn't even remember the boy he once was, he was taught to allow things to unfold on their own measure. Answers would come with patience and reflection whether it be through animals, people, or objects. That was the way of his people. Jorgen abandoned his people for Artros, whose revealing objectives were only to seek and conquer. Jorgen's people were lost to him now like the bloodline of a mutt. Occasionally he would catch a trace of their features through a stranger passing by, but like the stranger, their heritage was lost to him and it would never be found again. Only relics by the sea remained now.

He was in the middle, allowing the quest to lead him and using the Darkness to protect the chalice. If he failed, then he would make one last journey, when the light of his life was extinguished. Death was just an escort ticket for the soul. It would lead him to the final, unknown destination in which he'd watched so many of his brethren depart. He cheated it for centuries, rejuvenating himself through the Darkness. Maybe it was the time for time to end.

Jorgen stood on the edge of the cliff and the border of his life. The Darkness inside him boiled with his thoughts, along with a pool of water at his feet. It was too late to jump or flee. He would fight. He couldn't hide from himself any longer. Steadfast, he watched the Shadow Creatures across the morning horizon. They swiveled about as one black mass, tainting the air above Catherine's home. He knew wherever the shadows were she would be.

Suddenly the Shadow Creature's fluent stir started to jitter with a spasmodic twist about the shield over Catherine. It escalated into frenzy. The creatures started clashing, heating the air around them in their fury. Then the Shadow Creatures started breaking apart, slow in seeping movements, until they disbanded in a tidal wave, heading across the river to something, or someone else, on the other side.

Jorgen snapped around and walked toward his car. With an exhale of dark air through the parted knuckles of his hand, he blew the snow off of his car with a heavy gust, drying his clothes along with it. Driving through the field he had parked in, he pushed the foot-deep snow away along the road like a snowplow with the power of Darkness, and headed for Catherine.

The distressed town was quiet as he made his way through the lonely intersection in the historical downtown. Nonetheless, he moved with caution, coming closer to Artros' territory. Jorgen felt two of them. One was Artros, transmitting in the direction of where the Shadows Creatures fled to the west. The other was Catherine in the opposite direction on the other side of the river. Her emotions came to him in waves. He also felt the throbbing of the necklace, as the object pulsated from a recent attack of power. Catherine was safe, that much he knew, but Artros, in his broken line of energy, was wounded and in distress. But a third pulse disrupted this cord between Catherine and Artros. Jorgen detected it as another Master of Darkness infringing upon Artros. Jorgen wondered if Artros was wounded by another Master's dark power. *Impossible*, Jorgen thought, but he had been out of the world's timeline. Masters rose and fell through the ages.

Jorgen watched the skyline again as he drove. He hadn't seen evidence of a fight. Only another Master could attempt to bring Artros down. Jorgen surmised Artros had lost control of the Shadow Creatures upon injury. They broke free and came after him. *Could it have been Catherine?* Jorgen asked himself in denial. Catherine's strength was untold, but without the knowledge to wield the Darkness, she was nothing more than a loaded gun. One without direction, but one that could misfire at any time. This was not her energy he sensed. No. It was another Master's work that made Artros pulse like a rat with its tail cut off.

Far ahead, Jorgen saw a young man running across the street, the one from the hospital and at the footsteps of Catherine's home. Nathan. Jorgen slowed his car, and while the snow appeared to be powdering out from the front of his grill and to its back bumper, it never touched his car. Nathan slipped in the snow, before he got back up to run again. He was the only sign of life this morning, running in the opposite direction of the Shadow Creatures. Jorgen watched him scurry away, no longer an innocent bystander and playing his part in the role as Artros had intended. Leverage.

Until now, Jorgen disregarded the disbanded Shadow Creatures as nothing more than an opportunity to capture Catherine. But seeing the young man's panting, red face, running in haste as if the shadows themselves were chasing his heels, Jorgen needed to understand what became of Artros. A small rush struck Jorgen, thinking the black Daemons were taking their Master apart one thread at a time.

Instead of turning right as intended toward Catherine, Jorgen turned left in the direction of Artros. Dismayed, Jorgen saw a mass of Shadow Creatures above and through the bare limbs of trees ahead. They were pacing as if waiting for direction, subdued and controlled as before. He parked his car along a one-way street and got out to walk on foot, intent on discovering what became of Artros. Coming closer, he felt Artros' suffering. It gave him confidence that he could finish his old Master's reign here and now.

His caution rose with each footstep. He wanted to call the Darkness to him as if he was raising a blade, but he couldn't. If he let it grow before it was time to attack, he might give his position away.

Jorgen saw Artros standing a distance down the street, his back to him. The Shadow Creatures hovered afar. Jorgen's curiosity grew, but he only dared a few steps more. The short distance further allowed him to see Artros leaning on his staff, crippled, to Jorgen's pleasure. At their encounter by the hospital, Artros held more power than he'd ever known one Master to hold, but now it was depleted. Jorgen studied Artros' dark threads and realized that the power hadn't been drawn out, but slashed away from him like a cat's claw. Artros was trying to heal the loose lines of broken energy that flapped about him like beheaded snakes, dripping and draining more of his power until he could focus his energy and heal what was left of them.

Artros turned aside, tilting his staff with him, and Jorgen countered the move, stepping aside a large maple tree with the middle of its trunk gutted for the town's power lines. Jorgen sprung from the ground and straight into its center to crouch in the bowl of its wood and hid.

Artros waved his hand and staff in the air, directing the Shadow Creatures. The Shadow Creatures flew, slunk, and writhed past Jorgen through the air and upon the earth from whence they came. Jorgen watched them head back to guard what Artros coveted, Catherine. Jorgen tightened inside and clutched the bark, knowing he let his chance pass.

A part of him wanted to see if he could outrun the Shadow Creatures, but the abrupt movement would give his position away. Flexing his legs to look between the limbs of the tree, he peered through the V of the ancient Maple and saw Artros along with the outline of another behind him. The third pulse. Recovering, Artros started to walk in Jorgen's direction, but then paused as if he were sniffing the air in search of him. Then, the one behind Artros stepped forward. Jorgen saw her. After all these years she was walking with the man who betrayed him.

Esa.

Pain and time was supposed to be a tonic for forgetting. Not forgiving. Seeing her again, the memories he'd thought were lost came like the flood of one crashing tear. Her flesh still hued the same false purity as when she'd met him in the forest, in the small clearing of green moss that stayed soft and supple year round. Looking at her, he could smell the trace of rosemary she would crush and rub over her skin, intoxicating him with each embrace he'd spent centuries blocking out. She would come to him clothed in a white dress spun from lamb's wool, the color of innocence. In the time of their love, he tried hard not to soil her purity or her youthful spirit. Honor lived in him then, but she pushed until he could resist no further. Even after he'd laid her down in the moss for the first time and her dress was stained from their embrace, remorse lingered in him even as her laughter chimed in the forest to comfort his regret. She said that all things were equal and they had a future together and that this day was a part of their living past. All tomorrows would become yesterdays and he mustn't linger on doubt when there was a promise between them to belong to each other, forever. He believed her then, when the days were only a gap between the nights they would spend together. They professed their love to each other until dawn arose, until they could ignite their love once again in the darkness, pretending that one day they would walk as man and wife under the sun.

He used to recall those nights and wonder how he faltered and lost her. Back then, she was an eternal virgin in the forest, even after he had taken her. He'd brush her hair with the comb of his fingers, while caressing the curves of her body by moonlight. At night she'd come to him with a candle and he'd wait in the summer breeze of goldenrod, mixed with wheat of the swelling harvest, watching the flame flicker in and out between the trees as she came. When the candlelight disappeared behind a tree, his heart sunk wondering what he would do if he never saw that light again. Then, her flame would beam in the darkness once more when she had only wanted him. He thought she was the light. The only light that would ever glow in his life, but the flame extinguished, and he all but died trying to save it.

Jorgen recalled the touch of her skin. After all these years, she was timeless. He thought he knew her, the girl in white. After the sorting of memories, he saw her for what she truly was, and her desire. Power. It overruled their love, and the lust of its draw consumed her passion. Artros hungered for her then, and he fed her what she craved.

Seeing Esa made him ache in agonizing anger. Looking away from them, he braced his hands on the tree trying to cool the Darkness urging to take hold of his emotions and bind itself onto them, onto the world. The solitude of pain and loss was a heavy burden, and he'd kept it contained like a rabid black dog.

Artros' staff lightened with the crunch of each step as they passed. Esa's perfect lips spoke words he could not hear. But questions like thoughts appeared on her face, as the two disappeared around the corner.

Jorgen slid his hands down the tree's limbs. Violent hate was opening the scars in his soul. The Darkness inside him cracked the branches of the great old Maple, just enough to make it tilt on the point of balancing or breaking, only time would tell.

Nathan wondered how much time they had before Artros would discover his black rose and apprentice were making a break for the county line. Not much, he gathered.

Nathan said again, "Come with me."

"Come . . . come . . ." Catherine said bewildered.

"We have to go. Go now," Nathan pleaded.

"Now . . . I . . . I want to . . ."

"Catherine, are you listening to me? We can't stay. We have to leave now," Nathan said stepping closer to Catherine. She walked around, aimlessly, looking at everything and nothing. "I'll help you pack, but we don't have much time."

"Why, what . . . I want to go, but why are you leaving, I mean . . . where are we going?"

"Just . . . I can't tell you right now. We don't have time. We just have to get the hell outta here and then . . ."

"I can't leave," Catherine sighed, and placed her wandering hand to her throat where the necklace lay. "Just, I mean, not yet. I want to go, Nathan. I want to go with you, but I have to do something first."

"Does this have to do with Jorgen?" he asked, sinking, wishing he had time to explain the last few months. There used to be time, all the time in the world he neglected to share with her because of Artros and his greed. He wanted to know what happened to her, but time was thin ice now, waiting to shatter. Every second was another dangerous encounter with Artros, possibly the other man too, Jorgen. Nathan thought Jorgen dropped out of his life when he saw him walk out Catherine's door, but the man was everywhere now. Artros lost control of his power at the mention of

Jorgen's name and the necklace. Esa, in envious denial, confirmed Jorgen's gesture went far beyond a simple gift. It didn't matter Jorgen had somehow been a part of Catherine's life, or that she decided not to tell him about it. He understood the difficulties when it came to the men in black. Nathan watched Catherine grasp the silver pendant hanging down the necklace around her neck, her expression softening, almost like she was touching Jorgen as well. It was as if Jorgen were standing in the room, between them. Nathan walked up to her and grabbed her hand from the necklace and held it. Catching her attention, he said, "I know that something has happened to you, something you can't tell me right now, or maybe can't explain. I've had something happen to me too . . . and I'm sorry, so sorry, but we can't talk about it right now, because now we have to leave."

"I . . . I . . . have . . . have to get the necklace off," Catherine stuttered in abrupt reversal, staring into Nathan's eyes with pure dread. "If I don't get it off, he'll, he'll . . ."

"We'll get it off. We'll find a way," Nathan said, urging her with a tug towards the door.

Catherine pulled against him. "I need you to leave," she said softly. "It's safer if you're not around me right now."

"I will never leave you," Nathan said. Their eyes locked for a time, filled with the unspoken each desperately wanted to share. "What is it that you know, Catherine?" Her silence spoke volumes. He let her hands go and moved for the door.

"Stop. Nathan wait!" Catherine said running up behind him.

Nathan turned the knob, but waited. He felt the heat of a phantom hand longing to touch his back and turn him around. He willed himself to face her.

"I will come with you," Catherine said. Nathan needed to hear those words; he sucked them inside. "But, I have to do one thing first and then . . . I'll come."

He focused on the detailed features of her face etched in sadness. Why, he deliberated, should all this concealment stand between them? He was ashamed the Darkness seduced him this far. Now it was testing him and if he didn't follow it, he may never have anything left to chase after. If any man could walk away from power and not feel the slightest remorse, then maybe he wasn't a man after all, but a boy scared by the knowledge of power. He had been blinded by Artros' intentions and it pained him to confront the truth: the taste of Darkness was intoxicating. Even as he ran for Catherine, he thought of what he was leaving behind, but at least he knew what side of the line he was standing on. He chose to reject the power offered him.

He moved to embrace Catherine; he wanted to reassure her they'd work this through. But when she hesitated, his resolve to leave faded.

"You promise?"

"I promise. I'll come."

"When?" he whispered.

"I don't know, but today . . . tonight maybe, at the latest, I . . . I just have to . . ."

"I know. I know . . ." Nathan trailed off before he opened the door to a blaze of white light outside reflected off the snow. The clouds had given way to the sun's merciless beam. "When you're ready, I'll be waiting."

"Do you promise?"

He gave a weak smile, "I promise."

One hand on each side, they closed the door together.

With a trembling hand she held onto the doorknob, a prop against her wobbly knees. She tried to understand everything happening to her. Nathan came for her. At this moment, they could be in his car, heading out of town together, forever, but against all of her yearning, she denied him. It was for his safety; she had no choice. She let him leave without explanation. She would one day tell him about the forces behind her decision; today was not the day. The pain inside of her was gnashing its way into her soul. She wanted to rip it out before it devoured her. A silent scream rang inside of her head, causing her mouth to tremble, but she refused to release it.

Without warning, the trailer shook in short energetic pulses which swelled in rhythm and strength. The clock and mirror banged against the wall. Dusty trinkets fell from a crooked shelf. Dishes knocked against each other and the cupboards and Catherine saw particles of the ceiling crack off and fall to the floor. Frightened, she clenched the doorknob, closed her eyes and held her breath until she couldn't contain it anymore. She exhaled long and hard as she waited for the quake to pass. Oddly, the tremors responded to her breathing. Once again she inhaled and released a long controlled breath, her mind eased along with the tremors until they merged together like soothing waves upon the sand and the trailer was still. With slow hands, she reached for her boots and coat and tried to stay calm while she put them on, afraid to stir the daemon quake again.

She had to find Jorgen, but how? She needed him to remove the necklace—nothing more. She would leave him, Kathy, and the dark man of her nightmares behind. She started along the right side ridge of the half-plowed road. Artros had told her to walk endless streets, anywhere and nowhere . . . whatever that meant. *Who was he?* she asked herself.

She thought she caught flashes of the Shadow Creatures that filled the trailer park the night before. She disregarded them for paranoia, wanting to believe it was just the sunlight burning indentations upon her eyes from a tree, road sign, or bush along her path. She had a mission.

Her weakened legs relaxed once she reached a No Outlet sign at a road crossing that veered down an older subdivision in town. Leaning against a tree, she studied the sign and wondered if her life had reached a dead end like this one. Had her exit closed when she shut the door on Nathan and his plea for her to come with him? She looked further down the road into the little, unplowed subdivision. Not one footprint spoiled this landscape of refuge and harmony for the families living there. How would it be to live in one of these daydream houses? She imagined herself on the porch of the bungalow closest to her, waving a morning goodbye to Nathan as he left for work. The landscape appeared as a mirage, taunting her thirst that longed to be filled. The simple life, Utopia. Her inertia broke with a jolt at the sound of a car horn in the distance. She caught another flash of shadow. Then another. Their imprints grew stronger with numbers, obscuring her long-distance vision. Their appearance nudged her back into her complicated reality. She kicked herself off the tree and started walking again, frequently turning to see the shadow figures, imagining she could hear their soundless footsteps.

Trailing through the streets, aimlessly wandering to an undefined goal, she saw the city limit street sign ahead. She gave up. *All for nothing*, she thought, looking down at her boots, soaked to the ankle. Flexing and wiggling her toes to warm them gave no relief from the creeping numbness. She crossed her arms and held herself, unsure what to do next.

In the quiet morning a car engine sounded in the distance, full throttle and heading her way. Catherine snapped her head to the sound and pushed her hair back from her face. A black car was spinning its tires in the middle of the city limit intersection attempting to stop. It spun a half circle on the slick road and planted its driver side door parallel to where she stood a block away. The car looked like a beat up mutt with a smoking tail where the rear tires burnt through the snow and peeled rubber on the asphalt below. Her heartbeat increased as the driver's door flew open and a man in black jumped from the car and rushed her in long, running strides, covering the distance in a few easy seconds. Catherine instinctively turned to run from the advancing man until she realized it was Jorgen. He came to a sliding halt, forcing her to duck in fear from an impending collision that would take her down with its force.

Catherine braced herself for a confrontation. She *would* convince Jorgen to take the necklace off. Jorgen stood before her, taller than she remembered. She looked up at him with imploring eyes and simply said, "Take it off."

He gripped her shoulders. "You don't want me to do that, Catherine."

"Please, take it off," she said, feeling the strength of his hands on her. She never begged, but she would if she must. His touch made everything real.

"I want you to see Catherine," he said, abruptly spinning her around. "See Catherine . . . see." He let go of her shoulders and placed his fingertips upon her temples.

With her vision directed down the street, she couldn't focus on anything other than the invasion of his hands on her head. She uttered a sound in protest, but grew silent when searing fire entered her flesh. His fingers opened a heat wave in her mind. Catherine felt something loosen inside, as if a secret door cracked, opening a new world to her. The winter's white light that blinded her as she walked changed into shimmering colors like a stained glass window come to life. Multiple colors reflected onto and off the snow, all vibrant and full of life and emanating from everywhere. Mailboxes, garbage cans and vehicles discharged colors of their own. The blue siding of a house discharged other shades of blue that mingled with greens and yellows extending into the air, like the rest of the objects around her.

Organic life, from dormant trees to snow-laden bushes projected the primary colors they were made from. All colors radiated around her and a marveling conduction of a white light rolled off their surface like a fog, dissipating into the environment of the colored world. Everything appeared to derive and reiterate in its own breathing light cycle. It was as though life itself was one cascade of complex and fluent colors.

Catherine stood in awe of this colorful, unworldly wonder. Her spellbinding vision was suspended when, at the far end of the street, a large black mass appeared. It was almost a man, darker than any starless night she'd ever witnessed, and he was heading straight for her. She watched it swallow every particle of color it passed, devouring every raindrop of light. Then, the one black corpus became three black masses when two triangulated out behind the leader in formation. Involuntarily, she leaned back. Jorgen supported her with his body, his fingers continued to pressure her temples, causing her to focus on the images rapidly catapulting toward them.

Horror-stricken, she begged to retreat when she saw the leader grow in size as he came for her. The color of red, set in like eyes, targeted her.

"Make them go away," Catherine said. "Make them go away like you did before."

"I can't Catherine. Not this time. You have to see them. You have to see who's behind them. See . . ." Jorgen strained.

Catherine heard her Nana's voice chanting the same words she said in the hospital: *See baby girl see . . .*

"I see them. I see them. I do. Let me go." She closed her head and turned away.

"No. See *him*," Jorgen said as he willed her head to move with his fingers back to the black masses.

"I can't. Stop . . . stop!"

"See him!" Jorgen commanded.

Emboldened, she turned to the dark masses coming her way. Jorgen needed her to pay witness—only then would he release her.

Through the trio of black masses, she saw another black mass appear. But this wasn't a shadow. A man, his long black coat swelling behind from the wind he created in his speed. He was wearing a hat, tipped down like a bow waiting to break a wave while something long spun around his hand, like fan blades.

The man was closing in, commanding the shadows that advanced in their sinuous current of movements. She didn't have to see his face to know he was the dark puppeteer at work. She knew this was the man of her dream.

"I see him. I seeee himmm," she yelled pivoting to face Jorgen, feeling the overbearing essence of her dream and its threat of harm. Seeing her nightmare in the flesh released a terror inside of her. He was the haunt of buried memories and stifled dreams. He was the man in the dark alley she could never see and the emptiness of the morning sun. He was with her always, and in this awakening, Catherine came to know he'd been with her for as long as she could remember. He was a faceless captor, forever watching her. Even with her back to him, she felt the proximity of his presence and his ruthless will to get to her. He was Artros.

"We have to go," Jorgen said pulling her to his idling car.

"No," Catherine said, resisting. "Take the necklace off and he'll go away."

"How can it be you know so much, and yet nothing at all,"

"He said he wouldn't hurt . . . me . . . Nathan . . . if . . ."

"Artros is the riddler of lies. He won't stop until he possesses what he desires."

Jorgen's face was filled with honest concern. Were the words Artros vowed to her that night in the dream, merely false promises? She glanced behind. The Shadow Men and Artros charged them.

"Run," Jorgen yelled, pushing her in one heave toward his car. She had no choice. Run from the shadows and run from the dark Artros of her dreams.

Catherine ran without looking back. The world of brilliant colors and black shadow beings had vanished with the release of Jorgen's grasp. The only truth she could see was her shoes hitting the ground as she ran. She jumped through the open driver's door and slid across the worn leather interior into the passenger seat. She gripped the door handle, preparing for escape if need be. Holding tightly, she looked back for Jorgen. He was on the street, steeling to challenge the dark masses moving their way.

His left foot extended out to ground himself, while his right was bent behind. He brought his arms to a full extension in front of him and cupped his left hand over the back of his open right hand, then dipped his knees for impact. Could he stop them like roadblock with only his hands?

The atmosphere changed as if the air and her body were being sucked toward Jorgen like a vacuum. She saw Jorgen's body vibrating as though he was trying to control the air rushing toward him. His body jolted in one great spasm before the surge came.

The force of his expelling power punctured the ground, the air, and everything within sight. Suffering impact, she was forced to close her eyes as the shear rocket of its power exploded all the glass in the car and made it jerk sideways as if struck by an invisible vehicle, driving her body sideways and half into the driver's seat. Thundering glass shattered over her body. A wincing pain shot through her as she listened to the sound of destruction and mayhem. Then, all was silent. Someone tipped her upright from the driver seat where she lay. Wiping the glass from her eyes in careful sweeps, she saw Jorgen. He was shifting the car into gear and accelerating. The car sped forward.

Cuts from glass beaded her skin. She turned to look out the shattered back window at loose pieces of metal, cars, shutters, upturned asphalt, all piled in a giant heap of refuse as if a great tidal wave blew through and buried the black masses and their leader.

Porches of the houses buckled, while shingles and siding had taken flight along with the shattered glass of their windows. But it was the trees that stuck out the most to Catherine. They had parted in the pathway of Jorgen's power like a splintered toothpick, some crashed into rooftops or lawns, while others had uprooted, and snapped power-lines which now whipped about with electric tongues. Catherine could only be thankful these were not the great old Oak or Maple trees of the west side of town which could have caused more damage. There was a chance no one was killed.

Jorgen drove, leaving the city limits, and headed deeper into the country. At first, the cold wind blowing though the empty windshield refreshed Catherine, as it beat on her face, and cooled her fear. She needed rest, no matter how small. She refused to look or speak to Jorgen who in turn, remained silent. She suspected the power he used to help them escape was also the same power that allowed them to drive freely now. She didn't understand, nor did she want to. Not at this moment. Glass particles hummed to vibrations on the dashboard before falling to the floor. Watching them fall in twos and threes and then by ten and more, Catherine was seized by a panicking notion that Jorgen had no intentions of stopping.

CHAPTER FIFTEEN

Jorgen pushed through the snow in one continuous plow, bringing a bitter wind through the broken windows. Their silence was unspeakably eerie to Catherine.

Ahead, a large forest bordered the distant farmlands and they were heading towards it. This countryside surrounded Catherine all of her life, but confined by city limits she rarely saw it. They passed farms with metal rooftops covering modest two-story homes next to slender hillsides. The farmers managed to work the land for generations, surviving off the patches of earth with what livestock the land could maintain while leaving enough left over to till and pasture the animals. All was still in the early morning of the aftermath of the storm. Like the townspeople, even the animals seemed afraid to come out of their shelter instinctually knowing another storm had yet to pass.

Catherine remained quiet for a time, soaking in the image of the Shadow Men and the man named Artros who came at them, at her. Her body shivered with little hope of reprieve. Putting her wet boots next to her on the seat she curled her knees to her chest and wrapped her arms over her knees, burying her head into them. But nothing could shield her from the icy blasts. Turning to Jorgen, she saw he hunched further into the steering wheel, determined to keep pushing forward, but his body looked worn and tired, about to collapse right into the wheel he gripped.

Jorgen's driving became sporadic as the snow billowed in spurts. Twice, he almost lost control of the car as the snow ceased to plow in front of the grill, but he held strong somehow regaining control of the car and snow once again.

"Pl–please–st–st–stop," Catherine stuttered from the cold that leached into her bones, afraid to ask where they were going.

"No," he said in a hoarse whisper, and turning down another main road lined with a forest of trees.

"Stop–th–the–car," she said louder.

Jorgen didn't answer. The car swerved a slight left, and then a wide right, and Catherine looked ahead wondering which side of the road they might plunge into. Jorgen's head perked up from its weakening bow and whipped the steering wheel left again, but this time with intention. Catherine braced the door handle believing this time they would crash as they headed for a row of standing pine trees along side of the road.

Instead, a turn of the wheel drove them down another road, a narrow seasonal two-track, indistinguishable in the forest and snow. Traveling for half a mile, the car slowed, finally resting in a snow embankment. Jorgen turned the ignition key off and slumped forward, his head and chest planted on the steering wheel.

Catherine didn't know what to do. She thought about running and placed her hand on the door, but sighed, it was useless. Where could she go? This enigmatic man somehow saved her from Artros and the pursuing shadows. Jorgen was dangerous, she reminded herself, thinking back to the blast that came from him, which destroyed streets, homes and all surrounding.

Jorgen's chest rose and fell in shallow breaths; he seemed weakened. But even if she could run, her frozen limbs wouldn't make it very far. She couldn't face Artros again; she felt a certainty he was hunting for her now, riding a black Shadow Stallion. Where did these men and their shadows come from? What made the necklace important, and why did Jorgen place it around her throat? Jorgen could answer these questions. Without him, she'd only have more; she needed him. He needed her too, but why?

His eyes opened and closed despairingly. They finally opened to face her. His head shot up, and the movement startled her to attention.

"I need you . . ." he said half choking on his words. "Help me."

"I—I don't know how," she said.

"I need you to heal me."

"Heal you? What? I can't . . . I don't . . ."

"I used it all, all I had . . . to keep him from you . . . to protect you. Please," Jorgen beseeched, "help me."

"I don't know what you're talking about. I don't know how to . . . to . . ."

"I need . . . need just a little . . . a little . . ."

Jorgen spoke through a pain she didn't recognize. He wasn't physically injured as far as she could tell, but the pain was as real as if he had been. A part of her knew she owed him something in return for protecting her from the shadows and Artros. But then again, it was his fault. He put the necklace on her. He had no intentions to harm her; she was certain of this.

Now she was given the opportunity to make her own demands.

"If I help you . . . do whatever it is you—you want—then I want to make sure you'll do something for me."

Jorgen opened his eyes, half-staffed, and waited for her to say more. "If I help you, then you have to promise me you'll take me home."

"You don't want me to do that." His words were long, drawn out, and faint.

"Yes–yes I do. You have to promise me you'll take me back."

"A promise is nothing more than a word," Jorgen said gazing down.

"That's it . . . give me your word," Catherine said, unfolding her legs. She placed her feet on the floorboard and reached for the door. "You'd better tell me you're going to take me back or–or I'm gonna start walking back right now." She opened the door and stared at the deep snow.

Jorgen grabbed her arm. She looked at his hand which slid down to limply rest on the seat beside her.

"Heal me, and I will tell you all you need to know. Then, you may decide if you still want to return."

Well, Catherine thought, that was some kind of assurance, if anything. But there was one more thing she needed from him, more than the first. "Tell me you'll take the necklace off too."

She saw he was slipping farther away, into himself. His mind eased away and Catherine feared he might not awaken from this unseen affliction.

"Jorgen . . . Jorgen," she said, shaking his right shoulder. "Wake up."

With one swift motion, his right hand snapped up to her wrist and clenched it with a strength she thought impossible given his current state. She withdrew it by instinct, but he held strong, pulling her hand to his chest, and turning his body to face her. His free hand gripped her shoulder as he took command.

"Forgive me." Catherine felt something release from inside her body and drift towards him. The sensation throbbed in vibrations at first, and then a steady stream, generating heat as it discharged from her body and into his. The draw was frightening, and she recoiled, but he held onto her. His strength grew with each pulsating vibe.

"Don't be afraid. It's almost . . ." Jorgen said trailing off.

Catherine tried to relax, listening to his voice. She wanted whatever was happening to be over. Closing her eyes, her breath leveled and she felt her body spin like a turbine. She submitted to him and surrendered all her will. She felt the invisible wavelength between them grow from a vibrating line to one surge of energy, tireless and seemingly irrepressible as it pressed forward.

As the energy passed, Jorgen's body quaked. The car shook and in a distant, dark voice unlike his own, he uttered the word: "Ragnarök."

It was over. The car was still. His hands slipped from her and the connection was broken. His body still rocked in violent shudders as hers drooped from exhaustion. The chill in her bones returned and she sat back in a seat of cold fatigue.

A benumbed heaviness took over, forcing her to close her eyes. She drifted off with a sensation that Jorgen was looking at her, willing her to face him. She pushed against his will only to finally open her eyes. She panicked when her eyes met a crystal darkness, beaming and pulsating, desiring to devour her with their dark animalism.

Catherine had a flashback. A memory she'd hidden in the depth of her mind that only awakened now, looking into Jorgen's eyes. In her memory, she was her child-self. A little girl she vaguely remembered. In this memory she was at the hospital with her Nana. But not just with Nana, on top of Nana while she laid on the gurney. She had pried Nana's eyes open for a reason, a game, she now recalled. But this wasn't a game. She was looking for hope inside of Nana's eyes. Nana, however, looked back at her with eyes like

Jorgen's now, a tunneling darkness that threatened to consume her. As Catherine remembered staring into Nana's frightening eyes, she recalled a tantalizing voice as well, beckoning to her—they were the words of the other that was inside her grandmother. She remembered the puzzling taunt of the forgotten voice. It spoke clearly to her now, "The Devil is an Angel. An Angel is the Devil." And then Catherine spoke the answer to the riddle that hung in her subconscious all of these years.

"The Devil and Angel are one," Catherine said aloud.

The body beside her was no longer Jorgen. Protector or otherwise, didn't matter.

Catherine flung herself out of the car only to land in a bed of white—her blanket of death. Catherine lay physically drained and depleted of hope and looked up through the dense evergreen limbs, rich with life in this desolate tail of winter. The blazing sun came down in shards through the trees and one small sliver of light rested at the corner of her eye. Catherine thought this could be death, bright and white with all the teasing of life trapped in hibernation, like her. She related herself to the forest around. Feeling one with the trees, which looked as though they were growing and thriving, but she knew they were just waiting on the inside for the growing season to begin, like she waited for her life to begin. Each day was winter to her. Every year had been one long wait for the sun to break, and when it did shine, it was just like this, a cold false light in the forest of waiting. She turned her head just enough to let the slice of light burn into her left eye, blinding her. She lost faith in herself and the future.

She felt herself picked up and taken into Jorgen's arms. She saw him with two different visions, one clear from her right eye but the left one, burnt by the sunray, was full of colors. At first his face was luminous and indistinguishable from the warm colors of red and yellow by the sun's searing.

Then, they cooled and became darker shades of blue and purple, until that too passed, leaving his face an ashen shadow where the gray imprint started to outline the curves of his face, one by one.

Watching the illusion, manifested through sunrays or a greater purpose of the whole, Catherine thought about Jorgen as he held her, feeling no threat by his touch. The black in his eyes receded. She held her fear at bay for a moment to consider what mysteries were yet to unfold. He was more than a man, but what else didn't she know? She understood that if he planned to harm her, he would have done so by now. He had taken something from her, something silent and unstated, that left her weak and drained, but he'd asked and she allowed him to. She felt diminished and chilled, but unharmed.

She sunk in his arms, willing whatever to come, to simply come. She had no strength for anything else. She melted into calmness and imagined herself floating away.

Jorgen said in sorrow, "I've never touched . . . forgive me, Catherine. I had no idea the power within you." With his words, she felt gentle waves of warm water wash over her and soak deep into her skin, nourishing her. Enveloped by its soothing sensation, she felt replenished. Despairing thoughts lifted as her mind stabilized and her consciousness sharpened.

Together they created an exchange as she inhaled a breath of him and an exhaled one of her. What she had given was being restored. A part of her understood this conversion. She knew she'd done this before, given a part of her, and accepted this sensation in return. Why it was familiar, she did not know.

When the power receded, she found a place of comfort in his arms, like the cradle of her dream. Speaking in a foreign tongue, Jorgen said, "Svǫrt verða sólskin, of sumor eptir, veðr ǫll válynd. Vitoð ér enn, eða hvat?"

She looked to him for understanding. A radiating heat flowed from his body and warmed her left side. Even though the pulsation had ceased, he continued to throb with it, whereas she only felt warm and restored. "What did you just say to me?" Catherine asked.

"Ah," Jorgen sighed, "it's best if you don't listen to tales of the sea that are less than a whisper of the forgotten."

Catherine lifted in his arms and said, "Please don't speak in vague riddles. Just explain to me what you said. Tell me what it means."

"It was something and nothing. A part of a tale I was told as a child, if I was ever a child at all . . ." He hesitated, but then continued, 'Black becomes the sun's beams, in the summers that follow, weathers all treacherous. Do you still seek to know, and what?'"

"But what does that mean?"

"Never mind, Catherine. We don't have time for tales now," he said setting her down, still bracing her with one hand behind her back, and opening the rear door of the car. Assured she could stand on her own, he ducked into the backseat. Pieces of glass could be heard falling as they were brushed from the seat onto the floor. Then she heard the odd sound of something being unzipped.

"Take off your boots," he said.

"I'm fine, really. I'm warmer now."

"You may feel warm, but once the Darkness has settled in, your body will remember itself. Darkness gives us power, but we must always take care of the vessel that contains it, lest the powers wither us into the nothing from whence we came."

"What is Darkness?"

"Take your boots off and I will tell you more."

Catherine did as she was told, and unlaced the long boot strings patched with snow and ice. Peeling off her socks, she set them on the floor next to her boots.

He gestured for her to slide over in the back seat. She saw a large inviting black blanket, unfolded and open. She wrapped herself up in it as Jorgen slid next to her and closed the door.

"What do you mean by Darkness? What is it?" she asked.

"It is a metaphor for the opposing side of light. It's wild by nature, raw and unfeeling. When Darkness is harnessed, it is used like a tool."

"I don't understand. I mean I want too. I'm trying, but I have no idea what you're talking about."

Jorgen sighed and said, "I used the Darkness, its power, to block Artros' pursuit. He maintains great strength, Darkness if you will, and I couldn't understand how he obtained such power, until now." Jorgen looked away from her for a moment and then back again. "But we will come to that. Blocking Artros exhausted my power, but somehow we managed to make it this far, but if we stay here long, he will find us. You have healed me and I thank you for that. I needed the Darkness, the power you hold inside, to heal me. However, once you relinquished it completely, it overwhelmed me. It was . . ."

"Wait a minute. How could I possibly . . . this is crazy," she said placing her hand to her forehead, "ever–I mean me– have this something. Do other people have it too?"

"One can harness power from anyone, but you are unique, unlike any being I have ever seen."

"Unique? Are you kidding me? That's one for the . . ."

"Imagine each individual is like a snowflake, no two are alike. And the energy inside of them illuminates with the white fire of life which shoots off like a sparkler. Its burning embers disappear, but the webbed core itself is rejuvenated and the cycle repeated. The ends of these shoots are called threads, and one can pull them from an individual to obtain energy. Once these threads have been pulled, they transform from a white thread to black, and it can disperse if it is not harnessed quickly. But once it is gathered, even wielded, it is known as Darkness. Darkness is many things. However, each branch of the power comes from one substance, one invoking energy. The energy we call Darkness."

Catherine cringed, "Does it hurt—hurt the people?"

"If one is sick or wounded, it can lead to their demise, because it is an energy life force that is taken from them. Even an otherwise healthy person can become ill or die if they are depleted, but the human race has grown strong. Death hardly occurs unless it is intended. Harnessing energy amongst a mass is pliable and second nature once one has become a Master of Darkness."

"And that's what happened to me, didn't it? You took it from me," Catherine said, realizing the sensation had a name. "But why did you ask? You didn't need to, did you? You could have taken it without . . ."

"I have been a thief for many, many years, as I will continue to be. But I made a vow upon meeting you that I would attempt to uphold some of the honor I used to know, if that is possible after all this time."

"Why me? Why this?" Catherine said, shaking her head.

"Artros has been using your energy, Catherine. It has placed him at his pinnacle of power. He's been manipulating you, hiding you from the power you contain, and keeping you prisoner, insuring he could use you when he was ready."

"Use me? Ready for . . . what?"

"To take you for himself."

"What the hell does he want from me?"

"It's not you. It's what's inside you. But I don't think he can have one without the other," Jorgen said in thought. "I'm sure he hasn't taken you by now because he has to have you in complete control to acquire all you hold within."

Catherine lowered her head stunned by the notion Artros had been a part of her life all this time. Years possibly, and she didn't know it.

"You have," Jorgen continued, "a web of energy inside of you that shines brighter than I have ever seen, that in itself is exceptional. But there is another, which is a true mystery."

"Another?" Catherine asked.

"You have another one that radiates pure Darkness. The two interweave as they rotate and spin inside you and yet they never connect. I'm not sure if they are meant to. I don't know. I can only see what I do. But the Darkness inside you has yet to be fully awakened. It is the dark web, this power, which Artros truly covets."

"Can't I just give it to him? Like what I did for you . . . and you for me . . ." Catherine trailed off realizing the exact exchange at work between them moments ago.

"If that were possible he would have taken it by now. And he hasn't been teaching you the way of Darkness, because you have been too young, unbalanced. Teaching the art to someone before their time is a grave mistake."

"Wait. If I gave you this . . . whatever it is, then why did you give it back? Why can't Artros just take it from me?"

"That is your expanding life force, your threads. The Darkness inside you has never been known. Artros has been stealing your energy, the one that comes from the white web of your life force and it has given him strength beyond measure. But he's been taking it without your knowledge, when your mind is idle and your subconscious is vulnerable. When . . ." Jorgen paused for a moment questioning how much she could absorb, "when you allowed me to draw your energy with free will, I thought the force would harm me, or you. I have never known a life force such as yours. I broke the current just in time, and took control of the Darkness before it could master me. You gave me . . . so much willingly. What would have killed another only left you depleted. I could see your suffering from its withdrawal and I restored some of your strength."

"What if you couldn't stop it?" Catherine asked.

"Then it would have destroyed me and possibly, you . . ." Jorgen's thoughts drifted off.

In the quiet, cocooned in the blanket, both fell into deep thought. Jorgen worried he'd said too much. But for her own safety, she had to know, be prepared for what, he felt sure, was coming.

"What about the other one? The black one Artros wants. If you can take from the one, then why not the other?" she finally asked.

"It is . . . contained . . . and complicated in its purity. Unlike a web with shoots in which to pull threads, it loops into itself. The power you hold within is profound. To attempt to force it, to take it, could be catastrophic. It is . . . an unknown, as it has never existed in an individual, or anything I have seen, until now. The dark energy inside of you resembles . . ." Jorgen hesitated for the right words, "the Flower of Life. An ancient symbol which has opened the minds of men for answers they seek only to have more questions awake for all their understanding. That's the quest. The end. The Light. I seek to understand it, so that I might put an end to all of this . . . this Darkness that I have known."

"The more you tell me, the more confusing all of this is. I'm nobody. Nobody! And I don't want anything to do with this. And I don't care if I have to do whatever—let Artros take what he wants because I don't care. I just want him away from me. I don't want any part of this!"

"Catherine, you don't know what you're saying. If one can draw the Light out of someone's life force and it becomes Darkness, what if Darkness could be drawn out of someone? It could be the Light! It could convert into pure indestructible energy. I can't imagine what Artros would do if he obtained it and I can't allow that to happen. I have been searching for the Light, without hope of ever finding it. And as much as I see it everywhere, in everything, I have gone mad at times wondering if it even exists. But when I saw you for the first time—a webbed light entwining with the pure essence of Darkness—I knew it must. I decided that if you can't reveal the Light to me, then I would die trying to protect it—lest it become corrupt and tainted by a man who not only wields the dark power, but calls himself father of Darkness itself!"

"But then . . . really, you're just after what he wants as well," Catherine said. "To me you're no different. You just want what's inside of me. That's what you're trying to protect. Not me . . . it!"

"That is not true. I . . ."

"Yes it is. You just want to take it . . . protect it. This isn't about me at all, it's about—"

"Call it by name Catherine!" Jorgen roared, his anger was fuelled by insult. "Darkness and Light will be a part of you the rest of your life, whether you choose them or not. You weren't born with a choice!"

Jorgen turned away from her, reeling. She dipped her head, hugging herself inside the blanket, and pulled the soft fabric tight around her. There was silence for a time. The air inside the car grew colder, as the warmth she felt before slipped from her. Lost in the spilling revelations, she turned her head to the side in an attempt to rest her mind from Jorgen. Tilting her head, she saw the snow on the trees had started to glisten from the rising temperature. The snow flurries ceased and the topcoat of snow was starting to melt.

"I know," Jorgen said in a tranquil voice aside her, "that you lead an impoverished life, one that has all but crippled your spirit because humanity has failed you. But for these faults, this injustice that has been brought upon you, you are stronger in spirit and strength because of it. I believe that a part of this strength has been the reason Artros has waited this long to take you. And because, even though you feel tangled and angry by the life that challenges you, you have become a survivor, and survivors never surrender the heart, not completely."

Catherine's eyes welled up, hearing Jorgen's words. It was as if, for the first time, someone read into the depth of her soul. A part of her was saddened, hearing someone speak to her as if they had known her for years, but another part of her grew uneasy, wondering if he was swindling words so she might believe he cared. Believe he wanted to protect her and not what was inside of her.

"I was manipulated by Artros," Jorgen continued, "misled and betrayed. Since the Darkness came into my life, I have been forced to walk in the same shadows that ripped me apart. I don't know how to overcome all that I have lost and what I have taken," he paused for a moment and then said, "but I hoped saving you from him might be a start. A start, if not the end, and that at least will bring justice to the man I once was."

A tear trickled down Catherine's cheek and dripped on her neck. Only then did she realize one escaped. Wiping her face with the blanket to hide its evidence, she brushed the necklace around her throat. She felt the affliction of its weight and the touch fired her. After all their conversations, she didn't know what it was for, or why he put it on her.

"What about the necklace," Catherine said.

"Nothing gets in," Jorgen said, "nothing gets out."

"You know," Catherine said whipping around to face him, "that's about as vague as anything else you've told me. I understand some of it, but then again, not really. Nope, not nothing at all–all of this is crap. And I'm sick of it. I don't want anything to do with this. I just want you to take it off and take me home."

"I told you I would protect you. The necklace is a declaration of my vow."

"I don't care what it is—it has caused me nothing but trouble. And Artros said if I didn't take it off he'd—he'd hurt me and . . . and Nathan. And I can't stand it. It didn't do any good. He still can get me and . . . and . . ." Catherine said with despairing anger.

"When did he come to you?"

"Well, he didn't exactly come to me . . . it was a dream I had. He told me that I had to get the necklace off. He told me to find you and I'd have to convince you to remove it or else . . . or else there would be consequences." Catherine didn't want to tell Jorgen about the other parts of the dream, how she felt whole in the cradle and that Artros had tried to take something from her, or enter her. She wasn't sure. Withholding created a wall and helped her retain some of her defenses.

"If he has made himself known to you, then he is not far from taking you," Jorgen said to himself before he continued. "The necklace is a binding tool. It bears my name within the inscription, written with words that once worked alongside relic powers from a time long ago."

Catherine touched the pendant hanging in the center of her throat and thought about his words of ancient times and things forgotten. She couldn't cope with the thought that Jorgen could be . . . that he was . . . She tried to focus on something, praying her mind wouldn't shatter from what she'd witnessed and the answers she'd been given. She fingered the markings of the necklace and said, "It looks like a double R, one reversed, like they are back to back."

"That is one way to spell my name, with the runic symbols of my people, but it empowers the rune Raidho, which means, to travel. Combining my name and the element of the rune, I was able to create a protection against traveling, and entering. One that won't allow the spirit to travel, or be swayed by another, as long as the binding tool is in place."

"Once again, I have no idea what you're talking about."

"You can travel outside of your body on the celestial plane, or someone can enter your body and take control of you, if your spirit is persuaded by their possession."

"You mean like possession . . . possession?"

"Yes and foremost. If Artros can't take you willingly or by force, he may attempt to take control of your body and manipulate your spirit to do his bidding. He may have done this before. Your strength becomes you, which will make it harder for Artros to enter you without a fight."

Catherine's stomach churned, thinking possession was possible. But there was the Mad Hag, the incident at the hospital with Nana . . . She couldn't bear the thought, not right now. She needed to find a way out of this mess. She sat confounded, searching for the answer to save herself from Artros, and how to protect Nathan at the same time.

It was hopeless.

"I don't know what to do," she said aloud.

"We have wasted valuable time. We need to leave before he discovers you."

"No. I have to go back," Catherine said, thinking about what would become of Nathan if she didn't.

"No," Jorgen replied with a smoldering voice.

"If I don't, Artros will hurt Nathan."

"Who cares about that treacherous boy?"

"I do," Catherine hollered back. "And he has been nothing but good since the day I met him."

"I tell you, he walks with Artros. Who knows what role he has yet to play for his dark Master's wishes!"

"You lie!" Catherine said.

"I speak truth," Jorgen said, undeterred by her accusation. "I know what it is like to lose love to Artros, to the Darkness, but I tell you he is on that path right now."

"I don't care what you think. I healed you and you said you would take me back as long as I did it. You said I decide."

Jorgen slammed his fist into the passenger seat in front of him, causing it to buckle and fold in two. The hit, however, was devoid of Darkness. It was only the anger of a man who wanted to rebel against nature, and the promise of words he had long ago disregarded as another pretense of lies.

"You push me Catherine, farther than I have been pushed in a long time," Jorgen groaned. With his words he opened the door and slammed it behind him. It too almost came off its hinges.

To her dismay, he walked in front of the car. He stood still in silence with his back to her, appearing to look ahead. She wondered if he was studying the two-track road, the forest, or if he was consumed with thought, or thought of nothing. Time was lost as he stood there. She heard the snow dripping off the evergreens with the warmth of their promise that spring would break and the blessings of life would come with each drop of water that fell.

Eventually, Jorgen turned around and walked to the driver side door. Catherine refused to look at him, but she heard his voice as he opened the door and entered the car. "I will take you back, as you wish," he said, and then added, "but if Artros comes for you, then so will I."

"Take the necklace off."

"No."

Driving back, Catherine was apprehensive, but she needed to be sure Nathan was safe. Through solitude, and the spurs of its longing, she captured courage from the mere thought of him. Deep in thought, Catherine realized the wind didn't penetrate past the open windows as they had on their way out of town. Lifting her hand to where the glass should have been, she felt nothing other than a wall like gridlocked air. Pushing against the opening, her hand passed into a grating intrusion, stimulating something inside her that charged back against an electrified field which stopped the airflow from coming into the car.

"Don't disturb the shield," Jorgen said driving. Those were the only words spoken since they left the forest and she did not intend to disobey him as long as he was on course to take her home. She removed her hand from the window.

"How is it possible?" Catherine asked in regards to the blocked air and everything else passing through her head. Jorgen didn't respond.

They drove south and Catherine could see the outline of the town she grew up in. She thought she would be relieved, but the terror that made her jump into Jorgen's car and flee from Artros and his shadows, returned.

"What are they, Jorgen?"

"Are what?" he replied.

"The things, the shadows . . . that look like men, but aren't."

"They were men, or women, once. That is the belief. But their prevailing dark nature burned an imprint of them which has lasted beyond death. I do not know if they retain . . . what one might call a soul. But once they become creatures of the Darkness, they are called Shadow Men. Artros controls the ones you saw. They are a most treacherous leprosy when it comes to the forsaken."

"I saw one with red eyes. The others didn't seem to have any, but this one . . . this one . . ."

"Only a few are imprinted with eyes. And I have only known one to have chords for a tongue. While some are thought to have been tortured souls of this world, there are others some would call evil by nature's creation. Theirs is a malevolent seed. The strongest can direct their lost brethren and other Shadow Creatures. Through the centuries, some have been known to manipulate human flesh."

"You mean, they can . . . can control someone? Like me?"

"Yes and no. They are able to possess a weakened spirit, usually induced by a negative atmosphere or illness. It has been known for them to enter someone without complete control over the body. The world sees the victim infected by a Shadow Man as unstable and full of mindless wrath. Only the strongest spawn of Darkness can achieve possession. These poor souls reach asylum, never to be healed. It is thought death releases their soul. However, it is questioned if the energy of their soul isn't absorbed into the Shadow Man. That which does not carry the flesh will always crave the flesh and if it cannot have it, it will feed from it. Negative energy and ill health are sustenance for Shadow Creatures. Artros has enslaved them for the purpose of guarding you. But even the wandering waste of this world can have a vengeance against servitude. It is a dangerous game he plays, controlling so many."

"What does he need them for?"

"They have been summoned to guard you and attack anyone who attempts to take you from him."

"Then, how did we get away?"

"His arrogance defied him. He lightened his forces, confident as long as he remained nearby, you could not escape him. He wanted me to come to you and you to convince me to remove the necklace. When I challenged him, he was still calling the dark powers to revitalize him from an assault I do not understand, but one which left him weakened."

"Is he still . . . weak?"

"Weak to me is nothing compared to your perception of the word. And no, he will not be weak, if you are still thinking about going back."

Catherine was quiet, grateful she couldn't see Jorgen's face. Rationalizing her reason to return, she knew the dangers and the faith she placed in Nathan. A plan formed in her mind. It was simple and the only logical thing she could think of. She would find Nathan and run. Just run. It didn't matter where, just anywhere away from these men and their Darkness.

They crossed the city limit and Catherine didn't need to see Jorgen to feel his tension building. Tossing the blanket off, she shoved her soggy socks in her pockets and felt the wet cold leather against her feet as she tied the bootlaces.

Most of the roads were now plowed, but Jorgen drove slower as they came closer to the trailer park only a few streets away. Suddenly, he made a right turn, accelerating as he crossed the first block in the opposite direction.

"You're going the wrong way!" Catherine yelled.

"No I'm not," he said.

"Stop the car," she said kicking the back of his seat with her feet, but Jorgen sped faster. "If you don't stop the car . . . I'll jump. I swear I will. I'll jump. I will!" They passed another block. Catherine wondered how hard the impact would be and how far she would roll before she came to a stop. "If you keep going," Catherine said in accusation, "then you're no better than him."

Jorgen slammed on the brakes, but Catherine wasted no time with words. She jumped out of the car as fast as she could, hearing his door open as she started to run.

He yelled her name once, but she never looked back as she ran for home.

CHAPTER SIXTEEN

We should have left, Nathan thought in repeated cycles. *I should have told her to forget about Jorgen. We should have left. We have to leave. He'll be back. He'll find us. We should have left.* Nathan was sitting on the couch in his wet clothes, shoes, and coat on for almost two hours. Like a broken record he could neither move nor stop the skipping thoughts in his head.

Nathan heard his pa's alarm. With great effort, he removed his coat and shoes and plopped himself at the kitchen table, his thoughts riddled with worry. When would he get word from Catherine? He listened to his father move about in his room, a routine Nathan knew by heart—it was his pa's standard schedule, one he started once his wife walked out on them. At 12:20 the coffee pot would stop dripping and Steve would sit and read the paper he recycled from work, still groggy and stinking of the factory, despite the shower he dutifully took every night he came home.

Steve flipped through the newspaper, studying the photographs of the river disaster and reading the corresponding articles and added them to the tales he heard at work.

Turning on the transistor radio atop of the kitchen counter, he listened to the day's broadcast of the river's devastation, and the night's snowstorm. At one point the announcer paused mid-sentence and said, "This just in . . . South Hinder Road is closed until further notice, along with intersecting roads leading up to South Hinder Road. Details have not been released at this time. Reports have come in . . ." Steve turned up the volume and bent closer to the radio.

"What the hell is going on around here?" Steve asked aloud.

"What Dad?"

"They're saying there was some sort of explosion on Hinder Road, but they didn't say if anyone was hurt or what happened. All the roads round here have been shut down. They're not letting anyone in. The radio said it might have been a gas line, but I'm thinking otherwise. Too much shit's been coming down, it ain't natural and the storm made it worse. I got a fish of a feeling that things aren't right around here and I'm not the only one who smells it. Always been quiet, our town, and this shit don't fly with me. It's got stink all over it."

"Well . . . " Nathan began, not knowing what to say as he thought of Artros. Steve had his habits, his routine which never included going to Donnie's Bar. He hadn't heard the tavern gossip linking his son to the "unwelcome" outsider. He couldn't imagine his father's disappointment if he knew he was involved with the man in black. One thing for sure, these events were unnatural, but only he knew it was the Darkness at work. Nathan didn't know how, but he didn't need to. He didn't orchestrate the tragic events unfolding throughout town, but he was not an innocent man in all of this. His involvement with Artros, and the dark power, caused him to abandon Catherine for a time. He lost the simple life he once knew, along with friends and future dreams. Now he was going to lose his father, and through all of this Nathan knew the Darkness changed him into a liar as well. His guilty gut churned when he thought about his escape. For all of these thoughts the only thing Nathan could think to say was "Well, at least you don't have to go into work today."

"Oh, I gotta work alright. No matter what, a man's gotta work. There was that time the tornado came through town when you was little. Did I ever tell you about that time?"

"No."

"Well the factory use ta have windows, you know. You can still see where they was 'cuz there are bricks different from the others . . . but when the tornado was comin' through town, and the sirens was goin' off, they still made us work. And when the tornado came, we all ducked under the line to take cover. The tornado roared through like a freight train, everyone stayed quiet, you know. Quiet until the windows busted, I guess," Steve recalled. "But only then did some cry a little. I think most everyone was too scared to really cry or scream. It was strange watching all the glass and wind and rain coming in, and no one saying anything. I'll never forget it. Damndest thing when everyone's scared but no one makes a sound."

"Was anyone hurt?" Nathan asked, watching his dad recall the moment.

"Naw, not too bad anyway, so we was thankful for that," Steve answered shaking his head. "But you know what those sonsabitches did? They still made us work in the water on the floor, with the windows busted out, and everything."

"Why didn't you leave?"

"As long as you work for the man, you don't got a choice. You just keep doin' what he says so you can bide your time for something better. I didn't stay for the man; I stayed for you. Walkin' out on my job would have been like walkin' out on you, and sometimes a man isn't given a choice, long as he has someone he's gotta look out for."

"But they have to call it off today, I mean with the storm and . . . no one can get into work."

"That factory ain't shut its doors since they opened," Steve sighed. "I was thinkin' I'd go in early anyway and pick up some extra work from the guys who can't make it in yet, not till the county roads are clear. After yesterday, I think everyone's got to be running thin by now."

During the morning rush, Nathan hadn't thought about the country roads. He'd seen one plow run through town, figuring there were plows going down every road. If he made an attempt to skip town this morning, they wouldn't have made it far, especially in his two-wheel drive Celica, but he could have tried.

"Hey Dad," Nathan said, in pained words. He was going to say a parting piece he never thought he'd be able to make. "I just want to say thank you for taking care of me all these years. I know it's been hard since Ma . . ."

"Don't you think nothin' of it. I don't know where I'd be if you weren't helpin' your ol' man out like you've been doin'." Steve smiled and took a sip of coffee before he continued. "You know, tonight might be a good time for you to come in an' talk to my boss about that job I've been itching at ya. The line will be crawling, and they say they got an opening. Fact, they might hire you on the spot."

"Thanks, but . . . maybe I'll wait until tomorrow. I've got to get some sleep before I go to Donnie's tonight," Nathan said, adding another lie to his roster, knowing he would never return to the bar, nor home, or see his father again.

"Boy, you don't look like you've been sleeping at all these days."

"Just . . . just working for the man, Dad," Nathan said. In an awkward moment he bent down to hug Steve—a gesture out of character in their relationship, but Steve embraced him back and mumbled words of praise to Nathan. Nathan said, "Night Dad." And that was as close to goodbye as he was going to get. Once in his room, trapped in a purgatory, he crumbled, knowing he was walking away from a man he loved with every particle of his being. With that, he passed out on his bed, exhausted.

It was almost five o'clock when his eyes snapped open. He jumped off the bed, cursing himself for falling asleep. As he ran to the kitchen to grab his bag and coat, he saw that Steve's lunchbox and thermos were gone to the factory with him.

Worried he might have missed Catherine, he rushed for the door, but paused briefly before opening it. Yes, he could walk out that door, away from his father, but it would be a long time before he could walk away from the coward. *Man-up*, the men would say, but those men faced a rational world. He was running from something that couldn't be touched or bargained with—something he didn't have the right weapons to fight. Right now he didn't have a choice. If Catherine was ready, he would be too.

Hoisting the bag strap over his shoulder, he heard a voice behind him. "I have been a patient man—a giving man." Nathan's shoulders sank. He turned to see Artros lounging back on the couch, comfortable as a houseguest, inspecting his long hands as he extended and crunched them before he continued. "But nothing displeases me more than one who would steal from me. One whom I had hoped to lavish with intricate gifts of power."

Nathan's first instinct was to play dumb. Make excuses as to why he'd abandoned Artros in the street and why he was carrying the loaded bag, but he knew this man wouldn't accept his paper-thin lies. Artros was beyond them.

"You were after me to get to Catherine," Nathan said. "You used me so . . . so you could get close to her."

"Everybody is used for something, boy. That is the way of the world—the way of Darkness." Artros looked at Nathan without reprimand, but his words were an onset of strategic maneuvers to come. "Catherine will be a part of me longer than the sunsets of your eyes will ever see, as she is my dawn, forevermore." Artros rose, seeming to tower over Nathan. "You, however, were an advantage. One whom I would have used to make proper introductions between us," Artros sighed a false breath before continuing. "But all of that is spoiled now, and it's unfortunate because I'd love to be a gentleman when given the rare occasion. Now both of you force me, against my will, to punish you. Ease yourself Nathan. I have no intention of physically harming you, or Catherine. Not in the least."

"Catherine didn't do anything. I was leaving. Me. Not her so . . ."

"She left with him today," Artros said, catching Nathan off guard.

"Him?"

"Jorgen."

"What do you mean . . . she left with him?"

"She left, willingly I might add, without regards to you. But don't worry, she is coming back to me," Artros said as if he could inhale Catherine. "I can feel her closer with each footstep. She heads straight for me. But while we wait, you will open a present I've brought to pass time. One to entertain us until she arrives."

"What are you talking about?" Nathan asked.

"Won't you answer it?" Artros said pointing to the door. "She's been such a good girl standing outside, waiting in the cold. Waiting for you to open it."

Nathan turned toward the door. He'd have to do Artros' bidding if he were to survive a while longer. Nathan opened it to find Melissa standing proudly in front of him. Artros' coat never appeared as heavy as when Nathan saw it covering Melissa's frame. Her shoulders seemed to bow under the weight, as the hem of the coat laid around her feet in heaving lumps. If a chill crossed her body, as one shuddering sensation did Nathan's, she didn't show it. Picking the coat up like a Victorian dress, she giggled and bounced inside, teasingly nudging Nathan as she passed.

"What the fuck is this?"

"This is your punishment. A gift from me," he said, walking up behind Melissa standing with a beaming grin, "to you." He unhooked the coat from her shoulders.

Only then did Nathan notice the long red gloves Melissa wore, extending past her elbows midway to her shoulders. The rest of her scarce, scarlet garment of satin and lace matched the tips of her fingers now working playfully to free one of the gloves. Moving her bare hand down, she lifted the hem of her negligee, exposing her belly and lace underwear. She panted through parted lips. Her breasts rose and fell. Holding her gloved hand out, she dropped the other glove on the floor between them and then touched her naked thigh, streaking a line past her belly, chest, and up to her neck, while her bare hand tugged and twisted sections of her garment from the yearning within. Melissa's hand rose in an arc to Artros' face, skimming a line from the side of his brow, and down across his jaw line.

"The gifts I like to give," Artros said grinning, "are the ones that don't have to be forced into giving."

"I don't want her," Nathan said, pivoting his face away from Melissa who longed to be unraveled like a ribbon.

"Darkness has a way about it," Artros said, "An uncanny, efficient way, which allows men to become animals, and an animal to become a man. A man of power. You will learn that a body," Artros said stroking Melissa's arm to her delight, "is just that. A body and nothing more. A body is a tool, one to satisfy the deeper urge within us. One that aims to fire and consume all at the same time. Think of this as another gift of my teachings. One of using the body for nothing more than a purpose."

"I'm done with your teachings!" Nathan yelled.

"Ah, so you think," Artros responded, calm in his smile. "But we have a long way to go, you and me. I am going to break that vessel of the boy you are, slowly . . . starting with Melissa. And your body will respond according to my teachings. For your ignorance of the body, I may forgive your defiance today, but only once . . . because I am a gentleman at heart."

Nathan dropped his duffel bag and gripped Melissa's shoulders to shake her into reality. *Useless*, he thought, *she was here of her own will, or so she thought.* He could only attempt to reason with her, break whatever manipulative mindset Artros placed inside her craving eyes. Pleading, Nathan said, "You need to leave. You don't understand what you're doing—what is going on . . . you, you . . . get out!"

"Oh, I understand completely," Melissa said, glossy eyed. "You just don't see it yet. We were meant to be together. We're going to make purple. Artros said we would."

"Artros is a liar!"

With that, Artros grew full of fury. Enraged by Nathan's words, he tossed Melissa aside with a whisper of his potent hand and grabbed Nathan's outstretched arms. Clutching Nathan, Artros said in pure vehemence, "I never lie!" But the word *lie* came out of his voice like a serpent, gliding around Nathan's flesh until he could feel it spiraling around his arms, into his chest, up to his shoulders and into his mind.

Artros' seething voice echoed inside Nathan's head. The word lie—lie—lie pounded into his conscience, and hollowed out a residence. Nathan struggled and fought against the pressure from within. He fought the voice until his strength faltered and his thoughts were not his own anymore and the world blacked out.

Running down the street to the trailer park, Catherine looked back to see if Jorgen followed. She wanted his protection, but she was determined to make it to Nathan's doorstep. She knew that just because she didn't see Jorgen, didn't mean he wasn't nearby. The same held true for Artros and she grew cautious coming within range of the trailer park. She wanted nothing more than to escape town. She knew there was no time to pack or plan. Only flee.

Crossing the field in her usual route, she struggled through the snow, adrenaline flowing. The park's roadway was clear and she was thankful to step on level ground. Catherine moved to cross through the neighbors' yards, but hesitated. Behind the thin walls lining the people from the outside world, she heard voices rise in anger and crunching commotion, like a storm was brewing inside and soon it would overflow.

Walking along the road, she heard a shout, a crash, a slam. The serrated sounds came from every direction. People usually stayed clear of another's rented turf, but that never stopped their voices, idle chatter, or rumor-spreading gossip. But this was different. Something was taking hold of the people and working its way through them. It was as if they were caged by their heated emotions, seeking retribution from the poison of their toxic environment. The trailer park was suffocating and, through the choke, they were fighting each other as a means to escape.

The unsettled voices matched the ominous irrigation of dread overwhelming the park. It seeped like black ink into the hearts and minds of its residents. Passing by the houses, she heard insults met with retaliating abuse. Above the shouting, she heard abrasive clashing and crashing. She wanted to cut between the houses, but with each attempt another sound or voice would rise forcing her to backtrack.

Calamity was building in the park. Catherine dashed along the road, each curve tightened its knit closer to Nathan, but it wasn't fast enough. Cautious of detection, she made a decision to cut between the trailer yards and cross their unnatural battleground.

She veered through the lawns, crouching as she moved so she wouldn't encounter the wrath of a resident. Some voices were muffled like shifting gravel, while others rose in spikes. A viscous menace throbbed thick and deep into the people, spilling out in boiling passion. Its emotional gauge went up; it was steadfast and climbing. In one trailer, a claim of betrayal sounded, and in another, an argument of money. There were some without voices, only objects colliding against the walls. Sounds of the sick and children simmered beneath the volume, begging to be heard. But there were trailers which remained quiet like an empty soul, and their silence disturbed her just the same.

With only two coils of road left, she saw the first of many Shadow Creatures. It looked like a dog coming across her trail only to vanish at the aluminum base of the adjacent trailer. It slunk, dripping of a slop shadow mass, acting as though it were on the hunt, as pieces of its sod body fell away and disappeared as soon as it was out of sight. Then, she saw a shadow buzzard perched in a tree. Its head scrambled as its wings fluttered without flight. Black snakes slithered, leaving a dissipating trail. Down the road, stood a Shadow Man, stagnant in its floating black water, but watching her nonetheless.

Catherine stepped out and onto her road, the last spiral. An early mist of fog rolled across the park. Catherine saw her place, knowing Nathan's was just a few steps beyond, but a new crop of Shadow Creatures flooded the road between them. Shadow rodents, felines, and reptiles moved in feverish scuttles. A wandering yellow mutt walked across the street. Limping as he came, he halted on the road. Catherine thought the dog ready to collapse and by instinct she moved to help him. The dog turned, facing her, and snarled, just before three lamprey Shadow Creatures covered his neck like a black flowing beard. He was foaming at the mouth and his saliva which oozed down became a succulent treat for the creatures. A black feline Shadow Creature jumped on his back as he disappeared behind a shed. The white pathway in front of her was blotted with hungry creatures of all magnitudes.

Gathering courage, Catherine ran for the finish line. The Shadow Creatures parted as she headed for Nathan's doorstep. Just around the bend of the road she faced a man dressed in black. She skidded in her boot tracks and came to a stop. His hat was tipped down. His step was light and carefree as he strolled down the road. He swung his cane like the conductor of a deaf man's song and the Shadow Creatures dispersed.

Artros.

Artros reached for her through the haze of thickening fog, beckoning, and challenging her resistance. Standing before him, she felt dormant particles of her essence drawn to him, awakened by his presence.

Catherine was determined to fight. His magnetism pounded her as though she were threads of a loom and he the weaver. Catherine fought the urge within to submit and drew against him. She gained a foothold and ran for Nathan's door. For each one of her footsteps he gained ten. Close to Nathan's she halted, afraid Artros would crush her. Artros stopped. He tilted the cane towards her and she felt its threat, but she wouldn't back down.

She tested another step forward, challenging him with the move. He countered with one long stride of his own. She swelled with spite and took another step forward, willing him to dare and take her.

Artros stepped back. Each movement between them a tango until Catherine was confident she was leading. Encouraged, she quickened her pace. Then, Artros did something Catherine didn't expect. He halted and reached a hand up to his hat. Catherine feared it was a movement of trickery. But Artros simply tipped his hat to her and bowed gracefully before whirling around with a spin from his cane. He proceeded to walk in the opposite direction, without another motion of farewell.

Watching him walk away, Catherine felt joy—he'd merely left by her bold steps against him. With a snip of a grin, she ran up Nathan's porch steps.

Reaching for the knob, she was ready to enter Nathan's home unannounced. Her elation faltered with the sound of tussling inside. This wasn't the same as other trailers, filled with thrashing anger. No. This was the sound of panting breath and whispered words.

She listened at the door.

Another sound came from within. A giggle, followed by heavy movement.

Catherine hit the door with her fist.

"No," a girl's voice rang with laughter. "Don't answer it."

"Ahhhh," a voice like Nathan's sounded. "You don't know how much this pleases me right now." But the tone was different, tainted, and unfamiliar to her.

"Do I please you?" the girl asked with seductive ache.

"You will," Nathan's foiled voice said again. "Oh, you will."

Unable to withstand the torment, Catherine burst through the door.

The living room was ransacked. Cushions and pillows lay strewn from the couch, alongside torn newspaper and clothing. Dishes on the kitchen table were pushed back in a U-shaped form, where a cup of coffee was knocked over, drained of its liquid that soiled the floor. A chair had fallen on its side next to a radio playing static beeps and pitched squeals from an AM frequency.

The smell of sweat and flesh repelled Catherine. Quivering in revulsion, she witnessed Nathan on the living room floor, atop of Melissa who laid groaning underneath. Undressed to lace underwear, Melissa arched her body to Nathan's bare chest. One of his hands held him above her, while his other gripped her hair and pulled her head from side to side. She grabbed his belt, unbuckled it and slid it from his waist and proceeded to whip his back in a playful tease. He grazed upon her pink nipple with his lips and tongue before brushing it with his cheek. His eyes were closed as he turned his head toward Catherine in primal satisfaction. His hand moved from Melissa's head and down to her breast. He moved like an erect snake above her, only to dip back down to taunt his willing prey, who in turn, thrust her throbbing lust to him with each stroke. Her panting chest glistened with sweat. Both were oblivious to Catherine.

Nathan's back was marbled with claw marks. Melissa flung the belt across his back and held onto its ends. She wrapped her legs around the denim of his torso in an attempt to pull him down. She cried out in yearning, demanding him to face her. But Nathan's eyes opened and stared straight at Catherine.

Catherine saw the Darkness within.

"You punish me," Nathan's tainted voice said, "and I will punish you."

It wasn't Nathan, and yet the venom scorched her. It was the breaking key in a string of notes. A gagging came to her throat and she thought she might vomit. She wanted to yell "Nathan wake up," but she knew the sound of her voice alone wouldn't awaken him from this possession. She didn't know how to fight it. In grief and defeat, she wondered if Nathan was able to comprehend this nightmare. She recognized her folly when she congratulated herself for defeating Artros. What she watched in this room was the ringleader at work. This was punishment. The game was refined and she was a hostage to its outcome. Artros was inside Nathan, operating his body as though it were a machine with gears and eyes. He enjoyed her torment as she looked upon the only thing she loved in the world being manipulated because of her defiance.

A flood of tears followed her as she ran from the depraved scene. She had no choice, she could only return to her trailer. She slowly opened the door and scanned the dimming trailer for Artros. Its silence roared caution. The evening's sun and draping fog made the trailer glow a gray dusk of desolation. Within, all was motionless. Even the shadows.

Since she was a young child, Catherine wanted nothing more than to curl up in the arms of another. She moved down the hallway, taking soft footsteps to Kathy's door. She knew the woman on the other side of the door couldn't, wouldn't, offer her the solace she needed. And she'd never ask. She edged close and listened at the door. Again, she heard nothingness. She cracked a small opening, enough to peer in. A light flickered from a ceiling light fixture and two mice scattered into their hiding places. She choked at the smell of tainted flesh.

Kathy lay upturned, sprawled on the bed, cradling her empty bottle. Her face looked as blue as her eyes had been in another life, before liquor and death turned them gray.

Catherine quivered. Kathy was dead and her childhood with it. Once, she had wanted to call this woman Mother, the one who sheltered her in spite and showed her the world through a dark face. But like all children dream,

Catherine desired one of healing. She yearned for the bond that existed between a mother and daughter. She dreamed in nightly vignettes of a mother who loved her, dressed her in tidy dresses, tied her hair in bows and massaged away the aloneness in her tiny heart.

It would never be. That dream died like a tomorrow in her life and couldn't be salvaged. She closed the door to her mother's bedroom and stood in front of its pealing ply and crusted smudge. She started to beat and kick its hollow inlay, causing splintering holes and scraped bloody hands, but the room was quiet. Kathy left Catherine with a lasting emptiness.

She needed to change out of her wet clothes, but as she stood outside her bedroom door, looking in at the mattress on the floor, the garbage bags she'd used as drawers, and the pillow-towels as curtains, she feared if she stepped inside, she'd be swallowed up.

The furnace kicked on and off. The metal siding creaked. She heard voices of other residents next to her as their shouts carried through the walls. It was only she and her dead mother. No one came. Not Artros, nor Jorgen, nor Nathan.

And if they did come, no lock could stop them.

Catherine curled up on the couch and held herself, as she always had, with her eyes fixed on the door.

Watching a lamb run into a burning field was how Jorgen felt as he beheld Catherine's return to Artros. He had let her go. No matter her intentions, he gave his word to protect her despite driving her back to ruin. Anger rose up in Jorgen, and for all his attempts to soothe it, it was hovering on the edge of rage. If he allowed the anger of Darkness to consume him, then all hope would be lost for Catherine . . . and for him.

That was the nature of the beast, the Darkness. Once caged, it wanted nothing more than freedom. It was wild in substance and black of heart. If the Darkness took hold, vengeance would be merciless, and only the ones left standing would have wished they'd fallen, if only for beholding the sight of its retribution.

Anger and rage were sisters. Jorgen had to be careful they didn't make contact with each other. Only a Master of Darkness could balance the two and it had been a very long time since Jorgen claimed himself to be exactly what he was, one with the Darkness.

For the first time in decades, Jorgen hated. The heat of that hatred was building. It grew without boundaries. Love and Light. They were a song that would never compose itself. The wind between his fingers he couldn't catch. A portrait without a face. All inventions of his delusion. Searching, he realized he was lost on their path and he forgot himself. Watching Catherine run into Artros' snare, he saw himself, young and ignorant, embracing the arms of Darkness before he even knew what held him.

Jorgen contemplated a thousand thoughts in a heartbeat. He had little time.

He would save Catherine, if not for the Light, then for innocence. She was still pure, and that alone was something worth saving. In doing so, he was crossing the point of no return.

Incapable of redemption, he would attempt to rescue Catherine by using the power she had unknowingly given him. He would be her dark knight and use his cache of weaponry, no matter how brutal, to keep the chastity of her soul intact.

Catherine's power flourished within Jorgen. He soaked in its dark luster and used its strength to gather more from the outside world.

He despised the vow he made her, and the righteousness which filled it. But he couldn't keep the vow without invoking the Darkness. The Master he presumed to leave behind, and the one he wanted to become, a man of honor, could not exist when it came to the dark powers. Darkness had a way of taking a man and destroying any trace of what he once was. He was swirling and manipulating the power Catherine gave him, planning to use those powers against her.

Shadow Creatures were akin to the Darkness they were energized by. A multitude, free from Artros' command, hovered and rummaged around the grounds he claimed and more were coming to the town. Magnetized by the gluttonous and hyperactive Shadow Creatures inside of Artros' dome, they lingered at the borders like lepers to be fed. These sporadic offspring of Darkness were excluded from the inside border, as Artros had not yet called them into his army. And so they swayed and bent, burrowed and soared around Catherine. They tested its borders one at a time for a way in, to absorb and reap the threads their beastly brethren feasted upon, who mutated and grew stronger by the hour.

Inside Artros' dome, Shadow Creatures suckled the residents dry of their moral thoughts by leaching off their life force. It contaminated the people like poisoned water and these black parasites created a lunacy of bitterness and treachery from their strength in numbers and length of stay. Those on their deathbeds would lash out at their caregivers who in turn walked away from their loved ones without remorse. They would die first, the ill and injured. Next, the will that drives the soul and turns the wheels of a man's violent desires into action would be the ones seeded with vengeance, lust and greed. Last would be the children, flux in emotions and restraint, who even couldn't be trusted in Darkness such as this.

The Shadow Creatures were here too long. The people were caving in on themselves.

At the outskirts of Artros' guard, a band of Shadow Creatures lingered, searching for a way to break through the great dome. Jorgen saw them, knowing what he must do.

Jorgen needed to clear his thoughts and let the Master within take control. He longed to rise above the Darkness, to become a man of virtue and mercy. But if he were to stand against Artros, then he could be neither. He must transform into the man he couldn't face. A man of insatiable hunger filling his plate with wrath for the life he was starved of.

Jorgen was ready to balance the scales between anger and rage and see which scale outweighed the other. But they could never equal his pain. Only Catherine, or death, could lighten the burden he carried. No matter the outcome, he believed the end would set him free.

Alone with the Darkness, Jorgen let it direct the sails. A captain was hopeless without the wind, but Jorgen stood, feeling it come toward him in an energizing rush. Midnight waters moved at his feet. The inviting dark power broke through. He succumbed to it and let it blow and burn through him. He directed it, and its salty taste for vengeance, causing him to become stronger all the while.

Jorgen could almost talk to the Darkness. Understanding its nature, the way it moved and the way it breathed inside of him was an essence of the unspoken brought to words. The more he let the anger breed, the stronger its power and retaliation. If he couldn't control it, then it would come back and bite him with its wrath. That was a true Master's achievement, control, and as long as he held, the Darkness couldn't take over. To maintain focus, he visualized Catherine as the Light. Once he reached the dome, he would allow the Darkness its due, wreaking havoc to the Shadow

Creatures of Artros guard, and the unfortunate innocents within its path.

Jorgen was coming for Catherine without reservations. If it be a thief he was, then a bloody one he would have to be.

He called the wandering Shadow Creatures to him from outside the dome and from afar. They came. The Shadow Creatures harkened to his command and advanced with him, without mercy or status. All flesh and structures were equal through the indifference of Darkness. Compassion could not be known if he were to take her.

Unifying Shadow Creatures triangulated and multiplied behind Jorgen as he came for Catherine.

He was moving once again to challenge his old Master. This time without the weakness of love to hold him back.

To uphold a vow to save Catherine, he had to break a vow and use the wrench of Darkness, which shined absolute when its temper took over.

CHAPTER SEVENTEEN

A rabid fever overtook the trailer park. Catherine huddled on the couch, pulling her arms and legs closer, but she couldn't stop their quake. The door remained closed, but the madness was spilling out of the homes and into the street. Voices shouted in hatred at one another. With the bouts came the squealing of tires before a crash. She heard its aftermath in the screams of the collisions as metal crashed into windshields, car doors opening, and fights ensuing. Sounds of firecrackers cracked in rapid succession, followed by unmistakable gunshots. The people were ripping their world apart and the earth would be there to swallow them.

The only light in the trailer came from the lampposts outside. They flickered on and off, like silent lightning and people its thunder. When the lights went out, the gray fog became black curtains over her living room window. In false hope, she thought the chaos diminished with a break of sudden silence. Instead, it escalated as if it had reached the top of a cliff, ready to plummet into despair. Mercy was not to be found outside.

Through the shouts, Catherine recognized one of her neighbors' voices, Janice Peterson. She bellowed that her husband was dead as she wandered, lost. She'd nursed Harold since Parkinsons crippled his body. The love between them was never in question. And even now, as she shrieked into the night words of "good riddance" and "shackled me down," Catherine knew this was not to be her true feelings. *Lunacy*, Catherine thought.

Hearing a woman of character, like Janice, become one with the cyclone of insanity, Catherine lost faith Nathan would be able to save himself. She wanted to gather courage and go back to him, but even though his body was there, he was not. Artros was. He'd been true to his word and she blamed herself for Nathan's undoing even though Jorgen made accusations against Nathan. And if he wasn't possessed, he might be roaming mad like the rest of the people. To her, it was the same. She wondered if at any moment she, too, might walk out the door and join the people's fury and bloodlust. She didn't know what to do. She felt trapped on a deserted island surrounded by blazing fires and it was only a matter of time before they incinerated her.

Routinely, she clutched the necklace. She felt it in her hand and understood the gravity of Jorgen's gift, its protection, and the reality that even the body couldn't be trusted when it should be the one place a person could hide.

With a loud bang, something hit the side of the trailer where she lay. She didn't move. She heard footsteps on the porch, followed by a struggle and the grunting of men, but still she didn't move. Then there was silence, but only for a moment. The pounding footsteps returned and the door opened.

Catherine sat up.

It was Sam.

One of his eyes was swollen half shut. Splatters and streaks of blood covered his face and neck, but it was not his own. The top buttons of his flannel were torn off and his jeans were wet and stained reddish brown. His wild eyes caught sight of her. Panting heavy breaths, he kicked the door shut with his unlaced steel-toe boot. Sam cocked his head from side to side while cracking his inflamed knuckles. He straightened his neck, gritted his teeth, and said, "Come for payment."

"No!" Catherine yelled, jumping off the couch as he rushed her. Unable to withstand the blow, she was shoved back onto the couch as his weight plowed on top of her.

His body smothered her as he used his mass and strength to hold her down. Her legs were trapped underneath, but she swung her arms at him, clawing and hitting his face and shoulders. Broken couch springs dug into her back. Catherine felt him harden between her thighs as he rubbed himself in agitated motions attempting to keep her in place.

"You owe me," Sam said foaming above her while he spoke, slobbering onto her neck and lips. "And you're gonna keep owin' till I gits it all outta you. Your ever lovin' pussy is gonna love it too. That'll teach yah. You're gonna git a lesson in owing . . . soooo gooood . . . that when you're all paid up . . ." Sam cut off, finally able to grip her lashing hands within his and pull them back behind her head. His face bent over hers and she could smell his rancid breath of liquor and meat. He continued, "You're going ta gimme a deposit for the next month's rent, and the next, and the . . ." but before Sam could say anything else, Catherine stopped him with the only part of her body left to move, her head. She slammed her forehead into his face. His wet teeth imprinted her skull and broke the skin.

She was dazed. He tilted back and wiped some of the blood away from his bleeding nose. It was enough to free one of her hands struggling for escape. The moment didn't last. Sam struck back at her tenfold. He punched her in the stomach with all his strength. In that instant Catherine felt the air and life inside of her leave.

Her mouth gaped open for breath. She felt the top button of her jeans coming undone. In his fever, Sam fought to undo the simple hole and knob, as he pulled and ripped, instead of unfasten.

Watching Sam's hands claw at her jeans, Catherine felt her fear and pain drain away. She released it all. Sam broke the button and moved his hands across her waist and began to pull its denim down. Her body became numb and Catherine felt like she was breathing without air, but this strange breath filled her all the same.

In letting go, Catherine was awakened to another sensation expanding inside of her. The feeling started in her gut where Sam laid his blow and flourished outside of her body like a blossoming petal without a tip. Her head turned away from Sam, she could feel it reaching and lengthening in the dark. She lost herself to the awakening that grew inside her. Catherine tilted her head up and saw Sam scraping her thighs with his blunt nails as her jeans were pulled down to her knees and removed. Still, Catherine felt nothing other than the bloom in the dark.

Fear did not enter her mind as she lay in her shirt and underwear like a doll on the couch. Sam stood and unzipped himself. Catherine directed her attention on him and his rampant lust. While she was without feeling of the flesh, simple words entered her mind watching Sam. Vile. Disgust. Foul. Hate. She focused on him. She saw her essence extend and then retract in a bowing motion above her. It curved as it came in closer and spiraled like a seductive black lotus towards Sam.

Sam, now free to the knees of his pants and underwear, turned back to Catherine. As he moved to flop onto her, he found himself suddenly suspended in midair with his hands held out like he was pushing against an invisible wall of air. Shock and horror covered his face as he was pushed back and upright, trying to understand what unseen force was moving him backwards from the couch.

His open mouth was speechless and void of anything other than the spit it held. Terror solidified his face. He was erect in a standing position, but hovered a foot off the floor. His wide eyes looked down, but his face could not, as his flesh was frozen against him. Catherine sat up, filled with scorn and malice, unquestioning the power that held him at bay.

Then a word spoke in Catherine's mind. One of her own, but one influenced by everything she'd ever encountered by this monster of a man before her. *Undone*. The word in her mind rang. She wanted him *undone*, never to feel, or think anything from him again.

The word was ready to work her bidding. Sam's arms became unfrozen as his hands made their way to his chest and the flesh exposed under his unbuttoned shirt. His eyes rolled around like cue balls as his mouth opened for the wail he couldn't release. His fingers pressed on his skin and then entered the flesh of his body, soaking in like putty before they tore oozing red and blue seams into it. The skin of his chest rippled where his fingers moved inside as they stroked and then gripped his rib cage. Each finger hooked a rib of its own and cracked them, one by one as the bones chipped away. Sam's body started to piece itself out, one bone at a time.

Undone, Catherine pulsated. All of him—Undone.

Nathan awoke on his living room floor where the carpet imprinted his face. Sitting in the corner of the room, he saw Melissa's shuddering naked legs bent up to her chest. He was drained and disordered by a painful prickle covering his body. He hitched himself up on his elbows to look around, to try to make sense of the room he'd known all his life. The room started to spin, causing a state of vertigo. He steadied his eyes back down to the worn fibers of the carpet and tried to remember what color they were meant to be. A small whimper came from Melissa's corner.

"Melissa?" Nathan asked in a daze. Shouts and screaming from outside confused him all the more. For a short time he thought the voices came from his head, but realized otherwise. The trailer park was on fire and the people its matches.

As Nathan slowly perked his head up, finally able to focus on Melissa and her quivering lips, a black high-heeled boot stepped on his hand and ground its spike into it. The swing of a long fur coat brushed his face. As his memory returned, he knew it could be none other than Esa.

Artros . . . he thought, but lost his thoughts again. Then, he recalled a gift, a Melissa, but all was empty after that. Only his pants covered him. He could have thought of a hundred scenarios, but he knew one thing was evident and it stung through the claw marks on his back.

Esa's heel spun around on his hand as she pivoted to cross the room. Swinging away from them, Melissa's breast dragged on the floor as she bent to her side attempting to crawl towards Nathan steadying himself on his elbows again. The movement didn't go unnoticed. Esa whirled around and grabbed the back of Melissa's neck and hair with one hand.

"Artros wants Catherine," Esa said, lifting Melissa off the ground and up to face her. Melissa's legs were strings under Esa's clutch. Her body was spotted with welts where blood dripped. Some of her hair had been ripped from her head. A few of the loose clumps stuck to her wet face, bleeding mascara from her eyes. She whined as Esa looked at her with disgust and continued, "Jorgen wants her. But you know what?" Esa asked to no one. "I don't need her!"

Esa finished, crushing Melissa's neck like an eggshell. Nathan heard the crunching of bones. Melissa's face relaxed of all fear and life even though her body continued to spasm. Esa dropped her like a dirty rag and flicked her fingers to free her hand of the few strands of Melissa's hair clinging between them.

"The older Artros becomes the more weakness he shows in his reserve," Esa said to herself and returned to her pacing. Nathan was afraid to look at her or Melissa's empty eyes staring back at him. "That's why he chose me," Esa said with justification. "Above all women, he chose me. Because . . . I have always been a little reckless. Especially when it comes to the Darkness. That's why he wanted me," Esa gloated. "That's why he will want me still. I know what's best for him—for us. And I won't have another woman, not even a woman—a child . . ." Esa yelled before her voice simmered down, "come between us. I don't need to see her, to know she's nothing more than a vagrant girl who has captured his interest. But not for long." Esa stopped in front of Nathan, who was afraid to question or anger the goddess towering above him. "And you," Esa said, tipping her boot on his forehead, tilting his head up to her. "You will please me. It's been a long time since I've indulged myself."

"Get up!" she commanded, kicking her boot off him. Nathan struggled to lift his body, still unfamiliar to him. It felt as though it was weaving itself back together with pinpricking needles. Weakened, he attempted to rise as quickly as he could. Slouching before Esa, Nathan dared not look into her flaring eyes, knowing one cross move might crush him like Melissa's delicate pale neck.

"You are so naïve," Esa said, gently lifting Nathan's chin to hers in false sympathy. "We're going to have to tap into your raw innocence of youthful yearning and stir the Master awake. He is dormant, you see. Sleeping in his dreams. But I will shake him of his illusions." Esa let go of Nathan and stepped back. "I am going to give you a taste of the power he has been withholding from you." Her fabricated compassion dropped, along with the soft features of her face. Devious crafting spun within her thoughts. Nathan tensed and he braced himself, unsure of what was coming. But Esa quickly lost interest in him as her head snapped to the wall of the trailer. Nathan realized she wasn't looking at the wall. She was looking past it, to the outside, where Nathan could not see.

"Jorgen is coming," she said with distracted delight. Nathan saw a fleeting smile part her lips which quickly contorted into one of revulsion. "He comes with an army," she said aloud as if contemplating what she saw. "He knows I am here . . . but . . . he does not come for me . . . " Esa said raising her voice into a screaming spitfire. "He is coming for *her*!" The walls shook and the furniture rattled. Photos fell, lights swung, and a shelf came down with his little league plaque next to his father's bowling trophy.

Esa turned back to Nathan with soulless black eyes. He felt a hot surge enter his body that rejuvenated him with a flood of adrenalin. He stood face-to-face with all the misgivings, contempt and pining thirst he'd ever had and left unsatisfied. He never considered himself a man of vengeance, but this awakening anger inside him put his tepid nature to rest and the fuel of Darkness forward. He was empowered by it. He knew without Esa's explanation what she'd done to him. He could take Catherine, by will or force, and walk away from Artros at the same time. He wouldn't run. No. He had the Darkness now. He would leave, defiant to the men in black. He was immortal. He felt victory in anger, and it willed him to take exactly what he wanted in its vigor.

Esa looked pleased as Nathan reeled in the power she granted him. He was not afraid of her, only thankful she'd given him this gift, this Darkness that Artros had been too weak to bestow.

"Take her and go," Esa said in farewell. Nathan turned and left. He didn't bother with a shirt or shoes, walking outside to the anarchy of the street, where people ran, cursed, and brawled. He saw the Shadow Creatures swarming and feeding off the people and draining them. Engine and trash fires burned out of control and smoke rose from a neighbor's house. Nathan took no notice. He was invincible.

Jorgen came with his black pyramid of Shadow Creatures rippling out behind him with flanks of the stronger in front followed by the weakest. To his right and left were two Shadow Men. One he called from the graveyard, where mourners gathered to bury their dead and another from a rental complex where it resided to absorb the negative energy of its tenants. Anyone who looked upon Jorgen saw a man in black walking down the center of the road, but if they were close, they would see the snow melting underneath his black boots where he stepped and feel the rise in temperature behind his back. Behind, and to the sides of him, dead oak leaves rustled without wind, reflections of disfigured shadows scathed the windshields of vehicles, and the windows of houses, without a figure to connect them. Fire hydrants popped caps with a gush of water, car tires flattened, and streetlight bulbs shattered. The Shadow Creatures knew no borders of streets or walls and passed through the homes of innocents. Those crossing their path felt an uncanny dread followed by fatigue and the impulse to weep without reason. Electrical units flickered on and off. Dishwashers and disposals started, stoves ignited, televisions and small appliances fluxed with energizing pulses.

Jorgen tapped into Catherine's energy which would be bound with his for a time since she gave the dark power to him. Feeling her connection in wavelengths, she started to radiate a disturbing rhythm. It shifted to excruciating distress like her spirit was bracing itself in the middle of a typhoon and she was doing everything to hang on. Her vibrations whirled around him with great energy and strength. But then he was abruptly disconnected, blocked and inaccessible for all his reaching. The only thing he could connect to was the necklace which had been a staple of his protection for so long. The necklace was still at Catherine's home and that's where he was headed.

He saw the trailer park ahead where Artros' Shadow Creatures were unifying. Forced to cease their voracious feeding upon the residents, they gathered towards the edge of the dome in a spherical formation, directed at Jorgen and his army. The Shadow Creatures swayed with anticipation waiting for their Master's next command.

Jorgen stood on the hearth of his destruction or Catherine's deliverance. One would come either way.

The unifying mass of Shadow Creatures cast a windstorm in the park. Paper and loose debris tossed about and telephone lines swung. The gust of their movements caused sporadic flames to rise, threatening to engulf the park at any given time. Flames of those fires brightened as lampposts' lights flickered on and off. The park looked like it was under a gigantic strobe light, beating in radical pulses through the thick evening fog. The residents' life-threads were drained or sucked completely dry. In a few of those flashes, some residents witnessed the Shadow Creatures winding together in the massive dark ball. Some thought the Devil himself patched out a little piece of earth to call his Eden. Other people brandished guns, while some fired at the Shadow Creatures in the air or at one another. A young man chased a girl with a baseball bat. She screamed as she ran down the road before she failed to yield in front of an oncoming car that didn't bother to brake even after it plowed her over. A woman chased another woman with a bloody knife raised to her peer's bloodstained back. Pets turned wild and the birds pecked and tore out the intestines of their predators. Cats and people alike climbed trees to escape their tormenters, but no matter who saw the Shadow Creatures, none of them would want to remember this night and the phantom torture that brought a madness which ate away their souls and rotted their hearts against them.

The affliction of Darkness manifested in many ways. Centuries passed since Jorgen knew one to affect a community to this degree. But the devastation in the dome couldn't match what was coming.

As Jorgen advanced, his hands extended in front of him with his palms facing each other, appearing as though he was trying to sculpt the air into a sphere and hold it in his hands. But he was collecting Darkness and shaping it into an orb. The power caused his arms to shake as it took great strength and control to hold this form. Jorgen couldn't unleash it until his army had made a hole in Artros' shield of some kind.

Observing the park and Artros' army held at bay, Jorgen looked through the black mass, the residents and their homes, and farther into the trailer park to the Master's command post. Artros was working the dark art. He saw Artros holding an orb of Darkness like his, but Artros was sending this orb into his staff which spun rapidly with a gyrating motion in front of him. The staff could hold multiple orbs of Darkness at one time while Artros created another. The staff would disperse an orb in any path he chose, or a multitude of directions if he armed it with more than one. The staff worked like a cannon for orbs while Artros pulled more energy within him at the same time to refill the staff with power once it was released. Jorgen had only his hands and the use of one orb at a time. If Artros sent an orb at Jorgen now, he would take out some of his Shadow

Creatures inside of the dome. Like a bullet, the dark power knew not friend or foe, only direction.

Jorgen's army was half the size of Artros' and he didn't have a weapon of power like the staff. Artros carried the nature of an instinctive general in his thirst for power, whereas Jorgen was a man of solitude and studied the world and its refinement through its diverse elements. If he was to defeat Artros, he would have to find a way to overcome the tactics of battle with his quiet knowledge of insight.

The first flank Jorgen directed was the lesser of the Shadow Creatures. The lampreys, rats, hedgehogs and others of the like came from the back to attack the bottom of Artros' defense, while ones like bats, ravens, and owls soared above to dive straight into the top of the dome. Artros' creatures were ready to obey their Master and protect the gluttonous feast they spoiled upon. A quarter of Jorgen's army was overwhelmed instantly and the others were soon to disintegrate. He hoped to pull some of the larger Shadow Creatures away from the border, but Artros mastered them well and would not falter. Jorgen had to keep moving forward while he tried to think of a way to penetrate the shield.

Artros made the next move. He attacked with numerous ranging Shadow Creatures, lessening the protection of his shield, but in doing so created another obstacle in front of Jorgen. Jorgen held the burning black orb in one hand and used his other like a conductor, calling his shadows to rise and counter the attack. Creatures without sound, they tore into each other with their shadow mouths, hooves and talons all the same. Dark Shadow Creatures of the earth, and unknown, they fought without blood, screams and weapons. Only the dark shadow flesh and nothing more. Their clash and destruction felt like the aftershocks of a quake, an electric charging of the air, and dry heat which wouldn't allow the pores to bead. Jorgen sent his canine, raptors and thin stallion line to battle. His forces would soon be annihilated.

Still, Jorgen couldn't use the orb in his hands. Jorgen felt Artros' pride exhuming itself over the battle ground as another division of Artros' Shadow Creatures were sent in, and then another, and another. Jorgen sent in more to counter them as he watched his outnumbered army depleting. Soon, nothing would be left of them. *Nothing would be left of them*, Jorgen thought, *nothing*.

Shadow Creatures were made of nothing. A dark nothing. And like a disease, their dark essence infected the world. Yet, the Shadow Creatures knew how to survive in their nothingness. They knew without knowing. Shadow Creaturos knew combat. They knew the rage of man, the suffering of bloodshed, and the mourning cries of the battleground and the burial of the dead. They knew all of this because they had a purpose of their own and their purpose was to consume. Under a Master's hand, they are the wind to his pull, a feral canine to chain, and a savage trapped in ice. They thirst like a foaming horse to the bit, a rabid dog, and lockjaw. Jorgen had to find a way to overcome the Shadow Creatures, not in combat, but by their nature. And he had to do it now.

Jorgen divided what was left of his restless army and released his unholy mass, dispersing commands even as his hunger-driven black serpents, bulls and wolves rushed passed him. Two waves crashed into the battling Shadow Creatures in front. One joined the combat and the other broke around it and headed for the people, to the poor tortured souls within the dome. He commanded this flank to feed, to fill, and consume all they would for their empty hunger.

Jorgen watched the Shadow Creatures fight and his forces being destroyed. But like the shifting of sand through the sieve, Artros' army was rebelling against his command, sensing Jorgen's second battalion latch onto the residents in which they had feasted upon for so long. Greedy as their emptiness was, they started to pull away from the battle to protect and defend what was left of their banquet.

As the Shadow Creatures dispersed the battlefield and the wall of defense, Jorgen saw a small gap had been created and left unprotected near the top. If he could see it, then Artros would too. Jorgen pulled his arms back and threw the orb in his hands into the park, straight at Artros. The black ball streaked like a burning coal flame. Artros was quick to react and sent a large orb from the spinning staff in front of him as he supplied the staff with another before the first made impact. Jorgen was left with his hands, his only weapon which was working to gather another orb of Darkness against Artros' fully automatic staff.

Their orbs collided above the trailer park. The force of their power created a black explosion with a thundering shock. The remnants of its power trickled down in the sky like electric eels. The battleground of the earth and air sounded like the titans of old had awakened from their legend graves, swinging axe and sword against one another. The sound deafened the ears of the people rioting about, shaking them from their insanity. The innocents which befell the Shadow Creatures torments were not healed, only roused from their disease that had fed upon them. Instead of terrorizing each other in that sickness, they dispersed in all directions. Some fled the park. Others ran for their homes, even a few were set afire to see if their loved ones were dead or alive, crossing over immobile bodies and blood-stained snow.

The Shadow Creatures were not deterred by the sound, only heightened by its blast, tearing each other apart and absorbing the essence of the fallen. Bulls and boars fought against each other, while leeches and rats nibbled away on top of the black mass of the fighting pairs. Cougars jumped atop of stallions' backs, while snakes wrapped up the legs of another shades' body. Shadows on both sides fluxed, acquiring energy while others dispelled it. Some were climbing the ladder of supremacy, as their rat-formed bodies transformed into ones like felines, vultures, or boars from the energy they absorbed. Others, shred of their wild fibers of Darkness, were shrinking as their brethren fed off them and soaked in their essence. Now, the Shadow Creatures belonged to no Master.

The only ones Jorgen commanded to stay were two Shadow Men that walked like phantoms by his side, deviant as Shadow Creatures, but closer to the merciless nature of mankind. Artros had six under his control which were sent to annihilate Jorgen's forces, but even they were falling into the desire to ingest their own empty hunger like the Shadow Brethren they'd been sent to destroy.

The dome was shattered. Broken fragments of Shadow Creatures lashed about and the Masters would hold no reserves in destroying each other. Without a tool, like the staff, Jorgen was still balling another orb in his hands as Artros set two black orbs at him. One by land and one from the sky.

Jorgen didn't have time to harness the energy needed to defend against the two. He hoped the orb in his hands would be strong enough to stop the one rolling at him like a boulder of lava across the park, tilling trailers up like weeds and annihilating anyone or anything in its path.

Jorgen unleashed the orb from his hands. It crashed into Artros' orb. The explosion crumbled a side of the trailer park. The second orb was making its descent and closing in on Jorgen. With the hand of Darkness, Jorgen picked up one of the Shadow Men and threw it at the second orb in the sky. Quickly, Jorgen created a thin shield of protection over him as the two collided above him. The impact obliterated the orb and Shadow Man into a cascade of melting nothingness which liquefied the snow and scorched the earth in their diffusion.

Artros was fueling the staff with smaller deadly orbs, ones Jorgen knew he wouldn't be able to avoid. In a rash decision, he threw his last Shadow Man directly at Artros to divert the impending attack. As Jorgen thrust the Shadow Man forward, leaving Artros no choice but to block it, Jorgen used the dark power to leap through the air behind the Shadow Man and cross the trailers to Catherine's street where Artros worked the dark art. As the Shadow Man threatened to land a blow, Artros' concentration broke and the staff in front of him sent out a swarm of orbs without a course. In mid-flight, Jorgen bent to the side to avoid an orb, but in doing so another orb scathed his leg and tore a hole through his coat. It branded his calf and ate into his flesh with its fiery embers like black maggots.

Artros obliterated the Shadow Man in front of Jorgen. He shielded himself with his hands and flew through the blast. Molten cinders struck him, burning small holes into his clothes and hands. Jorgen landed on Catherine's street, cracking the snow-covered asphalt in landing, and washed the orb's remnants from his leg with the swipe of his hand. Artros seethed as he beckoned his Shadow Generals to his side. They did not harken to his call. His empty staff was still spinning, ready to be filled with another orb.

Something nearby was unsettling the air. It was the work of Darkness from a Master's hand, but it was different in its dark vitality and it came from Catherine's trailer. He wondered if Esa was stationed somewhere behind him, ready to protect Artros, but Jorgen did not feel the woman. With the slide of Artros' eye to Catherine's, Jorgen realized his old Master felt its presence too, but the presence would have to wait.

Jorgen knew he didn't have an opportunity left for maneuvers or strategy. The moment was now. It was one animal against another and he would degrade his opponent to the very beings they were, Beast of Darkness. Jorgen had depleted his power controlling the Shadow Creatures, creating the orbs, and taking flight. But Artros was weakened as well. Jorgen would soon find out their degrees of power as he was ready to unleash all he had upon his old Master. If he lived to be critically wounded, like the last battle between them, Artros would devour any particles left of his dark essence.

Jorgen summoned the Darkness. Every fiber of the power Catherine gave him, he built into a titanic surge. The power filled him to the limit of his being and he unleashed it onto Artros still harnessing the Darkness. Jorgen's power moved at turbine speed, spiraling and tightening as it came at Artros. He tried to thwart it off like a matador using the shield of Darkness for a cape. But the power struck Artros. He was propelled backwards. Artros' body flagged away with his coat rippling in the wind, over the homes and out of sight. Jorgen wasn't sure if he wounded his foe or delivered death's blow. He reached to find Artros' dark power, but with the Darkness afoot in the night and saturating everything around it was too hard to distinguish. Artros' hat and cane lay on the ground, powerless without their Master.

Jorgen's first impulse was to grab the cane and break it in two, but he didn't have time for self-indulgence. His blow was greater than he could have imagined, but how much time he had, he wasn't sure.

Within a few strides he made it to Catherine's. He ran on adrenalin only. The dark power was almost depleted. The presence was here. Catherine was here. Inhaling, he opened her door.

The atrocity before his eyes couldn't be matched for any soul he'd ever laid eyes on. Catherine was standing before an unstable mass of guts, skin and blood. It was only recognizable as human by the eyes that gyrated around the revolving flesh which still held a vision of horror in its pupils. The flesh was undone, but not extinguished. The intestines were shooting out and around like atom rings in brutal design. The bones started to liquefy, dripping marrow droplets onto the dog-eared carpet below. Catherine stood in her shirt and underwear. Her hair was knotted in sweat around her black eyes as she stabbed the pieces of flesh in front of her with a knifing gaze.

Astounded, Jorgen saw only one of the multiple loops of Darkness inside of Catherine free and working its profane rapture on the specimen before her. Whatever caused it to break loose from the weave within her, traumatized her enough to set this band out and into this revolving mangled mass. Jorgen saw Nathan inside the trailer as well, bracing his spread-eagled body against the wall. The Darkness was inside of him, but it had only one gear compared to the machine he witnessed at work now. Jorgen didn't have time to question his presence, or the one whom had bestowed the dark power into him. He had to find a way to contain Catherine before the power of her full potential could spread, allowing it to reign over her and anyone that came in contact with it, including him.

"Catherine," Jorgen commanded. "Catherine, you must call it back."

Only a flare of a twitch registered in her placid face, as the rolling fragments in front of her started to disintegrate. The dark band shooting out from her was eager to find something else to grab.

"It will kill you Catherine," Jorgen said trying to maintain control. "Darkness wants nothing but to feed. I know how you feel. I know. But you must call it back!"

As the dark band finished off the leavings of the pieced out flesh, a corner of its black ribbon extended to Nathan. It scraped his bare chest and a small flame arose where it struck as if it ignited by the blood it drew. The dark band acted like a serpent, testing the flesh in snapping strikes, before it twisted and coiled around his body. Nathan screamed in agony and buckled over. Jorgen knew that even if Nathan understood how to wield this new power inside him, the boy could not stand against Catherine, not even this one stretch of Darkness reaching from her now. And neither could he.

The distorted humanoid before Catherine was snuffed to nothing. The rest of the band followed, teasing intoxicating pain through slashes which now moved in a fever upon Nathan. Catherine's head turned towards Nathan without pity or recognition inside her black eyes.

Carefully, Jorgen came to stand behind Catherine. He never expected that tonight the one who might be his undoing would be her. He was ready to take that chance. He would not flee. He was ready for the hand of death, even if it was Catherine's. Nathan's screams became strobe screeches as the pain was too great at times to even voice his torment. Suddenly, Nathan burst into flames and his body thrashed about the room, but the band from Catherine would not release him.

Jorgen placed a daring hand on her shoulder and whispered in her ear, "If you are to destroy the one thing that you love, then you have destroyed yourself as well."

Nathan's body burned red and black flames as he thrashed into the walls and furniture, catching them on fire. The band pursued Nathan. The living room was ablaze and reaching for the kitchen and back bedrooms. Catherine unknowingly cocooned herself, along with Jorgen, in a protective shell, where not even heat existed.

"Call the Darkness back. Catherine . . ." Jorgen said. "Call it back for Nathan."

Just when Jorgen thought it was impossible to reach her, a whimper of a word came out of Catherine's mouth. "Darkness . . ." she said, and then in stronger understanding, "Nathan." The night in her eyes started to recede and the band retracted from Nathan's coal burning body.

Along with the retreat, the shield around them started to shrink. Confusion and beads of sweat covered her face. The band was fully withdrawn and secured inside her. She yelled through the blazing inferno, "Nathan!" and reached out for him.

Jorgen clasped her hand, pulling her back. She fought, but only with the strength of the girl she was and not the power within. Her hair singed in curling disintegration and her shirt started to melt like balling wax. Jorgen knew they had but a second to escape. He was too weak to push the flames from them, or spare the time to save Nathan as well. She reached for Nathan, whose body was blackened all the way to his charred, bald head, as he flung himself about. Jorgen grabbed Catherine into his arms and lifted her up. She didn't fight him. She only reached out to Nathan, screaming his name. Jorgen kicked the burning door open and rushed outside.

Catherine was wailing as they came to the middle of the street. Jorgen held Catherine tight as he scanned for Artros. He was nowhere to be seen. But a black clad figure stepped onto the road and Jorgen saw Esa with her flowing long hair, loose in the waves he would watch bounce through the forest in the time when she wanted only him.

"Jorgen," she said, calling to entice him near with the sound of her syrup-filled voice she'd used on him ages ago. He would not be seduced by her deception. Jorgen moved again with Catherine in his arms, confidant that if Esa were here to stop him, she would have made her intentions known before she even uttered his name.

Catherine was limp in his arms, when suddenly her sobbing ceased and she started to struggle in his grasp. "Nathan. Nathan. Nathan!" she yelled. Trying to maintain his grip on her, he glanced back and saw Nathan stumbling out of the burning trailer. Smoke rose from his blackened body as he fell into the snow. Esa walked slowly toward

Nathan and Jorgen saw nothing more as he turned away from them. There was nothing else here for him.

Neither Esa, nor Artros pursued them. The Shadow Creatures had either dispersed, or lingered in the backdrop to feed off of the remaining residents that chose not to escape their demolished trailer park consumed in flames. One Master was wounded, or dead, and held no power over them, while the other simply released his grasp. The park sounded like a giant wad of burning paper within the sounds of popping and crackling. An occasional explosion interrupted the air, heavy with fog and choking smoke. The sirens of screams and madness had ceased. Those who chose to stay in the park were the ones who knew they could not live to see tomorrow with the mayhem they had witnessed or themselves created.

Crossing the field and onto the main road, Catherine whimpered Nathan's name. Jorgen did not know if Catherine would eventually understand how Nathan came to be wounded, and by any mortal right, should have met his demise.

And Jorgen didn't know if he would be able to tell Catherine that fire alone could not destroy the power of Darkness Nathan carried inside when she lashed out upon him. That same power would heal the boy in time. Jorgen knew Nathan would survive, but he didn't know how Catherine would if she knew. He couldn't take that chance. He had to protect her above all else. He would take her far away from this town and to the only place he knew could protect them for a time. His home. The one he'd spent years of solitude in and left, never believing he would return.

Jorgen carried Catherine off like a thief of the night, one in which he'd always feared he would become. And for this night, he was.

Cinder and smoke covered the graveyard of the trailer park. The inferno was seen for miles, but only now in the aftermath did the flashing lights of the rescue teams shine their weary beacons to this part of the town.

As they rolled in a steady pace around the circumference of the park, all knew there was nothing left to be salvaged, only the death count which would rise by morning. Firefighters, policemen, and volunteers stood away from the embers, all in silence. None knew what to say to each other, or the townspeople, as to the catastrophic events which took place in their quiet town these past few days. None of them knew themselves. They were only helping hands, stretched hands, and exhausted by the extension of their reach. They came, but even if they'd been here earlier, they would have made better witnesses than heroes for all they'd endured.

Lights spun around in a multitude of colors. Red, yellow, blue and white pulsed through the smoke-filled air in case someone could be harkened from the wreckage, toward them, and they might have the strength of heart, if not of their body, to help whatever wayward soul found them. Hope remained, but no one came.

Esa stood over Nathan. His charred body melted the snow around him. Placing her boot on his chest, she compressed it and heard a faint moan from the boy underneath. Esa wouldn't release him. She continued to press slow and hard into his smoke-filled cavity, when another moan came, followed by smoke that fumed from his mouth. Nathan's eyes popped open and Esa studied them with disapproval, even as the deviled whites and red lines of them looked to her for comfort or release from his misery.

Artros voice sounded behind her. "My Mistress," he accused, "never liked to get her hands dirty."

"Artros," Esa said spinning around to him, willing an embrace that was thwarted off.

"You will not be forgiven," Artros said, all but spitting his words at her. "Not of this."

"Artros," Esa pleaded. "You know me . . . and I know you . . ." she said trying to finger the nape of his collar as her lips fluttered. "She was no good for you—for us. She . . ."

"After all this time," Artros said, lifting his wooden staff to her throat, causing her to yield in unaccustomed fear, "you know nothing!"

"I—I sent the boy in . . . to get her for you . . ." Esa beseeched with a lie.

"I know you better than you know yourself Esa," Artros said pressing the staff into her throat. "Lies are unbecoming of a woman of power. And as your punishment for betrayal, you are going to grind for spoiling my affairs."

"What do you mean? I never . . ."

"You," Artros snapped, "my spoilt dear, are going to finish what you started. You are going to teach this boy the reckless power you bestowed upon him."

"Me? I can't. I never . . ." Esa protested.

"That's right—you never!" Artros said pushing her back and off his cane. Esa's head swiveled as if slapped. "And because you have, you will sacrifice for the consequences of your actions."

"No! I won't! He is but a —"

"Your *apprentice*, Esa. That is what he is to you now. You will be his Mistress from now on."

"And if I don't?" Esa questioned with a challenge.

"Then you will never be another's," Artros said as he turned from her without a word of farewell and strolled down a white strip of snow salvaged between molten metal, burnt cars and liquefied plastic. He reached up with his left hand and placed his hat upon his head while he swung his cane by his side with the rhythm of his walk.

    Dawn had broken as Esa watched him walk away before she looked down onto the charred boy, still cooling in the aftermath of the power she'd given him, and the ruin that same power brought.

    Esa heard Artros' voice as it faded away through the wreckage, "I have felt her emptiness and stroked her silent soul. I smell her heartless scent and taste her breath. In the blinding sun her love echoes to me, Darkness. Light.

ACKNOWLEDGMENTS

I've come a long way from standing in my garage and deciding I was going to write a story one day to becoming a writer and author. It's been a journey, to say the least.

I must thank my wonderful children, Evelyn, Ishmael, Izabelle and Delilah for putting up with their mother, her newfound addiction to writing and the days they've watched her walk around like a zombie after late night escapades of hammering on the computer.

Ron Andrade, for all of your encouraging words, support, drive and a list that's too long to say how everything you've done has helped me through.

Shelly Towne, who never told me to shut up, even though she should have. And for Jeremy Towne who has put up with me because I'm his wife's friend.

Lynn Parsons, my dear friend and harshest critic, who never takes bullshit for an answer.

Bonnie Baumgardner, my mother, whose love is endless like her support and encouragement.

To all of you who have taken the time to read my writing, and, whether or not you know it, have carried me onto writing some more . . . Kyle Krainik, Ted Zahrfeld, Marlene Sophab, Penny Powell, Jim Breadman, and to all the other soul's I have tortured along the way—*thank you very much!*

COMING SOON

Shadows

The Second Novel in the Darkness Series

About the Author

Erin Eveland lives in Michigan with her four children. She is the author of several short stories. *Darkness* is her first novel. You can learn more about Erin at:
erineveland.com.